OLD SCHOOL BONES

OLD SCHOOL BONES

RANDALL PEFFER

BLEAK HOUSE BOOKS

MADISON | WISCONSIN

Published by Bleak House Books
a division of Big Earth Publishing
923 Williamson St.
Madison, WI 53703
www.bleakhousebooks.com

This is a work of fiction. Any similarities to people or places, living or dead,
is purely coincidental.

ISBN 13: 978-1-932557-85-5 (Trade Cloth)
ISBN 13: 978-1-932557-87-9 (Evidence Collection)

Library of Congress Cataloging-in-Publication Data has been applied for.
Printed in the United States of America
11 10 09 08 07   1 2 3 4 5 6 7 8 9 10
Set in Adobe Jenson Pro

Interior by Von Bliss Design
www.vonbliss.com

For Holden Caulfield, Sula Peace, June Jing-Mei Woo and the *tcipai* of Mashpee/Aquinnah

PROLOGUE

GRACIE Liu has been having nightmares these days. Like when she's awake. The same one. Over and over. She pictures death, murder. A fraternity of white pricks.

It always starts at the school's remote waterfront on Hourglass Lake. Far from the eyes of the faculty and the students at Tolchester who haven't been tapped for society membership.

There's this gang of teenage boys. Old-school preppies with haircuts like you see in yearbooks or in movies about boarding schools. A lot of bushy, longish hair. Tucked behind the ears. The way white boys in prep school let it grow when they're feeling too lazy or busy or defiant to get haircuts. Blond, sandy tones. She doesn't know how she sees that. It's always night in her dream when the killing starts.

Gracie is seventeen, willowy, Chinese.

But in the nightmare she's this guy. James Aaron Epstein. It's 1957. Initiation night. And she's being herded by the upperclassmen, in their chinos, Weejuns, orange fraternal sweaters. Driven into the freezing April water. Pushed off the docks at the boathouse into Hourglass Lake with eleven other boys who wish to pledge with Mystery &

Mayhem. One of the oldest societies at Tolchester. They're in their tighty-whities, nothing else.

The splash as she hits the lake blinds her. The cold of the water cuts her, a thousand tiny razorblades, slicing her feet, her legs, balls, heart.

The bottom of the lake is too deep for standing.

"Let's see how long you little fucks can tread water."

Several of the brothers have begun throwing rocks at the pledge class, driving them away from any chance of hanging onto the docks, bullying them farther out into the lake.

She feels the flailing of her fellow pledges, the random bumping of arms, legs struggling for warmth, buoyancy.

"This is bullshit," says some kid next to her. She thinks he could be her hero, this Holden Caulfield, this rebel. "We ought to storm those fuckers and pull them in here. Show them what mystery and mayhem really is."

"Ready when you are," she says.

"No talking!" One of the brothers on the dock throws a stone. It stings her in the ear.

"Hey! What the hell?"

"Shut up, Jewboy." A couple of boys throw stones at her.

She tries to float on her back, kick out of range. Holden is beside her.

Shit it's cold. Her fingers, toes buzz with pain.

"Screw these jokers!" says Holden. "Let's get out of here."

"Right," say several other boys in the water. "Let's get out of here before somebody dies. Those bastards just want to see if we have the balls to defy them."

Holden turns toward shore, starts stroking. The others follow. All those WASP boys. And her.

Until another stone wings her in the back.

"Not yet, Epstein. Stay the hell where you are."

Shit it's cold. Her legs and arms are tight as iron.

"Yeah, show us how a Jew suffers."

She wants to shout, wants to scream. *Fuck you. Take your stupid, secret, white-boy society and stick it up your asses.*

But her throat is too frozen to do anything but wheeze.

"I think the yid's in trouble," someone on the dock says. The voice sounds very far away.

"Naw, it's just a cheap-ass kike trick."

She looks around for Holden, for help. But it's like she's seeing the world through the end of a long straw starting to fill with water. It's in her nose now. Her ears are ringing. As she sinks.

*   *   *

Once upon a time there was a famous and wicked prep school… in a rich, little town on the fringe of Boston.

That is to say, *two* famous wicked prep schools, one for girls and one for boys, that merged in 1981. Domains of privilege, power. American castles built on old money and secret societies. Proving grounds for two centuries of merchant kings, statesmen and warriors. Ivory princesses locked in towers … And quite a few racist pigs.

The story's started. Rising out of some black place beneath Gracie's liver, some secret cavern where the ghosts of white boys spank each other silly.

She squints through the darkness at the Helvetica shouting at her from the laptop screen. Her eyes ache, feel on the verge of shriveling from the terminal dryness of the February night in Massachusetts. The purgatory of steam heat.

And she's wishing she were dead. Like in the nightmare. Really. Or at least asleep in a glass coffin for a very long time, waiting for a prince to show up and release her from this new hell.

She groans.

"I can't do this! I just freaking can't. Every time I start to write, it turns into some kind of sick fairy tale." Her bobbed hair is bushed out from static, her glasses nearly slipping off the end of her nose, a half dozen pizza stains on her pink flannel pajamas.

Tory Berg-Dreiser pulls her comforter over her head and screams into her pillow.

"I need Red Bull."

"Liberty always has at least a six-pack stashed under her bed. She's addicted."

"I drank her last one."

"She's going to kill you."

"You think I want to write this shit? I'm doing it for her. And now I'm ..."

"Will you shut the hell up and go to sleep? It's just writing a freaking précis for American History, not *Crime & Punishment*. I bet Allen never even reads that stuff."

Sleet taps against the leaded windowpanes of the ancient dorm room. The radiators warble, hiss. Hibernia House is a Gothic Revival mansion-turned-prep-dorm at the Tolchester-Coates School. A faculty starlet resides in nine palatial rooms on the first two floors. The four eleventh-grade girls in her charge board in the servants' quarters on the third floor. Two gabled bedrooms and a bath surround a central common room with nothing but a TV, a fridge, a broken couch, and a huge fireplace with a nonfunctioning gas log. Above the mantel James Dean keeps watch from a black-and-white poster tacked to the wall with pushpins.

"It's just not coming out right. I think this place is giving me a nervous breakdown. I swear! Winter in a New England prep school, ugh! I wish ... I wish I were back in Hong Kong. Chinese New Years starts tomorrow and—"

"Earth to crazy roommate. You're keeping me awake and—"

"I used to like this place! Everything was fine until I got into this ridiculous history paper. Why did I ever let Liberty talk me into doing this project with her?"

"Girl, you need a boyfriend or something. Get a life!"

"Me? What about Liberty? What the hell was she thinking researching all of this secret society stuff at the school? So sick! They had names like Mystery & Mayhem, Ryley's Raiders, Sparta. And we just found another one, I think. Red Tooth."

"I'm going to Red Tooth you if you don't shut the hell up!"

"You don't understand. It's the underworld taking over my life. Did you know some guy actually died at one of the initiations back in like 1957 or something?"

"Gracie!"

"I mean, the guy—"

"Will you just fucking stop with the Nancy Drew shit?"

"Really. He disappeared during some secret society's midnight treading water initiation in Hourglass Lake. They found him a week later floating facedown among a mess of lily pads near the dam—"

"Jesus. Stop!"

"He was a Jew. They wanted to see him suffer."

"No kidding!"

"That's what brought an end to the secret societies. The school banned them. Just like that. It was a big deal. The dead guy's parents sued the ass off Tolchie.

"Good. Make them pay."

"But it wasn't over … I mean it ISN'T over. Liberty thinks some of these societies went underground. They still exist."

"Conspiracy theory crap."

"Yeah, well, tonight Lib found a note tucked in her physics book. A really awful note. You think it was a coincidence?"

"What did it—"

"BACK OFF YOU STUPID WOG, GASH. YOU ARE OUT OF YOUR LEAGUE!!!"

"What's a wog?"

"It's like the British equivalent of the N-word. Your basic upper-crusty racial slur."

"Oh!"

"Yeah. Oh! I bet Liberty went down to Doc P's apartment as soon as Doc got back tonight, from like whereever, to talk about this racist crap!"

1

"DON'T answer the door!"

"What?" Awasha Patterson pushes skeins of black hair away from her cheeks, rubs her eyes, tries to blink them awake. But she feels strange, still floating in a dream. It is the middle of the night.

Someone is knocking on the door to her apartment, the door leading into the dorm, into the stairwell for the students' entrance to Hibernia House.

"Ignore it. This is our time. Kids have no sense of boundaries." A husky voice beside her right ear.

Danny spoons against her hips, her back from behind. An arm curling around her, tightening across her breasts. The tension of muscles, a body in heat. The scent of oil, her own and her lover's. Pungent, steely. She is suddenly a child again, cutting open fresh oysters on the shore of a salt pond in Aquinnah. The Vineyard. Her first home.

Downstairs, the door to the dorm stairwell, the students' entrance, clicks open. "Dr. P? Are you there? Please!" A desperate teenage girl's voice echoes through the apartment. The student has let herself in.

"Jesus. These girls. Can't they give us a break? They know I'm in here with you. Are they spying on us?"

She feels Danny's breath on her ear, smells pinot grigio. Tastes the evening's wine in her own mouth. It rises in her head again. She floats with it. The sweet brilliance of grapes. Of a new lover. Of someone with eyes for only her. So not Ty. Never Tyrone. So tempting. So tender. For once.

And a little forbidden. A secret tonight. *I'm your Danny, sweet. Always your Danny. Your only Danny.*

But a child is calling for her. One of her girls. She can hear the pain in the voice. Knows that ache. A tearing loose of the soul. A heart in free fall. *The tribal drums. Flutes. Dulcimers. Pounding. Pleading. Satin sheets damp beneath their backs.*

"It's Liberty. I've got to go down and see what she wants."

"Awasha. God!" Danny's voice half growl, half moan. "Stay with me. I can make them all go away."

"Not them. Her. Liberty!"

"Please stay."

Lips kissing along the neck, chest. Tongues hot, sticky. Fingers tracing a cheekbone, jawline. You want to kill me? Kill us ... ?

"I can't."

She tries to peel out of Danny's arms, slowly. A reluctant rising out of a warm pool. Sitting up in bed, she stares out the window at the light of a streetlamp filtering through the branches of an ancient oak. The light washes her torso in a glow, more aura than light. She is nude but for the curtain of dark hair falling to her elbows. Petite, almost anorexic except for full breasts. Her cheekbones high, prominent. Nose fine and proud. More than a few of her old boyfriends have told her she looks like the actress Penelope Cruz. Except for the skin, of course. Her Indian skin. What her brother, her twin Ronnie, calls "Wampanoag hide."

But in this pale light her skin's cinnamon luster—the slight reddish hues of her cheeks, on the bridge of her nose, her lips, her neck—these are only things her lover can imagine.

She feels a hand glide over her left shoulder, along the edge of her jaw, her teeth counting the finger tips as they slide slowly toward her lips. Spreading soft fire.

"Don't leave me!"

Footsteps downstairs. A sob. "Dr. Patterson???"

"I've got to go."

Lips on her shoulders.

A strong, smooth hand taking to her tummy, to the inside of her thigh. A hand that seems to know her better than she knows herself. This new hand. Gentle fingers. This Danny. Who craves her. Now when the night seems a sea. Restless, warm.

"Dr. P … ? Are you awake? I really have to tell you something. I have to … Something happened …"

That voice. The child needs her. The girl's struggling for purchase.

But this hand. Good Lord, this hand like no other. This hand seizing her body and soul. Fingers of fire. Her brain starting to boil. Until she almost tastes the ringing in her ears. Hears these lips on her cheeks. Calling her back to love. Lips on the edge of her mouth. Jesus. Satin lips. Hungry lips.

She strains. "Liberty …"

The larceny of Danny's tongue.

"Can this possibly wait … ? I was sound asleep."

"Oh … I'm sorry."

She tilts her head back, gulps for air one last time. "Tomorrow. OK?"

* * *

The wind is up, churning the waves on the south coast of the Vineyard. Coating her skin with brine. It dries almost instantly in the bright sun to leave her feeling scratchy in her yellow fleece pullover and jeans. Eel grass piled up by the waves. With the tide high, the walking is hard. Almost no sandy strand. Her bare feet and thin ankles hurt from the strain of balancing on rocks, jagged granite. She reaches out for Ronnie's hand, takes it like she did when they were kids here on the Vineyard. Here at Aquinnah. On the old tribal lands. Before they moved off-island. Before their new lives on the Cape. Moving from town to town. Mashpee, Barnstable, finally Chatham. Chatham for middle school and high school. When they knew that being Indian made them different. But years before Ronnie's war.

"Alice loved it here," she says, and squeezes Ronnie's hand a little tighter.

"I used to call this place Black Squirrel's Beach."

She gives a little laugh, thinking of how they never called their mother "Mom" like most kids. That short, stout woman with the pillow breasts and sparkling black eyes. They always called her either by her Christian name Alice or her tribal name Black Squirrel. Just as their father had.

"So she's come home now for good."

"To the land of Maushop." She pictures the giant who in tribal lore left his footprint south of Cape Cod. One of those prints this island, whose spiritual center is the promontory on these looming, red cliffs. Gay Head in the language of the white man. But Aquinnah. Always Aquinnah for the People of the First Light.

She feels the sweat in her twin's hand.

"We have to let her go."

The greenish hatbox, containing their mother's ashes, suddenly feels almost too heavy for her free hand to clutch to her chest.

She looks up at her brother's face. This big man in the red plaid work shirt and dirty khaki pants. Moccasins. He is tall and heavy like their father Micah, Strong Deer, had been. His eyes are wet. The wind is blowing tears over his face. He tries to wipe them away, but the thin, jagged lines *of fluid keep coming, coursing over his broad, tan cheeks. His hair is long now, black, much curlier than hers. He wears it Indian-style, tied back in a bushy pony tail. His hand feels suddenly jittery. She knows he is really starting to feel his hang-over now. Remembers how he had always been the strong one, never a drinker. Before his war.*

They mount a large, round boulder, the sea rushing around it, turning it into a tiny island with each surge of the waves.

"How do we do this, Ronnie?"

Gulls are swooping. Diving on the bait fish that the stripers are driving to the surface. Screeching.

"Christ, Awasha. I don't know."

It is early October, but the air suddenly feels almost too hot to breathe. Scorching her lungs. Like the air from a desert. The air she imagines in Baghdad, Iraq. Land of Allah. Land of a thousand and one Arabian nights. Lands of flaring skies weeping sin too dark to name.

"We have to say something."

She feels a convulsion starting to rise in her brother's chest, in her own. A black rattling.

"Help me, sister."

Something, some power beyond her will, maybe instinct, guides her. She means to speak of love, of farewell.

But her heart has other ideas.

"Forgive us, Black Squirrel… ," she murmurs. "Forgive your children all of our trespasses."

Her hand lifts off the cover, opening the box as she swings to face downwind. The breeze starts to swirl the ashes out of the box. Their mother. Alice. Black Squirrel scatters. A small cloud drifting away over the rocky beach, the breaking waves. Vanishing. With no word, no sign of hope or pardon for her babies.

2

"ALL that coffee is killing me." Gracie groans.

"No kidding. I have to pee so bad. And someone is in the freaking bathroom!" Tory stares at the closed and locked wooden door to the bathroom on the top floor of Hibernia House.

The two girls are just back from pounding double latte espressos at the school's Tuck Shop after their three o'clock swim-team practice. Cranked to the max. And dressed for the blizzard raging outside. Gracie is doing her alternative thing in full Red Army surplus gear: olive drab great coat, watch cap pulled down over her ears. As she pulls off her woolen mittens, she is mumbling about the new year celebrations in Hong Kong today. The bobs and weaves of dragon clans through the crowd. The relentless snapping of firecrackers that lifts you right out of your body. The heavenly scent of spiced pork sizzling in a wok. The warm, moist air.

"You gotta love a school that thinks four healthy, teenage girls can make do with a one-stall bathroom and a tub/shower." Tory pulls off her Yankees ball cap, starts shaking tiny ice pellets out of her long, blond hair.

"Idiots!" Gracie drops the rucksack she uses to carry her books. It hits the floor with a thud. She raps on the door with her knuckles. Stomps the floor with her Doc Martens. Clumps of wet snow scatter over the ancient hardwood floor. "Hey, who the hell ever is in there! Shove it along, will you? We're dying out here. Hey Liberty ..."

"Hey, Justine?!"

"Did you call me?" A voice from the stairwell. Footsteps plodding up the stairs. Slow, labored. Justine Agoropolis crests the staircase and stumbles into the common room, a tall, slender girl staggering under a backpack loaded with textbooks. A black Northface anorak sheds melting ice and snow in streams. Her face little more than a shadow beneath the hood.

"Yeah, we thought you were hogging the bathroom."

"Well, I'm not ... but I'm thinking about it."

"After us, girl scout."

Justine, still just a specter with eyes beneath the black hood, pivots on her left foot, looks around the room, takes in the situation. Three of the four residents of Hibernia House are lined up outside the bathroom door.

"Is Liberty camping out in the potty again? Yo, Lib, there's a waiting line, give us a break will you?"

"Damn it Liberty, we have to pee!"

Gracie grabs the nob to the bathroom door. She rattles it, feels that the door has been locked. *Like who the hell ever locks this door anyway?*

"Liberty, unlock the goddamn door and get your black ass out of there!" It is clear from the tone of Tory's voice she thinks that playing the race card should get action.

But the only sound coming from the bathroom is the faint beat of dripping water.

"I don't think she's in there ... Liberty?!"

"I really have to pee."

"Maybe she locked the door by accident before she left." Justine is sticking up for her roomie. "She's supposed to have a singing lesson now."

"Well, someone sure the fuck locked the door."

"I'm going to wet my panties if we don't get that door open soon."

"Relax, Gracie." Justine throws down her book bag. "Stand back."

Gracie and Tory barely have time to step out of the way.

Their tall friend in the anorak makes a three-step, running leap for the bathroom door, a foot connecting with a marshal arts kick at latch height.

The brass doorknob flies free, hits the floor as the door snaps open.

"Oh, shit," says Gracie, the instant she sees the blood. "Oh, Jesus, no!"

*   *   *

By the time the ambulance arrives, its flashing lights cutting through the darkness and the blizzard, the Hibernia House common room reeks of stress, urine, puked latte. Two campus security officers stand guard in front of the bathroom door. Two uniformed town cops and a detective move in and out of the bathroom with paper booties on their feet, vinyl gloves on their hands, digital cameras.

A police radio crackles a garbled question.

"We're still waiting for the state boys, the M.E. and the headmaster to show up. But we got the dean of the Academy here." A cop talking into his radio. "She wants to see what we're dealing with. Any objection?"

His eyes shift to this dean, Denise Pasteur. She is a tall woman with a pretty, angular face, bobbed blond hair. Even in her overcoat, turtleneck sweater, and wool slacks her body puts the cop in mind of a pro tennis player. He just can't remember which one; some Russian maybe. She stands in the middle of the room hugging Tory and Justine to her chest.

The girls are crying. Choking, shrieking. Tory's red-and-black school sweatshirt is stained from the latte that spills in small bursts through the hand she holds over her mouth. Justine's olive skin has turned the color of the snow outside, her lips tremble as if trying to speak. But she can say nothing, just howl between fitful gasps for breath.

"Shsssssh ... Shssssh. Just let all the pain go. Let it all go, girls."

The dean looks a little shaky herself as her eyes dart around the room to the police, the school security guys. Her gaze settles on her colleague Awasha Patterson. Reads the urgency, the give-me-strength, in Awasha's eyes. She sits on the couch cuddling Gracie in her arms. The girl's Red Army fatigues and Doc Martens are soaked with her own pee. Her face red from tears and something else. Terror maybe.

"Oh, Liberty! Oh, fuck, why? Why?" A litany bubbles from Gracie's mouth.

"Did you see, Dr. Patterson? Did you see the blood? The bathtub so full of blood? Not like in the movies. Not delicate swirls and trails of red curling through the bath water. But purple. Purple like a barrel of wine poured out of Liberty. Poured over Liberty. Her body just a shadow beneath blood. Only the side of her head, her black hair, her long braids. Those copper highlights, floating above the ... She was sticky with it. Her nose and mouth buried in it ... as if in the end she wanted to suck back her life. Did you see it? I saw. I saw. My friend. My dear friend. My Liberty. Our Liberty. Wrists sliced open. Torn envelopes, the letters gone. Help me, Dr. Patterson."

The police radio crackling again. Someone outside in the blizzard, the night, looking for clarity. Another plea.

Awasha hears it, shivers. Holds Gracie to her breast even tighter, to give warmth, feel warmth in this storm. As her own soul unravels.

"Dr. P ... ?

"Are you awake? I really have to tell you something. Something hap-pened ..." The larceny of Danny's tongue ... *"Liberty, can this possibly wait ... ?"*

She squeezes her eyes shut. Remembers the giant Maushop, her mother, the red cliffs. Aquinnah. Sees the gulls swooping. Diving on the bait fish that the stripers are driving to the surface. Screeching.

"Forgive us our trespasses."

3

"SIT, Dr. Patterson ... Do!"

She feels a flash of color in her cheeks, the fine black hairs in the small of her back rise as her boss Malcolm Sufridge closes the door to his office behind her. It is barely seven in the morning. The snow plows are gnawing loudly at the drifts outside, cutting paths from the dormitories to the chapel for an all-school meeting in less than two hours. Classes canceled on account of death.

"We have suffered a terrible loss. Terrible. That poor misguided child. Poor child ... Alas, our Juliet is dead!" Sufridge paces the floor of his butternut-paneled office, looking tormented. Hands plowing his wispy gray hair. An actor in what he surely sees as the final scene of a tragedy. His stage this cradle of power, part library/part throne room/part Gothic castle. Domain of headmasters for centuries. A place of reprimands and punishments, private coercions and mysterious pacts.

To Awasha the room reeks of authority and privilege unknown to her own people and her gender. She prefers to stand. Let the weird old man rant.

"Sit, I say, Dr. Patterson." The baritone voice commanding.

Awasha winces. The posh English lilt, an accent descended from ten generations of Eaton dons. An accent polished by advanced degrees in letters, in British Romantic literature, in theatre. At Oxford. A tall, thin man who wears his black academic gown like a royal robe. Both students and faculty call him Bumbledork behind his back, a rude twist on the name of the folksy titan who rules the school of witchcraft and wizardry in the Harry Potter novels.

"Over here, Awasha."

She follows the voice, its familiar female tenderness. Blinks. For the first time since she has crossed the threshold she realizes that she is not alone with her boss, with Bumbledork. Denise Pasteur is settled into one of the three armchairs circling a baronial fireplace where an immense oak log burns.

"Yes, Dr. Patterson. Come. Sit by the fire. Let it do what it can to melt our pain."

She can feel Denise looking at her with deep blue eyes, telegraphing a sense of urgency. A need for company. For an ally. *Like swallow a little bit of your pride, girl. Sit by me.*

In spite of the fire the room feels freezing to her. When she sits, she has the urge to reach out with her fingers for the warmth of her ally's hand.

Sufridge, looking lost in his own thoughts, a player searching his brain for his next line, settles into his throne, a faded orange Windsor chair.

"We should be hugging each other in grief right now ... but there are things we must talk about. Things that we must do first for the greater good of our school, our students, and all of us who serve them.

*   *   *

"I know this is hard for you, Dr. Patterson, but for the sake of the school, I need you to support me here. This morning our minority students certainly, but truly everybody, at the all-school meeting will be looking to you for reassurance. You are our belle weather." Sufridge gets up from his chair. He is ready to end this meeting.

"But, sir. My girls need me. They are devastated. We are like a family ..."

"This is not up for debate, Doctor. This morning shortly after nine o'clock the three of us will stand in the front of the chapel before the students and the faculty. We will lament the foolish choice of Liberty Baker to end her life. We will sing our hymns of sad farewell, we will say our prayers of forgiveness. We will offer counseling services for those in need. Then we—"

"Sir!" She rises from her chair to face Sufridge, tossing her hair out of her eyes. Something fierce, defiant, Indian has come over her. "I beg you ... don't close Hibernia House. Don't separate the girls and me."

They jut their jaws at each other. Tall vs. short. Headmaster vs. director of minority affairs. Europe vs. America. White vs. Indian. Man vs. woman. Employer vs. employee. She feels all of the old rivalries, the classic tensions. The bullying. And she looks to Denise Pasteur for support.

The dean of the Academy gets to her feet. Standing as tall as Sufridge, she rolls her shoulders beneath her woolen turtleneck sweater. Ever the athlete. "Can I say something here?"

Sufridge turns away from the women, away from the confrontation. Stares at the fire as if commanding it to roar. "I should dynamite Hibernia House. If it were not such an historic building ... I would wipe it off the face of the earth. This used to be such a happy school!"

"It will be again, Malcolm. I'd like to make a suggestion: Awasha's girls need her."

Sufridge continues to stare into the fire, runs his fingers through his hair. "We will be sending out our acceptance letters for next year's class in just a few weeks. If we let the emotions surrounding this senseless death fester, it has the potential to devastate our yield, and the trustees have—"

Awasha throws her hands in the air. "I'm not really hearing this. A girl dies. A school is buckling under grief, and we are going to talk about admission yields, about what the trustees want, about the school's public image?"

"Please. Each of you has a point. Hibernia House is a lightning rod for grief right now. We need to get everyone out of that place for the time being. But there is no need to scatter Awasha and these girls among other dorms. It could only serve to spread the trauma."

"But where do you put them then?"

"How about my place, Beedle Cottage?"

She gives Denise a look. As if this is too much.

"Why not?! For the rest of the year. I know it is not a place of your own, Awasha, and you value your privacy. But it is a huge place. I have four extra bedrooms that I never use. And you can have the study. I don't use an office at home. The girls can have the game room in the basement for their TV and cooking."

Sufridge has turned away from the fire, is looking at his dean of the Academy with a subtle squint of recognition. She has once again demonstrated her uncommon ability to navigate clear of disaster and chaos.

"Well, Awasha?"

She rubs her hands over her eyes, suddenly feeling drunk from a lack of sleep, grief, butting heads with her boss. Something feels wrong about this plan, but she cannot figure out what. She is too wasted to fight.

Denise cocks her head, a little smile of encouragement.

4

"WHY are they trying to cover this thing up, Dr. P?"

Gracie and Tory are sitting on the spare bed in Awasha's new quarters in Beedle Cottage. She squints at them from her own bed. Her head in her hands, feet on the floor. Even though it is well past midnight, everyone is still wearing their clothes, shoes.

"I don't know what you mean, Gracie." She doesn't see any cover-up. The funeral was three days ago, the school still thick with TV trucks and reporters camped all around the edge of the campus. She has made this point about a dozen times during the last hour and a half of unloading from the girls. Knows it is her job to listen, and not to judge, for as long as these girls need her.

But, damn, this is getting hard. How do you take a vacation from death? And the girls' conspiracy theory paranoia.

Tory's eyes suddenly focus on her mentor, widen. "Are you OK, Dr. P?"

She rubs her eyes with her index fingers, feels the tears starting to pool. "I'm fine Tory, I guess. Just a little off-balance. I was starting to feel alive again after Liberty's funeral. Justine's leaving today came as such a shock."

"Her parents are assholes."

"They think she would be better at home, Gracie. Who knows, maybe they are right."

"I doubt it. They want to put her in some kind of religious school for white girls. Like where they all wear uniforms. Can you picture someone all Greek and ethnic like Justine there?" Tory is shaking her head.

"My mother called me yesterday and said my old school in Hong Kong was willing to have me back. I told her to fuck off."

"Gracie!"

"Well, I did. And you know a week ago, I was so sick of this place I would have jumped at the chance to leave? But not now, Dr. P. Liberty needs us. If I quit her now … I freaking know I'd regret it the rest of my life. I'd be like one of those pretend friends in *The Great Gatsby*, who just walked away from Gatsby after he was killed."

Tory huffs. "They sucked. Daisy Buchanan, Myer Wolfsheim. Only Nick Carraway did the right thing."

She thinks back to her days as an English teacher before becoming a dean. *The Great Gatsby* always seemed a bit effete to her. Precious. Give her a Tony Morrison novel any day. Still … Gatsby died. She felt the loss of the hope he inspired in others. "Not everyone has that kind of courage, girls. Gatsby was shot to death. Murder is a pretty scary thing."

Gracie stiffens, moving to the edge of her seat on the bed. "That's what I'm talking about, Dr. P. I'm telling you we are not dealing with a suicide here. Liberty loved her life, loved her biology, her singing, her track. She loved us!"

"She was going to be a doctor, find a cure for cancer. Almost everybody liked her. Lib was always the one to cheer the rest of us up in Hibernia House when we got down."

"She wouldn't have hurt herself. Lib always said she had seen way too many blades growing up on the streets of Roxbury and Mattapan. She hated razors so much she never even shaved her legs or under her arms!"

"Really?" Something stings her in the back of the neck.

"Yes, really. Bumbledork knows it. The cops know it. We told them about twenty times!"

"But it's like they're deaf. Like they don't want any complications."

"They just want to write off Liberty as some troubled minority kid who couldn't take it anymore so she offed herself."

"Yeah, the detective kept asking me about her relationship with her mother. Like 'We heard her mother was a crackhead. That's got to be hard.'"

Awasha pictures Liberty's mother Teddie visiting on Parents Weekend, the addict's high-voltage eyes. She bites her lip. "It's true."

"But. Dr. P, you could just feel the love when her mom took us all out to dinner this one time last year. She was so proud of Lib. Damn, my parents have only been here twice in three years. I'm not slitting my wrists."

"Your parents live in Hong Kong, not just down the street in Mattapan."

"My dad has business in New York and New England about once every six weeks."

"I'm sorry, Gracie."

"Don't be sorry, Dr. P. Just stand by us now. We need you."

Tory closes her eyes and growls. "I'm just so angry. We told the police about that threat that Liberty got, you know? The one that said something like 'Back off, you stupid wog.' No one seems to give two shits. Help us, Dr. P. How do we know Gracie isn't next on someone's list? Maybe the killer or killers aren't finished. Maybe there's more death."

Her feet, ankles hurt from the rocks. She feels the sweat in Ronnie's hand. The greenish hatbox clutched to her chest. Gulls are screeching. A black rattling in her chest. And her brother begging, "Help me, sister." Her heart seizing with things she should have done differently. For her mother. For Ronnie. For Liberty. "Forgive your children all of our trespasses."

"I'm not a private detective or a lawyer."

"But maybe you know somebody."

5

MICHAEL Decastro is crashing. He's splayed out in his orange foul-weather overalls, facedown on his berth in the forecastle of the fishing trawler *Rosa Lee*. His head is buried beneath his pillow, when he feels something shaking his shoulder.

"Get up, Mo. You got company!" His father Caesar's voice impatient, annoyed maybe.

"Christ, Dad. What? Huh … ? Tell them to come back later. I'm wrecked."

He has just spent the last thirty-six hours of their trip home from Georges Banks nursing a sick fuel system on the fishing boat's diesel. At one point they had drifted for hours, rolling viciously in twelve-foot seas south of Nantucket while he changed out all of the fuel filters, drained sumps, bled the lines. But now he is finally off watch. The *Rosa Lee* at the dock in New Bedford, lumpers unloading the gray totes of iced haddock.

"She don't look like she's going to leave. She has that kind of come-hell-or-high water look on her face."

"Who?"

"Some pretty little thing. You been keeping secrets from me?"

"Huh?"

"You been romancing *uma menina?*"

"Where?"

"I don't know where you do your tom-catting. Your time ashore is your own business."

"No. Where is she?" He takes the pillow off his face, sits up.

"Wheelhouse. She was looking kind of wild-eyed, nervous, so I had her sit down in the steering chair. You gone and got some poor girl in—"

"Jesus. Hell, Dad! I have no idea what in the … who … I was so asleep. A woman? Are you setting me up? Tell me it's not Filipa, tell me this is not another lame attempt by you and Tio Tommy to patch things up between Filipa and me."

Caesar Decastro gives his only son a fake wounded look. Boyish, innocent. He looks much younger than his fifty-five years. A Portagee fish boat captain with piercing eyes. The green fisherman's sweater and yellow slicker mask none of his wiry frame. Longish salt-and-pepper hair looks like it has not been combed since he left port for the fishing banks six days ago.

"Dad?"

"Go see for yourself, buddy boy. Destiny waits."

*　*　*

When he comes up the stairs into the wheelhouse, he sees her sitting in the captain's chair before she spots him. And for a second he just stops, stares. Tries to make sense of what he is seeing, read his visitor.

Her skin is darker. But not African. Her facial features very fine. Her cheekbones high with a slight reddish tint that is not make-up because it spreads across the bridge of her nose. In her long, camel hair overcoat and maroon scarf she seems high-born. Regal is the word that comes to mind ... until he sees the way she is wringing her hands in her lap, the bitten-off fingernails.

She seems to sense his presence, turns her gaze away from the brilliant blue of New Bedford Harbor, the snowy docks, roofs, steeples of Fairhaven on the far shore. Sees him staring. Twitches with surprise. "Oh!"

"My father said you ..."

She drops out of the chair, looks petite now that she is standing in front of him. Shorter than Filipa, than his long-gone fiancée.

"You must think I'm pretty strange, coming here like—"

"We don't get too many visitors. Not women." He almost says except for his mom, before she died. Thinks better of it. Too complicated. "But ... anyway ... well ... Welcome to the *Rosa Lee*. I'm Michael Decastro. I don't think we've—"

"No. But I've heard all about you. My mother was your landlady on the Cape, when you lived over her liquor store in Chatham. She showed me your pictures. In the papers, the magazines."

He feels something growl in his belly. "That was somebody else."

She smiles a little, *like maybe not*. Her cheeks and nose really start to color.

"You're going to think I'm really crazy now ... but you're my only hope."

"For what?"

"... I need a lawyer. A really smart lawyer. With a heart."

"I'm not in that business anymore."

"But you don't understand. A really wonderful girl is dead. There's reason to believe somebody killed her."

"I think you need to talk to the police."

"They don't care. They say it was a suicide."

"Maybe it was. The police are pretty good at their jobs."

"Her best friends say this was murder. They say this may not be the last. They're afraid. And so am I."

"I think you need to talk to a P.I."

She heaves a heavy breath. "My mother thought someone should give you a medal. She showed me the articles. She called you Robin Hood."

He scowls, remembering all the hype that came in the wake of the Provincetown Follies murder case. His client Tuki Aparecio. The biracial drag queen from Bangkok he helped escape a frame-up. The one who vanished into thin air ... and left him feeling half-dead.

He rubs his eyes, steps into the center of the wheelhouse, stares out at the harbor, spins the ship's wheel for something to do with his hand. "I'll tell you something. Your mother is a sweet, kind lady—"

"Was. She died last fall."

His heart stops for a second, thinks of losing his own mother, Maria. "I ... I'm sorry. Alice was one of my favorites ... But that time out on the Cape. That time I lived over your mother's store in Chatham was the worst time of my life. I had this case in Provincetown ..."

"Alice said it was hard on you."

He nods, spins the wheel with more energy.

He doesn't say it destroyed his relationship with his fiancée. That after those stories in the papers, every nutcase east of Hartford started calling him for representation. Doesn't say it has been a lot of months since he quit his job as a public defender, turned off his phone, left Chatham. Since he started fishing again. On the *Rosa Lee*. She must know all this. Someone in the P.D.'s office told her, and told her where to find him.

She approaches him from behind.

"You gave people hope. You made people think that sometimes the little guy, the stranger, the outcast, the poor person could maybe get a fair shake."

He feels her nearness, stops fiddling with the wheel. Keeps his back to her. "There was a time when I thought maybe I could do something to save the world. When I wanted to do my share. But the cost was too high. I found out I couldn't take a case without getting emotionally involved."

"But that's what makes you different. That's what makes you great."

He turns. Looks down into her black eyes. "No. That's what makes a bad lawyer. I can't help you. Really."

The wheelhouse is suddenly boiling hot, reeking of stale coffee, Doritos, diesel fumes. This is uncomfortable. He just wants her to leave.

"I'm sorry. I bothered you. It was a terrible mistake, a vain …"

He sees her upper lip beginning to quiver.

She turns away, looks around for an escape, a door. Can't find it.

"Damn me! I must have been out of my every loving …"

"Don't cry."

"I'm not crying. I just can't find my way out of—" Suddenly she doubles over, hugging herself across her chest.

A sob bursts from her core, dark and heavy.

"Look, I've got a bunch of gear I got to weld and—"

"I'm going."

"Sorry … I don't know what to say. The law just ripped my heart into little pieces. You know what that feels like?"

She wipes back some tears on her face. "It's how I felt when my mother passed. How I feel right now … OK? Don't you have a mother?"

He could just scream.

*   *   *

"*Give me a big hug, Mo,*" she says. "*We may not have all the time in the world,* meu menino."

He's not sure what she's telling him, can't quite figure out why she has driven all the way down here to Chatham on the Cape from Nu Bej.

But now here she is. Maria. His mom. Taking his hand, hugging him to her chest as they stand in the shadow of the band concert gazebo. This bright, late-October day. The leaves on the maple trees in Kate Gould Park a faded yellow, red, brown. Falling in slow-motion spirals.

"*I'm leaving town,*" he says, *staring off at a fisherman in a pick-up coasting along Main St.*

He thinks maybe she has come because she knows, a mother's intuition, that he has quit his job with the law firm, resigned as a public defender. That he already has his clothes and books stuffed into garbage bags in the little studio over the liquor store down the street.

"*I know this is a bad time for you. That case with the drag queen. You put your heart and soul into—*"

"*It's OK, Mom. I'm coming home. I'm going to start fishing again with Dad and Tio Tommy.*"

She pulls back to arm's length, leads him to a seat on a bench.

"*That's why I'm here. I wish you would reconsider.*"

She's looking oddly pale, thin. Almost as thin as the drag queen Tuki. When did she lose the weight? All his life she has been a fleshy earth mother with soft caramel skin. Wild, black curls, sparkling brown eyes, a laugh that rolls through a crowd and makes everyone smile. Not a Portagee Princess like his ex, Filipa. But a woman whose royalty roots in her capacity to make everyone around her feel safe, admired, with the touch of her hand, her boisterous smile.

"*What's the matter, Mom?*"

"You're so good at the law, Mo. Don't give up all that you've worked for just because your client has disappeared. Think about what you did. You actually found the real killer in that Provincetown Follies case."

"Is this why you came? You're trying to give me a build-up?"

"Hey, you're my talented son. Can't a mother be proud?"

He smiles. "Yeah, but something's up. I can tell. Why don't you want me to come home? Why don't we have all the time in the world?"

She takes a deep breath, seems to wheeze as she inhales.

"Things are not so good at home."

"Between you and Dad?"

"Not exactly."

"Well what then?"

She inhales deeply again, holds his eyes firmly in her gaze.

"The doctor says I have a cancer growing in my ovaries."

"Shit!" The word explodes from his mouth.

"Yeah, really. Shit!"

She puts her head on his chest and lets him hold her.

"I'm definitely coming home. You're going to need surgery and—"

"The cancer has already spread."

"Cristo! Does Dad know?"

"He was with me at the doctor's."

"Why … ? I mean, I don't understand how this kind of … ?" His voice breaks. He can't find any more words.

"Remember when you were a teenager. How I used to tell you to go gently, go slowly with your girlfriends? To stand in awe?"

"You said be patient, a woman's body holds a thousand mysteries."

"Well, this is one of them, meu menino."

6

HE can't believe he's back in Cambridge, in Harvard Square, ordering a second double-espresso in the little Spanish café where he used to court Filipa. But, OK, he's here. The dutiful son. For his mother. And for Alice Patterson.

Alice of Chatham. Alice the sweet. Dead Alice. Indian Alice. Mother Alice. Alice who used to leave hot three-bean casseroles covered in tin foil outside his apartment door. Alice who said a busy public defender could not live on pizza and beer alone. Alice who cried when he told her about the end of his engagement to Filipa. Alice who offered him free rent after he quit the law. Alice whose son is a mess with booze, whose daughter a wreck with loss.

He said he would meet her here. Neutral territory. Not New Bej. Not the fancy prep school where she works. But now she is a half hour late. He is having queasy thoughts that maybe any minute Filipa will pop in here—she still lives in Cambridge—and he will have to deal with a boatload of guilt and sadness and ...

This whole thing is a freaking mistake.

"Michael?"

He looks over his shoulder, sees a woman's form, stiffens, turns.

He sees the cinnamon tint on the cheeks, the nose. Exhales. Not Filipa, thank god. This new person. Meeting here in this café was her idea. Not his. For four years of undergraduate school, Pamplona was her oasis at Harvard. A Spanish *querencia* for an Indian princess.

Awasha.

Her name short for Awashonks. She has told him proudly that she is the direct descendant of her namesake. When local Wampanoags clashed with colonists in 1675, King Philip's War, Awashonks was the *squaw sachem* of the Sakonnet clan. Her support for the English colonists turned the tide of the war against Metacomet, King Philip.

Awashonks, woman warrior.

"I want you to meet someone."

He sees a Chinese girl standing next to her, a teenager wearing a full set of vintage Red Army gear, including the weird, double-flap hat with the ear lugs. She is taller than Awasha by several inches. Wisps of dyed purple hair push from beneath the hat. A petite diamond nose stud flashes in the light. She eyes him, head-to-toe. Back again.

"She didn't tell me you were so cute!"

"Gracie!" Awasha elbows the girl.

"Well, Dr. P, you didn't." She pulls off the woolen mitten on her right hand, thrusts her large, soft hand into his.

When he tries to free his hand, she squeezes.

"I'm Gracie Liu. Pleased to meet you … And I am not going to let go of your hand until you agree to help us find out who killed my friend, how we stop them from killing again."

*   *   *

It's just the two of them now, walking in fits and starts across Harvard Yard. Gracie has taken the subway, the T, back to school for her English class and swimming practice. Awasha stares at a clutch of coeds laughing loudly as they climb the steps to the Widner Library. Has a little memory of college days, girl pals. The bright afternoon sun has turned the snow to slush under their feet.

"I want to apologize for Gracie. She's a great kid—but she can be a little outspoken. And now she's wound up tighter than deer gut … with her grief. Fear."

He nods. An acknowledgement. "She—well both of you, actually—sure know how to get a guy's attention."

"I told you. We're desperate, we're hurting."

He nods again, suddenly feels too warm. Maybe from all the caffeine … and now the sunshine. He unzips his black Northface.

"This death has to be scary as hell for both of you. And that other girl, the one I haven't met. Tory? But … I just don't see how I fit into this mix. I'm a fisherman."

"You know you're more than that."

"I don't want the life of a litigator any more. That stress. That feeling of scattering like bits of seaweed in the wind. I know I said I would do what I can for you and Gracie. But I just don't see—"

"I will pay you … somehow."

"For what?"

"Counsel."

"What?"

"You know the legal system, how the police work, how to get their attention. You know what questions to ask to help us find Liberty's killer. It could be someone right at Tolchester-Coates."

"I told you before. I think you should be talking to an experienced P.I. You want me to help you find an investigator?"

"We want you. We want someone with courage and conviction. Someone who cares about Liberty. For the underdog. For us."

He squeezes his cheeks with his hand, a nervous tick. "Look. You don't really know me. I am not a superhero, maybe not even a good guy. I can give you a whole list of people, starting with my former fiancée and the state police on the Cape, who can testify to that."

"Please! My mother could not have been wrong about you. And … and don't you see … we're drowning here."

He hears a hitch in her voice, feels the storm rising in her again, just as it did back on the *Rosa Lee* before he agreed to meet her here in the city.

"Christ!"

"What?"

He spots a park bench in the sun just steps ahead. "Why don't we sit down?"

She stops walking, purses her lips, scowls. Seems to be considering whether or not to give up on this guy, just turn her back and stride away.

"I'm sorry. I must sound like an arrogant, callous bastard."

"Pretty much, yeah! If you want to know the truth. What happened to the amazing legal navigator who saved Tuki Aparecio?"

He sits down on the bench. The air suddenly gone right out of him. Eyes on his slush-soaked sneakers.

"Your mother used to talk about you some."

"Did she tell you that I'm stubborn? That I'm used to getting my way?"

"She was really proud of you. She said you had a doctorate in Literature and Native Studies. A really good job, too."

"And … ?"

He opens his mouth, almost says her mother worried about her. Wondered if she would ever find the right man. Wondered when she would stop picking up and putting down lovers like she was shopping for apples.

"What?"

"You're mother had a big heart."

She settles beside him. "Don't fold on me."

He feels her gaze on his face.

"What makes you so sure Liberty Baker was murdered? What kind of kid was she?"

"Come over to T-C with me. I want to show you some things. You ever go on MySpace?"

7

"LOOK at this," she says.

They're sitting in her gray Saab, parked between the piles of plowed snow behind Hibernia House. A laptop wedged between the seats whirs, giving off little popping sounds as her fingers flick over the keyboard. Locks onto a wifi signal from the dorm. Images coming, going on the screen. Blue banner—myspace.com, a place for friends.

click

She's logged in.

click

Hello, *Awasha Patterson*

click

Friends Space

click

Liberty

On the screen, a thumbnail of a photo Gracie showed him back at Pamplona. A black teenage girl in her track uniform, sweat running down her face, smiling at the camera. Her arms are hugging the shoulders of three other girls in track uniforms: Gracie, a cute blond, and a tall Mediterranean-looking girl. The young women of Hibernia House, a sprint relay team. The black girl, Liberty, has a baton in one hand. Her teammates are making the V-for-victory sign with their fingers.

click

Videos

click

Sistahood

click

Soundtrack playing. Marvin Gaye and Tammi Terrell singing "Ain't No Mountain High Enough." On the screen a grainy, badly lit video. The camera is hand-held, unsteady, struggling to stay in focus. The music fades.

"So, hey, y'all. This is my crib. See? Welcome to the Sistahood."

Liberty. Live. Smiling into the camera. A huge grin. Perfect white teeth. Eyes more electric than in the track photo. They seem to almost pop out of her face. Amazing long, black lashes. Skin not nearly as dark as he expected. Almost as light as his own Portagee hide, with a shade or two more of *café com leite*. His mother's skin. Hair a glossy black. Not quite African hair, it's finer. Pulled back tight against her head. He can see a long ponytail swaying down her back. Her head and shoulders doing a cute, subtle bob-and-weave as she talks.

The camera pulls back.

She's sitting on her desk, waving a stuffed, pink, floppy-eared bunny in front of her. Wearing a simple wheat-colored cardigan and jeans. They fit her long, slender body like skin.

"This is Mercatroid. He's a magic rabbit. He keeps me safe, gives me love while I'm here at school. Wave to the folks at home, Mercatroid." She waves the bunny's paw.

"So check it out, y'all. This is how a sista lives at the big, bad boarding school ya'll wondering about." She waves a free arm to show off her room. "See, it's not so whack as you thought, right? Pretty, pea green walls all gussied up with homegirl's hotties."

The camera pans to a poster of Denzel Washington in *Training Day*, Kanye West in a pair of mega-shades. Justin Timberlake. Bruce Lee.

"And this is where yours truly gets her beauty rest." She stands up, walks three steps across the room to a bed piled with orange-and-green polka dot comforters, lacy pillows, more stuffed animals.

"We got to hit the books. Later, peoples. This is the first edition of the Sistahood Video Blog, signing off. Peace y'all."

Both girls laughing, Liberty flashing the peace sign as the camera fades out.

* * *

"Did you see what I saw?" She's staring at the blank space on the laptop screen where the video has vanished.

Long shadows of the trees fall across piles of snow outside, across the Saab, across her, him. It will be dark soon. His head hurts. Maybe from squinting at the video. He closes his eyes.

Almost sunset. They have been drinking Bacardi and the local Kalik beer since the middle of the afternoon, when she stops dancing, takes him by the elbows. Pulls him against her slick, wet body.

"Michael."

"I don't know."

"Didn't you feel her spirit?"

"Yeah." His voice sounds frayed.

"Why would anybody want to kill such ... such amazing energy, that sweetness?"

"You really think I can answer something like that?"

*   *   *

"Check this out."

click

Another Sistahood Video Blog.

Old School Bones—work in progress.

Liberty's room again. Dark outside. The room full of shadows cast by a couple of floor lamps. The posters of Denzel, Kanye and company gone.

The camera zooms to the walls. Pans. Shows taped-up photocopies of old articles from *The Tolchie News* and *The Tochester Alumni Register* hanging where the posters of Denzel, Kanye and company once were. Time lines drawn on a roll of paper towels. Lots of photographs. Stacked on Liberty's desk, and in piles around it on the floor. About fifty old yearbooks and what look like history texts.

The camera picks up Liberty standing beside her bed. She's dressed for winter. Thick, long, red turtleneck sweater, black Lycra running tights, furry snow boots. Ponytail twisted on the crown of her head.

"Greetings, peoples. We're back. After a long pause. But, yo, the amount of homework they give us here can really get in the way of our artistic expression. Anyway, Sistas Liberty and Gracie coming at you with some like serious shocking jive we found while working on our history research paper. Dig?"

She holds up a book in her hand. Camera zooms on the book cover. SECRETS OF THE TOMB: SKULL & BONES.

"For those of you who don't know, this book is about a secret society at Yale. Powerful old white boy stuff, OK? Like the Georges Bush and their cronies. Naw mean?"

The camera follows her as she walks a section of the wall papered with photocopied pictures of scores of teenage boys with the words DEAD or LOST scrawled in red marker over their faces.

"Ninja Girl Gracie and I have found a possible link between college societies like Skull & Bones and secret societies here in our very own Tolchester-Coates School."

She puts down the Tomb book, picks up a newspaper.

"Our happy, multicultural school claims they abolished secret societies here more than fifty years ago. But check it out. In the last two weeks I have found subtle references to secret societies called Red Tooth and Mystery & Mahem in Tolchie yearbooks from the last five years."

The camera zooms to the features page of *The Tolchie News*. It's the current edition of the school's weekly newspaper that Liberty is holding up.

"The headlines on the page have a code hidden in them."

She reads as someone's finger, ninja camera girl Gracie's probably, points out the headlines. It moves from left-to-right, top-to-bottom on the page:

RED BLAZERS MAKE A COMEBACK AT T-C

TOOTH DECAY CITED AS REASON TO BAN CANDY MACHINES

STILL WATERS RUN DEEP: MR. LYNCH, ARTIST IN RESIDENCE

RULES COMMITTEE FACES TOUGH CHOICES.

"You don't get it, homies?" She gives the camera a mock frown.

"Look at the first word in each headline. Read them in sequence. RED TOOTH STILL RULES."

The camera pulls back, shows us Liberty full-on. She puts the newspaper down, walks toward the camera.

"I'm telling y'all, this is bad business. Devils' work, wait and see. Stay tuned for more from your trusty sista detectives. From the Danger Zone. Old School Bones is a work in progress. Ya hear?"

Fade to black.

*   *   *

"Now what do you think, Michael? You think this is a girl who would have killed herself ... or could Gracie's conspiracy theory have some weight?"

She stops dancing, takes him by the elbows. Pulls him against her slick, wet body. A soft whisper in his ear. "You're not lily white, are you?"

"Can I see the room in the video?"

8

SHE unlocks the door with her master key, bites her lower lip. Feels like running. Anywhere, just away from here where she can still smell the death, the fear.

"God, this is so hard," she says.

The door swings open into Liberty's room, on the third floor of Hibernia House.

"It's empty," he says.

The room has the stifling smell of chlorine bleach. The faint scent of urine, puke.

She tells herself to find her courage, takes two steps into the room. Except for a spider just starting to spin her web in the corner, the room is empty. EMPTY empty. Not even the standard student desks, the chests of drawers, iron beds, chairs, mirror. All gone. Floor swept clean and mopped.

"I don't understand."

"What?"

"All Liberty's stuff was here yesterday. I checked."

"Maybe her family came for it."

"Her mother wouldn't take out the school's furniture. Or clean the floor."

"You got a point."

"Bumbledork!" Her voice echoes in the empty room. The late afternoon sun casts a reddish glow on the polished hardwood floor.

"What?"

"Bumbledork must have done this, had the whole room cleaned out." She peers into an empty closet.

"Bumbledork? Isn't that the name of the guy in Harry Pot—"

"Sort of. It's what everybody calls Sufridge, our headmaster."

"He's not a wizard."

"He thinks he is. Dresses like one."

"What kind of school is this?"

"It always had its dark side, but … now!"

She spins on her heels, walks out of the room. Crosses the central common room with its TV, couch, the fireplace with the dead gas log, poster of James Dean over the mantle. Keys the lock in the door to Gracie and Tory's old room.

"Look."

A draft from the door swinging open scatters dust bunnies across the room.

A small cloud drifting away. The rocky beach, the breaking waves. Vanishing. With no word, no sign of hope or redemption for the babies.

The school furniture in disarray. A cardboard box overflows with trash. Old graded essays and math tests lie discarded on the floor.

"What?"

"No one has touched this room since Tory and Gracie moved out over a week ago."

"Maybe the cleaners ran out of time."

"They don't punch out of work for another hour."

"You think something funny's going on here?"

She puts her hands on her hips, stares at him. "Don't you? Doesn't it look like Bumbledork is trying to erase every last little bit of Liberty from this school?"

"I couldn't say. This is all new territory for me."

"I guess if you are going to help us find a killer, you better see the scene of the crime."

* * *

"Look, Awasha, I'll admit your headmaster may well be in a hurry to put this death behind him, behind the school. But who wouldn't be?"

"That's not the point."

Her back teeth are starting to grind as she looks at him sitting there on the toilet lid, staring nonchalantly at the claw-foot bathtub where Liberty died. Can't imagine how she ever thought he might be her great hope. A savior. Sometimes all men under the age of about forty seem to look and act the same to her. Like her twin brother Ronnie. Loveable. But meatheads. Large children.

And this one could use a shave and a haircut. Can't he feel anything? Does he get off on hearing himself theorizing about bullshit, avoiding the murder that is staring him in the face? Listen to him rambling on.

"The death of any kid, let alone a popular kid like Liberty Baker, has got to be a major trauma for a school." He reaches out and rubs the fingers of his right hand over the clean edge of the old tub. The porcelain gleams. "I just don't see how you can come to the conclusion that Liberty's death is anything but a desperate act. A suicide."

"You saw those video clips. Liberty loved her life. And she was afraid of knives and razors. She couldn't cut a banana!"

"Maybe she was drunk or on drugs. A lot of people get high before they try something like this."

"I thought of that. I asked the police. They said that the medical examiner always runs a toxicology test on what they call *unattended deaths*. Liberty tested clean. Besides, she wasn't a druggie. She treated her body like a temple. She was an amazing kid. Understand?"

He doesn't respond. He is still staring into the tub ... as if he is looking for something. Or just lost in a daydream about fishing.

She stamps her foot. *Like look at me, man!*

"Sorry. What?"

Her teeth grinding again. "You know what? Let's forget about this, OK? I'm sorry I troubled you. Go back to your fishing boat."

She snaps off the bathroom light, Hibernia House suddenly almost immaterial. A collection of gray and violet shades in the low light of late afternoon in mid-winter.

He doesn't move.

"Hey, let's go! I've got places to be, a job. Three dozen students needing me."

"I can't picture how you could kill someone and make it look like she slit her wrists on purpose. It seems almost impossible ... like ..."

"Forget about it. It's not your worry."

"But you said she was threatened a couple days before her death. Somebody called her a name, a ... ?"

"A wog. It was a note. It said, 'Back off you wog cunt. Don't stick your nose where it doesn't belong.' Something like that."

"And wog is a racial slur?"

"In England."

"I hate that kind of thing!"

She switches the light back on. "Join the club."

"You saw Gracie's Old School Bones video. Maybe she was really onto something. Maybe she stepped on the wrong toes."

"With the history term paper?"

"And the video, for that matter. Anyone can access the stuff kids put up on MySpace."

"You mean like these fraternities?"

"Yeah."

"You have the note?"

"Gracie said Liberty threw it away."

"Shit!"

"What?"

"What have you got to go on but a lot of hearsay and—"

"Shsssh!" She snaps off the light. "Someone's downstairs. Coming up. Get in a closet!"

IT smells like baby powder, athletic shoes, rose cologne. And something else faintly. Spiced rum, maybe. Like someone spilled some Captain Morgan in here once upon a time. Even in the dark, he can tell that a steam line for a radiator runs through here. The heat baking his right calf as he leans into the deepest corner of the big walk-in closet in Gracie and Tory's room. His ear presses against the wooden door, listening to the muffled voices out in the common room. Awasha's. And another female's. A throatier voice.

"When I saw the light on up here, I figured it had to be you."

"I guess I still need some closure with all of this."

"It has to be horrible for you. Well … all of us. But especially you. Not just losing that beautiful … but losing your home."

"I keep thinking, I should have been able to stop her. You know, the night before …" A choking sob. "She wanted to talk. And … told her to come back … was too late … trying to sleep. All the while …"

He hears another sob. Maybe she is trying to distract the new-comer, cover for him, but her emotion sounds so real. Raw. And now he hears the lower female voice. Cannot make out the words. Something, something. Soft, tender. Trying to comfort.

A long silence. The steam heat hissing in the pipes. His right calf burning again.

"... madness for me to come back up here ... don't think I'm ready. I ..."

A long pause. He hears something. The slow, awkward shuffling of feet maybe. Fish squirming on a deck after the net spills. Their death upon them.

"Why don't we go downstairs for a while?" It is the other female voice. The rough one.

"I ... getting back to the office. I told some Muslim kids I'd ..."

"Just for a little while—for some tea."

Another long pause. Fish on the deck again.

"OK."

* * *

After she is gone for maybe a half hour—no voices, no signs of life from the floors below in her apartment—he tip-toes out of the closet. Stretches out on one of the girls' beds. Flat on his back, forearm over his eyes. A position practiced every night for nine and a half months. In another dorm, another school. When all he wanted in life was to surrender to the gods of forgetfulness. While he waited to be released, waiting for graduation from all the preppie madness.

With his eyes closed, he sees her. The black girl in her track uniform.

Sweat running down her cheeks, a baton in one hand. The other making the V-for-victory sign.

The camera zooms to her face. Come-hither smile, those immense lashes batting. Suddenly her hand reaches up and tries to cover the camera lens ...

She has the long-legged gate of a ballerina, her bare toes hitting the floor a split second before the rest of her feet. Something little-girly about the fluid, effortless, unselfconscious way she moves ...

The camera at arm's length captures herself leaning against the desk next to Gracie, throwing a long arm around Gracie's shoulders. "Wave goodbye to the folks ..."

* * *

"I'm so sorry!"

Her voice startles him. His eyes burst open. He doesn't think he was asleep exactly.

It is night outside the window. His eyes try to find her form, her silhouette as he sits up on the bed, peers into the dark room.

"I don't want to turn on the light. It would not be good for me ... for us to be seen up here now. Come on."

He feels a hand reach out of the gloom and take his. A small hand. Soft on top, but the fingers dry, a little leathery. A hand that has known hard work. Like his own. Maybe a fishing hand.

"Who was—"

"Shssss." Whispering, "Just a worried colleague. We need to be quiet."

He wonders why. Aren't they alone?

"Follow me." Her hand tugs. He rises. She walks, soft cat-steps. He tries to do the same. For some reason he has a memory of dancing school in the North End of Nu Bej. "The Blue Danube Waltz." What the hell's that have to do with how Liberty Baker died ... or murder?

* * *

When her Saab stops to drop him back at his jeep on Mt. Auburn St. in Cambridge, it is snowing again. He can feel the tires skid a little on the road, knows yet another winter storm is winding up in the Gulf of Maine. Pictures twenty-five-foot waves, pounding seas.

"Well, that was a pretty different afternoon."

She cocks her head, eyes him.

"What do we do now?"

He puts his right hand on the door handle.

"My dad and Tio Tommy want to get back out fishing as soon as they can. Prices of cod and haddock are sky high."

"You're going with them?"

He bends at the waist so he can see her better, peers into the car.

"Yeah, sure. I'm a Portagee from Nu Bej. I fish." His eyes look through the windshield into the sheets of falling snow.

"What about Liberty and—"

He opens the door. A gust of wind cuts his cheeks. He pulls his navy watch cap lower over his ears.

"We're in for a hell of a storm, Awasha. The Rosa Lee won't be going anywhere for a while."

"So… ?"

"I don't like that ugly word."

"What?"

"Wog."

"You'll help? Even though I made you hide in a closet for God knows how …"

Sweat running down the deep brown face. Cheeks and young breasts covered with fine white sand. Fumes of gin, lime. And something rank. Marley singing "One Drop" from the distant bar. Or was it another song, like "Africa Unite?"

"Michael?"

"Nobody ever made me do that before, hide in a closet. I didn't know I was so important."

She smiles. A shy smile. In the glow of a streetlamp and the reflection from the swirling snow, her skin, eyes, lips seem to shine. "Can you close that door?"

He pulls it shut, pinches a cold cheek with his hand. The nervous tick again.

"It's all about learning how and why."

"I don't follow you."

"Understanding a crime. Understanding death."

"How and why Liberty died?"

"First we have to check out the official cause of death."

"Suicide?"

"Yeah. Maybe she really had a motive you don't know about."

"There was no note."

"When I was in the closet, I heard you tell your colleague that Liberty came to you the night before she died. Wanted to talk. Right?"

A long pause.

"Yes."

"She sound upset?"

"No … Yes. I don't know. We didn't talk."

"Why?"

"It was late, I was already in bed. Jesus. I screwed up, OK?"

"I'm not judging you."

"Yes, you are. I can feel you are!"

"Maybe she talked to someone else."

"Not any of the girls in the dorm, not her stepparents. Nobody heard anything from her that night or the next day."

"What about her mother?"

10

"I don't know, Dr. P, I don't think Michael Decastro believes us!" Gracie squirms in the over-stuffed chair, eyes dart around the office.

The Director of Minority Affairs Office is a converted classroom in the foreign language building. She has decorated it with amazing art. Theatre masks from Malaysia, mahogany statues from Africa, Chinese scroll paintings, a Wampanoag medicine stick carved from the rib of a pilot whale. Stuff she used to keep in her classroom when she was an English teacher here. Stuff from before she gave up teaching to play Mother Teresa to Tolchie's minority kids.

"He thinks we're tripping on grief and paranoia." Tory leans back in her chair, runs her hands up the back of her neck, rakes the last of the melting snow out of her blond hair.

"Give him a little time, girls. I can see why he wants to talk to her mother. A healthy skepticism can be a good thing."

As soon as she says the words, she feels something starting to shrivel in her chest, her hands going numb. Has to spin in her desk chair to bring back the flow of blood. She hates the idea of having to defend him before these girls. *Damn Michael Decastro.*

"Well maybe skepticism is a good thing when you are conducting a chemistry experiment ... or watching some cheesy love triangle thing on *Grey's Anatomy*. But what if there's a killer on the loose? You know, like what if he's coming after Gracie?"

"Yeah, what if right this minute Freddie Kruger is stalking my tender, young, Hong Kong booty?"

She can't decide whether these girls are just impatient and milking the drama or are genuinely scared. "You want me to call the police? If you feel in danger, we have to tell them."

The girls look at each other, scowl.

"They'll just tell us we better take a leave of absence. Like go home you twitchy chicklets."

"Maybe they're right."

"Doc. We've been through all this before. We're scared, like hell yes. But we don't want to leave. We have to stand by Liberty. If we quit on her, then maybe this whole thing is going to happen again to someone else. Maybe these secret societies are—"

"You realize all this about secret societies is a lot of speculation. A conspiracy theory?"

"You think that note Liberty got just came out of the blue? After almost three years of clear sailing at T-C, someone suddenly decides to hit her with that racist crap?"

"I don't know. The police didn't seem too suspicious. So that's where we hope Michael Decastro can help us. Let's give him a chance. We just dragooned the poor guy into being our knight in shining armor!"

She feels the shriveling in her chest again.

"You said he was all hung up about how someone could have faked her suicide."

"I don't think we should be talking about this. It's too awful, too—"

"Doc! We're not little kids. Come on!"

She swallows a thick mouthful of saliva, wishes she could rush out of here. To someplace where she felt safe herself. Her lover's long arms.

"He said that if someone had tried to slit Liberty's wrists there would have been some signs of a struggle."

"Not if she was unconscious." Tory's voice sounds suddenly pumped, defiant.

"But how... ?"

"You know, Doc, like in the movie *ET*?" Gracie shifts to the edge of her chair. "When the science teacher made the kids drop those cotton balls soaked with chloroform in the jars. To put the frogs to sleep before the dissection."

Her face sours. "I think that kind of thing only happens in Hollywood. If someone had drugged Liberty, the medical examiner would have discovered it during the autopsy."

"Maybe not."

"What are you saying?"

"You ever hear of roofies?"

"What?"

"Date rape drugs."

"Yes."

"They leave your system in hours. And they can kill."

11

WHEN he unzips the side curtain of his jeep on the shotgun side, she leans so far in she is almost close enough to touch her nose to his. Her breath is smoky with the sharp scent of cinnamon Altoids. Her hair a bleach-blond fro, epic proportions. Tina Turner.

"You want to party?"

He glances ahead down the business strip of Blue Hill Avenue in Mattapan, then into his rearview mirror. Looking for cruisers or the plain Ford sedans of the vice squad. Except for a pusher and a pimp sharing a forty from a brown bag outside a convenience store and three hookers passing a spliff at the bus shelter, no one else has come out tonight. Besides the snow plows. A gang of three grind south away from him just now, their orange lights flashing against three-foot banks of snow.

"Tedeeka?"

"It's Teddie, honey. Can I get in? Do you have any idea how fucking nasty it is out here?"

He pauses for a second, catches her eye, tries to read her face. But it is a mask. Part rock star, part pirate wench. Beautiful, cruel. The eyes on fire from a recent fix. Crack or maybe crystal meth.

"Hey, cha cha cha, baby! Let me in or move it along. It's freezing on the street."

"Sorry," he says, opens the door.

Her faux leopard coat flashes as she pounces in beside him. "What you have in mind?"

Your dead daughter, he thinks. *Lost girls.*

"Talk to me, honey."

"You drink coffee?"

*   *   *

"She was a good girl, an angel, that one. Liberty. You hear what I'm telling you?"

"Is that why you sent her away to that boarding school?"

Her eyes sear him. "Fuck you, honey. She got a scholarship. Fuck you for asking!"

He takes a sip of his coffee, knows that after fifteen minutes of her flirting, bullshit, digression, he has finally touched the mother in her. The raw core. He rolls the coffee in his mouth. Now he wishes he had added a fourth pack of sugar.

"Yeah, right, fuck me for asking!"

She reaches across the jeep, puts her hand on his thigh. "Leave it be. You know what I mean? The hurt just too deep. I loved that child! And she knew it. Word! But nothing anybody can do to bring her back."

"Sorry, but—"

"Dead is dead. We going to do something here? I got bills to pay. I can't be wasting the night away … getting no action." Her thumb rubbing the inseam of his jeans.

"*Cristo*, Teddie. Talk to me."

"I got to get back on my corner. My regulars will be coming by looking for me. You know what I mean?"

She tosses her empty coffee cup on the floor, grabs her enormous red purse, reaches for the door latch.

"Wait!" He grabs her hand away from the door. "I've got money."

She tugs, tries to free her hand. Her eyes dart wildly around the inside of the jeep.

"Let me go. I don't want your money. I don't want your honky-ass questions. Why can't you let my daughter rest in peace?"

He sees the tears pooling in those big black eyes. Hears her breathing, fast and shallow, sees her free hand going into the calf of her red vinyl boot, probably for her blade.

The end of the road for this chat.

So he drops her hand, hits the latch.

Her door swings open.

"OK. Go, Teddie. Sorry to have troubled you. My bad. I guess the cops got it right. Liberty couldn't hack it anymore. So your daughter took the easy way out."

She splits the jeep in a swirl of snow.

"Fuck you. Easy way!? The child was scared out of her mind. Thought someone might try to kill her."

"She called you, didn't she?"

*   *   *

They are in a diner now. Almost midnight. Her skin dusky, eyes red, glaring at the stack of pancakes on a plate in front of her.

"It was the night before she died?"

"She didn't call but once a month or so. But when she did, we always talked good. Long."

He toys with a forkful of Spanish omelette. Takes a bite. Listens for a lie, but feels something else. The miracle that was Liberty maybe.

"Like I said. She was an angel. Never held it against me what I do to earn the bread. She had a powerful faith, growing up in that church school she went to before Tolchester. Said it was God's will. God's will we love each other to death … I lost my baby." Tears.

He feels the pain flow, ebb. Waits a while before he speaks again.

"But that last call … it was different? She was scared?"

"I don't know what time she called. Late. Like I was at this after-hours joint in Roxbury. Me and some of the other girls, partying, looking for maybe one last trick to make our night."

"She called you on your cell?"

"She said she wanted to come home. Like to the hood. Like fuck all those white folks. Some kind of terrible racist thing going down."

He takes another bite of the omelette, screws up his face. Swallows hard.

"The note? It called her a 'wog gash.'"

"She said it was something awful. I didn't really understand. I couldn't hear her very well. Lot of noise in the club, you know?"

"Anything else?"

"She was crying. I told her be cool. Give it a day. That school was a big opportunity for her. Don't just piss it away because of one ignorant threat. There are ignorant people everywhere want to bully you. But …"

"But what?"

"She just kept saying, *I feel so lonely tonight, Mama. So scared.*"

"She mention any names? Another student, a teacher?"

"Just her friend, that China girl Gracie. Said Gracie was the only one who knew about the note."

"I've got to ask you. You think that note could have put her in such a dark place, she would take her life? Or was there something else tearing her apart?"

She takes a tentative bite of pancake. "Liberty was always such a happy kid. You said you saw her videos. Sure she would get down sometimes, but it was like for fifteen minutes or so. We talk on the phone, she tells me some problem. Work it out for herself before we ever done talking. She was like that. A survivor."

"But that last time … ?"

"I thought it was pretty much the same old thing. She was on top of it when she hung up. Said she was going to pray on the problem, talk things over about the note and such next day with that Indian lady, Dr. Patterson. She was good to Liberty, you know? But she had her own life, too. Good-looking single woman. Boyfriends. Lot of guys sniffing around …"

He feels a jolt in his gut. Maybe he has been missing something, like the Drag Queen Tuki Aparecio's boyfriend who ambushed him a year ago when he was representing Tuki in the Provincetown Follies murder case.

"What about boyfriends? Did Liberty have a boyfriend? Problems with a romance?"

"Kevin."

His hand drops his forkful of omelette on his plate. He stares at the omelette like there's something foul about the taste. "You ever meet him? She talk about him much?"

"Some. He's a white boy."

Sweat soaking the brown face. Fine white sand crusting over the cheeks. Her long, black hair trailing in the seaweed. The roar of the surf. What you going to do now?

"I think his father teaches at the school."

"How long had she been seeing him?"

"Since last fall."

"Any problems?"

"We didn't talk that much about him. She just said he made her laugh."

He suddenly grabs the bottle of squeeze ketchup and starts squirting it all over his omelette. "You think she was sexually active?"

"She said she was saving herself for marriage. I kid you not. It was something she picked up from that church school."

"You get any sense he might have been trying to change her mind?"

12

"WHAT'S the matter, sweet?"

Danny's hand starts raking up the back of her neck, lifting her hair in waves.

She shudders, pulls away. Lying on her side. Her eyes trace the shapes of tree limbs in the shadows cast by the moonlight on the bedroom wall. The comforter crushing her into the lumpy bed. Not her bed.

"Please … !" With a violent heave, she throws off the covers. Sits up.

"What?"

"I feel all itchy inside."

"Just lie back … close your eyes … let me help you …"

She feels Danny easing her back onto the sheets. Lips on her belly. A gentle hand rising up her thigh. Her lover's tenderness, desire. What she has always wanted, maybe, a focus on her own needs. For once. Not a man's needs. But a lover whose body can give and give and give. Maybe unto death.

"Danny …"

"Relax ... you've been under a mountain of stress." Lips and tongue gliding along the horn of her hip. Fingers, frighteningly smart, finding their ways into secret coves. Her loins begin to roll, rise with the voice of Billie Holiday calling from the stereo: "All of Me."

But her heart shouts. *Stop. Please.*

"Stop!"

She sits up again, puts her face in her hands.

"Love?"

"I feel like I want to rip off my skin."

"Have a sip of wine and ..."

She pushes the offered goblet away.

"I can't do this tonight, Danny. God knows I want to ... But I just can't."

"If it's this place, we could go to somewhere more private like—"

"No. I don't ... I just can't ..."

"It's OK."

"No it's not. You've been so patient and kind and generous and ..." Her voice wet with sobs.

"Shsssssssssss ..."

"I feel like something has been tearing me in half. Ripping me into short, hard little pieces."

"Is it me?"

"Why did I let you stop me from seeing Liberty that night, from helping her?"

"You want to talk about it?"

Praise Allah. The tribal drums. Flutes. Dulcimers. Pounding. And now tears. Pleading. You want to kill me, American? Kill me now? Like the others?

"I can't."

*   *   *

"Did I ever tell you about Liberty's mother?" She tries to relax the iron rods that are her arms, legs. Settle back in Danny's arms. The bed frame creaks as they put the full weight of their backs against the antique maple headboard.

"The hooker?"

"Michael went to see her."

"The fisherman you told me about."

"The lawyer. My mother's friend."

"The hired gun Gracie made you—"

"He was my idea. I just need someone outside this whole mess with Liberty to help put this behind me. Tie up the loose ends."

"You could have asked me."

"You're so busy … And I need you for this." Snuggling.

"How'd this guy find Liberty's mom?"

"On the street."

"He picked her up?"

"I don't know."

"But he's one of these sick people you were talking about?"

"No. Damn. How do I know? My mother liked him a lot."

"I heard that drag queen client of his on the Cape did too."

"She told him something."

"The queen?"

"Liberty's mother."

"What?"

"Liberty called her the night before she died."

"Really?"

"Like while we were … you know?"

"Oh."

"Yeah. She told her mother that I had a boyfriend sleeping over."

A child calling for her. Pain in the voice. A tearing loose of the soul. A heart in free fall. Needing her.

"So? It's nobody's business but our own. We're adults. Just because you live in a fishbowl doesn't mean—"

"I don't like it. Him asking about me. About us."

"You don't have to tell him anything. He works for you."

"Not really. I'm not paying him. No one is. I think he sees himself acting on Gracie's behalf. You know? If someone really killed Liberty, maybe Gracie is in danger too. She's started calling him. She says she talks to him. A lot."

"Jesus, I don't know. I think these girls have gone way down the rabbit hole with their conspiracy theories. If it looks like a suicide, and smells like a suicide, it's probably a suicide. Awful. But understandable."

"But what if somebody wanted to hurt Liberty?"

"Why?"

"Maybe she found out something nobody wanted her to know about the existence of secret societies at T-C."

"You think kids would kill her because of a club?"

"OK, it's a long shot, I admit. But she did get a threat."

"Did it mention one of these clubs?"

"No."

"Well?"

"I don't know. OK, maybe it was something else she did to make an enemy. You know Liberty had a boyfriend? Kevin Singleton."

"Jack Singleton's boy?"

"Captain of the track team. A senior."

"Ummm."

"What if he wanted more from her than she was willing to give?"

"So he slit her wrists, dumped her in the bathtub?"

"It makes me feel like there are nails exploding inside my heart."

"I'm sorry you feel so miserable. I wish there was something I …"

"This talking helps. I need perspective."

"There is absolutely no evidence that Kevin Singleton or anyone except Liberty hurt Liberty Baker."

She says Michael has been saying the same thing—with great conviction. Until this afternoon.

"What changed?"

"I'm not sure."

"Can I ask you a question? What do you think is in it for this guy Decastro? What does he care about Liberty Baker or Gracie or Tory or you?"

"I don't know. Maybe we all have some debts to pay the gods?"

"Maybe he has a thing for dead girls."

13

"THIS better be good."

She sees him squinting at her across the steel table, a bunch of *lo mein* noodles pinched between the chopsticks in his right hand.

Her gaze drifts away, off to her right, toward a vendor's counter as if she's looking to see if her plate of spring rolls is up yet. But what she's really doing is giving him permission to look at her. *See me, Michael. See the strength in my jaw. See my observant eyes. See the way my breasts swell beneath the V-neck sweater, too. Ninja Girl.*

She wonders if he sees anything, feels anything. Wonders if he knows she dressed for him tonight. That no matter what he thinks, she's not a kid anymore. That she's got to find Lib's killer. That she's scared. That she's heading way out on a limb here. That she can't do this without him.

And now she's got something to show him that could change everything. Maybe even the way he thinks of her. Maybe make him see her as something more than some crazy chick with a conspiracy theory.

He's playing with his noodles with the chopsticks, not eating.

"What's the matter, you don't like Chinese food? Want to try some of this soup?"

She pushes her bowl of *won ton* toward him, offers her spoon. Looks into his dark eyes, surveys those high Latin cheeks, the shadow of his heavy beard, the cords of his neck. Smiles. Smells the ginger, the hot pepper, steamed onions. Basil. Lots of sweet basil. Music's rising in her head. One of Lib's favorites. Beyonce Knowles' "Green Light."

She tries to imagine herself as one of Charlie's Angels. As Lucy Liu. Tough, no-nonsense ninja. But the picture in her head keeps morphing. She can't help it. She's seeing the inside of a dark Hong Kong bar in the Wanchai district. A girl in a thong working a pole dance to the rhythm. Her. *OMG, if he only knew how much I want him to really see me. To be a ninja knight.*

"Hey, Michael! You with me here?"

He blinks, coming out of a secret place of his own, maybe. Seems to see for the first time the bright lights of this busy food court tucked above a fortune cookie bakery in Boston's Chinatown. Seems to see her, too. This girl full of yearning opposite him at the table. Her nose stud a tiny ruby today, winking at him.

"I was just thinking … What was I saying?"

"This better be good."

"What do you mean?"

"That's what YOU said. I think you were talking about the *lo mein* I ordered for you."

He shakes his head no. "I was talking about what you want to tell me. I'm not in the habit of having secret rendezvous in backroom restaurants with high school girls."

Ouch.

"Come on. Admit this is a cool place."

He looks around. Takes in a dozen different vendors stirring their woks, ladling out soup, blending shakes of durian and strange red beans. Street people, a few suits, lovers waiting in line for their food. Inhales the smells again.

Can he smell the tamarind, my Tommy Girl perfume?

She gives him an urgent smile, feels her hair frizzing in the steamy air.

"Definitely funky!"

"See, I knew you'd like it. A great date place, don't you think?"

He sighs. "We're not having a date, Gracie. You said to meet you here because you had something you wanted to show me. Please, can we get on with this?"

Put a knife in my heart.

"If somebody you know sees us here, they might get the wrong idea. What? What was so urgent that you had to sneak off campus tonight?"

"You mean that you had to drive the whole way up here from that fishing boat, or wherever you live?"

"Yeah. OK. Come on. What couldn't you tell me on the phone?"

Whoa, adrenaline rush. Work it.

She feels the power of her secret. "Swear you won't tell anyone."

"Sure. I swear. What?"

"Swear. Look at me."

He levels those lazy bedroom eyes on her.

Oh yeah … Hang on, baby.

"Are you ready for this?"

"Gracie!"

"I've got Lib's journal."

"Her what?"

"Her journal. You know, her diary. She's been keeping it like forever."

"Where did you—"

"Stole it. Bumbledork had it in his office, shoved under a bunch of papers on his desk. Tory spotted it yesterday, when he called her in to ask her how she was doing. You know, with Liberty's death and school and all."

"You just snatched it?"

She smiles. *Like how cool am I now? Ninja Girl warrior.*

"It's not his! He's the one who stole it. I just got it back this morning when it was my turn to go see the great and powerful Bumbledork for tea and sympathy.

"How … ?"

"Girl power. I threw like a major crying fit. When he went looking for a box of tissues, I scored Lib's journal. Here!" She opens her messenger's bag, removes a ragged, red, cloth-bound notebook. Laminated to the cover is a magazine photo of Denzel Washington dressed as a Civil War soldier for the 54th Massachusetts Brigade. A promo shot from the film *Glory.*

"Wow!"

"Denzel was her hero."

"So there's something in here?"

"You said you wanted to know all about her thing with Kevin."

"Singleton? Her boyfriend?"

"Feast your eyes."

"You read it, huh?"

"You don't think I'd make you come all the way to Chinatown just to buy you noodles."

She sees something shift in his shoulders, his back. He's suddenly leaning toward her across the table. Eyes widening. His cheeks a little darker.

"Well, you know, I …"

Is he flirting?

She blinks, wets her eyes, hopes they really catch the light now. Her lip gloss, too. My god she's such a little slut. Woman warrior.

"Check it out."

She hands him the open journal, pages in green script. Feels the warmth of his fingers as they brush hers in the hand-off. Watches the smile burst across his face. Glowing at her. Only her. Not Doc P. Ninja Girl. In this kick-ass black sweater.

Score.

14

HE reads.

Kevin's being kind of a dick tonight. I called him to tell him about this awful note I found in my physics book today. I was crying. I told him I wanted to see him. Please come over to Hibernia House. Or meet me at the boathouse down by Hourglass Lake. Like PLEASE! He said it was too late. He couldn't get out of the house without making his parents suspicious and they were already on his case because his grades had started to suck.

Go talk to Doc P, he said.

Yeah right, like thanks a whole lot, pal!!! I'm always there for him whenever he has a bad day. How many times have I snuck away after lights-out to meet him at the boathouse to give him some TLC? Why isn't he here for me the same way? Are all guys like this? Can you ever trust them to take care of your heart? And if you can't trust them, how can they ever in their wildest dreams think you are going to give it up for them? That's what I want to know.

I think I'll give him the cold shoulder for the next couple of days. See how Mr. Stay-at-Home likes that.

For some reason he feels hot, sweaty a little around the temples.
Maybe it's the MSG in the *lo mein*. Maybe just the weirdness of this
place. Or the way she's looking at him. Way too intense.

"She's sure not too happy with him," he says.

"Yesterday you asked if they were having trouble. I told you I
thought things were pretty good between them. But now you see ..."

Her eyes glisten. Proud eyes, hungry eyes.

He wipes the sweat at his hairline with his fingers. "What happened to your theory about a secret society being behind Liberty's
death?"

She leans toward him. Elbows on the table, chin in her hand.
"I don't know. I still think it's a real possibility. I mean, there was
that note. But on *CSI* the boyfriend or husband is always the first
guy the police want to talk to. So, maybe she tried to dump him
and then he ... ?"

"If they had a fight. If anything leading up to her death was violent, the medical examiner would have found some evidence." Sweat is
beading on his chest, tickling his solar plexis.

Dude?

"But maybe he just slipped her some roofies, first."

"Why?"

"Maybe he wanted to date-rape her." She pauses, seems to scan his
face with almost imperceptible shifts of her eyes. "Like to get even, you
know? Maybe he got carried away."

Something deep in his head has begun to smoke, burn. Anger, for sure.
And something else. "You think Kevin Singleton is that kind of kid?"

She scrunches up her face. "I don't know."

"Is it hot in here?"

Her hand reaches over, covers his as she turns the page. "Look.
There's more."

* * *

I went downstairs and tried to talk to Doc P about this racist note and Kevin and everything. But she couldn't talk. OK, it was late, and she said she was in bed. Fair enough.

But Doc P almost always has my back. Tonight, I know she couldn't talk because she had someone in her bed with her. She thinks I don't know about her boyfriends. But this is an old house, and sometimes I can hear things going on downstairs. Like sappy, whack music. The bed creaking. Moaning.

This one guy, who looks like Tupac Shakur, is always sniffing around Hibernia House. Laying down his lines. Like trying to relate to me b/c I'm a sister from the hood. Maybe he's trying to hit on me. I don't know.

Fool. She ought to drop him like a hot potato. She said things were all over with him. But you never know. I don't see his car on the street, though. So maybe she is branching out. With Doc P, it's like that book Smart Women, Foolish Choices. *Sometimes I feel her hurt. Lonely lady.*

Anyway, I needed to talk. So I called Tedeeka. She's a good listener. Pretty amazing how we connect.

But she's not a big one for advice. Especially about love. She's got a pimp whips her butt all over Roxbury.

Take care of number one, baby, she told me!

Word, Teddie, I think. How do I do that when I got a boyfriend afraid to come out and comfort me, a house counselor like to lose her mind for one faithless fool after another, a mother turning tricks on the street? And, oh yeah, the KKK or Red Tooth or whoever breathing down my neck?

What I need is a big hug and some action. Not some of Teddie's street jive. Well, it's 4:00 in the morning, and I got to catch some ZZZZZZZZ for my beauty sleep. Then help Gracie with our history project. Secret societies? Probably a lot of male nonsense. More later.

The rest of the journal is blank.

He wipes away the sweat on his forehead again.

She still has her elbows on the table. Her chin cupped in her hands. Staring at those last words in Lib's journal … and him. Wondering about all those black whiskers on his cheeks, whether she really thinks they're sexy.

"So?"

"I don't get it, Gracie."

Sometimes guys can be so clueless. It's kind of cute.

He squints at her. She's the knower here. The mystery. Ninja Girl.

"What's not to get?"

He says he doesn't see how any of this adds up to murder. Or points a finger at a suspect. He just sees a desperate, depressed girl.

"I thought you were Sir Lancelot."

Smile, babe.

"Cut it out. I'm a fisherman, not one of those guys on *Law & Order*."

She wonders whether she's laying it on a little too thick. But what the hell, this is her time to shine, right?

"Gracie?"

"You sure don't get females …"

He shifts in his seat, looks like he's going to stand up. Walk right out of here.

She grabs his left hand—it's like this involuntary thing. "Don't you see? Liberty wasn't really depressed. When teenage girls are REALLY depressed, they stop eating, they shit on everything, even themselves. They totally lose their sense of humor. They stop thinking about schoolwork. And they don't sleep. Or they sleep ALL the time. Trust me on this."

He looks at her hand holding his hand. "What are you saying?"

She tells him to read between the lines. Pauses. Unhands him, doesn't want him to think she's clingy. Just real. A force. The ninja warrior in the killer sweater.

"I think I'm out of my league."

She smiles, says Liberty was bitter and confused about how males treat females. That seemed to bother her even more than the awful note. But she still had the ability to feel for Doc P and her mother. Still the same girl as in the videos. Still had her sense of humor, her whack sarcasm. Still thinking about her beauty sleep and working on the history stuff.

He says that's not exactly a smoking gun. Why would your headmaster want to steal Liberty's journal?

She swallows a bite of *Moo Shi* pork. "That's the sixty-four-million-dollar question. What was he looking for in here? What did he find? What was he trying to keep out of the public eye? And does it point to Liberty's murder?"

She watches his mouth. Sees him roll a noodle over his tongue, swallow. There's a buzzing starting along the insides of her legs. A bubble building in her chest. *Fuck, would you just look at this guy's beautiful face.*

"Maybe Awasha will shed some light on this."

"You can't tell her about the journal."

"Why?"

"First, you promised ..." She licks her lips. "And, second, it would break her heart."

"Damn." His voice arcs. She can hear the lightning, feel the strike.

"Yeah."

Exhale.

"This is between us."

Exhale.

"So now what?"

"Maybe I should have another look at Hibernia House. I missed a lot the first time around."

Exhale.

"The school has posted No Trespassing signs. But Ninja Girl knows the secret passage in."

"We can't go in there alone. It could be dangerous."

No shit, Sherlock.

15

AWASHA has seemed on edge since before they entered Hibernia House through the back alley, the basement door. Gracie's secret passage in.

Now as soon as he asks if he can see her apartment, it's clear he's really hit a nerve. She has been staring out the dormer window, probably watching for one of the school's green and white Honda SUV's the security folks drive. Now she wheels back toward him, her long, black hair cutting a perfect arc through the harsh morning light. Her eyes suddenly a ghost crab's, on sticks.

"Why do you want to see my apartment?"

Tory shoots Gracie a look. Like *what the fuck?*

"Is it a problem?"

"No. But it would not be cool at all if someone found us in here. And I just don't see—"

"You said Liberty came into your place the night before she died. She let herself in. I want to see how she did that, where she was. Maybe … I don't know."

"Whatever. Come on!"

She leads him and the two teenage girls out of Liberty's empty quarters, the scrubbed walls and oak floors giving off a mercurial glow. Across the moth-eaten oriental rug in the common room, James Dean still leers from the poster over the mantle. They go down the students' stairwell. Treads, creaking. Two flights to a dirty white door. She tries the door. It's locked. She hisses, fishes in her bag for keys.

"Was the door always locked?"

"Never. Doc P left it unlocked for us," says Tory.

"I guess the maintenance people must have locked up."

She keys the lock, opens the door into a small study. Everyone files in.

"Was it locked last week when I was here?"

She looks confused. "What do you mean?"

He says that when she hid him in the closet upstairs, she came down here with someone—a colleague, she said. For tea.

"Oh … right. I don't know. Why is this … ? No. It was unlocked. I remember."

"So someone has been in the building since last week? Maybe in your apartment?"

She frowns. "These damn people. Nothing is private. I don't know why I work in a place like this."

Tory and Gracie shuffle in their thick winter coats, hugging themselves. The school has dropped the heat in Hibernia House to about fifty degrees to conserve energy. Vapor puffs from the girls' lungs, Awasha's, his. They are all panting. A cloud rising toward the ceiling. Her private rooms overhead on the second floor.

She had someone in her bed with her. She thinks I don't know about her boyfriends … It's like that book Smart Women, Foolish Choices. *Sometimes I feel her hurt. Lonely lady.*

"You want to show me around?"

"Can we do this fast, someone might …" Her voice sounds raw.

He understands. This seems fruitless. But if there is one thing he learned from the Provincetown Follies case, it is that absolutely nothing tops a thorough re-creation of events leading up to a death when it comes to getting beyond speculation and misunderstanding.

"What would Liberty have done when she came in here that night? Would she have stayed in this room?"

"No. If Doc P is not in her office, we usually go into the living room and call for her." Gracie gives a little shrug. "It's a big house. She never hears us call if we stay in here."

Awasha sighs, leads the crew out of the study into an immense Victorian salon. High ceilings, huge marble fireplace. Antique furnishings, a grand piano in one corner.

"The living room. I just don't get what you expect—"

"This place is pretty amazing."

"The furnishings belong to the school. An historic house, they expect me to entertain. So they decorate the public rooms on the first floor. Lot of old WASP stuff."

"You sound annoyed."

"I really don't want to have to explain to someone why we're in here. Why these girls are in here when they are supposed to be at the all-school assembly."

"But look at this place."

"Yeah." She eyes oils of a half-dozen portraits of the American gentry, circa 1850. And one of Edgar Hibernia by the piano. "A memorial to a bunch of dead white guys."

Tory clears her throat. "It's kind of spooky when you come in here late at night, the lights off. Like all those dudes on the wall watching you."

He looks around. Even on this bright morning the room reminds him of a funeral parlor. Purple, filtered light. He tries to picture Liberty in here sometime after midnight. A black girl in a room full of dead white men. Bruised by the words *wog gash*, craving a hug. But his mind blanks on an image, keeps picturing the scene he cannot talk about. Awasha with Tupac Shakur.

The bed creaking. Moaning ... Sappy whack music.

He spots the stereo. An old-school component set-up tucked on a bookshelf beside the fireplace.

"Can we go now, please? It's just a matter of time before security or some maintenance worker shows up to check on the heat."

"You listen to a lot of music?"

The girls roll their eyes.

Maybe she blushes. Her skin just the tiniest bit redder across the bridge of the nose.

Suddenly he has this urge to see her music. Maybe hear it. Just plain, dumb curiosity.

He spots an album box, empty, in front of the tuner. Next to an open can of Red Bull. He picks up the box. Squints to read its contents. It's a homemade mix of love songs. Luther Vandross. Al Green. Oleta Adams, "Get Here." Mariah Carey, "Vision of Love." Cyndi Lauper, "Time After Time." More. A duet, "Can't We Try?"

He cocks his head, squints at her. Gives her a silly smile.

"You going to disrespect my taste in music? We didn't come in here so that—"

"Doc P, you have to admit—"

"Hey, if I can't control what's on my walls, at least I can control what I listen to. How do you think it is down here when you girls are raging with Bow Wow, Puffy, Public Enemy and that crowd twenty-four seven. Sometimes hip hop can ..."

He says he likes this stuff. He's got every Al Green album ever made. His mom and dad were addicted. Dad cranks "Sha-La -La" every time they are hauling back on the *Rosa Lee*.

"Great, Michael. We need to get out of here. There's nothing in here that has to do with Liberty."

"Hauling back?" asks Gracie.

"Bringing in our net. Full of fish ... hopefully."

"We should get out of here. Before somebody sees ..."

He's clicking on the stereo, suddenly feeling a little giddy, for no reason other than memories of love songs blasting over the deck of the *Rosa Lee*. The scent of fresh cod squirming in the net.

"One song, OK?"

"Not now!"

Harold Melvin and the Blue Notes Launch into "If you Don't Know Me By Now."

The violins are just winding up, sweet, up-tempo, when she kills the power. "We're out of here. This is a dead end. Show's over. Come on before we all have to answer a lot of uncomfortable questions."

"Can I borrow your mix?"

She gives him a totally exasperated look. "If you swear to stop snooping around my apartment and get the hell out of here."

"Scouts honor."

She opens the CD tray, reaches for the album box to put away the mix.

"Hey what's this?" The open can of Red Bull is in her hands.

He shrugs. "You forgot to finish your can of rocket fuel?"

"I don't drink this stuff ... Girls?"

"Liberty," says Tory. "She craved it."

"Maybe she left the can in here the night she ..."

Gracie shakes her head, says maybe not. She's pretty sure she drank her last one trying to write that freaking précis.

He clears his throat, then asks in a low voice, "I'd like to take this for awhile."

16

"JESUS, let me guess. This isn't a social call. You drove all the way out here on the Cape to ask me for a favor. Like a big fucking favor. Am I right, Rambo?"

Detective Lou Votolatto leans back in his swivel chair, pushes back from his desk. Stretches his long legs out, exposing mismatched socks. One blue, one gray. He cups his nose between the fingers of both hands, sighs. The little cubicle in the West Barnstable state police barracks seems the size of a squirrel cage.

"I'm on my knees, Lou."

"I thought you quit the law ... The fishing sucks right now, eh?"

"We've been stormed in ... so I'm trying to help out a friend."

"Oh Christ. I can't even imagine what you got yourself into this time. Please don't tell me your dragon lady client has reappeared in Provincetown, and we are going to be dancing a tango around her immigration status again."

"I haven't heard from Tuki."

"Well consider it a minor blessing. That little petunia had you so tied in knots, most of the time you didn't know your asshole from your ear."

"I need to get this tested." He hands the detective an open can of Red Bull.

"What's this?"

"Maybe evidence a kid was murdered."

"A little kid?"

"Seventeen-year-old girl. She died about two weeks ago at the Tolchester-Coates School."

"That place on the edge of Boston? Where our illustrious politicians send their kids?"

"Some of them. The smart ones."

"No shit? A girl died there? How come I didn't hear about it?"

He says the M.E. ruled it a suicide. The school seems to have kept a pretty tight lid on publicity.

"Yeah, and news seems to travel by dogsled on the Cape at this time of year. Can you believe all these freaking blizzards?!"

He looks out the window at ten-foot piles of snow rimming the parking lot.

"How in hell does a nice Portagee fisherboy like you get involved in a prep school scandal?"

"I'm not involved. I'm just trying to help out a friend."

"Ten to one there is at least one really pretty woman involved."

"Come on, Lou."

"You think someone offed this poor kid with a can of Red Bull? Are you pulling my chain, Rambo?"

"What do you know about rohypnol?"

"You mean roofies? R-2, rope? Someone date-raped this kid?"

"I don't know. I don't think so. The autopsy doesn't say."

"Then what? She died how?"

"Wrists slit. Razor blade. She bled to death in a bathtub. Girls dormitory."

The detective winces. "I hate that one."

He asks if Votolatto has ever heard of someone knocking out a victim with some kind of drug, then killing her.

"Yeah, sure it happens. But I've never seen anyone make a murder look like a wrist job. At least not well enough to fool an M.E."

That's what bothers him, he says. Could be this really is just a suicide. Rohypnol is undetectable in the body after less than twenty-four hours, but if this girl had been knocked out when someone cut her open, wouldn't traces of the drug remain in the corpse? If she was dead, she couldn't metabolize the drug.

"What put you onto roofies? I mean, who thinks someone wanted to harm this girl?"

He tells him about Gracie and the other girls that lived in the dorm. About Awasha. How they all swear Liberty Baker was too emotionally grounded to kill herself. And she was afraid of knives.

"But here's the thing. She got a threatening message the day before she died."

"So why aren't the local cops and the CPAC guys up there all over this?"

"The M.E.'s report. No signs of violence, no alcohol, no drugs."

"Sounds like a done deal."

"Will you test the Red Bull for me? So some of these survivors can get on with their lives? Isn't there a standard toxicology kit you guys use to test for this stuff?"

"Yeah, but it doesn't test for roofies. And quite a lot of other stuff."

"Is this the same kit the M.E. would have used for the autopsy?"

"No doubt."

"So he might not have tested for roofies at all?"

"Not if he had no reason to suspect them."

"Shit."

"Yeah." The detective sets the can down on his desk. "Maybe I can get some tests run ... You want to tell me about this dead girl?"

"A real superstar. Track, biology, singer. A disadvantaged kid on scholarship from Mattapan."

"Race?"

He pauses. Takes a deep breath. Swallows some saliva. "Black. Well, biracial actually."

"How come that was hard for you to say?"

* * *

A soft whisper in his ear. "You're not lily white, are you?"

They are in a crowd of spring breakers at the swim-up bar, a saltwater pool at a hotel on Paradise Island, Nassau. The Republic of the Bahamas. More than a hundred teenagers are dancing in the pool, flirting, getting trashed. Mostly college kids from the South. But some preppies from New England, too. Like him and his three pals from St. John's of the Harbor, Newport, RI. This is a yearly ritual for his friends, real preppies, born and bred. But totally new for him, a one-year post-grad student on scholarship to St. J's to play football.

Ziggy Marley's jamming over the PA system. "Tomorrow People." People are singing along, the song their anthem.

He feels his arms slide around her smooth, dark back. Holds her against him. Sways a little to the music. He smells the mix of salt, gin, lime on her face. Long African hair pulled back tight against her head, ponytail hanging from a bright orange band. This island girl. This Bahamian.

She's from Nassau, a district called Over-the-Hill. Here with a few friends for the Break. For the Americans. A high schooler like him. Crashing the party.

"Are you black?"

"Does it matter?"

"Maybe." *Her breath on his neck. Her hips easing against his.*

His head buzzes from the beer.

"It's kind of a long story ... Want to walk down to the beach?"

She looks anxiously at her three friends. They are mounted on the shoulders of his buddies, having a water fight in the middle of the pool.

Her eyes black, wet. Begging a question he can't hear, can't even imagine.

"It's getting dark. The beach can be a dangerous place."

"God's own truth, Cassie. You'll be safe with me."

"Promise?"

17

WHEN she finds Gracie and Tory, they are in the girls' locker room after swimming practice, wrapped in towels, fluffing their hair with blow dryers.

"We need to talk!"

"Now?"

"Just keep your towels on and follow me."

She's wearing a flannel maroon robe, so long its hem drags on the floor as she leads the girls into the faculty women's locker complex. The place seems empty. Beyond the rows of lockers, she opens a door that leads into a conference room with a TV, dining table, sofa, stereo, phone, kitchenette, sports magazines.

As soon as the girls are in this room, she locks the door behind them and grabs three plastic bottles of water from the fridge.

"What's going on, Doc P?"

"I'll tell you in the steam room, Gracie." She hands each girl a water bottle.

"What?"

She nods to an opaque glass door. Steam hisses from vents on the other side.

"There's a steam bath in here? The faculty gets a steam bath?" Tory's eyes are big, black agates.

"Let's go. In girls! Private times and places to talk around this school seem in short supply these days."

* * *

The steam room is a hot fog, the vapor so thick she can barely see the silvery silhouettes of the girls sitting on the white-tiled bench seat to her left, backs against the wall.

"Come on, girls. Help me out here. Are you hiding something from me?"

"I don't know what you mean," Gracie says.

"Really, Doc P, whose side are you on?"

"That's not fair, Tory. And you know it. I'm putting my job on the line for you girls and Liberty."

"But all of a sudden you've gotten so suspicious … and, well, paranoid."

She wipes the sweat from her eyes. Takes a long drink of water, tries to feel its smooth chill sliding down her throat, cooling her heart.

"Just tell me about Kevin, OK?"

"I don't see why you're suddenly so interested in everything about Kevin. And why we can't talk about all this at Beedle House, your office, or the Tuck Shop?" Gracie's voice echoes off the walls, pained, annoyed really.

"I don't trust those places anymore. I swear this school has ears. You know, Kevin's father is an old friend of the headmaster. The last thing I want to do is start a rumor, OK? Please just bear with me … and trust me. Be honest."

"So you think Kevin hurt Lib?"

"Didn't you tell me he was the one who started Liberty on her Red Bull kick, Tory?"

"Yeah ..."

"Well Michael gave it to a detective friend of his to check out."

"They found something nasty in that can didn't they, Doc? That's why you're acting so freaked."

She says she doesn't know. But the Red Bull suddenly appeared in her apartment. Out of the blue. Liberty couldn't have put it there, because she was out of Red Bull. But what if she saw Kevin that night and he gave her a can? Or maybe he left the can himself?

"I don't think he gave her the Red Bull," Gracie says.

"Why?"

"They were having a fight. She was mad at him."

She suddenly feels dizzy. "When did you plan on telling me this?"

"I'm sorry, Doc. It seemed like no biggie. Just the usual guy trouble. You know how that goes?"

She needs to gasp for air. But when she opens her mouth and inhales, the steam sears her lungs. "Christ!"

"We're sorry, Doc ... You think someone else left that can at your place? Like went in there on his own or something?"

"I don't know. But it sure as hell is not going to look good for me if that Red Bull turns up poisoned."

"You really think Kevin was snooping around in your apartment? It was like his can?"

"Tell me. Is he into drugs?"

Nobody says anything. The heat kicks on again. Awasha is listening to the bubbling and crackling of the steam when she hears the faint clunk of a door closing outside in the conference room. She stiffens, is rising to her feet to see who's outside, who could have a key to unlock the door, when Tory speaks. She says she smoked pot a few times with Kevin. Just a little bud. Down by Hourglass Lake. Well they did some X together once before a dance. Actually, twice.

"Liberty, too?"

"No. She really wasn't into that stuff, Doc."

"Kevin just shared these drugs?"

"Well ... we gave him money to get the stuff."

"So he's the go-to guy for drugs around T-C?"

"He has his connections. Like it's high school, Doc."

A viper's uncoiling in her core.

"Does he write racist notes, too?" Her words sound halfway between a scream and a prayer.

18

HE'S draining the oil in the *Rosa Lee*'s big Caterpillar when he gets the detective's call. The engine room smells of hot sulfur, baking paint, batteries gassing off a little. He doesn't know why he isn't wearing rubber gloves to do this job. Maybe he still gets a thrill from getting covered in hot, black oil up to his elbows. Whatever. It takes him so long to wipe off his hands and fish the phone out of his jeans pocket, that he misses the call.

All he's left with is the message:

"Where the hell are you, Rambo? I got some news on your Red Bull. You want to meet me about four-thirty to talk about this? We're not dealing with roofies here. But you sure as hell hit pay dirt."

Votolatto's message says the lab rats found of GHB. Gamma hydroxy butyrate. Another date rape drug. Called *liquid-X* and *scoop* on the street. The Red Bull had something like ten times the normal dose or GHB to knock out somebody. Enough to put a person into a coma—or stop a heart if she had finished the whole can.

He feels the blood draining from his eyes. Drops the phone away from his ear, Lou Votolatto's message still playing. A scratchy voice, saying something about meeting for chowder at a bar in Woods Hole, then fading to nothing. He hears only the whir of the nor'west wind topside, the groan of the Rosa Lee tugging at her lines, the squeal of the steel hull against the heavy rubber fenders of the fish boat rafted inboard. Waves slapping the boat windward.

His back sags against the metal wall, knees buckling as he slides slowly down the bulkhead. He is sitting on the diamond-plate catwalk around the engine, staring blankly at the knees of his jeans. Already the sharp scent of salt, gin, a whole lot of limes, rising in his mind.

*   *   *

On the beach in the dark. The sky raining stars. They sit facing each other in their bathing suits on the sand, warm surf swirling in tiny waves around them. His bare legs, bare feet, stretching out before him, pressing the soles of her feet.

They both lean back, braced by their arms. Cassie wants to try this odd form of intimacy she read about in a Kurt Vonnegut novel, Cat's Cradle. *Boko-maru.*

"Close your eyes," she says. "When two people are like this, you know, sole-to-sole, they cannot lie."

He feels a little surge of pressure, the tips of her toes rolling gently against his. Knows he may soon admit to things that he never talks about with anyone.

"So where did you get your dark blood?"

The question is a wasp in his head. His mind filling with pictures of the long-dead woman he called Vóvó Chocolate.

"It came from an island a long way from here. But maybe not so different."

"In Africa?"

"Near. São Vicente. The Cape Verdes."

"The green capes." Her voice is lazy from an afternoon of gin and tonics.

"My mother's mother. She died when I was little. Spoke the old language."

"You mean she sang her words Bahamian style, mon?"

"Only in Crioulo.*"*

"African."

He says Criuolo *is a blend of African languages and Portuguese.*

"A callaloo stew, we call that. Kind of like you … and me."

"Oh …"

"Except you got more from your father, the European side, right? I got most of the African."

He opens his eyes. Looks at her, lids still closed, the face of the moon's daughter tilting toward Venus. Her body a mermaid's at rest. Cristo.

"And you don't pay no never-mind, to your African blood."

"Until I come to a place like this …" The words gush out.

His heart quivers.

"Is that a confession?"

The surf thunders offshore on a reef. He says nothing. Just wonders who this new self is. This Crioulo.

"So maybe we could be long lost cousins." She reaches out for his hand. "Kissing cousins."

* * *

"What are you going to do now, Rambo?"

He eyes the detective over his nearly-empty mug of draft. Watches from his barstool as the fire in the wood stove at the center of the room sputters and flares. Outside the bay windows of this Woods Hole pub called Captain Kidd's, Eel Pond is a wind-whipped snowfield dotted with a few lobster boats and a small sloop frozen at their moorings.

"That's why I'm here, Lou. I need some serious advice."

"You are totally fucked when it comes to the chain of evidence."

"What about prints?"

"A lot of people have touched that can of Red Bull, including you and me. Didn't you say you found it like two weeks after that poor girl's death?"

"It was in her dorm counselor's apartment, by the stereo in the living room."

"Which is not where she died."

"Not even close."

"And no one saw your dead girl with the Red Bull?"

He says no. If you believe her friends, she was addicted to the stuff. Usually kept a stash of it. But the night before she died, one of Liberty's pals drank the last one.

"What you're saying is the very existence of this can is a mystery. That the house counselor doesn't drink the stuff. Never saw our can before the morning you found it."

"She found it."

"How do you know she didn't plant this thing?"

"Why?"

"As a distraction? As manufactured evidence to make it look like there's been a crime here? As bait to keep you around? Maybe she wants your bod. I don't know. I can think of a million reasons."

"She's not like that. Her mother used to be my landlady. A total sweetheart."

The detective shakes his head. Disbelief. "So that excuses everything."

He says she seemed totally surprised to see that can. It was not in some obvious place. Next to a stereo on a shelf. Nobody would have been looking in that corner of the room if he hadn't gotten interested in her album collection. She didn't even want him or the girls in her apartment.

"So maybe she does have something to hide."

"We all have our secrets. But I don't—"

"Someone died, pal. We're talking about more than Miss Lonelyheart's private collection of peekaboo undies here."

"Hey. Come on, Lou. That's not fair to—"

"You want another beer?"

"Yeah, but—"

"Look, my young fisher friend, you got a serious problem. You just found a smoking gun and somebody nearby turned up dead."

"You think I should tell the local officers? The M.E. and the state CPAC guys in Middlesex county?"

The detective leans back on his bar stool, locks his hands behind his head and stares at the ceiling. "Why the hell did I ever get mixed up in this?"

"I don't know. Because you're a good guy? Because you don't go for people killing the children of the world?"

"Naw. That's you, Rambo ... I just fucking felt sorry for you. Now, Christ, I could be up to my ears in another one of your vigilante justice schemes."

"What?"

"If you tell the cops about the Red Bull now, they'll be all over you, your buddy the Indian chick, and those high school girls. There are laws, you know, against withholding or tampering with evidence."

"But isn't that what you are telling me to do?"

"Whoa, pal. Hold on here. I, Lou Votolatto, am not telling you to do anything. I'm just saying the system will make a lot of people's lives miserable if you hand over that Red Bull now."

"So now what?"

The detective signals the bartender. Suddenly he wants two shots of rye with his bowl of chowder. "This is your gig, buddy boy."

He sighs, squeezes his eyes shut. Thinks. "I've got to ask you again. You think you could get the can dusted for prints? Maybe we will find something interesting. Maybe we can at least learn if Liberty Baker ever held this can. And maybe there's some DNA."

"Do you know how many laws you are asking me to break?"

19

NOON. Bright and sunny. The dry snow sugaring out of the oaks and maples. Tiny diamonds. She waits in her Saab at the far corner of the freshly plowed parking lot of the public boathouse on Jamaica Pond.

Surely no one will see her here. See them together.

When his jeep rolls up, she feels the bridge of her nose flush. Knows that she is happier to see him than she will tell him. This is the way she used to feel every time she saw her brother Ronnie.

Before his war. Before he came back from Iraq with his hideous confession. Land of Allah. Land of a thousand and one Arabian nights. Land of flaring skies, weeping oil, and sin so dark it should never be named.

I have to tell you something, Awasha. I HAVE to tell you, but you have to promise not to tell another living soul. Promise. By the Great Spirit, the Medicine Circle, Maushop, and …"

"Hey!" He's knocking on the passenger-side window. Smiling. "Want to walk around the pond?"

She is out of the car, taking both his gloved hands in her deerskin mittens.

He's an old friend, now, right? Sort of.

"I was going to ask you the same thing."

"*Cristo*. You look amazing."

Her coat is knee length, pale white deer hides stitched together, the fur visible at the seams, at the hem, inside the collar. Her boots, reaching above the calves, the same material. Her hat a beaver crown. Long black hair in braids tailing over her shoulders. Lips deep red.

"My mother made these clothes for me. They are stitched like the traditional winter wear for our people, but the style is all her own."

"Your mother had an eye for it. Beauty. I think she would be embarrassed for me to come to meet her daughter looking so shabby."

She looks at him. Slightly-too-large black hooded sweatshirt, jeans, black clamming boots. Beneath the hood, his cheeks dark with the shadow of a beard coming.

"A swarthy stranger in our midst!"

"Is that good?"

"I don't know yet. Are you still my ally?"

She gives him the slightest wink and wiggle. A devilish smile.

He wonders for a moment if Lou Votolatto could be right. That she's possibly playing him. Maybe so. But well, screw it, he is already breaking the law. A girl's dead. Others may follow. Unless he hangs with this lady … who sure as hell does not look lonely or desperate today! A lady who could have every man she wants.

She takes his arm. Leads him along a path through the fresh, eighteen-inch snowfall cut by nordic skiers and dog walkers. Into the woods.

"My friend is checking out the can again. For fingerprints, and other stuff."

"I could be in a whole lot of trouble if someone finds out about what's in that can and where we found it, couldn't I?"

"We both could."

"What about the girls? Do they know about the GHB?"

"I haven't told them. Should I? Maybe they have a right to know."

"Why put them outside the law, too?"

The trail through the snowy woods narrows. Now she takes the lead.

"You mean we are actually ... already ... technically ... a conspiracy?!"

"Sweet, huh?"

"We could go to jail?"

"Oh yeah."

"And somebody might actually try to pin a murder on me." She sighs. Resignation.

"Unless we find some prints on that can other than yours and mine and Lou's."

"So what do we do?"

"You said the girls told you Kevin Singleton supplied them with drugs."

"Pot and ecstasy. He sold them some."

"And we know from Gracie that he and Liberty were having some kind of spat."

"Right."

"Did he have access to chemistry equipment at the school? I mean could he have cooked up that batch of X for the girls?"

"His father is the chair of the science division, one of the faculty old-guard. He has keys to the labs, chemicals."

"You know anything about GHB?"

She says just what she has learned in drug seminars. It's a lot stronger than other popular date-rape drugs. Pretty easy to make if you know a little chemistry.

"Some addicts like to use it to add zip to their crystal meth and heroin. You can take it with booze too."

Her stomach feels on fire. She stops so fast to ride out the pain that he crashes into her from behind. Grabs her in a bear hug to keep from falling.

"Hey!"

With his arms around her, the burning beneath the waistband of her wool skirt begins to melt away.

"We definitely need to talk to Kevin Singleton, don't we?" she says at last.

He releases her. "Sooner rather than later, Awasha."

"This isn't going to be easy."

"Whatever it takes … at this point."

She's silent for a minute, just watches a pair of cardinals chasing each other among the branches overhead. Thinking. "You want to pretend you're a cop, Michael?"

"Not really."

*   *   *

"I thought you said you were taking me to see Liberty's mother, Dr. P!"

Kevin Singleton stands just inside the threshold to a guest room in the Tolchester Arms, a boutique hotel serving the school's alumni and guests from a little nob of a hill on the western edge of the T-C campus. He has an uneasy look on his face, the corners of his mouth turned down in a frown as he looks around for some sign of a black woman.

Awasha closes the door quietly behind her.

"Hi, Kevin. Have a seat." Michael motions to one of the vacant chairs next to his at the little breakfast table by the plate glass window.

He is doing his best to look like one of the plain clothes detectives on TV. Black trench coat, his father's gray gabardine blazer, white collar shirt open at the neck. Blue tie, tightly knotted but pulled down a few inches, manila file of papers in front of him. The wooden grip of his gas pellet pistol peeping out from under his left arm, held in place by a shoulder holster contrived from a bungee cord.

"Where's Mrs. Baker?"

"She had another commitment." Awasha nods toward Michael. "The special agent's here from homicide."

His chest nearly buckles from the boldness and inaccuracy of her bluff. Hopes this kid doesn't know that neither the local nor state police have any officers called special agents working their murder detail.

The boy glares at him with the righteous indignation of someone who has fallen for a bait-and-switch scam.

Kevin is a tall kid. At least 6'2". Unkempt curly brown hair. Brilliant blue eyes, very anglo facial features—the fine nose, thin lips, cleft chin. No facial hair at all. Clear skin. His style mostly preppie. Layers. An over-sized green zip-up fleece over a plaid flannel shirt, red waffle-weave undershirt, ski gloves. Jeans just a touch too baggy and low on the ass. Hiking boots.

"I don't understand. What's this about? You said Lib's mom wanted to talk to me."

"Please sit, Kevin. We really need your help." Her voice sounds oddly deferential.

The boy doesn't move. Seems to be considering his next move. "Did you say homicide? You think someone killed Lib?"

"We need to talk." Michael holds the boy in his gaze, tries not to blink.

"What? You lure me to this room with some bogus story about how it would mean a lot to Lib's mom just to talk for a while? And then you do this: a cop ... No. Hell no, Dr. Patterson. You deceived me. I'm not going to talk to you or this man. But I am going to report you to the headmaster for harassment."

"Kevin. Look, I'm sorry, but—"

"You can't treat people like this. Jesus Christ, my friend just died!"

"Kevin—"

"No! Absolutely not! I'm out of here."

The boy turns for the door, but Awasha stands in his way.

Michael feels the hair rising on the back of his neck, takes a deep breath, tries to assume the professional cool Lou Votolatto projects in an interview.

He clears his throat so that his voice will sound low, a confident whisper when he speaks.

Then he starts to lie. Hates it. But the words keep bubbling forth. Because a girl is gone in the prime of her life, because her friends feel sick and threatened. Because this kid's arrogance is starting to piss him off.

"Go ahead, Kevin. Leave. But if you do, leave with the knowledge that you've blown your chance to be on the side of the good guys here."

"What?"

"We're pretty sure your girlfriend did not kill herself. And we think you know it too."

"Wait, are you saying I—"

"I'm saying you can talk to Dr. Patterson and me, now, off the record ... tell us what you know. Or some folks in blue will be back here tomorrow to haul you out of class in cuffs under suspicion of murder."

"Are you threatening me? Screw you, mister. You have no reason to think I had anything to do with—"

"We have it on good authority that she had a fight with you the night before she died."

"What?"

"We also know about the pot and ecstasy you've been selling. Have you been stealing your father's keys to the chem cab and mixing up some recreational flavors to earn a little spending money?"

"No."

"Then you better talk to us because you never know what will turn up if we get the narcotics boys to search your room. Your house."

"They can't do that."

He can see that this kid is not going to fold unless he calls his bluff with a bluff of his own.

"They can and they will." He pulls a phone from the pocket of his trench coat. "What is it Kevin? You want to talk, off the record? Or do I hit speed dial to send the narco squad over to 1122 Union Ave. right now? Which?"

The boy wrings the loose gloves in his hands. The Adam's apple begins to pulse in his throat, his ears suddenly red.

"Can I think about this for a second?"

"Take all the time you need," she says.

"Here." Michael stands up, walks to the mini-bar in the room, fetches a bottle of Poland Springs, offers it to the boy. "Sit down. Have some water."

20

HAPPY hour. They are sitting at the bar, drinking black coffee, in the Dolphin Restaurant on Main St. in Barnstable village, the Cape.

The detective, looking shaggy and rumpled this afternoon, eyes him between sips.

"Jesus H. Christ, you were impersonating a police officer? Are you crazy?"

He shrugs, dips a wheat roll in a large bowl of clam chowder, stirs. Sops up the broth. "It seemed like a good idea at the time."

"I must have been out of my mind to have ever, I mean EVER, gotten involved in this. When this caper turns sour—and the way this is going, it most fucking assuredly will—I'll be kissing my pension goodbye and begging for a job as a night watchman at the power plant over in Sandwich. You know that?"

"Well you could always come fishing on the *Rosa Lee* ..." He smiles, teasing the cop a little. *What the hell else can you do?*

"That's supposed to be funny, but I lose my day job over this and I'm going to be your worst nightmare."

"Come on, Lou. You're my new best friend." He doesn't know why he's in such a fuck-all mood. Maybe way too much coffee. Or denial bred from fear. Or the memory of the way her body molded to his for a few seconds during that accidental hug at Jamaica Pond. Or …

"Screw you, Rambo. Stupid Portagee squid peeler."

"Hey, is that any way to talk to a guy who has just brought you a perfect set of prints from perhaps the last person to see Liberty Baker alive?"

Votolatto looks at the half-empty Poland Springs water bottle in the Ziploc bag on the bar. "At least you did one thing right."

"Yeah, well maybe. I guess we'll see if you can match Kevin's prints with the ones on the Red Bull. But … shit … I don't know, Lou."

"Oh Jesus, here we go. Now, NOW, that you've got us into this cesspool up to our necks, you tell me you're starting to lose your nerve?"

"Not my nerve. It's too late for that. I'm just not sure Kevin Singleton is our boy."

"You mean you think you got bum information about his fight with his girl? He didn't really sell drugs to her friends?"

"No. All that stuff seems solid. And maybe he was lying about what happened the last time he saw Liberty. But his story kind of held together for me. At least on a gut level. And then there was that racist note. I can't see him writing it."

"Could be the note has nothing to do with the crime. Ever think of that? Just a red herring."

He says he remembers fights with his girlfriend in high school. And with Filipa. A whole storm of emotions, anger to denial. The urge for revenge followed by self-loathing. He heard all of that in Kevin's voice yesterday at the hotel.

"That's when people kill. Their emotions fry. They just lash out. But slipping someone a GHB cocktail, then slitting her wrists with such finesse that even an experienced M.E. buys the suicide, seems like a pretty tough act for a teenager whose heart is in meltdown."

"So what are you saying?"

"Maybe we have to chase down some of these rumors about a secret society."

"Don't say that word again. Or I walk right out of here. You won't see me again, hear?"

"What word?"

"WE. You want to try playing hero, have at it. I'm going to watch from the bleachers."

"But you'll see about the prints?"

"Think about this. Everybody has secrets. Especially teenage boys who pedal drugs, and guys with dead girlfriends. What do you think this kid Kevin is hiding? Why? And ... how long do you think it will be before he tells someone that you and Pocahontas tried to roast him at the stake?"

21

"MISS Liu, you're next!" Malcolm Sufridge holds the immense paneled door to his office open to the great hall of the gothic administration building, sweeps Tory out with a shoveling motion of his hand.

Her face is red, blotchy, her blond hair looking stringy, lifeless. Eyes drop to the floor when she sees Gracie. "Sorry," she mumbles, then scurries away.

Sufridge points to an empire chair next to his desk. "Please take a seat."

She settles hard into the chair, takes a deep breath, tries to gather strength for what will surely come. Her eyes, flat, unreadable, watch his black academic gown flow behind him as he scoots across the room to face her over the corner of his huge desk. The judge and the accused.

"I think you have something that belongs to me."

"Excuse me?"

She's stalling. The moment she got the email requesting her presence in the headmaster's office after classes, she guessed this was all about Liberty's journal. No surprise. The mystery is why does he want it back? How badly does he want it? What will he do to get it? What does he know about Liberty's murder?

Maybe she can find out, if she plays this scene right. That's the only way to think of it. Just another play, another role. The drama tank all over again. Improv. Sometimes she's pretty good at it. And if she nails this bit, maybe she can help Michael find the killer. Maybe he'll see her more clearly, see Ninja Girl ... before the killer tries to get her too.

"Please don't be coy with me, young lady."

"Dr. Sufridge, I don't know—"

"Of course you do. The last time you visited this office there was an important notebook on my desk. It disappeared."

She stares at her hands folded in her lap. Gone are her defiant Red Army clothes, nose stud. Now she's all about subtle make-up, lip gloss, eyeliner. A camel cashmere coat, flowing ruby scarf, navy turtleneck sweater, brown suede skirt, fashion boots. She has wallowed in films like *Crouching Tiger, Hidden Dragon*. Hopes she knows what it takes to play the role of the seemingly submissive female who can disarm even a man of immense power.

Her head lowers slightly, her palms press together, the traditional Chinese sign of obedience. She purses her lips ever so slightly, then raises her eyes to meet his. Her look, the studied pose of a concubine in the royal court.

He looks away, clears his throat, fondles his fountain pen.

"Do not play games with me, young miss."

"I'm sorry, Dr. Sufridge. I don't understand." She wonders what Tory told this bastard. What he knows. But really, who gives a flying fuck. She has her role to play. Her mask.

"I want that notebook."

"What does it look like?"

She gives him her most demure smile, the hidden dragon.

He stands up. Runs his fingers through the waves of gray hair at his temples. His jaw starting to grind, eyes glaring down at her.

"Stop this!"

"But, Dr. Sufridge, I just ..." She crosses, uncrosses, recrosses her bare legs for his benefit.

Looming over her, he cannot help but look.

"My god, Grace! You ... Do you wish to destroy this school? Do you want to remain a student here? Do you still hope to go to an Ivy League college? Pursue a career in theatre and art?"

Here comes the threat, she thinks. The I-could-kick-you-out speech. It's time to lie, at least about the college and career stuff.

"I'm not so sure anymore. Maybe it would be better if I went home. Should we call my parents?"

She looks him straight in the eye, just lets him catch a glimpse of her tiger.

He turns away, his academic gown rustling, fanning open. A blurry shadow in the middle of the room. Some raw noise escapes his mouth. Maybe a clearing of the throat, maybe a growl.

"So that's how things stand? Well ..." His voice strained, frazzled, desperate to find any means to take back the advantage.

She stares at his back as he stands before a huge gothic window facing west. A silhouette. Shuddering with anger.

He wheels around to face her. Bars of red rising on his neck.

"Listen to me, my defiant young friend. If you care about your beloved Dr. Patterson, you will find that notebook and give it to me."

"What? Doc P?"

"This is not just about protecting the school. Perhaps that does not matter to you. This is about protecting Dr. Patterson. If I do not get that notebook back, her life is ruined. Do you hear me, Grace? Utterly ruined!"

"Dr. Patterson?"

She had someone in her bed with her. She thinks I don't know about her boyfriends …

His face is suddenly ashen. As if he has lost his grip on something.

"I don't understand," she says.

But maybe I will, she thinks. *Someday.*

Because she has seen it. This lost thing. Just for a second. A shadow escaping his hands. A suspicion. Or a secret. It floated out the window. Rose into the pale blue sky of this winter afternoon, disappeared. Leaving nothing but the taste of dried blood in her heart … a vague sense of victory. And a clear view of how to end this scene. With one more lie from Ninja Girl. A lie to buy herself time to figure things out, to tell Michael.

"I REALLY don't understand, Dr. Sufridge."

"You heard me. This is all in your hands now. I have nothing more to say. Stop trying to make a fool out of me and give me Liberty Baker's journal!"

"Oh! That's what you are looking for? I'm so sorry Dr. Sufridge. It's right here. I guess I accidentally …"

She opens her green backpack, produces the red, cloth-bound notebook. Denzel Washington, Civil War soldier, staring solemnly from the cover.

"Smart girl."

Ninja Girl smiles, pushes the journal toward the center of the headmaster's desk. The photocopied version folded safely in the back of her American history text.

22

EELS twisting in his guts, scowl frozen on his face, he climbs up the steps from the galley to the wheelhouse of the *Rosa Lee*. She is the outermost boat in a raft of trawlers at the dock.

The sun, inching above the horizon, has turned the length of New Bedford Harbor into a sheet of gold. The wind calm. He can see gulls just starting to test their wings, their voices mocking.

"What's the matter with you?"

His father sits in his captain's chair, wearing jeans and a gray sweatshirt. He twists a pencil over the knuckles of his left hand. A mug of steaming coffee in his right. The VHF radio is playing the National Weather Service loop for the offshore waters south of Cape Cod.

"I've got to go to Boston this morning."

"What?"

"I just got a call." His voice is still gravelly with sleep. He's wearing the blue long-johns that he slept in below.

"Don't mess with my morning like this, Mo. I've been waiting for something like two weeks to get back out there. Now we've got the weather. It's March, the fish are running, and I'm behind on the boat mortgage."

"Dad—"

"Tell me you're not going to do this to Tio Tommy and me. Leave us short-handed. Soon as he gets the groceries, we load ice and fuel, shove off. Georges Banks here we come. *Cristo Salvador*, what a forecast we have. Looks like more than a week of high pressure!"

"Dad, I feel awful … but I can't go. I have to meet someone at the Braintree T-station at eight-thirty. I think it's an emergency."

His father flicks the pencil that was in his hand across the wheelhouse. "Goddamn it."

"I'm sorry."

"I thought you were done with lawyering."

"I did too, but … now … people are counting on me."

"Hey, I'm counting on you too."

"This sucks."

"You're telling me."

"Do you hate me?"

His father drops his mug into a cup holder and wipes his face with both hands.

"No … Hell no, buddy boy. I just can't take these surprises the way I used to. You do what you got to do. Tommy and I will deal … But just tell me something."

"Sure, anything."

"Do you think you can really find this girl-killer, or are you simply looking to get laid with that Indian honey?"

"I don't know, Dad."

"You sure you don't want to try to patch things up with Filipa?"

* * *

He has just seized a pole by the door in the subway car for balance, when the train jolts, tossing her into him. He staggers amid the crowd of morning commuters, spreads his legs to absorb the train's acceleration, the shock of her body.

The Red Line lurches forward out of Braintree station. Her arms circle his waist. And the tears start.

"Shit," she says. "I promised myself I wouldn't …"

This is awkward. People looking. Coats and scarfs and knit caps hiding everything but their faces. Everyone, even the black men's cheeks, silver in the neon lights of the car. Chestnut eyes rolling his way. Watching what he will do next. With this teenager, this Chinese, this girl called Gracie who won't let him go.

"She's gone … she's …" Her words are more air than noise. Little bullets against his chest.

He does not grasp what she's saying, but he comforts.

"It's OK. Gracie, everything is going to be OK."

She hugs him harder. He feels himself stiffen. But his left hand strokes the purple highlights of her bushy hair.

"Just let it go."

"We … we lost her … she …"

She cries. Harder now. The howling of a cat. Pressed against his chest. On the third day of March. In a subway car. At 8:53 in the morning. In front of two hundred other people. Shit. Just shit. And him missing what's no doubt going to be the first slammer trip of the spring on the Rosa Lee.

The train, screeching and rumbling through the tunnel, slows for the Park St. Station in the heart of Boston, stops. More than half the people in the car get off. Finally, as the train picks up speed again, her sobs sputter, end.

Still she does not let go of him.

He waits several more minutes, the train popping out of the tunnel to cross the Charles River Bridge, diving underground in Cambridge again, before he asks. His mind racing.

Who have you lost now? Who have we lost? More than Liberty? Awasha?

"Who's gone, Gracie?"

She pulls her head back from his chest, looks up into his eyes. Her cheeks wet and pink.

"Tory."

"Tory?"

She says Bumbledork scared the hell out of Tory yesterday afternoon. She left this morning. She didn't even say she was going. Wouldn't talk last night. Her mother came for her in a car. It was not even sunrise. Not even day yet.

"And that's why you asked me to meet you in Braintree on this train?"

"I don't know, Michael. Maybe I should go home too."

"No one would blame you."

"It's so weird. Just a few weeks ago, of all of the Hibernia House girls, I was the one who really wanted to leave. Now … I'm the only one left. What do I do?"

"Why don't we get off at Harvard Square? Get some breakfast. My mother used to say you always think better on a full stomach."

She finally lets go of his waist, takes a seat in the nearly empty car.

"Really?"

He sits down next to her.

"I'm living proof."

* * *

"Sorry you missed your fishing trip. I'm sorry I melted down on you like that." She stuffs the last bit of her second cheese croissant in her mouth and smiles a little. "Forgive me?"

She's turned a corner, he thinks, knows he should feel some relief. But his heart is still surging against his ribs.

"You think the school is missing you yet?"

She looks around, maybe seeing where she is for the first time. The tables at Au Bon Pain are packed with Harvard students this morning, bubbling with anticipation for their coming spring break.

"I have to tell you something important. I almost forgot. With Tory suddenly leaving. Shit, what was I thinking?"

"You mean something about your headmaster bullying you?"

"More like blackmail, wouldn't you say? Like with his threats about Doc P?"

"Extortion. You gave him back Liberty's journal to protect Awasha?"

"Well yeah."

"Let me ask you something hard about her."

"OK?"

"You think she had something to do with Liberty's death?"

"Jesus, Doc P? No! Liberty was like her favorite. Why?"

"What about Sufridge?"

She bites into her third croissant, powers down a half-cup of latte.

"That asshole! How should I know? He's obviously trying to hide something. But ..."

"What?"

"But that's not what I forgot, Michael. I had to see you. I had to give you the photocopy of Lib's journal for safe keeping. And I couldn't tell you this stuff on the phone. Someone might be listening, right?"

He shrugs. Kind of doubts it. Who would bother bugging her cell calls? But whatever.

"So talk to me." He can hear his heart in his ears.

"I went to see Kevin last night after Bumbledork tried to beat up on me."

"Singleton?"

"You know he thinks you're some kind of cop."

"You didn't tell him something different?"

"No. But he's pretty scared."

"Good. Maybe he'll tell the truth."

She says he's really freaked. Like he thinks maybe he is going to get busted for killing Lib. He's pretty sad, too. She thinks he really loved her.

"From what I've seen, lots of killers do."

"Huh?"

"Love their victims."

"Yeah, but I don't think he killed her anymore. Do you?"

"I don't know. I'd say that's an open question. Why?"

"Because he said he's worried about me. I guess you made him think I could be in danger. He wants to help."

"Who?"

"Me."

"How?"

"He said he's heard stuff about a rebel secret society."

"What do you mean *rebel*?"

"I don't know, that's just what he called it."

"It still exists?"

Kevin's not sure. But he told Gracie his older brother—the guy is twenty-five—said that when he went to T-C, Hibernia House was still a boys dorm. There were rumors about a secret room.

"Yeah … ?"

"I think I should take a look. But I can't go back to that school yet. I feel too crazy."

"What do you want to do?"

"Take a long walk. Like to another country. And then I want to buy you dinner."

"I don't know."

"Don't try to weasel out of this … unless you want to see me throw another fit."

He shakes his head. "Why didn't I go fishing?"

She shoots him a warning glare. Then her lip starts to tremble. "I think I'm going to cry again."

"You ever eat *moqueca* or *lombinho?*"

A ghost of a smile. "There's a first time for everything."

"Let me make a phone call first."

23

"WE need to talk!" Denise Pasteur closes the door behind her, steps into Awasha's office. "Gracie Liu is missing."

"What?" She puts down a copy of *Sula* by Toni Morrison that she's been rereading for a seminar she's running for African-American kids. Kicks her chair back from her desk, stares up from her seat at this tornado that has just blown into her life.

"She missed all of her classes today. I just got the attendance reports from her teachers. When did you see her last?"

"You were there."

"This morning when Tory's mother came to get her at Beedle Cottage?"

"Yes."

"You didn't see her in the dining hall at breakfast later?"

She didn't go. She was way too disturbed. Tory's leaving came as such a shock ... She just beat it over here to the office. Put on her headphones and lost herself in Al Green and her book for hours.

"You check Beedle Cottage?"

"She's not there. Did she seem desperate to you this morning?"

"How should I know. I was a basket case. Why?"

"Because she and Tory had a couple of tough meetings with Bumbledork yesterday afternoon. Didn't they tell you?"

No. When would she have seen the girls to talk? Doesn't Denise remember they went to *The Winter's Tale* together last night, then they ...

"I guess I'm kind of out of it."

"What happened with Bumbledork and the girls?"

"That man plays everything close to the vest. I was hoping you could fill me in."

"How do you know about his meetings with—"

"Edith. She's not only his secretary, she tallies the daily class attendance lists. Called me when Gracie turned up absent and was not on the infirmary's sick list."

"Oh."

Did you see the blood? The bathtub so full of blood? Not like in the movies ... but purple ... Her body just a shadow ...

They both know the two of them are going to be in the hot seat if Gracie doesn't turn up soon. They're the ones responsible for her safety. Dean and house counselor. First Liberty dies on their watch, now they lose her best friend. What else can go wrong?

"You want my opinion? I think your friend, that ex-lawyer, has something to do with this. I think this is about that man's encouraging those girls in this misguided fantasy that Liberty did not take her own life."

"He's a good guy. He grounds us. He has the perspective of a man who has been through hell over a murder case. And a man who knows the law. Didn't I tell you my mother really—"

"How do you know he doesn't have Gracie with him right now? Doing god knows what? The girl is a risk taker and vulnerable, I mean really vulnerable, right?"

Something snaps in her head.

"Why don't you call him?"

"I think he was leaving on a fishing trip today."

"Maybe he changed his mind. Maybe he lied to you."

Streaks of pain are shooting up her throat. She picks up the phone, punches in his cell number, waits. The receiver shakes subtly in her hand. Her skin burns as the dean settles into a free chair, reading her from head to toe with impatient eyes.

The phone rings once, twice, a third time. Then a forth.

She is just about to click off when he picks up. His voice annoyingly cheerful. A bit like her brother Ronnie's when he's been drinking for hours. There's some kind of noise in the background, the buzz of voices, a restaurant … or a pub maybe.

Suddenly she feels her throat flooding with stomach acid.

"Have you got Gracie with you, Michael?"

"I told her we should call you. That you would be worried."

Denise Pasteur's eyes still searing her.

"What the hell is going on?"

"It's OK. We've had some bumps in the road. But I'll have Gracie back at school in an hour."

Some kind of Latin music—lots of drums—coming out of the phone, singing.

"What language do I hear? Where are you? It sounds like—"

"Awasha, I can't hear you very—"

"What?"

"Meet us at Hibernia House, seven o'clock. Alone."

The dean leans closer, trying to listen to the conversation … just as it ends.

"What's going on?"

"He found Gracie. It seems they're having dinner. She'll be back around eight. We can get the story then at Beedle Cottage."

"Those two are in a world of hurt!"

*   *   *

She has been waiting in the dark for at least a half hour inside her old apartment at Hibernia House, looking out the kitchen window. Now two figures are trudging up the alley. Staying in the shadows. As soon as she hears footsteps coming up from the basement entrance, up the basement stairs, she flings open the door from her study into the stairwell, pounces.

"What the hell have you two been up to? Were you in a bar when I called?"

"Not exactly."

"Not exactly?"

"It was a *churrascaria*."

"What?"

"A Brazilian place. Kind of a barbeque. In Inman Square."

"But it's a bar."

"Well …"

"Doc P, it's not his fault. I asked him—"

"I'm in no mood for lame excuses, Gracie. You cut classes and you end up at a bar in the city with … with … Do you have any idea how this looks?"

Michael clears his throat. "I can explain. Things got kind of complicated today. But maybe a little clearer, too."

"What are you talking about, Michael? Oh, yeah, they sure did get clearer. Can you even guess at the shit storm that is about to descend on your head from the administration of this school? The dean is freaking out."

"The dean?"

"Denise Pasteur. My god, I went to you. I pleaded for your help. I trusted you because of my mother. And now—the two of you. Michael, she's a child and you ... What were you thinking?"

Gracie's face darkens. "Jesus Christ, Doc. Stop! Just stop. Please! And listen for once. While there's still time."

"What do you mean?"

He blinks, trying to clear the static from his head. "We need to start looking through Hibernia House for a secret room."

"I made Michael meet me this morning because he was the only one I could turn to ..."

"What about me? I was right here."

Not last night, she says. Not this morning after Tory left. She couldn't find Doc P. She needed to talk to an adult. Really needed to talk. About Tory and Bumbledork. And Kevin.

"Kevin?"

"Gracie thinks he wants to help us."

"He could be the guy who killed—"

"Maybe ... maybe not."

"What?"

"I called my detective friend this afternoon. He said his lab rats looked for a match between Kevin's prints on the water bottle and the prints on the Red Bull. No match."

"So?"

"There are two unidentified sets of prints on the Red Bull, plus yours and mine."

"Kevin is out of this?"

He says maybe. Unless he was smart enough to use a pair of gloves when he was handling that Red Bull. Lou Votolatto thinks the kid is hiding some secrets. Who knows? But gave Gracie something new.

"I went to see him last night, Doc P. He's taking things pretty hard."

She tells Doc P about Kevin's older brother Clyfe in California, about the rumors of a secret room in Hibernia House back in the Nineties.

"You mean a party place?"

"Yeah, I guess."

He slips four cinammon Altoids into his mouth, figures it would be smart to mask the scent of the two Brahma beers he drank with dinner.

"I told Gracie we better all have a look."

"Where?"

"Kevin's brother thought it had to be somewhere upstairs."

"You think this kid is sending us on a wild goose chase, trying to distract us?"

"Have you got a flashlight?"

24

"DAMN, we have less than a half hour before I told the dean you would be back at Beedle Cottage, Gracie." She sweeps the floor of the Hibernia House common room cautiously with the flashlight beam, even though they drew the shades on all the top floor windows twenty minutes ago.

"We've been through all of this, twice. Not a sign of a hidden room."

"Maybe Kevin's brother was wrong."

Gracie drops onto the couch. "What about the attic?"

"There's a hatch above the landing in the stairwell. We'll need a ladder."

"I'll just stand on a desk," says Michael. He already has one in his arms and is lugging it out into the stairwell.

A second later he is mounted atop the desk. With his arms extended, he pushes up on the overhead hatch, slides it out of the way. But even standing on his tip toes he is eighteen inches short of being able to see into the attic.

"Give me a boost, Michael." Gracie clambers onto the desk. "Come on!"

He makes a stirrup for her foot with his hands. She puts her hands on his shoulders for balance, steps into the stirrup. Up she goes, the flashlight in her hand probing the space overhead.

"Shit!"

"What? What do you see?"

She drops back down to the desk, slides to the floor. "Two dead rats with their necks broken in traps. It looks like they've been up there for about a hundred years."

"What else?"

"A stack of ancient window screens. And water pipes from the bathroom, I guess."

"No sign it was ever a party place."

"Sorry, guys. It doesn't even look like there's a floor. Just a few boards to walk on. And a lot stuff that looks like pink cotton candy."

"Insulation." Michael slides the hatch back in place, drops off the desk. "Looks like we're back to square one."

"And we're almost out of time."

Gracie has settled onto the couch again, legs stretched out, eyes closed. "Kevin said his brother sounded so sure."

"Another urban legend bites the dust."

Suddenly the girl leaps to her feet. "Hey! What about the chimney!"

"You think it was some kind of secret tunnel?"

"No. But when I looked in the attic, I didn't see it."

"I don't understand."

"Shouldn't I have seen it going up through the attic to the roof?"

The adults shrug.

"You can see the top of it rising above the roof on the north side of the house. It's black with white trim," says Awasha.

He has his eyes closed, trying to picture the design of Hibernia House. "Maybe there are two rooms in the attic. The hatch over the stairwell is on the south side. Maybe there's another way to get up there from the north side."

"Which way is that?" Gracie suddenly has the look of someone who depends on the GPS mapping function in her cell phone to keep from getting lost.

"That way," he says, pointing toward Liberty's room.

Awasha is muttering. "Danielle is going to be looking for us at Beedle Cottage."

But Gracie and Michael are already in Liberty's room. Gracie pounding on walls. Michael tapping the ceiling with a broom handle. An urgent cadence. In the dark. Listening for someplace that sounds hollow or loose.

It's on his third tap of a closet ceiling that something gives way overhead. Falls.

Dust, plaster clinkers, cardboard come showering down on his head. A choking cloud.

"*Cristo Salvador!*"

"What?"

He sniffs to clear his nostrils, looks down at the pile of debris at his feet. Awasha shines the flashlight.

"I think I found something ... or else the maintenance crew has been patching this ceiling with plaster of Paris and cardboard from an old case of Pabst Blue Ribbon."

* * *

He drags Liberty's desk into the closet, stacks a chair on top of the desk, climbs. Disappears through the hole left by the false ceiling.

From the bottom of the closet, she can hear his footsteps take several steps across the wood floor overhead.

"Unbelievable."

"What?"

"You won't believe this."

She stares up through the open rectangle in the top of the closet, watches the flashlight beam flickering through the dark above. Outside, the clock on the school's classroom building chimes.

"Damn! It's eight o'clock, Gracie. I promised the dean—"

The teenager's suddenly hugging Awasha's arm with both hands, shivering. "Do we have to go, Doc?"

Something claws at the back of her mind. An image trying to get out. She sees Squibnocket Beach, its rocks, boulders. The scent of eel grass beneath the cliffs of Aquinnah. And a greenish hatbox that feels almost too heavy for her free hand to clutch to her chest.

"Doc?"

"What?"

"What do you want to do?"

She pictures her mother, Black Squirrel. A faint gray cloud, blowing off over the Atlantic.

"I want to see!"

* * *

By the time she and Gracie reach the attic, Michael has found an old lava lamp, turned it on. It casts a red and golden glow, the shadows changing with the ebb and flow of the lamp. The gabled roof of Hibernia House makes the space seem a mix of stunted alcoves and vaults. There are fewer cobwebs than she would have imagined, but a film of silvery dust covers everything. No sign anyone has been up here in years, maybe decades.

She can see that once this was a living space. Servants' quarters possibly ... or a writer's garret. With no windows. There's a regular pine floor. The walls a web of peeling blue wallpaper, cracked plaster, exposed lath. Naturally stained wainscotting. One wall is lined floor-to-ceiling with empty Pabst Blue Ribbon cans.

"I don't get it," says Gracie. "How did they get all this stuff up here?"

He flashes the light around. "There's your answer."

The flashlight beam settles on the remains of steep stairs circling the back of the big chimney on their way down to the third floor. But the steps stop short of a landing. Studs, drywall, insulation where once there must have been a door.

In the center of the room, three crudely made tables. Two with several decks of cards stacked in the center, one with a set of science lab scales and an immense, blue, glass bong. A dozen folding chairs sit in no obvious order. When she squints her eyes, she can see several crumby mattresses tucked into the remote recesses of the room. Closer inspection shows each with its own stack of *Playboy*, *Hustler*, *High Times* magazines from 1973, '74, '75. On the floor near the lava lamp is a phonograph. The Beatles Yellow Submarine LP on the turntable. Books of matches and half-burned candles of all shapes and sizes dot the landscape.

"Check this out." Gracie points to the chimney. Above the bricked-up hearth hangs a green nylon banner. Two-by-four feet. Words on the banner proclaim CLUB TROPICAL in large orange script. Beneath the words someone has scrawled in what appears to be pink paint, SUCKS SHIT. And in fuzzy red lettering, maybe from some kind of marker, RED TOOTH RULES!

"Red Tooth again. Like in the News: Red Tooth Still Rules. This is secret society shit, guys. We've found a club room like Kevin's brother said. You think this is the name of another secret society, Doc? Club Tropical?"

She doesn't answer. Can't think what to say. Something has stolen her voice. It's as if she's watching a movie, can't talk to those people on the screen. Gracie drifting away from the banner, taking the bong in her hands, sniffing at the dope bowl. Michael starting to thumb through one of the *High Times*. On a distant wall a crude oil portrait of Jimmy Hendrix, in browns and yellows.

Her eyes fall upon a small box on the fireplace mantel. When she picks it up, she sees that it is an open six-pack of Trojan condoms. Two remain sealed in their red foil.

Her ears are ringing. She closes her eyes and sees her brother's face. *Ronnie in his red plaid work shirt, khaki pants. Moccasins. Tall and heavy like their father. His eyes wet. Wind blowing tears over his face. He tries to wipe them away, but the thin, jagged lines of fluid keep coming over his tan cheeks. A convulsion starting to rise in his chest. In her own.*

"There's something very wrong here."

"What, Doc?"

"Come on Gracie. We've got to go!"

He puts down the *High Times*. "I'm thinking somebody might have been dealing dope up here. Stashed some drugs or money. Kind of looks like they left in a big hurry. And never came back. Mind if I look around some more?"

She feels a black rattling behind her eyes. "I'll call you. Give me at least an hour or two … And try not to get caught, will you?"

25

THE living room in Beedle House is nearly dark. Reeking from the wet, smoky maple sputtering in the hearth.

It's after eleven o'clock.

Denise pours herself a fourth or fifth glass of white. None for her Wampanoag friend, the long-term house guest. The one still nursing her mug of tea. She would rather watch the ripples of blue flame dying on the last burning log than say one more word tonight. Rather wonder if it might be better to be Liberty Baker right now. Maybe her mother and the tribal elders were right. Death could be a canoe ride to a better place.

Gracie is long gone from the scene. Dean Pasteur having told her to get her defiant little ass upstairs in her bedroom and do some homework for a change. She's restricted to campus indefinitely, required to be in her room every night by eight. Like shape up or ship out, young missy.

The dean settles onto the sofa. Raises her glass, swallows deep. Sighs. She's in her red silk pajamas, ready for bed, but looking across the room hoping to catch Awasha's attention. Get her to come out of herself, out of the fire. This mystery with long silk hair, with the old Indian robe wrapped around her, feet tucked under her in the winged-back chair.

"That girl should have gone home with the others!"

She hears frustration, and something else—anger maybe—in Denise Pasteur's voice. Suddenly wishes she had never agreed to leave Hibernia House to come to Beedle Cottage. Not after Liberty's funeral. And not tonight. Especially not tonight. She wishes she could just settle down and read a few chapters of *Sula*. But barring that, she'd rather still be back in that attic, searching for god-knows-what. Peace of mind, probably.

"Don't be like that. Gracie's had a rough time. She just needs some TLC." Her eyes arc, reflecting the last of the fire.

"So she's running off to get it from some thirty-year-old fisherman who takes her to Brazilian bars in the city? Shit, Awasha! Talk about risky behavior. If her parents knew she could get away with this sort of thing at school, do you have any idea how many ways they would sue us and T-C?"

"Michael Decastro is a good guy."

"Why is it you feel the need to tell me that just about every time I see you? Do you have a crush on that man too?"

She says he's salt of the earth. Like friends she had growing up in Barnstable, Mashpee, Chatham, the Vineyard. And some of her cousins. Portagees. Fishermen's kids. Honest and loyal and steady. Hearts as big as …

"God. Enough already. I'm sorry I ever raised the topic. But I just wonder how you are going to feel when Gracie turns up pregnant … or worse."

"That's mean. You're so mean tonight. Why are you being so cruel?"

"Because I can't get through to you. It's like you're on some other planet."

"I've had one hell of a day. I don't need to be badgered ... Please!"

"Let's call it a night and go to bed. I'm just afraid that if word of any of Gracie's mischief gets back to Bumbledork—or the rest of the faculty—we're all screwed. Gracie's getting to be ... Fuck. I'm sorry. Forgive me, OK?"

She smiles. "Of course! I just need to stay down here by the fire for a while and chill." Beneath the robe her right hand fishes for the cell phone in the hip pocket of the sweat pants she wears for sleeping on these frozen nights.

*　*　*

He thinks maybe he was too pushy, too weird when she finally called him. When he said he needed her to come back to the Club Tropical. He couldn't help himself. He was getting into something messy. Something freaking him out. Something he didn't want to deal with alone.

Now that she's back in the attic, he's still not sure he feels any relief. It is after midnight and the two of them are down on their knees in front of a small door leading into a crawl space over the eaves. He found it concealed behind a steamer trunk. But the door won't budge. It has been fastened shut with a random collection of steel screws, the kind that you usually see anchoring the legs to chairs you might find in a dormitory.

"Somebody totally jury-rigged this. Had to have been kids, not a tradesman. I think they were trying to hide something. But I can't get this open!" His fingernails ache from clawing at the edge of the door.

"Try this." She grabs a spoon she sees on the table next to the scales.

It's a soup spoon, heavy silver plate, probably stolen from the school dining hall. And it works well enough as a jimmy. One-by-one he pops the screws loose as he pries with the spoon around the edges of the door.

Then he curls his fingers around the loose edge and pulls. Hard. The door pops open with a loud crack, the sound of screws clattering on the floor.

He drops back on his haunches, stares into the dark crawl space.

"You first." Her voice warbles slightly as she hands him the flashlight.

He looks into her black eyes. Soft and deep and scared. Sitting there on the floor, she's shivering, too, even in her sweats and parka. It must be below forty degrees in this attic. His hands and throat feel dry, bony from the dust and chill. He can't take even another second of this nonsense, and maybe neither can she.

"Miller time."

"What?"

"I found a bottle of peppermint schnapps tucked back in a corner by one of those mattresses."

"You want to drink? Now?"

He lights a big candle made in a mason jar, warms his hands over the flame, and pushes the candle toward her hands.

"Yeah, I'm going to see what peppermint schnapps tastes like. What the hell. Take a break. Like what the hell are we doing here in the middle of the night?"

"You really think a bunch of dumb teenagers would kill Liberty to protect something like this?"

He shrugs, doesn't have the faintest idea. If there is one thing he has learned from his time with the Public Defender's Office, it is that people, even the gentlest of us, can kill.

"Michael, this place is creeping me out!"

"You think the kids buy this stuff 'cause they think it smells like mouthwash on their breath? Stuff's got to be older than we are."

He wipes the dust off the top of the ancient bottle with his jacket sleeve, breaks the plastic seal, twists off the cap.

"You're really going to drink it?"

He sniffs at the open neck of the bottle, the sharp scent of mint, the tang of alcohol. "Yeah, why not? I don't think booze goes bad."

"Then give me a sip too." She stretches out a hand. "I damn well need something to get me through tonight."

*   *   *

He picks up the flashlight and rolls from his butt onto his knees. "Time to find out if the Club Tropical stowed any swag in this crawl space."

She giggles, takes a long pull from the bottle of schnapps, a half-dozen candles now burning in a circle around the two of them.

"Do your thing."

He crawls headfirst into the crawl space.

The first thing he notices is the faint scent of ammonia, the subtle stench of the fish hold on the *Rosa Lee* the day after the lumpers have toted off the catch and the ice is all melted.

"Shit."

"What?"

He backs out.

"It's full of broken furniture ... and a couple of dead squirrels. They've probably been nesting in there for years."

"What do you want to do now?"

"If anyone stashed something back in here, it's buried under a lot of crap."

"Maybe we should just call it quits."

"And do what?"

"I don't know. This is just way too weird."

He sits, rubs his eyes, takes a swallow of schnapps, slaps both his cheeks with his open hand. "Get your net in the water, Mo!"

"What?"

"Nothing. Just something my father says to me when I'm dragging my ass over something I know I have to do."

"Oh ... Well, then, get your net in the water, Mo."

He scrambles back into the hole, closes his eyes against the cloud of dust that rises as he pulls out the pieces of three or four old chairs. A cold wind blows through a hole the squirrels have gnawed in the cornice. When the debris is all out, he sees four stacks of old porn mags rising right up against the eves.

"Those horny little buggers were in here."

"What?"

"Standby."

He drags the magazines out of the crawl space. Brushes away the dried-up carcass of a squirrel still curled in its nest of oak leaves. Suddenly, the scent of ammonia is so strong his throat seizes and he has to bail for fresh air.

"*Cristo!*"

"What's that smell?"

He grabs some Kleenex from the pack in his coat pocket and jams it up his nose.

"What are you doing Michael?"

"Fishing." He crawls back through the hole and shines the light around, notices that the floorboards that had been covered by the magazines are lose.

As soon as he lifts up three of them and tosses them out of the way, he can see something black, vinyl or plastic, stuffed between the floor joists.

"I got something."

"Really?"

He tears away more floor boards, passes them out to her. They come up in four- and six-foot lengths. Now he knows what he is seeing between the joists. It is a plastic garment bag. There's a Brooks Brothers logo on it. Something lumpy inside. An old suit maybe. The scent of ammonia is nearly gagging him even through the Kleenex in his nose.

"What did you find?" Her voice sounds distant, muffled by the ringing in his ears.

"Come on, Mo!" he coaches himself. "Don't puss out now!"

His right hand finds the zipper on the garment bag, pulls. But the zipper seems stuck.

"Shit." He pulls again.

This time the zipper gives.

He is looking down into the bag. At a coat sleeve. A blue blazer. Three brass buttons on the cuff.

"Oh fuck, Awasha!"

He whacks his head on the door jam, leaping backwards out of the hole.

"There's somebody …" His voice breaks.

She looks at him with flat, blank eyes. As if she suddenly sees on his face the nightmare that is in the garment bag. The grimy, sleeve of a blazer, pushed up on a leathery, shrunken forearm … and a hand. The fingers squeezed in a fist.

Her arms are already drawing him to her chest, when one of them starts to sob.

26

HE wants to run. *Cristo Salvador*, he wants to run. As soon as the first rays of the sun cut through the gap in her curtains. As soon as he knows the sun will rise again. God, he should be fishing. At the canyons right now with his father and Tio Tommy, setting out the gear. Not here. Not with her.

But she holds him in this bed, her bed, her apartment. Hibernia House. Her legs a vice on his waist. So he lies still, looks at her face. A fine face. A sleeping face. All the worry locked away in those legs. Yet the peace of honey and cinnamon in those high cheeks, the thin nose, the crest of the brows. Full, bowed lips to make a man forget he ever felt the harpoon of loss pierce his heart.

She stirs. Eyes opening one at a time. "Tell me this didn't really happen."

He kisses her forehead, has no clue why.

"If it's any consolation, we still have our clothes on."

She grabs the comforter with her left hand and tosses it off them, looks to see his jeans and knit shirt, her red sweats. Her legs release his waist, then tighten around him again. He feels something contract in her loins. Then his. A testing. A shift of mud.

"You got me drunk on thirty-year-old schnapps."

"We found someone dead in the attic. I'd say we had a right to do whatever it takes not to just wither up like those bones."

"Danny's going to kill me."

"Who's Danny?"

"Another fool."

"Come on, Awasha."

"You think those bones have something to do with Liberty's death?"

*   *   *

She has already gone off to work when he gets Lou Votolatto on the line.

"Jesus Christ, Rambo! You didn't touch anything did you?"

"No way."

"Good."

"But I saw. One second I was down on my knees staring into this garment bag, looking at this coat sleeve, the dried-up hand. Next thing I know it's like something is watching me from back under the folds of that bag. Then I see the eye sockets, teeth, what's left of a face all tangled up with the uniform."

"Uniform?"

"Yeah, the Tolchester school uniform: navy blazer, pinstripe shirt, necktie, gray flannel pants, penny loafers."

"Another kid. A student?"

"Yeah I'd say so. Seems like a little fellow. You know, like maybe just a first former."

"What?"

"Ninth grader."

"A boy you say?"

"We're talking mostly bones here, some skin."

"Dead that long, huh? Long-ass fingernails?"

"I didn't look that carefully. Awasha was in pretty bad shape."

"Pocahontas? The Indian chick was with you, huh? Jesus, Rambo, you are a real fucking piece of work. You go digging around in other people's attics for dead bodies and you take a date?!"

"She used to live in this place. She was the house monitor, remember? She wanted to know what was in that attic as much as I did."

"Yeah, right. Don't kid yourself, Don Juan. She was there for you, not the stiff. Middle of the night. Tell me you weren't drinking."

"What's that have to do with anything?"

"I'm just trying to get the whole picture. You know, like *Scary Movie 6.9*, the one the D.A. will be featuring for the jury after he hauls you off to trial for murder?"

"Murder? All I did was stumble onto a body."

"In a house posted for no trespassing, in your girlfriend's ex-attic, in the middle of the night. The same place another kid got killed less than a month ago. Where she got drugged from a can of Red Bull that has yours and Pocahontas' prints on it. You getting the picture?"

"But Lou, I—"

"You score a little nookie to chase the fright out of your veins?"

"Screw you, man. No. OK, no. Alright? *Jesús Cristo*, I call you for help, and this is what I get? No! She already has a boyfriend. We didn't have sex, you sick son of a—"

"Good. Score one for the rookie. One smart move in a cascade of fuck-ups ... Don't freaking touch anything. Get the hell out of there.

Pronto, pal. Meet me at the McDonalds by the Sagamore Bridge in three hours. This could be the clue you've been looking for."

* * *

A warm wind is whipping the rain when he starts for the Cape and Votolatto. The rain and melting snow make a slurry out of the back roads as his jeep winds through the hills of Tolchester toward the interstate.

His mind is only vaguely on the road. It has been almost a year since Filipa dumped him, since Tuki disappeared. Eleven months since he has smelled the scent of a woman on his skin, the taste of her in his mouth. And now he feels a low howl stirring beneath his skin.

* * *

Her breasts warm against his chest, her pelvis pressing against his hips. They kiss. Long, slow. Her hand feels for him. His fingers under the hem of her bathing suit, slipping along the curve of her thigh. Long legs struggling to clutch his hips to hers. As he sucks on her neck, lost in the garden of her hair. On the beach in the dark. Nassau. Paradise Island. The sky raining stars on her face. Chocolate cheeks tilting toward Venus. Her body a mermaid's. Jesús Cristo. Surf thundering offshore on a reef. Marley singing from the distant bar, "Turn the Lights Down Low."

* * *

The same song playing now on the jeep stereo. Well almost the same song. It's a remake on the *Chant Down Babylon* CD, Lauren Hill singing a duet with the long-dead Marley.

Hill is just easing into her last chorus, pleading for love, when he sees the SUV or truck in his rearview mirror round the curve behind him. Its paint gleaming in the rain. Silver or maybe white.

Barreling down on his little jeep at twice the speed. The headlights magnesium flares. The pale face of its driver, grinning with wide-eyed delight.

He hears the thud of impact with a guardrail ... just before his head snaps forward, his face slams into the airbag.

The green jeep vaults off the road, rolls on its side, plows down a snowy embankment, and settles into a wood of young, white birch.

27

SHE bites her lip and tells herself it's not that bad. She can look at him. Must look. He's alive at least. The bruised and swollen nose and lips will heal. The long, jagged gash on his right cheek, where the gearshift handle ripped him open, will someday just add character to a face that may have been just a touch too pretty before. The broken left wrist secure in its cast.

But the look in his eyes makes her stomach churn. Gone are the soft come-hither eyes. He looks up at her from his bed in Brigham & Women's Hospital with a gaze that seems a cross between regret and rage.

"Someone tried to kill me."

"Just try to rest."

"I want to tell you—"

"It has only been a few hours." She turns away, cannot look at that devastated face a second longer, stares out the window of his fourth floor room. Rain is still coming down. The piles of snow along the curbs down in the street almost gone now.

"But I need to tell you. Listen!"

* * *

"Just listen, sister. Don't judge me. I have to tell you something, Awasha … Promise not to tell another living soul. Promise! By the Great Spirit, the Medicine Circle, Maushop, and the soul of our father.

She looks up at her twin's face. The sunburn. The short-and-high cut hair. The slick black stalks just beginning to curl again. He is tall like their father Micah, Strong Deer, was. But thinner. A toy soldier knit of wires and fish bones, unraveling beneath that dress green uniform. Specialist First Class Ronald, Water Bear, Patterson, mustering out of First Battalion, Ninth Cavalry. Right here, right now, on the Vineyard. On the shores of Manemsha Pond. On his own terms.

Saying fuck you to the master sergeants, the generals, the president. Fuck you to FBO Camp Headhunter. Fuck you to sand and MREs. Fuck you to Baghdad. Fuck you Haifa St. Fuck you Talil Square. Fuck you M-16. Fuck you CLP gun oil. Fuck you Camp Independence.

THIS is his independence. He is not going back there, he tells her. No second tour. No more scorching lungs. No more desert. No more land of Allah. Land of flaring wells, skies weeping oil, weeping sin too dark to name. His sin!

"I'm sorry, sister. I have done a terrible thing. I have …"

She sees his lower lip quivering, the tears starting to overflow his eyes. The southwest wind, the breath of Maushop, blowing tears across his cheeks. He tries to wipe them away, but the thin, jagged lines of fluid keep coming, soaking his skin. And hers … as she draws his face close, wraps him in her arms, shudders with his convulsions. Her twin.

"Everything's going to be all right."

* * *

She says it again. Things will be OK.

"I don't think so," he says. "A white truck hit me, ran me off the road. He was laying for me. Do you understand?"

"Maybe it just seemed that way."

"The driver had this look. Like he knew me. Knew what I had found in the attic. Knew that I'm on the trail of Liberty Baker's killer. And he was shredding me. I had this weird thought that I could already be dead. That you might already be gone ... Gracie too."

She takes his good hand.

"We're OK. Don't worry about us. Get some sleep, Michael. I've called your aunt in New Bedford. Your uncle and your father are due back from their fishing trip in two days. You're safe here. I'll see you in the morning."

* * *

She presses her head against Danny's shoulder, smells the subtle scent of ewe in the sweater's wool as the arms of her lover draw her in.

"Just hold me, please!"

Even at this time of the night, even after the hospital visiting hours are over, the parking garage at the Brigham is full of cars. None moving. When she looks out through the windshield of Danny's car the place seems a tomb, complete with transports for the afterlife. Florescent lights cast violet pools. But mostly the shadows rule. The mist, the ceiling leaking rain, the concrete walls slimy with dampness.

"Can we go now?"

"Not yet, I need this touching. I've been through hell."

"You know I'm here for you."

She nuzzles Danny's neck, chest.

"But I'm feeling a little—I don't know—stupid, I guess."

"Why?"

"What kind of fool sits in a parking garage at night, for hours, waiting ... for a girlfriend who's off mooning over someone else?"

She lifts her head, searches for Danny's eyes, finds them. "That's not fair. Someone tried to kill him. You know that?"

"You believe him? You sure he didn't just make this up?"

"Why would someone ever invent such a thing? I mean, the poor guy almost died. I don't think you're being exactly …"

"Hey, why was he even in Tolchester? Shouldn't he be fishing or something?"

She takes a deep breath, not sure she wants to tell about the Club Tropical. Or the rest.

"We heard a rumor about a kind of clubhouse for a secret society in Hibernia House."

"You went looking?"

"Yes."

"You and him. He's gotten to be kind of a nosy guy, don't you think?"

"I wasn't going in that place alone."

"You could have taken me."

She kisses the heal of Danny's jaw. "You're right. It was a really dumb idea, but …"

"But. But you didn't find anything, right? He was going back to wherever. To New Bedford?"

"We found a room. In the attic. A hidden crawl space with loose floor boards. There was a body."

"No way!"

"Mostly bones. And a school uniform like they used to wear when Tolchie was a boys school."

"Another dead kid?"

"This one sure wasn't suicide."

"Did you call the police?"

"We were going to do that today, but now …"

"Don't do it."

"What?"

"Maybe the fisherman's right. Maybe someone really did try to kill him. Maybe keeping that room and that body a secret is important enough to kill for."

"You think this has something to do with Liberty, too? This body's a clue to who killed her?"

"My advice is to leave it alone. Unless you want to end up like Liberty or your pal Michael."

"What do you mean?"

"If anything happened to you, I … Can you just let Liberty rest in peace?"

"But—"

"Walk away from that house for good. Leave that room the way you found it. Close up the floor on those bones. I'll give you a hand."

"But after what has happened, how can we be sure any of us is safe? I mean, Liberty and another child are dead. Look what happened to Mi—"

"Did you let him make love to you?"

28

GRACIE hears the shouting even before she reaches the side door to Beedle Cottage. She has forgotten the novel *Heart of Darkness* in her bedroom. Needs the book for English class, has hiked all the way across campus in the rain to get it.

Now this. Shrill women's voices. And Bumbledork's bark.

She can see him through the living room window, pacing in front of the dean and Doc P who sit side-by-side on the couch. She knows that scowl on the headmaster's face. The bully, the dickhead.

But she is not used to seeing fear in the eyes of these women, a gray pall on their faces.

She backs away from the window so they cannot see her.

Something's going down in there. Like maybe this is about her little excursion on the Red Line, and that Brazilian bar, yesterday. Maybe Bumbledork thinks the dean and the doc have not been aggressive enough in their supervision, punishment.

She wants to listen. But from outside, all she can hear are the high and low notes of the voices. No words.

When she reaches the side door of Beedle Cottage that enters into the back stairwell, she squeezes the latch slowly, softly, until it releases. She unlaces her Doc Martens, leaves them and her black umbrella on the threshold. Slips inside in her stocking feet. Does not move until the voices swell in fierce debate. Then she tiptoes up the back stairs to her room, grabs the novel she needs off the floor by her bed, starts down the stairs again. Voices in the living room swell and fade, her ears a cheap radio tuned to a distant station.

Until she hears Bumbledork's posh Midlands accent utter Liberty's name and launch into a tirade.

She stops halfway down the stairs, puts her right ear to the wall separating the stairs from the living room. Listens.

"Do you have any idea the kind of things that child wrote in her journal?"

One of the women groans.

"Well, I'll bloody well tell you. Enough dynamite to make the three of us look like fools and knaves and ... You get the picture?"

A long silence. She feels sweat starting to bloom on the back of her neck. The rain makes a low drumming sound on the roof and the half-frozen ground outside.

Finally a woman clears her throat. The dean speaks.

"Don't worry, Malcolm. Everything is under control. What happens behind closed door stays behind closed doors."

He says something under his breath she can't understand until he clears his throat, booms, "Dr. Patterson, do you think you can let sleeping dogs lie? Can we all be on the same page here? For the good of the school?"

Gracie gags at his clichés, calls him a filthy prick in her mind. Holds her breath until her mentor breaks the silence.

"Why not, Dr. Sufridge?! Sure. But maybe Gracie Liu and I have over-stayed Denise's hospitality here at Beedle Cottage. We should find permanent accommodations, don't you think? Say, back in Hibernia House?"

She pictures Bumbledork's face scalded red with Doc P's proposal. Her *quid pro quo*.

Then she slips into her shoes, slides out the door, heads for English class. Wondering whether Doc P wants to move back to Hibernia House to take a longer look at the Club Tropical, to investigate it in depth, to protect the evidence. The clues to Liberty's killer. Maybe stuff she doesn't even know about.

29

THE cop told her, "You want to talk, you got to meet me over chowder. I'm a sucker for chowder ... and pretty girls!"

So ... So she has canceled her appointments, split from Tolchester, school, Boston. Left Michael in the hands of his nurses. Now she's driving down South County Road on the Upper Cape. Wimpy's, a local seafood place in Osterville, seems like an odd place to meet this man who Michael calls, *o padrinho*, the godfather. Lou Votolatto.

And, Jesus, she could use a godfather right now. If he's not just an old lech.

*   *   *

"Hey, Pocahontas. Over here," a guy shouts at her from across the street as she exits her parked Saab.

"Excuse me!"

"We going to have a chowder fest, sweetheart?"

"Detective?" She squints into the sunlight at the shaggy figure leaning against the blue Ford.

Michael has described the *padrinho* as a sort of Dirty Harry type, but the man she sees reminds her more of a vacuum cleaner sales-man: thick salt-and-pepper hair bushing out in about five directions, shadow of a beard.

"*Minga!* You're a knockout. I mean the way Rambo talks about you I got the impression you were easy on the eyes, but, honey …"

For a moment she feels like getting back into her car, just driving for about a hundred hours. *Who the hell does this guy think he is calling her "Pocahontas," a knockout?* Is this how Michael sees her too?

"Hey, good lookin', how about putting a little smile on your face for Uncle Lou."

He's crossing the street to her. Weird guy in the Sears suit and topcoat. Before she knows it, he holds her hands in his bony fingers, kisses her on both cheeks. *Crazy damn Italian!*

"Yo … ! Detective!"

"Yo? What's with this yo? Am I making you nervous, *princesa?*"

She steps back, her eyes darting off, seizing on the only cloud in the sky to carry her away from this creep. Maybe all the way to Aquinnah.

"I've got to go. This is a mistake."

"No, this is an obligation. A mistake is finding a can of Red Bull laced with GHB at a crime site and not telling the police. A mistake is conspiring to impersonate a police officer. A mistake is protecting the killers of children."

"I didn't …" Her cheeks color. "You know what? I don't care if you're Michael's friend. Fuck you, asshole!"

He bows deeply. A stage bow, from the waist. In the bright sun of a March morning, on the main street of Osterville.

"I'm sorry. I deserved that. And more … But …"

"What?" She turns her back on him.

"I had to press your buttons. I had to know, Awasha Patterson."

"Know what?"

"Whether you can be trusted. Whether you have any self-respect. Whether you have the courage to spit in the Devil's face ... Or whether you're as strung out as you brother."

"You know Ronnie?"

* * *

She takes her soup spoon, scours the bottom of her bowel to capture the last of the chowder, licks the spoon clean.

"Pretty good stuff, huh?" The detective smiles at her across the table. They are in a booth in the darkest corner of the restaurant. The light in Wimpie's today more of a brassy haze than anything else.

"I forgot how much I missed Cape cooking. My mother used to always keep a pot of fish chowder simmering on the stove during the winter when Ronnie and I were kids."

"Can I ask you what went wrong for your brother?"

"Ronnie's my twin. My little brother by ten minutes."

He rubs his eyes. "I've sat in a couple of his bail hearings. He seems like a decent guy. A sweet guy. But he's way into the system. DUI, disturbing the peace, assault ... Should I continue?"

"No."

"What happened?"

"First it was always being the odd kid in school, the Indian, and moving around the Cape and the islands a lot. Then it was the Army and Iraq. After that ..."

"Alcohol, pharmaceuticals, violence."

She stares at the specks of pepper stuck on the bottom of her chowder bowl.

"Sounds like a good candidate for a rehab program. I could maybe help if you ..."

She shakes her head no, feels tears flooding her eyes. "He won't listen to me. Only our mother. Now with her gone ... Do you know how I've tried to ... ?"

"It must tear you up."

"You have no idea. Liberty Baker killed. And poor Michael. That jeep wreck. I must have really done something terrible in another life to bring on all of this. You know, Detective?"

"Lou."

"Michael thinks the world of you."

"The boy's lost his marbles."

"No ... Someone just ran him into the woods."

"I think he's probably lucky to be alive."

"Maybe he should have just gone fishing with his father and his uncle. It sounds like he loves to fish."

The problem is, says the cop, Michael hates injustice like a bull hates red. He's also a sucker for long shots. And damsels in distress. The kid's got an Indiana Jones complex that's going to get him killed someday if someone like her doesn't take him out of the game.

"What are you saying?"

"You don't think the boy has feelings? You don't have a crush on him?"

"You don't even know me."

"But I know him. And he's forgotten almost everything he knew about the law since he met you. He's a complete loose cannon."

"Then thank the heavens he has you for an angel."

"I'm no angel. I can't save him. Can't you see that? Look what's happened to him now!"

"Someone killed one of my girls. And now we've found another dead kid."

"You can't help them."

"There's something evil at work in my school, Detective. It needs to be stopped. And the school seems to want to push the whole thing under the rug."

"Maybe you're right. But I'd say you've stumbled into something toxic. You need to leave what happened to Liberty Baker, and that bag of bones, for professionals. Or you, Rambo, and this teenager—Gracie Whoever—are going to end up in the morgue."

"Are you saying you can take it from here?"

"No! Jesus. Word gets around I'm connected with this scheme, I may as well just march myself before the judge, get down on my knees and plead for mercy."

"Last night a friend told me to close up those bones in the floor, seal the attic and avoid the police in Tolchester. Said they were no doubt tied in with the school and the cover-up around Liberty's death. Like someone is probably paying them off."

He shrugs. "It happens. Don't take this the wrong way. I'm not saying I'm in favor of letting a killer, or killers, go free. I can't tell you what to do. But if you value your job, your life—and the lives of Michael and that Chinese girl, the student—maybe you should listen to your friend and try to let go of your suspicions. For everyone's sake. If you drop it, Michael will have to find a healthier outlet for his passions. Know what I mean?"

She feels a fit of the jitters starting in her thighs and upper arms, spreading to her fingers, toes. "I'm scared. I have this feeling something really bad is about to happen, and there's nothing I can do to stop it."

"I know, sweetheart ... But wouldn't it be useful to know what kind and color of car Kevin Singleton drives?"

30

WHEN he opens his eyes, there is a soaking wet Chinese girl standing over his bed. Her bobbed hair plastered to her cheeks, the purple streaks brighter with the gloss of water. Her Red Army overcoat steaming in the hospital heat.

"In case you're wondering, it's fucking raining again."

"So I shouldn't be in any hurry to get out of this place?"

"What's the point, right?" She forces a smile. Sets a little potted jade plant on his solar plexis. "I almost forgot. Here's something to remind you that spring is coming."

He can see her trying not to wince as she looks at his battered, bandaged face.

"It's good to see you, Gracie. Take off your coat. There must be towels in the bath. You can—"

"Michael ..." She doesn't move. Just stands there, dripping, holding the jade plant on his belly. Looking down at him. Her lower lip starting to quiver. "I'm sooooo sorry. This is all my fault. I should have never—"

"Hey. It's OK."

"If I hadn't begged you to help us, none of this …"

He puts his good hand on one of hers. "I'm an adult. I make my own choices. It's your job to take care of Gracie, earn good grades. Write smart essays. Get ready for your swimming championships. And spring break. Isn't that soon?"

She wipes her eyes on the sleeve of her coat. "Next weekend. Swimming interschols are up at Andover. And then the break."

"It will be good for you to get away from here for a while."

"Tory and I were going to visit Justine in California. But now … I don't know. I mean what with your accident, the Club Tropical and …"

"And what?"

She puts the jade plant on his nightstand, wipes her eyes and nose on her coat sleeve again. "I went back up there, Michael. Like after I heard about your wreck."

"Back to the attic?"

"I saw the bones."

He tries to rise off the bed. "*Jesus Cristo!* Why in the name of God?!"

"I had this feeling. Like something was going really wrong and so I—"

"You have to stay away from that place."

"But—"

"No buts. Will you sit down? Promise me you will stay away from Hibernia House."

Suddenly she feels like that girl June Woo in *The Joy Luck Club.* Like dumb, inadequate, not Ninja Girl at all. "I had to go up there and see what … Before … Please don't be mad at me."

"Before what, Gracie?"

"Michael, I'm sorry. The day of your wreck, I came back to Beedle Cottage to get a book I forgot for class. Doc P, Dean Pasteur and the headmaster were having some kind of like really heavy talk in the living room."

"I don't understand."

She tells him about Bumbledork's coercion tactics. About how Denise Pasteur was quick to close ranks. How Awasha seemed to buckle under the pressure, but angled for her old apartment back in Hibernia House.

"That's it?"

"Except that after seventh period I got called into the dean's office. She told me I am being moved into a room with a new girl in Briarcroft Hall. And Doc P is going to an off-campus apartment."

"Is that OK with you? With her?"

"Shit, I don't know, Michael. I'm sick of living with the dean. It's like being in a fishbowl. But I feel like Bumbledork is trying to separate Doc P and me, you know? It's like he's up to something. And he's got something on Doc P."

"You don't trust her anymore?"

She shrugs, says that right after she heard about moving to Briarcroft, Doc P told her about his wreck. She was fucking freaking. So was Doc P. Then she wondered if maybe someone was going to clean up the Club Tropical the way they cleaned up Liberty's room. Like make a clean sweep of the place. And wipe out her and Doc P too. Shit, look what happened to him. It's like the clan wars back in Hong Kong. Freaking Chinatown!

"So you went back to Hibernia House? To the attic?"

"Yeah. With my camera. I shot about two hundred pictures, put them on a CD and sent them to Tory for safe keeping. And I got this—like maybe we're going to need some DNA."

She hands him something wrapped in a paper napkin.

He hits the button that raises up the back of his hospital bed, peels back the napkin.

There's a bone about the size of a pencil tip. A bit of fingernail attached.

"What's … ?"

"Pinky. Right hand. It could maybe tell us something about who killed Liberty, right?"

* * *

As soon as he's alone again with the beep of the heart monitor, the hum of the morphine jamming his veins, he turns off the lights in his room, bathes in the darkness until his mind starts to flow in long, rolling ocean swells. Then he fishes for the phone on the nightstand. Punches in Lou Votolatto's number.

He gets a voice mail box, tells the detective to give him a call. He's afraid he's got to ask him for another favor. There's this funky little bone …

31

THE steam is just starting to make the skin on her arms glow when the door opens. Gracie steps in, wrapped in a rainbow beach towel.

"This is kind of weird, Doc. Are you sure we should be meeting like this? I mean here?"

"You have a better idea, Gracie? The walls in this school have ears. And yesterday Dr. Sufridge came down pretty hard on me. I can't afford—"

"I heard." She sits down on the bench.

"What?"

"Well, I heard some of it. I was back at Beedle Cottage looking for a book and—"

"So then maybe you know I wanted to move out of there. Get us both back to Hibernia House. Now look what's happened."

"I already hate my new dorm ... How's your apartment?"

"Modern, sterile. And now I have to drive over here to work."

"So Bumbledork is trying to divide and conquer us. You think the dean is on his team too?"

"I don't know. I mean no. Denise Pasteur is her own woman."

"If you say so."

"Trust me."

"Anyway. Fuck 'em all, right?!"

"Why did you want to talk. What's bothering you?"

"I went back up into the attic yesterday after I heard about Michael's wreck."

"Accident."

"You really believe that?"

"No. Not really."

"I saw the body."

"Oh … Gracie!"

"It's OK. After finding Liberty, nothing seems to shock me. I just don't sleep much these days."

"I'm sorry." The steam vent spews. She feels waves of heat searing her.

"Is it baking in here or what? Christ!"

"Maybe we need to dial down the temp. But, come on, talk to me …"

She gets up. Leaves her towel on the bench where she's been lying. Walks naked across the tiled cubicle, opens the glass door, turns down the thermostat. The steam jets sputter off. But the room feels just as hot. She lies back down, folds the huge towel over her tight, trim body.

"The Club Tropical must really be evil."

"First, Liberty … and now that poor boy."

"We don't know the Club Tropical has anything to do with these deaths."

"Come on, Doc. The note in Lib's book. The secret room. That dead boy up there in the attic."

"How do you know it was a boy?"

The Tolchie blazer, the shirt, the tie. The school uniform from about thirty years ago before the merger and the school got rid of the dress code.

"You think this stuff is going to lead us to Lib's killer?"

"I think we should leave it all alone, Gracie!"

"What? Hey ... did somebody threaten you?"

"No. Not exactly. I talked to a police friend of Michael's. He thinks we're dealing with something really evil. And who knows how many people it involves? He said we should just back off, OK?"

"Did you see all the empty beer cans and booze? The sex mags and the mattresses and condoms? You think that place was some kind of love shack for the members? You think they had girls up there? Like what the hell was going on?"

*   *   *

"Just listen, sister. Awasha, OK? Her name was Aaserah. She was Sunni. She lived near Talil Square ... I was on patrol, going door-to-door in an apartment building looking for armed insurgents and locals who could use some attention from our medics. Looking for people who had gotten caught in the middle of a rough fire fight that had gone down the day before with some of the bad guys on Haifa St. ..."

She pictures it all.

Ronnie's face, sunburnt beneath his helmet. He is tall. Slender. Ever the Indian warrior. Assault rifle at the ready as he pushes open the unlocked door. A soldier beginning to unravel where no one can see beneath the desert camouflage fatigues. Even as he bulls his way into the little apartment.

And her, Aaserah, sitting on the pale green bedspread in her black abaya. Fumbling to pull the golden hijab over her long, braided, brown hair as she sees him, trying to hide herself from the soldier. From the man. Brown eyes flashing.

"You want to kill me? Kill us all? Kill the rag heads, American?"

He looks around the room, wide-eyed for his wingman, the rest of his squad, the guys backing him up. Wants to say, "Hey, Scooter, this one speaks English!" But he's alone. The only witness. The only one to absorb her anger.

"Shoot me. Just shoot me now!" She's on her feet, giving up on the hijab, the modesty. To hell with it. Balling the golden head scarf in her hands. Maybe to cover something else. Maybe a bomb.

"Stand your ground. Don't come any closer!"

She staggers toward him. Limping. Her right leg dragging. Still balling the hijab, working her hands. Not hesitating. A gray Persian cat scoots out of the way.

He raises his weapon, tilts the barrel toward her. "Stop!"

"Go ahead, kill me, shoot the Sunni bitch."

Now he sees the blood on her abaya. Slick, wet. A dark stain, almost as wide as the leg beneath, running from above the arc of her hip to the hem. Red droplets falling on the floor, smearing under her slippers as she presses closer.

"You're hurt."

She keeps coming, just three or four steps away now. Raising the gold ball of cloth in her hand ... as if she intends to throw it. To blow him to bits with an IED. Destroy herself too.

He looks around for his buddies. Like what the hell. Is this how he dies?

"Fuck you, American. Shoot me. Don't you have any balls? Come on, shoot the soldier's wife. Shoot! The way you killed him. Kill me."

She lunges at him, throws the golden ball of cloth.

His ears, eyes, are suddenly boiling. His right hand tightens on the grip of the assault rifle, index finger feeling for the trigger.

Just as the hijab hits him square in the nose, blossoms. A veil of wrinkled gold.

It falls. Shrouding his forearms, his weapon.

And she falls too.

Right against the veil, the gun. Him. Knocking him backward a step.

Even as he releases the weapon, catches her. His hands somehow now in the pits of her arms. Her head hitting hard against his thigh. As he waits for the explosion to shred them both.

But it never comes. There is no bomb. Only a woman, unconscious in his hands. Bleeding the blood of ancient Babylon on his boots. A day-old bullet wound in her flank.

And a Wampanoag brave screaming for the medic. His lower lip quivering. A southwest wind, the breath of Maushop, blowing tears across his cheeks.

*   *   *

"Something's wrong with the heat in here, Doc. Let's get out of—"

"Just one last thing, Gracie. Do you know what kind of car Kevin Singleton drives?"

Gracie rises off her bench. Heads for the exit.

"His dad has a silver Murano."

"Is that a truck?"

"I don't know what you call it, but I'm fucking baking. And the door is jammed!"

32

HE'S never been so glad to be out of anywhere as he is now to be out of that hospital after three days. Never so glad to be driving his jeep, even bent and dented from the plunge into the woods. Never so glad to be back in Nu Bej this fresh March morning. The air over the harbor crystallizing his breath into little clouds that shimmer in the sunlight. Laughing gulls wheeling in flocks through the sky.

The *Rosa Lee's* the only trawler at the fish buyer's wharf, first boat home from the banks with a trip of fish in her hold. She's just back late last night.

When he enters the wheelhouse, he sees his father, lying on his back in the berth at the back of the building. Snoring.

He grabs the big toe on Caesar Decastro's foot, poking out of the rotting white sock.

"Huh?" His father cocks open one eye, sits up. "What?"

"It's me, Mo, Dad."

"*Cristo*, what the hell happened to you?" The fisherman rubs his eyes with his fists, takes in the red scars, scabs, stitches on his son's cheek. The wrist cast.

"I think I've gotten in way over my head."

"In what, a fucking meat grinder?" His black eyes suddenly pop wide open, shoot rods of intensity through the hazy morning air. More questions. The hooded Celtics sweatshirt and jeans give him an urban look. Longish, graying hair pokes out around the edge of the hood.

"So???"

"So what?"

"You OK?"

"I wrecked my jeep."

"Shit."

"Yeah."

"But that's not why you're waking me from my dreams of glory. My god, I thought I was a boy again, your mother the fairest Portagee princess in all of … Jesus."

"I think someone tried to run me off the road. Some guy in a white truck."

"On purpose?"

"Yeah, maybe."

"Damn, Mo … ! Where?"

"Tolchester."

The older man rubs his jaw, stares out through the windows at the harbor. He grabs a pack of Merits from the pouch in his sweatshirt, taps out a cigarette, lights it with his Zippo. His hand is a little shaky.

"Dad?"

Caesar Decastro gets to his feet. Moves across the wheelhouse to one of the two swiveling captain's chairs that look out over the bows. "Take a load off."

Michael drops into the other chair. "I'm all screwed up."

"So it appears … Shit, Mo!"

"What?"

His father takes a long drag, squints at his son. "Look, you want to square things up with me? Is this about that Indian honey?"

"I don't know."

"Come on, dog. Be real!"

"Don't be like that. Look at me, Dad. I need your help right now."

"I swear to *Cristo*, I told you this would come to no good. I practically begged you to come back out fishing with me and Tommy. Stay the hell away from that lawyer business. It messes you up. You can't go near the law without some kind of Clark Kent thing kicking in."

"What the hell are you talking about?"

"Clark Kent—as in Superman."

"Yeah, I get it, Dad, OK? But so—"

"So enough with trying to rescue all these Lois Lane types. You want to get yourself killed?"

"Huh?"

"How come you feel like you need to save every weepy woman?"

He squeezes his eyes shut. "I'm really in trouble!"

"You want to talk about this prep school stuff you've gotten mixed up with in Boston? Or maybe about Vietnam again? You want me to tell you how my romance with Meng almost got me killed over there? How a hard-on is like a time bomb?"

Something seems to smack him between the shoulder blades. Drive right through his lungs. He chokes. "No."

"You want me to remind you how that murder case you had with your half-black, half-Vietnamese drag queen client out in Provincetown destroyed your engagement to Filipa? And turned you into this ghost of the son I used to have?"

"No! Damn it, Dad. Help me out. Please. Something's really tearing me up. I feel like I'm being crushed in a vice, and there's no way out. And don't tell me all I need is to go fishing. Get out to sea. I've tried that."

"You telling me fishing isn't the answer?"

"I love it. And I used to think it was magic for me. But right now it just feels like another way to run from shit."

"What's wrong with that? Jesus, Mo, someone may still be trying to kill you. Get the fuck out of Dodge City!"

"I don't think I can."

"Why the hell not?"

"I have this sick feeling Dodge City's inside of me. How do I sort that out?"

Outside, a breeze whines through the fishing gallows, the outriggers, the nets.

"When you were a kid, and you had girl problems, you used to take long walks on a windy beach."

"You think that works when the girl is dead?"

33

DENISE Pasteur's face seems even more angular than usual, cheeks almost gaunt. Lips thin, less glossy. Her bobbed platinum hair whiter as she closes the door behind her for privacy.

"People are talking."

"Excuse me?" She can't believe what she's hearing, kicks back from her desk, spins in her swivel chair to face the dean. The chair screeching as she spins.

"About you and Gracie in the steam room."

"We could have died in there!"

"Well, since you kicked out the glass door, hit the panic button and brought the cops on campus, everybody at T-C is going to know about your little interlude by the time they get back from spring break."

"I don't believe this! A chair was wedged against the door from the outside so that it wouldn't open. We were stuck. Somebody wanted us to bake to death in there. And you're worried about people talking?"

"Don't be so dramatic. No doubt it was an accident. The custodian was cleaning up, moved a chair, didn't know you were in there."

"I didn't call the police." The words boil out of her throat.

"Somebody did. And now the police and the media are going to be all over this. You wait and see."

"Please. Why are you doing this. I thought you were my ..."

The dean walks to a bookshelf, picks up the Wampanoag medicine stick carved from the rib of a pilot whale, pretends to examine it.

"Put that down."

"What?"

"Leave my medicine stick alone."

"Jesus."

"Yeah, Jesus ... Maybe you better leave."

Denise Pasteur shoots her a look like you-must-be-kidding, still holds the medicine stick, taps it in her free hand.

"Please. Stop. Put down my stick. Go. Just go. Before I say something I wish I—"

"I'm serious. Think about it, Awasha. Think about how it looks. A teacher found alone with her female student in the women faculty's steam room. You were only wearing bath towels. Can you imagine the fit Bumbledork is about to throw at you? At us? Fuck!"

She jumps to her feet. "Us?"

"Us. You think you are the only one under the microscope around here?"

"I don't understand you."

"Damn it. You're smart. You ever listen to Bumbledork talk about women? It's right there under his patronizing tone of voice."

"What?"

"He thinks we're all psycho vampire Amazon dykes. You know he's watching our every move. We threaten his fragile sense of male superiority. He tolerates us because his job depends upon his appearing open-minded and inclusive. He has a mandate from the board to be

PC. But he would like nothing better than to see us shame ourselves with a really ugly—"

"A girl's been murdered here. Liberty Baker's dead. There's a body in the attic of Hibernia House. And we're talking about ... about perceptions? Perceptions?! What's gotten into you? Why don't you say what's really bothering you."

Denise finally puts down the medicine stick on the bookshelf. Her eyes welling with tears.

"I feel so betrayed. Why, Awasha? Why did you do it? First you spend the night with that ... that fisherman. I know you did. And now Gracie? What the hell was going on in that steam room? My god, you're a piece of work."

"You really believe ... ? I thought you knew me. You actually think I would hit on a student? That something was going on with me and Gracie? And with Michael? That's what's really getting under your skin? You're jealous? Danny?!"

She moves toward the taller woman, reaches out a hand, but Denise, her Danny, steps away. Turns her back, stares out the window at a collection of students dragging suitcases from a nearby dorm toward a queue of limos and taxis. The kids are all heading off to the airport on spring break. The campus will be empty by this afternoon.

"We had something good, you know? But you've pissed it away. For what? Some needy teenager ... and that n'er-do-well from New Bedford ... I could just ..."

"Just what?"

"I'm such a fool. I knew the rumors. About you and all those men. Why the hell did I ever think you could change? Why did I think you were the one?"

She heaves a sigh, drops onto her desk to steady the sudden weakness she feels in her knees. Sits among towers of books by Sherman Alexi, Julia Alvarez and Amy Tan, Spike Lee videos. Looking tiny, but

fierce, in that gray business suit. Her eyes growing wider, cheeks flushing as she starts to speak.

"You're not going to do this to me. You're not going to make me
responsible for your happiness. Not now. Not when there's a killer out
there who right now could be—"

"You know what the students call you behind your back? Pokey.
They call you Pokey. Short for Poke-Her-Hot-Ass. They think you're
the faculty ho. A native slut. Did you know that?"

She grabs the door nob, flings open the door. Points to the hall.

"Out. Get the hell out of here!"

"Don't do this."

"Fuck you, Danny."

34

CAESAR Decastro's only son, lapsed fisherman, failed lawyer, doesn't know why exactly—maybe he's hoping to resurrect an old ritual—but he's walking on Lighthouse Beach in Chatham. Middle of the day. He has dropped off a finger bone with Lou Votolatto, driven out on the Cape to this place that was a retreat for him during the Provincetown Follies case.

He's thinking about Liberty, the bones in the attic, Awasha, Gracie, killers. And his mother a year dead from uterine cancer. Feeling the bright sun and a southerly breeze warming his skin for the first time in months, when he realizes that the phone in his pocket has been buzzing intermittently for quite some time.

Now he stops walking, watches a pair of gray seals basking together on a pillow of sand, nuzzling. Nipping. Feels an odd urge to bark at them. But finally he turns away, climbs the dune toward the twin lighthouses, fishes in his pocket for the infernal phone.

There's a message from Gracie. She's at the airport in Boston, needs to talk to him before she boards her flight. "*Like this is really important, Michael.*"

* * *

"I'm heading to California, you know?" she says when he calls her back. "It's my spring break. Like I really need to get far the fuck away from that school. Tory is meeting up with me. We are going to Justine's house. Maybe take a little road trip to San Diego or ..."

OK. Of course. She ought to get away. Not feel the least bit of guilt about leaving him. He's going to be just fine. He's a fast healer. Doc P will be just fine, too. Everybody needs some time off. Things were getting way too intense. But ... her message sounded stressed. Is she OK?

"Not really, Mich ... if you want ... know." Her voice fades in and out. She's not holding her cell phone close to her lips, doing something else while she talks. Maybe carrying her bag. "Before I left Tolchie I did ... research and ... shit, they're calling my plane. I think I've got to ..."

"Gracie! Talk to me. Please."

"Michael."

"Yeah."

"They're boarding my zone. I—"

"Just hold still a second. Tell me what's bothering you. Don't get on that plane until—"

"It's a girl, Michael!"

"What?"

"The body. Our big new clue."

"What body?"

"The one we found in the attic."

"A girl?"

"I'm almost sure."

"But the clothes were—"

"I know. Boy's clothes ... Shit everybody's pushing ahead ... I've got to get in line."

"Talk to me! A girl? How do you know?"

He sits down on a fence rail surrounding the lighthouse parking lot. Pictures her. Purple-streaked hair, Chinese Army coat, black leggings, Doc Martens. Shuffling, backpack on one shoulder, toward the jetway, the ticket agent.

"Those bastards, who ... they are. The ... Tropical. All their porn and pot magazines ... from...Seventies. Like 1973 ... '75, right?"

"The ones I saw."

"I checked ... *Tolchie News* ... those years. Like ... library's archives. These freaking people ..."

"Gracie, can you hear me?"

"Sorry Michael it's a bit of a zoo ... bloody jetway ... Some lady with two kids ... stroller ... OK, I'm in my seat. So ... ?"

"So you were reading old school newspapers ..."

"Right. Ninja Girl's on the case. Wouldn't you think if a kid disappeared back then, there would be serious coverage in the school paper?"

"Sure."

"Nothing. I just read a lot of stuff about some kind of rebellions on campus. Like the boys walked out on mandatory chapel one Sunday, the student council wanted the dress code abolished. That kind of stuff."

"Nothing?"

"Well, nothing except that the first *Tolchie News* in the fall of '76 had a story about a girl from Coates who left for her summer break in June '75 ... and never arrived at her home. Poof. Vanished into thin air."

"Really?"

"No shit, Sherlock ... Hey, can I call you back once I get off this stupid airplane? They're telling us to turn off our phones."

"Wait! You think we found her?"

"I think those pricks in Club Tropical did something terrible to her. Then they disguised her body as a boy's in case anyone ever found the bones."

"Whoa! I mean maybe, but—"

"You think I'm crazy? Just some wigged-out chick? Michael the flight attendant is giving me the hairy eyeball."

"This is big, what you found. This missing girl. But the hair on the head was really short and—"

"What about the finger? I swear it had what looked like nail polish on it."

"I haven't heard anything from my guy. He's pretty busy and I just dropped off the—"

"Well when he gets unbusy, ask him if he knows anything about a missing person report on Roxana Calder—"

"Calder? What?"

"Calderón. Roxy Calderón from … Michael the flight attendant, she is like about to …"

"Roxy from where?"

"I got to go, Michael."

He wants to tell her she's an amazing kid. Wants to say, *Be careful. Call me from LA.* But she clicks off.

Down on the beach the seals still nip and nuzzle. High above on the dune, the ex-lawyer pictures Liberty Baker drowning in her own blood and starts to bark.

35

"FROM San Juan, Rambo. Roxana Calderón from the lovely city of San Juan, Puerto Rico. You ever been there?"

"No."

It's a late morning, western omelettes and home fries. The former public defender and his cop pal. This time, they're sitting at the counter in The Fishmonger's Café near the Cape-Islands ferry terminal in Woods Hole.

"How come? You don't like the Caribbean? You don't like to dance to *salsa?*"

"What about this Roxana?"

"I guess you're too young to remember, huh? When were you born?"

"Nineteen seventy-seven."

"No wonder you're such a fuck-up. You're still wet behind the ears, boy!"

"You sound like my old man."

"He must be a hot shit."

"Come on! Roxy? Tell me."

"It was a big deal for a while. The girl's father was a high-roller. Some kind of big-ass developer in San Juan, turning crack houses and bordellos into upscale condos."

"You were on the case?"

Votolatto rolls his eyes, shakes his head. "Dream on. I was just a couple of years out of the academy, still trying to get off road detail and into a CPAC unit."

"Wet behind the ears ... so to speak."

"Knock it off, OK, Rambo? Point taken."

"But you knew about the case."

Yeah, he was living in Allston-Brighton at the time, taking a criminology course at Northeastern. Had this professor who was a retired Boston dick. He was teaching, trying to get some traction as a crime novelist. He was kind of obsessed with the Calderón case. Talked about it a lot. Told the class missing person cases were some of the most overlooked and creative crimes they would ever see. Hardest to solve. The "Case of the Magic Airplane" he called it.

"What? Why?"

"The girl. Roxana. Pretty weird. She disappeared on a flight between Boston and San Juan."

"How's that happen?"

"See what I mean? Pretty creative stuff, huh? I don't think they ever figured it out."

"She vanished from an airplane?"

"TWA something or other. Big jet. One of those L1011s, I think. Or maybe a DC-10."

"They were sure she got on?"

The limo driver recalled taking her to the airport, the ticket agent remembered checking her in, had the canceled portion of the ticket. Two of the flight attendants saw her, virtually the whole flight, remembered serving her two rum and cokes.

"But she disappeared."

"Zip. Gone."

"She never got off the plane?"

The detective pushes his empty omelette platter away from him, burps into his fist. "Another coffee?"

"Come on. How do they know she never got off?"

"As I recall, her whole family was waiting for her at the gate, going to throw her a party. Her sweet sixteen was coming up, I think. Or was it fifteen—what do the Latins call it, a *Quinceañera*?"

"Really?"

"Yeah, they waited and waited and waited. No Roxy Baby."

"Crazy."

"It was a big investigation, you know what I mean? In the papers and on TV for a month … The father wouldn't let it go. Got himself in the media daily for a while …"

"He wanted revenge?"

He nods. "But in the end, nothing. They checked every inch of that airplane. Even checked the lavatory holding tanks in case someone cut her up and …"

"But they didn't check her school."

"Oh yeah."

The school, Coates, was pretty pissed off about it, called it an invasion of privacy. But the cops did their job. Nothing. No rumors, no traces of fowl play, no body.

"Until now."

"Where are you going with this?"

"The bones we found in the attic. The finger."

"You said it was a boy. Uniform from Tolchester Academy. Necktie, the whole works."

"Looked like a boy. Short hair, uniform. But what if ... ?"

"This place, this dorm where you found the bones was a boys residence?"

"Until about ten years ago, I guess."

"So how the hell did the Puerto Rican *princesa* get there? The attic of a boys dorm back in the 1970s? The whole place, Tolchester, was a boys school."

"The campus is basically right beside Coates School."

"You think she was involved in this secret society shit you've been telling me about? The ones that your Liberty Baker and the Chinese kid were researching?"

"Like I told you, the place we found the bones, the attic—"

"It was some kind of secret meeting place for one of those societies, right? Old boys club."

He tells Lou he's pretty sure they called themselves Club Tropical. From the magazines he found there, the club seems to have been active right around the time Roxy Calderón disappeared. Then the attic looks like it was suddenly abandoned. Sealed up.

"Like those boys had something to hide. Like they killed that girl."

"Or they all graduated and went to college."

"Yeah, that could have happened too."

"Maybe the police never searched Tolchester Academy, Hibernia House."

"So it seems."

"But she got on that plane."

"Those flight attendants ID-ed her from a picture. I guess this kid was rather memorable. Kind of a flamboyant dresser, as I recall. Hot pink mini. Big hair. Lots of make-up. Jewelry."

"A babe. Like fifteen going on twenty-five."

The detective shrugs yes, takes a long sip of his fresh coffee.

"When do we get the DNA results on the finger?"

Votolatto closes his eyes, massages his temples with both hands. "I don't know, damn it. My lab girl is doing this on the sly. I can't pressure her."

"We can get gender and race from it, though, right?"

"Yeah, probably. But Christ, kid. I'm going to tell you what I told that nice Indian girl. What do you say we drop this vigilante justice sh—"

"One other thing ..." He looks away, fiddles with his coffee mug. "Maybe there's some nail polish on the fingernail. Can your lab friend check that?"

The cop rocks back on his stool. "You're a pisser. You know that, Rambo?"

"What?"

"Somebody tries to kill you because you got your nose way deep into someplace it don't belong. Knocks the shit out of you. And now here you go with that nose again."

"Hey, Lou. Come on, this is important, right? Two dead kids."

"I gotta get home. Taking the missus to Boston tonight. We're going to see *The Phantom of the Opera*. It's our anniversary. You need a ride somewheres?"

"I'm going to catch the ferry."

"You're going to the Vineyard?"

"I've got to meet someone."

"Don't tell me. Ronnie Patterson's sister."

"None of your business."

"Ask her if she found out yet what kind and color of car that Kevin Singleton kid drives ... And leave your phone on, Casanova."

36

SHE'S running late, and, damn it, he's switched his cell off. No way to reach him except speed.

Her Saab squeals to a stop in the Steamship Authority pick-up circle at Vineyard Haven. When she jumps out to look for him, it hits her for the first time all day: the heat. Maybe seventy degrees. She feels suddenly silly wearing her rabbit fur parka. The wool leggings, deerskin boots. Stupid for being late. Crazy for ever asking him to meet her here.

She's not sure why she wants him to come, whether this is a good idea. Or just another one of ten thousand mistakes she's made with men. Mistakes born of what? Loneliness, insecurity? Missing her father Strong Deer? Maybe she should patch things up with Danny, stick with women. Maybe she's just like her brother, just as twisted up inside as Ronnie, by killing, by romance. Maybe it's a twin thing, this dark hollow in her soul that she tries to hide from herself and the Great Spirit. Maybe she really is a slut.

But she's back on the island, right? Back home. Her real home. Away from that school, Danny, Bumbledork, Liberty's ghost. On vacation. Spring break never looked so good, felt so right. The sky bright, light wind stirring her hair, long black threads floating in the air. The water on the harbor a pale blue. Except for the emptiness of the streets, the closed shops and restaurants, the complete lack of leaves on the maples and oaks on the hill above the ferry terminal, it could almost be summer.

And maybe, just maybe, he has come. With or without his phone. And then, well, she'll see. See if Lou Votolatto had a clue when he said the boy has a crush. Or whether all Michael wants to do is feel like a winner again. Bounce back from his wrecked law career, his failed engagement, his ...

Stop thinking!

She finds him standing on a small pier next to the Steamship Authority dock. One leg cocked up on a safety rail strung between two pilings, his hands cradling his jaw. He's wearing a fresh pair of jeans, a white fisherman's sweater. His eyes are staring out at the wooden schooners moored in the harbor. She can tell he is thinking about the sea, his mind probably a hundred miles offshore, with the cod fish and the shearwaters. So maybe this is good for him, coming here. Maybe he can heal on the Vineyard, too. She wonders if he has ever heard about the Giant Maushop or the beaches of Aquinnah.

"Hey, sailor!"

He turns to her voice. Pulls the silver Oakley sunglasses off his face. Smiles.

She feels his eyes on her. Tiny explosions rippling from the roots of her neck and arm hairs, across her breasts, down her flanks to her toes.

Then she is in his arms. They hold her with a strange fierceness. As if he will never let her go. *But right now, maybe that is OK*, she thinks. As she kisses his cheek before she can stop herself. She can smell the heat rising from his sweater. Not the pungent, oily scent of Danny. But something sharper. Flinty. A man's fear. Or his yearning.

She feels herself beginning to shiver, starting to remember the anger frozen on Danny's face when she said, *They call you Pokey. They think you're the faculty ho.* And now two girls are dead. One a clue to Liberty's killer. A convulsion rises in her chest.

"What's the matter?"

"I promised you we would not talk about Liberty ..."

"It's OK. You can tell me anything."

She disengages, takes his rough hand. "Come on. I want to show you something. A secret place."

* * *

She leads him down a trail through fields of brown salt hay. They skirt the edge of a large salt pond, pass onto a stony beach. The breeze has begun to stir, a warm wind urging small waves ashore. They rush onto the land, then hiss away, dragging trails of small stones, lady slipper shells. Gulls dive, scoop bait, soar on the up-drafts. Chattering to each other. The air smells of clams.

With the tide out the beach on the southwest tip of the Vineyard is a long strand leading to a point under high red cliffs. She stops short of the ribbons of eel grass marking the surf line. Pulls off her boots. Drops her parka. Hikes her woolen leggings to the tops of her calves.

"Come on."

He tugs off his Nikes, his socks, rolls up his jeans. The stones and shells hurt his feet, but he follows her to the water's edge. Feels the icy water swirl around his ankles.

"What is this place?" Part of him watches for seals, feels a bark coming deep in his belly.

She squeezes his hand as she did Ronnie's when they were kids here. Before they moved off-island.

"The tribal lands. My mother loved this place. I used to call it Black Squirrel's Beach after her."

"I used to call her, well, Alice the Great."

She gives a little laugh. "She really liked you, you know? She would be happy I shared her shore with you. She said you were a committed beach walker."

He thinks of the short, stout woman with the sparkling black eyes who stood for hours behind the counter of the liquor store downstairs from his apartment. Dead too young like his own mother. Like Maria. How was he to know she was Black Squirrel? He barely knew she was Indian. She reminded him of his *vóvó*.

"She was like a mother to me for that year I lived in Chatham."

"We scattered her ashes here last fall, my brother Ronnie and I."

"So she's come home."

"Yeah, can you feel her here? We believe this is sacred ground. The land of Maushop ..."

She tells him of the giant who left his footprint here, whose spiritual center lies among these ponds and beaches and cliffs of Aquinnah. How the boulders beneath the cliff were once the children of Maushop and his wife Squant. How on dark nights you can hear Squant calling to her children in the language of the ancient ones.

"You must feel so ... I don't know how to say this. So ... connected, so much a part of things here. So ... hugged."

She squeezes his hand tighter. "I thought you might understand. Black Squirrel said there was something Indian about you."

He shakes his head. "I just like beaches. I feel things on them. Like I do when I'm out fishing. But when I'm fishing, I feel the water, the air, birds, fish, sometimes whales. A place out of time. On the beach, I feel ... I don't know, something else. History maybe. Evolution."

"People."

He hesitates. "Seals, actually."

She drops his hand, faces him. Laughs. "You're kidding."

He shrugs. "No, I think of seals ..."

"You wish you were a seal, Michael?"

"Sometimes. You?"

"Maybe."

"Ever bark?"

"You?"

"The truth?"

"Down and dirty."

"Only when I'm feeling threatened … or really horny."

"Which would that be right now?"

He's opening his mouth to answer, or maybe bark, when she throws both her arms around him, drives her tongue between his lips. A basic impulse.

She pulls him tight against her hips, slides her hands over the lobes of his buns. The wench rising inside her skin again. Pokey. Fallen angel of lost girls. Of Liberty. *Maybe this is the only choice now. The only truth for seals.*

*   *   *

From what he can tell, the place where they bed each other is some kind of bait shack on the edge of a salt pond. He has to admit he likes the squalor of it all. Not just the place—the musty scent of scallop shells, its cobwebs, the light filtering through salt-crusted windows, the mildewed quilt beneath them on the floor. The oboe calls of seabirds. Her raw nakedness.

Who could imagine a body as tiny as hers as such a hot coil? Both of them slick with her sweat, his. They nibble, slither against each other. Faces lost in tangled hair. Her tongue twisting to his own. Tasting his ears, his breasts. The core of his navel. Lower.

His hands finding the soft, dark places in the arches of her feet, behind her knees. Tracing the curve of her moon. Gliding through the film of oil on her inner thighs. Until his lips find her fingers.

And the rest of him stretches for her soul.

She rises over him. Taking charge. Doing this her own way. Her hands under his arms, squeezing his lats. Her nails piercing his skin. The pain almost too much as she bends to him. Groans from someplace that seems impossibly far away, while her mouth sucks the flesh at the base of his neck.

"Hey, what's this?" she asks. The small, pale red bloom beneath his Adam's apple. In the vee between the cords in his neck.

A rose tattoo? What you gone tell you mama now?

She draws his blood to its surface.

Not again!

Even as their torsos surge forward, plunge down. Bucking, spiraling creatures, diving through schools of silver cod. Racing with the currents into a thermal vent. Trying to find the planet's molten core. Volcanic annihilation. Beyond the bite of a razor's edge on a girl's wrist. Beyond the *Playboys* and the *Hustlers*, the Dannys, the Filipas. Beyond Liberty. And death.

A place of bones and no bones. A place where his *vóvó* draws him to her breast and sings the lullabys of Cape Verde. Of Africa.

Until they rise up. Break the surface. Whole again. Their hearts chanting in some ancient language of hunting, fishing. Barking.

And they lie still.

37

"I hope I'm not interrupting anything."

He can almost picture Lou Votolatto on the other end of the phone connection, poised over a glass of Seven Crown at some road-house on the Cape, grinning wickedly into his cell phone.

"No, what the hell, call me anytime. It's only 11:45 at night."

"Hey, don't get all uppity with me, Rambo. Like who's doing who the favor here? You ever check your phone messages?"

"It was turned off until about an hour ago so—"

"No shit, I've been trying to reach you for about eight hours. I thought I asked you yesterday to leave your phone on."

"Sorry."

"You got distracted by that dolly didn't you?"

She stirs at his back, molds against him. Her right hand sliding across his belly. He feels her breath on his neck, catches the scent of Bacardi Limón as she exhales.

"Come on, Lou!"

"Don't come-on me. I know what you're up to."

"You have no idea."

"You're shacking up in some hotel over there in Vineyard Haven thinking about what it would be like to make a little Wampanoag papoose."

"Actually, we're in Edgartown, if you have to know, at a B&B. I was giving a foot massage with a cream made of raspberries and almonds. So … eat your heart out. *Cristo!*"

He hears the buzz of distant conversation coming from his phone. Music. Country and Western. Alan Jackson and Jimmy Buffett, "It's Five O'clock Somewhere." Feels her lips on his free ear.

"Lou?"

A clearing of the throat. "Well … do your thing, kid."

"What?"

"At least this one's a real lady, a fine young female. Not some nutso drag queen, like the last time you went on a campaign to join the Knights of the Round Table."

She presses her cheek to his. The phone sandwiched between them so she can hear too.

"Right. OK. Look, I'm sorry. I just sort of fell off the edge of the Earth here for a while. You know?"

"What else is new."

"Why don't you tell me?"

"You were right, Rambo. The finger belongs to a female … probably with Southern European, West African, and Caribbean Indian DNA."

"So?"

So this is a gene stock usually associated with Puerto Rico, Cuba, and the Dominican Republic. And, by the way, there was a trace of nail polish.

"Roxana Calderón?"

"Yeah, it's beginning to look that way."

"*Jesus!*"

"No shit. Could be you and your girlfriend just solved the mystery of the Magic Airplane."

He feels her breasts against his back.

"Well, sort of."

"Say again."

"We found Roxy ... but we haven't found her killer. Or Liberty Baker's."

Her fingers stop their crawl through the plume of hair rising from his groin.

"A bit of a problem, isn't it? Because it looks like maybe he's already found you."

"And now we know he's not Kevin Singleton."

"You sure about that?"

"Come on, Lou. Roxana Calderón disappeared more than fifteen years before he was born! Kevin usually drives his father's silver Murano. And the guy that ran me off the road was in a white SUV."

"I thought you said it was a truck. A white truck."

He shrugs. "I could have been mistaken. There was a lot of glare from the rain and the headlights."

"No shit, Rambo! You were hung over weren't you?"

* * *

She throws off the bed comforter. Sighs. "God, it's three-thirty!"

He stirs. "What's the matter?"

A shaft of light filters through the curtains, paints the antique sea-captain's bedroom with shadows.

"I can't sleep. I'm all jumpy inside. Now there are two dead girls and ... and you were making really horrible sounds."

"Sounds?"

"Groans sort of. No. More like the call of a loon."

"A loon?"

"Something like that. Spooky. Sad."

"Sometimes I have bad dreams."

"About all this killing? About Liberty?"

"Yes and no."

"I don't understand?"

He sits up in the four-poster bed, the light from a streetlamp outside making the hair on his chest silvery. "Can I ask you something?"

"Sure."

"Are you black?"

"What?"

His words seem to come from another world, another universe maybe. She runs her fingers through her hair, forehead to behind her ears, clearing the tangles away from her face. The oversize, red and white T-C DANCERCISE! T-shirt hanging from her shoulders makes her feel impossibly young, or shrinking, masks her breasts almost completely.

"I mean, I know you are Wampanoag. But I always heard that Cape Indians and Portagees have some common ancestors. Black ancestors. You know, from back in the whaling days when the Yankees made all the rest of us live together like—"

"What are you getting at?"

"I'm sorry. It's none of my business. I shouldn't have—"

"Yes." She hears the word flow out of her mouth. Soft but steady. Feels his hand reach across the foot of bedding separating them, take her fingers, her palm. Squeeze a little.

She squeezes back, sending him a code, a signal. "You too, huh?"

"My mother's mother, we called her Vóvó Chocolate. She was from São Vicente."

"Where?"

"The Cape Verde Islands."

"We got some of that too ... Where are you going with this, Michael?"

She closes her eyes, lowers her cheek against his shoulder. His arms draw her into a hug. Stiff, but warm.

"Sometimes I dream about beaches and black people. That ever happen to you?"

"Bad dreams ... with loon noises?"

"Yeah."

"No." She pulls away. Her hands releasing his arms from their hold on her shoulders.

"Forget it then, OK? Lie down, let me rub your back. Maybe you can sleep."

She kind of doubts it, with this question boiling from her throat. "You have some kind of problem with being part black?"

"It's more like ... I don't know. You believe in destiny?"

"Fate?"

He looks deep into the pools of her eyes. Tries to ignore the play of shadows over her nose, her lips.

She shrugs. "The Wampanoags say the Great Spirit shapes us all."

"But do you believe that?"

Something twists, a spring or a little animal, at the back of her brain. "I have to believe I carry all my pain for a reason. Otherwise what's the point, you know? Things are pretty messed up right now, wouldn't you say?"

"You mean Liberty and now this other girl, Roxana?"

"Yeah. And your wreck and Kevin Singleton and ... I don't know ..."

"Talk to me."

"Even this." She's still staring into his eyes, his face getting a little blurry as the tears begin to gather. "Look at us. Middle of the night, talking about black folks and the dead. Holding onto each other like we're the last roots on the side of the cliff."

"I'm sorry. Sometimes ..."

"Maybe we're both going crazy, Michael. Did you ever think of that?" The words burst out of her throat. "Maybe Liberty's taking us down with her. Maybe we have to let her go like your buddy Lou says. So we can take care of our own business. Just walk away, you know, and try to breathe a little?"

His face freezes, the wide-eyed look of a man who has been ambushed, clubbed from behind.

"If you can, go ahead. But ... I don't think I ..."

"Is this all about race for you? Liberty's death?"

"No. Yeah. Maybe."

"Why?"

"I was hoping you could tell me."

She leaps out of bed, goes to the window, flings it open. The night air blasts the room. Rattles pictures on the wall. "Why are you laying this at my feet?"

*   *   *

A cat scatters. The Iraqi woman staggers toward him. Toward the soldier. The Wampanoag brave in his desert fatigues. Ronnie. She's limping. Her right leg dragging. Still balling the hijab, working her hands. Not hesitating. Screaming. Daring, begging him to shoot her. Aaserah.

Then she falls. His hands catching her by the pits of her arms. A day-old bullet wound bleeding from her flank.

*   *   *

He has carried her onto the bed, onto the pale green bedspread, pulled the black abaya above her waist, stripped away the sash she wrapped around her middle to staunch the flow of blood and yellow ooze from her torn guts. His left hand is pressing a field dressing to the ragged hole above her hip, trying to stop the leaking fluids, the stench of shit, when the medic enters the room, takes one look.

"She's toast, man."

"She wanted me to shoot her."

"You should have. You would have been doing her a favor, believe me, dude. You know how fast gangrene spreads in a crap hole like this city?"

Ronnie's face hardens. "Goddamn it, help her."

The medic shakes his head, starts back out the door. "I got a soldier down up the street."

The Indian brave picks up his assault rifle, cocks it, points it at the medic's head. "You want to make that a medic down? Or you want to start an I.V. on this woman, white motherfucker?"

38

WHEN he comes out of the bathroom in his red boxers after showering, shaving, he has a bath towel in one hand, a razor in the other. She's sitting on the captain's bed naked, half-wrapped in a sheet, staring blankly out the window at Edgartown Harbor, empty of its summer fleet of yachts. His phone in her hand.

"What's the matter?"

"Gracie just called you. I recognized her cell number so I picked up."

He rubs his face with a bath towel, tries to hide his annoyance that she felt free to answer his phone.

"She's in Boston … and freaking out."

His forehead, eyebrows squint in confusion. "Your school doesn't start until next week sometime."

"I know … But I just can't leave her there on her own."

"Cristo!"

"Exactly."

"You're going back to Boston?"

"This is what I get for answering your phone."

He doesn't say anything for a while, dries his hair with the towel. "Doesn't she have friends she can stay with?"

She gives him a look like *Wake up. Liberty's dead.* "We're her friends, remember? She called YOU."

"What's that supposed to mean?"

"Nothing. She called Ronnie too."

"Who?"

"I never told you about my brother, my twin?"

"No."

"You'd probably like him. Gracie does."

"Why?"

"He likes to rescue women. Just like you."

"Ouch."

"Sorry, Michael."

"That was mean. Why—"

"Maybe Gracie thinks she needs a knight in shining armor ... but I don't. I'm not a seventeen-year-old girl. I don't need to be rescued. OK?"

"What did I do to—"

"I'm just saying I need an ally right now, not a white knight."

"Who ever said I wanted to be a white knight?"

"Gracie. That's what she calls you."

He tosses his razor through the bathroom doorway. It drops into the sink. Clatters. "So now it's goodbye Martha's Vineyard, hello Boston?"

"At least for me. You can go polish your sword, if you want."

"Stop!"

"Do you know what Gracie was doing in California?"

"Hanging out with her friends Tory and Justine."

"Along with Kevin Singleton and his older brother Clyfe."

* * *

Gracie's waiting on the curb in front of Boston's South Station when they roll up in Awasha's car at about noon. The weather has turned cold again. She's hugging herself in her Red Army coat for warmth. Her hair shimmers with a fresh application of purple streaks. Something about her looks older, more adult, maybe because she is not wearing her glasses or her face has lost its adolescent puffiness.

"I've screwed things up haven't I?" She throws her travel bag on the back seat, climbs in. "You guys were …"

"It's not important. We're here for you, OK? You can stay at my place." Awasha turns her head over her shoulder, looks back from behind the steering wheel, gives Gracie a smile.

It is a tight smile, maybe forced, but it's the first smile he's seen on her face since last night after they made love, when he was nuzzling her breasts.

Gracie leans forward and gives them both a wet smooch on the cheek. "I love you guys, you know that? I mean, REALLY love you."

Awasha's smile dries up.

"Hey, you want to hear something freaky? I got solid proof that some of these secret societies still exist. And Bumbledork knows about it."

The Saab accelerates into Boston traffic.

"What?"

"Kevin Singleton was visiting his brother down in Long Beach. As in California. Tory, Justine, and I met up with them. They took us clubbing."

"Terrific." Awasha's voice curdles with sarcasm.

"Just listen, will you, Doc P? Kevin's brother got a little baked. When he was dancing with me, I sort of teased him about being a fac-brat geek when he was at Tolchie. He said, maybe not. Like I obviously didn't know shit. 'Yeah, well what do you know about secret societies,' I ask him."

"So?"

"'You ever hear of Red Tooth,' he says."

"He's a member?"

"Kevin may be too."

The car veers toward the curb next to Boston Common, screeches to a stop. The driver turns in her seat, looks hard at the teenager.

"You're sure. This wasn't just some guy boasting to impress a girl?"

"Hey, I thought you knew me better than that. I always get evidence. Don't I, Michael? Ninja Girl."

He rubs his eyes, too little sleep, too much raw coffee on the ferry back from the Vineyard. His vision is fading in and out of focus. The face of the Chinese girl suddenly melting away into a blur of white skin, purple hair, pink lips.

"Check this out." The girl fishes into the waist pocket of her woolen coat, pulls out a key ring. Hands it to him.

He fingers the stainless ring. Looks at the old-school golden skeleton key on it. And something else. A charm that looks a bit like a miniature acorn. The cap gold, the nut itself ivory and sort of wrinkled. With little brown stains around the edge where it meets the cap.

"What's this?"

"Clyfe called it a society key."

"For Red Tooth?"

He hands the key ring to Awasha. She rolls it over in her hands, suddenly tosses it back to him. "Jesus. Damn!"

"What?"

"That's a human tooth."

"No shit. Gross, huh?" Gracie makes a gagging face.

"Is this Clyfe Singleton's key? How did you get it?"

"You don't want to know."

"Gracie!"

"I had to get down with the snakes."

"You stole this from him."

She says yeah. He showed her the key at the club. Later the two of them went back to his apartment. Way early in the morning. They were both pretty trashed. He was all over her. But then he passed out. So she just put her hand in his jeans pocket, grabbed the key and split.

"Where were Tory, Justine, and Kevin?"

"Out to breakfast somewhere. I had to call them to come get me."

"Oh, Gracie!"

"You guys think I'm a slut?"

He looks at Awasha out of the corner of his eye, hopes she's going to field this one.

"You want me to lecture you about the risk you were taking?"

"No."

"Then just promise me you'll stop with this Ninja Girl stuff."

"I just saw a way to catch a break in the case and—"

"There's no case! We're not detectives, Gracie. This is not *CSI*! We're more like victims. And how can I impress upon you that Kevin Singleton is not to be trusted. Not him or his brother."

"OK, Michael, I get it. But catch this. That tooth on the key chain. That's actually Clyfe's tooth. That's the Red Tooth initiation. The brotherhood pulls out one of your twelve-year molars and makes this key charm out of it."

"Christ!" Awasha closes her eyes. "Only white people would do this kind of crap."

He takes a deep breath, tries to clear the images of amateur tooth extraction from his mind. "You said something about Dr. Sufridge, Bumbledork earlier …"

"The ruddy bastard is one of them."

"What?"

"Yeah, he's Red Tooth."

"But he's English."

"Right. Seems that's where the brotherhood began. Fucking playing fields of Eton. Real old-school."

"Shit."

"Did this guy Clyfe, or Kevin, say anything more about the Club Tropical? Besides the rumor that led us to the secret room?"

"Not yet."

"What's that supposed to mean?"

"Clyfe is going to be looking for this key … I know how he can find it. And maybe how we can find out who killed Liberty, too."

39

"HAVE you no shame, Dr. Patterson? I hear you've got that child living with you now."

She's in Bumbledork's butternut-paneled office again. Still wearing her camel hair overcoat, maroon scarf. Winter has returned to New England. The oak log crackles, hisses, beneath the flames this morning in the immense hearth.

Her: sitting in one of the three armchairs circling the baronial fireplace.

Him: pacing back and forth across the room behind her, his black academic gown fluttering off his shoulders. Hands raking his thin hair.

The office with its shelves of books, its granite gothic arches makes her feel like she's in a Harry Potter movie. Again.

"I say, have you no shame?"

"Excuse me, but what are you insinuating?"

"Don't be coy with me, Doctor. You know very well ..." His posh English lilt falters.

"Are you talking about Gracie Liu?"

"Of course … Of course, I am. Who bloody else would I be talking about?"

"Just exactly what do you think is shameful, Dr. Sufridge, about a student staying at my apartment while she waits for school to open in a few days?"

"My god!"

"She's here from Hong Kong. We always ask faculty to provide rooms in their quarters if they can for overseas students who cannot totally fit their travel plans to the school schedule. What's so different about—"

"I have it from reliable sources that … that child was not overseas. She was in southern California for her spring break, cavorting with those friends of hers who left us back in February … and Jack Singleton's boys."

"Really?"

"Do you take me for a fool?"

She rubs her cheeks with her hands, tries to picture the blue seas south of Aquinnah, tries to hear the calls of the gulls.

"I came to you a couple of weeks ago with Dean Pasteur, and asked you to exercise dignity, a little decorum, a bit of restraint. All but asked you to keep your sexual proclivities to yourself and not flaunt them in front of the students. Lord, they are just impressionable children! And the school, don't you see, has been through so much already this year with that dreadful death and—"

"You're saying I'm a lesbian?"

"Well aren't you?"

"What does it matter?"

"Or are you what Americans call a switch hitter? I've heard something about a fisherman who—"

"I don't believe … What I do behind close doors is none of your business."

"You're wrong there, Doctor. So very wrong. You are a teacher. This is a school. You are living in school-rented housing … And now you're keeping a teenage girl, one of our students, in your apartment. A girl who half the school knows was found with you by the police in the sauna of the women's locker room. Naked!"

She takes a deep breath and stands up, faces him. "Are you or are you not accusing me of sexual misconduct, Dr. Sufridge? Because if you are, I want my lawyer present to hear this."

He stops pacing, puts his hands on his hips, drills her with his eyes.

"If you are not accusing me, I will consider any further conversation along these lines as harassment and report it to the Board of Trustees, file a complaint with the District Attorney's Office, and alert the media. Do you understand me?"

He lowers his voice, tries to speak in fatherly tones. "Why don't you just sit down, take a deep breath and collect yourself. Have a bit of a think there, my dear, before you try to threaten me again."

She throws her hands in the air, feels her brain screaming. "NO! I won't sit down. You know what? You're unbelievable! I don't have to listen to this anymore. You are so far out of line, I can't even … I … I'm at a loss for words!"

He picks up the fire poker, shoots her a squint-eyed look, turns away. Stirs the burning logs on the hearth. When he faces her again, his face is pale, teeth clinched, cheeks shaking.

"I am going to send someone over to your apartment this evening. If that child Grace Liu is still cohabiting with you, I will have no other choice but to—"

"Let me make this easy. I'll move out. Gracie can stay at the apartment until you find an *en loco parentis* situation that meets with your approval. Fair enough?"

He rolls his tongue beneath his lips to wet his teeth. "Don't think by any means that just because you have the privilege of being the only Native American in this academy, a woman, and an administrator, you can dictate policy in my school! This attitude of yours is most abrasive. And ... and I have not finished with you yet."

She tosses her long maroon scarf around her neck and starts for the door. Drums thundering in her head, her mind pictures looped snares for catching rabbits, fox. She stops in the doorway, turns back on the headmaster.

"Maybe you can put Gracie up with Jack Singleton. Then you and the Singleton boys can tell her all about the joys of tearing out each other's twelve-year molars. How about that?"

No sooner are the words free of her mouth than flames arc, twist, in her stomach. She hears her brother's voice in her head saying she's as screwed as a herring on a low-tide beach. Lost like one of Maushop's missing Children of the First Light ... when the giant's wife Squant begins keening. A howling hurricane of wind and memory.

* * *

The Iraqi woman stares up at him from the hospital bed, her eyelids heavy from sedation and buckets of antibiotics. A week after her surgery, she is still fighting infections. But she returns his smile, faintly.

"They tell me you saved my life. Is it true?"

The soldier shrugs. "I did what anyone would do."

"I don't think so. This city, this country, has become a slaughterhouse. Your people killed my husband."

He purses his lips. "I'm soooooooo sorry."

"You do not look like the other ajaneb, *the Americans. Is your family from the Middle East?"*

"No. We are from Aquinnah."

Her brows wrinkle. "Aquinnah. I do not know this place. It is in America?"

"Sort of ... It is on an island off the coast of ..."

"So is it a colony of the white men?"

"You could say that. My family is Indian."

She furrows her brows again. "Muslim, Seik or Hindu?"

"No, no. We are Native Americans. Wampanoag."

"Wamp a ... ?"

"Wampanoag. The People of the First Light."

He tells her where he was born. The tribal lands of Aquinnah. His people are from the island of Martha's Vineyard, Cape Cod, the south coast of Massachusetts. All of this was Wampanoag land before the English came. Before America was America.

"So you serve in the army of the occupation?"

He shrugs. "Sometimes that's how it feels. But in America today, we believe that every person no matter what race or color or creed has the right to ..."

Something catches in his throat.

"What's wrong?"

He dry heaves into his hand. Doubles over, hugs his belly. Maybe he has a stomach ulcer. The bootlegged vodka and the hash he smoked last night burn his blood.

She reaches out, takes his hand, the skin suddenly clammy. "What's your name, Wampanoag?"

He feels the dry leathery touch of her fingers, her palm. They are like his mother's. A hand so small, but so strong, so seasoned by manual labor.

"Ron," he says. "Folks call me Ron or Ronnie. But my people, the Wampanoags, call me Nippe Maske, Water Bear."

She squeezes his hand. "My people call me Aaserah. Thank you for giving me back my life. The divine spirit must work through you, Nippe Maske. Allah akbar. God is great. He needs me still."

40

HE'S hiding from everybody, everything—especially death. He's sleeping in his berth in the fo'castle of the *Rosa Lee* tied at the state pier in Nu Bej, when his phone chirps, wakes him. Even before he speaks into the mike, Gracie's voice erupts in his ear.

"Michael, everything's turning to shit."

"*Cristo*, Gracie. What time is it?"

"One fifty-seven."

He pulls the sleeping bag over his head, burrows into the pillow.

"Oh god, why … ? I'm exhausted. Can you call me back tomor … ?"

He clicks off the phone, sinks back into a raucous dream about *salsa* dancing with a dark stranger in a Brazilian club.

The phone chirps again.

"Come on, Michael. Wake up! Listen to me. Clyfe Singleton wants his key back, and he asked Kevin to come and get it. I told him I'd trade him the key for some information."

"In the middle of the night? What's Awasha say about all of this?"

"I don't know. She's not here."

He stirs, gets one foot out of the berth onto the cabin sole. "What do you mean?"

"What do you mean, what do I mean? I thought she was with you."

"Where are you?"

"I'm at her apartment, remember? You guys picked me up at South Station and brought me here, before you caught the bus back to New Bedford."

"She's not there?"

"And Kevin is really hassling me about the key."

"Hey, just hold on! When did you last see Awasha?"

"Bumbledork called her into his office this afternoon about three. It was the second time she had to see him today. She never came back."

He has both feet on the floor now, rubbing the sleep out of his eyes as the tiers of other berths come into focus in the red nightlight of the cabin. The wind is up. *Rosa Lee* tugs at her lines, groans as she rubs against the trawler tied outboard of her. No one will be going back out fishing for days. All the crews have gone home. There's a nor'easter moving up the coast. By morning there will be twenty-foot seas offshore. *What next?*

"She just left you there ... to fend for yourself?"

"I thought she wanted to hook back up with you, you know? She seemed pretty distracted when you guys picked me up. I can tell you two have got something ..."

"Leave it, Gracie, OK? She's not here. Not been here."

He looks around the fo'castle, wonders how she'd deal with this place. The tangled mounds of bedding in the berths, the half-empty coffee cups on the table. Ashtrays full of butts. A Cape radio station playing Dire Straits "Roller Girl" softly over the speakers. Everything stinking of fish and sweat. Would the *Rosa Lee* disgust her, or could she dig the rawness? Like the bait shack in Aquinnah?

Are you missing her, Mo? Damn right!

"I've called her a bunch, but she doesn't answer. I really need some advice about what I should do about Clyfe's key."

"Maybe she went to see her brother, the twin. What's his name?"

"Ronnie. I tried him. He doesn't answer his phone either."

He takes a gulp of cold coffee, tastes the bitter grains as he swallows, tries to think. *Shit!* "First things first, do you feel safe staying where you are?"

Well sort of, she says. Dean Pasteur is there. She brought over some Chinese take-out around seven o'clock, saying Awasha had to go out of town suddenly. Now the dean of the Academy is sleeping on the couch. But what about Kevin Singleton and the key?

He feels the cold coffee gurgling in his belly, struggles to focus his mind on the Singleton kid for a second, not Awasha. "He really wants the key back tonight?"

"He just called me for the fourth time. Right before I called you."

"Can you put him off 'til tomorrow? I don't want you meeting him alone."

"Yeah, sure. I guess. Like it's my move, right?"

"Right."

"Do you think Kevin knows who killed Lib?"

"How about you and I meet him someplace tomorrow around noon. A really public place."

"How do you feel about the bowling alley? You ever roll?"

He pictures his days as a kid on Saturday mornings at Wonder Bowl in Nu Bej. "You have no idea."

"What about Doc P? Should I be freaking out?"

"You should try to get some sleep. Her phone's probably just out of juice. I'm sure she's OK."

"No you aren't. I can hear it in your voice. You're worried."

"Gracie. Why do I always have to keep telling you to take care of yourself? Please! I'll find Awasha, OK? I think I know where she went."

"Really?"

"Really," he says.

If only it were true.

41

AN hour after sunrise. She wakes, turns on her phone, sees the long log of messages. Realizes that she better let Michael know she has been sitting in the West Barnstable state police barracks all night.

And she has to check in on Gracie to see how she's getting along. Thank god, Danny could step in to look after Gracie while all of this other shit was going down. It was a gift. At least she has peace in the Danny corner of her life right now.

She better make her calls.

But first she needs to see if Lou Votolatto is still here. If he will finally talk to her.

*   *   *

She's just come out of the women's room, her face still wet from the dousing of cold water she gave it, when Lou slides up from behind her and takes her elbow in his hand.

"Here's the word, young lady." He guides her to a chair at a small table. "The arresting officers, we're talking DEA as well as the guys from this barracks, have your brother cold, found enough pure cocaine stashed in his boat to charge him with possession and transport—a Federal offense. They could put him away for at least five years."

"You were in on this?"

It was the Feds' call. But he heard this could be coming. He tried to warn her when they talked in Osterville. Remember? He offered to help her find Ronnie a rehab program?

"You're saying he's an addict? He's dealing?" Her voice rising. Frustration, anger. With everyone.

"Does it surprise you?"

She almost shouts, *No. Fuck no*! But she bites her lower lip instead, turns away to hide her shame. "Can I ask you how the DEA and your pals came to be looking in his boat?"

"You can ask … I can't answer. Not now."

She drops onto a bench in the lobby. "How long until we sort things out? I've never done this before, get someone out of jail."

"You better count on spending today and part of tomorrow. He'll be arraigned in Boston at the Federal Court, bail set. The paperwork takes time. How about I buy you some breakfast?"

"I have to return some calls first."

"Tell Rambo for me, he sure as hell better be staying clean as a whistle. I'm not kidding!" He gives her a look, steady, unblinking iron eyes. A clear warning.

She feels her stomach tense. "Is my brother really in bad trouble?"

"It's not a bed of roses."

* * *

Nippe Maske, the water bear, is not in his battle gear when he knocks on her apartment door, just his desert camies. His sunburnt face smiling as he holds the pink roses in his hands.

When she answers the door, she seems taller than he remembered, her black abaya catching the curve of her shoulders, a breast, her hip as she steps forward to greet him. A crimson hijab covers her head. But when he looks into her brown eyes, sees them smile, he can picture her long, braided, brown hair. He thinks she has the lips of an Indian princess. His sister's maybe. Ripe, always in bloom. Not that he thinks of Awasha in that way, but you know …

"Allah akbar, Wampanoag."

"Asalaam alaikum."

She smiles again at his awkward use of the Arabic greeting.

"I thought you could use some flowers to brighten up your day. Things must be hard for you here on Haifa Street."

42

THE bowling alley smells of stale pizza and foot powder. He can't believe Awasha's stuck on the Cape. Can't believe the stateys have taken down her brother on narco charges. Can't believe he's actually rolling a line of candlepins after all these years. Or that he's having yet another *falso* date with a seventeen-year-old. Ninja Girl. As Tio Tommy says at times like this, *Welcome to Wonderland, asshole.*

"Your roll, Michael." Gracie is working a china doll look today, hair in pigtails, bright red lipstick, face glitter, baggy black cardigan, plaid thrift-shop pajamas pants. Red bowling shoes.

"When's this kid going to show up?"

"Don't look now, but he just came in the door."

"So do I roll, or do we stop?"

"Come on. You got a spare, and it's the last frame. Forget Kevin. Play the role, Michael. He thinks you're a bad-ass detective. Like don't fuck with the Jesus."

"What?"

She says it's a line from *The Big Lebowski.* The bowling movie, you know? Coen brothers?

No.

"Man, you need to get a life. Where have you been for the last eight years?"

Ah … law school, public defending, getting engaged, getting dumped, fishing …

"Just roll, dude."

The ball kisses the two and four pins just as Kevin Singleton drops onto the seat next to Gracie at the scoring table. He's wearing his usual: gray polar fleece over a blue waffle-weave undershirt. Baggy jeans. Hiking boots. His lanky body looks seven feet long as he slouches on the bench seat, faking nonchalance.

"How come he's here?" Kevin nods toward Michael.

"Maybe a girl needs a bodyguard around you Red Tooth types."

"Give me a break."

"No," says Michael, sitting down next to the pair, "give US a break, Kevin."

The boy runs his fingers through his curly brown hair, closes his blue eyes. "Look, man, I just came here to get something back that she took from my brother, OK?"

"Nope. Not OK. Gracie, your roll. Finish the frame for me. Kevin and I need to talk."

"Come on."

Michael tries to put on his best Lou-Votolatto-fuck-this-shit face. "Pay attention, Kevin. Did you forget you're still a suspect in the death of Liberty Baker? Did you forget the police have reason to believe her death has something to do with these secret societies at your school?"

"Are you going to start with more of your cheap-ass intimidation?"

"Did you forget that your brother told Ms. Liu that you and he and your father and the head of your school are all members of one of these secret societies? Do you remember that Miss Liu has evidence of this? That you told Ms. Liu last night that you were willing to answer her questions about these secret societies?"

"Yeah, man. I remember. Gracie, help me out, OK? Can you get this guy to just back off?"

Gracie takes her last roll, the ball wobbles down the lane, strikes, leaves four pins standing. "What, Kevin?"

She comes back to the scoring desk, enters the score, starts totaling the game.

The boy shifts his blue eyes. "Gracie. I thought you were my friend. I thought …"

She puts her hand on his knee. "I am your friend, Kevin. I know you didn't have anything to do with Liberty's death. I know you loved her."

"What do I have to do to get Clyfe's key back?"

"I want to know more about the Club Tropical."

"I already told you. Clyfe said he heard they had a secret room in Hibernia House."

She says she needs more. Somebody in Red Tooth knows more. This is really important.

He takes a deep breath. "Does this guy have to be here?"

She shoots Michael a wink. "Can you give us a minute … please?"

*   *   *

She finds him in the parking lot outside the lanes, sitting in his Jeep, listening to a Portuguese radio station. He's submerged in *fado* music, remembering how his Vóvó Chocolate loved these songs.

"Hey, bad cop." She pops in beside him.

He turns down the music. "Hey, Ninja Girl … What'd he say?"

"There are stories."

"Whose stories?"

"Red Tooth stories. Kind of society lore or something."

"Yeah?"

One of these stories is about a rebellion. Some kind of rift in the society. Back in the 1970s, some guy who was like a big deal in Red Tooth got pissed off with the brotherhood. Quit and started his own society with a bunch of friends. Kind of anti-establishment. The new society was the Club Tropical.

"The old boys thought it was a threat?"

"According to Kevin. The societies became arch enemies at Tolchie. Sounds pretty juvenile doesn't it?"

You couldn't have said it better, he thinks.

"How does this connect to Liberty's death ... or Roxy?" she asks.

"I don't know. But I bet Kevin can find someone to give up the names of Red Tooth's vanquished rivals ... You didn't give him that key back yet?"

"Are you kidding me?" She puts her hand down the front of her black cardigan, fishes in her bra, pulls out the key ring. "This stays over Ninja Girl's heart ... until we get answers."

43

SHE thinks her head is going to split at the ears. No sooner is she off the phone with Michael and Gracie for the fourth time today, heard about their pressure tactics with Kevin Singleton, than Denise Pasteur calls. Bumbledork wants another meeting with her. And Lou Votolatto is in her face again. He's asking if she's ready to meet with her brother, whether she can get an attorney before Ronnie's arraignment.

She almost says Michael Decastro, he's her lawyer. But then she remembers. He left the law under a cloud of suspicions when his drag queen client in the Provincetown Follies murder case disappeared ... before being totally cleared of charges. And ... and he dumped the rest of his cases in the laps of other poor slobs in the Public Defender's Office, went fishing. Dropped off the face of the Earth, really.

So now what?

* * *

She says flowers are little gods. But, please excuse. It is not proper in Iraq for single women to invite men into their apartment. Even if it is just to show how she will give these roses a most-honored home in the middle of her table. And, of course, she must keep to herself since it is the custom that she grieves for her husband for four and a half months.

"I feel so stupid," he says. "I just wanted to see how you were getting along."

She takes the roses from him with both hands, lets her fingers linger a few fractions of a second across his knuckles before slipping them away. Her eyes blink. Three times. Maybe it is a kind of code.

"You are a good man, Nippe Maske. Bring me roses again sometime. When my grief is not such a heavy shadow over my life ... and it is not the hour for midday prayer."

*   *   *

Ronnie's wearing an orange prison jumpsuit when two guards walk him into the interview room. His long, black hair falls over his shoulders. Not as long as his sister's, but with more waves, even some tight curls. Serious plumage now that the cops have taken away the leather thong he used to tie it back in a pony tail. His cheeks are dark with two-day growth, his eyelids drooping from no sleep ... and—can she admit it—withdrawal.

Goddamn it, Nippe Maske. You've really killed the hen this time, she wants to tell him. But what she says is, "Are you OK, Ronnie?"

He nods. They sit down, face each other across a metal table. The guards back off to the door.

The wind is up, churning the waves, coating her skin with brine.

Part of her is hoping that Lou Votolatto or Michael will show up here to help now. But maybe that would be a mistake. This is family business. Private. Better just to reach out her hands for his hands. She smells the peppery scent of his fear. Feels Ronnie's big, rough fingers. The calluses on the heel of his thumb. Damp palms.

"I wish Alice was here."

He's afraid to be alone with me too.

"Awasha?"

"Don't you think we've hurt her enough?"

"She would understand. She would know I did not do what they are saying ... I never ..." The big man cannot finish. His throat choking with sobs.

He tries to wipe tears away, but they keep coming.

Her hands take his again, tighten.

Gulls are swooping. Diving on the bait fish. Screeching.

"How did this happen to us, Ronnie?"

He says he had been tending his lobster pots in the bay most of the day with some of the other guys. Later they were drinking at a joint by the inner harbor. Suddenly in rolled the cops. Not Hyannis boys. State and DEA. Told him he was under arrest for possession and transport. Read him his rights. Buttabing, buttabang, buttaboom. Next thing he knew he was in cuffs, riding off to the stockade.

"I know one of the detectives here ... and a lawyer. Maybe they can help you. But you have to level with me. Was that your cocaine?"

"Come on, Awasha. You think I'd put that skanky shit in my body?"

She doesn't say anything, just remembers about three dozen wicked drunks he's pulled since he got free of the army, all the pot they smoked together in high school. The mescalin they took on Squibnocket Beach when they wanted to see the Great Spirit and the *manitous*.

"Why are you looking at me like that?"

"I don't need this right now, OK, Ronnie? I just can't deal ..."

"This is it, isn't it? I thought I paid for everything in Leavenworth. I thought I paid again when Alice died. But the payback is just beginning isn't it?"

She feels a painful screech starting to rise from her lungs. "I don't know."

44

HE stares at the text message on the screen of his phone as he sits at the counter of a Nu Bej diner next to his father, cutting into a western omelette. Another morning in fish town.

"*Cristo!*"

His father grunts through a mouthful of eggs. A questioning noise.

"She actually pulled it off."

"Who? What?"

"Gracie. The Chinese girl I told you about. She got the names. Look." He passes his phone to his father. Gracie's message is a list.

Club Tropical 1974:

Marcus Snyder

Jason Su

Thomas Merriweather

Jean-Claude Rausche

Caesar Decastro digs his fork into another piece of omelette. "Who are these guys?"

"Maybe the killers of Liberty Baker I've been looking for."

"Oh, hell, here we go again!"

"I'm afraid so."

"How about we go mend some nets first, OK?"

* * *

It's a fresh spring morning, already forty-eight degrees and heating up in the bright sun. The huge green net is partially unrolled on the steel work deck of the *Rosa Lee*. Michael and his father are sitting side-by-side on the net, repairing a fifteen-foot tear with seven-inch-long steel net needles and spools of green twine.

His father stops sewing and knotting for a second, eyes his son. "You ever think you might be on a suicide mission, Mo?"

"Because I want to bring Liberty Baker's killer to justice?"

"What else?"

"I told you the other day. I'm a mess."

"You can't leave these killings alone."

"No."

"I don't get it. What's in this for you, except maybe a bullet?"

"I don't know, Dad."

"That's no kind of answer."

"I never told you about ... Nassau."

"The Bahamas?"

"There was this girl ..."

* * *

Caesar Decastro spoons two cups of Folgers instant into a mug. Father and son stand in the fish boat's galley, the noontime sun casting a bar of light through the companionway.

"This is *saudade* talking. You're missing this girl. The Bahamian. What's her name?"

"Cassie … It was more than ten years ago!"

"That's what I'm saying. *Saudade*. We miss the things and places and people we've lost. It's the Portagee way, Mo. We grieve forever. It's like me with your mother. I know she's gone, but she's never gone."

"I miss Mom every day."

"See what I mean?"

"But I only knew Cassie for a few hours …"

"She put her stamp on you. It happens. Like Meng marked me in Vietnam and your mom …"

The fisherman seems to fade away into another world. He fills his coffee mug with tap water, claps the mug in the microwave, sets the timer for ninety seconds, starts the machine. It hums, rattles.

"Dad?" He leans against a bulkhead, drives his hand through his thick dark hair, realizes that it is out of control and oily. Gracie says he looks like a guy called McDreamy on some TV show she watches. More like McGreasy. Or McDamaged.

"I'm thinking …"

"Dad!"

"Well, just give me a minute here, Mo … So … it was spring break? You were just a dumb high school kid. And she came on to you, her a bit baked on gin-and-tonic."

He can feel her breasts against his chest, her pelvis pressing his hips. Long legs struggling to clutch him to her. Stars raining on her face. Chocolate cheeks tilting toward Venus. And the surf thundering offshore.

The microwave beeps. Coffee ready.

"We had sex on the beach."

"That's not the end of the world, pal. Give yourself a break. You've just been in a hell of a car wreck, you're tore up with this Liberty kid's death. Your mom's only been gone a year or so. And probably that Indian chick has been chewing on your heart."

"Dad!"

"Women, man, who the hell knows? You would hardly be the first man to feel blue, a little lost in memories. You know?"

"Aren't you the guy who told me a hard-on is like a time bomb? Sooner or later it takes you out. Or ... did I just imagine that?"

His father snags his coffee mug from the microwave, takes a long sip. "Forget about it, Mo."

"I feel like shit."

"Let's go back uptown and get some lunch and a beer. Then we'll find Tommy, come back here, finish up this net, huh?"

"Dad. I don't know ..." His voice breaks.

Caesar Decastro sets down his coffee, ever so softly, on the galley counter. Looks ready to wrap his son in a hug when Michael's phone rings.

He takes the call. There's a short exchange.

"OK," he says. Clicks off. Then he cups his face in his hands and takes three deep breaths.

"What?"

"We'll have to finish this later. I got to go, Dad."

45

SHE'S sitting at a table in the food court of the Hyannis Mall outside the Barnes & Noble. Been waiting for an hour when she sees him appear around a corner, search the crowd for her. She almost doesn't recognize him at first in the blue, three-piece suit, starched white shirt, gold tie. Fresh from meetings with Lou Votolatto and the U.S. attorney who will be prosecuting Ronnie. And she can't help herself. She gets up from her plate of shrimp fried rice and runs to him. Throws herself into his arms. Kisses his jaw, his cheeks.

"Thank god," she hears herself say three times. Then, "I feel like I'm drowning."

He holds her, lets her float against his chest. Says don't worry. Everything is going to be alright. Lou has convinced the D.A. that Ronnie could be telling the truth, that he was set up with the brick of coke. An anonymous caller dropped a dime on Ronnie. Twice. Maybe someone who wants to create a distraction ... or get even.

She's still holding onto him, breathing deep. "So now what?"

Everything with Ronnie is all set. The U.S. attorney has agreed
to a continuance. She won't set a trial date at Ronnie's arraignment
tomorrow in Boston. And bail's reduced to $20,000.

"I've already contacted a bondsman I know."

"Ronnie's going to be out tomorrow?" She lets go of him, stares
around at the food court, the corridors of the mall, the shoppers. As if
she's seeing everything for the first time. This culture that has hijacked
the Cape from the People of the First Light.

"We got lucky. The U.S. attorney on the case is new to the district.
She has no history with me."

"So now what?" She takes his hand, leads him into the bookstore,
totally forgetting her plate of noodles.

"Did you get that list of names of the members of Club Tropical
from Gracie?"

"Yeah, but I've been so distracted that…" She is not looking for
books, really. Just suddenly has this urge to be somewhere with this
man where they are not such a spectacle. Not Pocahontas in a Disney
mall. Somewhere that feels private. Safe.

"I forwarded the list to Lou."

"So?"

"There's a guy named Thomas Merriweather on there. I should
have recognized him. He got Lou's attention right away."

"Who?"

"Merriweather's a judge."

"Really?"

"Middlesex Country Superior Court."

She drops his hand, turns to face him. For the second time in five
minutes, she feels dazed. The lights in this bookstore way too bright.
Suddenly she hugs him to her chest. Wishes she could just take him
back to the bait shack … and make like seals.

"I should be happy, right? Why do I still feel like I'm being sucked down by a whirlpool, Michael?"

* * *

Lou Votolatto is walking with Michael on the seaside promenade in front of the Boston Harbor Hotel, their trench coats flapping in the early April breeze. Ronnie Patterson's arraignment over. Water Bear released on bail. His weeping sister has dragged herself off for yet another required audience with her headmaster.

The defense attorney and the cop are heading from the Moakley federal courthouse toward the North End. Lou's niece Adela has a bistro that serves up some wicked good lasagna. A little Compari on the rocks, too.

"Your Chinese sidekick. Amazing kid, huh?"

"A bloodhound. She calls herself Ninja Girl."

"She already knows shit the FBI never had a clue about in the Magic Airplane case. Merriweather's not the only heavy hitter on that list is he?"

"Not a chance."

Gracie hacked into the T-C alumni files last night. Turns out everyone on the list graduated in 1975. Back then Marcus Snyder was a nerdy Jewish boy from the Philadelphia Main Line, nicknamed "Brainiac" in the yearbook. Now he's a neurosurgeon with a house and office on Beacon Hill. His daughter Rebecca is an eleventh grader at the school.

"This Jason Su. A venture capitalist?"

"Has a house in Back Bay. Summer place on the Vineyard."

"A muckity muck."

"Last year Merriweather got the Massachusetts Bar Association's lifetime achievement award or something. Like African-American scholarship kid from Roxbury makes good and scores a house in Brookline."

"Jean-Claude Rausche?"

"A sculptor in Provincetown. Never married. Gracie thinks he's probably gay."

"I don't get it."

"What?"

"A bunch of things."

"Like?"

"Like what these guys had in common back in the Seventies? They come from different planets."

"Didn't you say this Club Tropical was some sort of short-lived rebel entity? These guys had a feud with one of those other secret societies?"

"Red Tooth."

"That one. You said the headmaster, the Singleton boys and their old man, whose some big deal on the faculty, are all part of that operation."

"You make it sound like we're talking about gangs here."

"Aren't we?"

"More like just a bunch of Harry Potter hocus pocus."

"But two kids are dead. And you and your little Justice-for-Liberty-Baker cabal are up to your eyeballs in nasty secrets some powerful people clearly do not care to share."

"What are you suggesting we do?"

"Don't start that *we* shit again."

"Seriously."

"Have you ever thought about moving to a little island in the tropics?"

*   *   *

The night scatters stars on her face. The beach a pale sugar.
He feels her arms tightening around his back. Holding him against
her. The African body. Slippery. Tasting of salt, gin. A basket of limes. Her
breath on his neck. Bare hips tugging against his.

Jesus Cristo. *Nipples hard against his chest.*

46

"THAT'S it, Dr. Patterson. We are through here. School reopens tomorrow … and you will not be on board." Malcolm Sufridge rises from the chair behind his mammoth desk, a smug smile on his thin lips. "The students and faculty will be told that you have been granted a leave of absence for personal reasons."

"But you have no grounds. You …"

He says that if her personal effects are not out of her office and apartment by the end of the day, he will have a moving company pack them, put them in storage first thing tomorrow morning. At her expense.

She leaves her seat, stands up. As if she cannot help herself. As if her body is submitting as Bumbledork herds her out of his inner sanctum before she infects the place. Before she stains the butternut paneling, the trophies of football victories over Andover, Exeter. Splinters a pair of rowing oars crossed over the fireplace. Shatters the porcelain vases stolen from Chinese emperors by Yankee merchant captains in the nineteenth century.

And Danny. Standing there like a statue. Her advocate, friend. The woman she tried to love. With her fucking clipboard cradled in her arm. Saying nothing. *Why?*

Screw it, she tells herself. *Why would a footloose and soul-torn Indian girl want to be a part of such an artificial, white, male-dominated, privileged world? Take your school, Bumbledork, and your secret societies. Shove 'em! You sterile, priggish, Anglo piece of raccoon shit!*

But then a calmer voice in her head reminds her that like it or not, some of her people are white, too. And there are a lot of good students and teachers in this school. That the Great Spirit, her own *manitous* and *tcipai*, have chosen her for vanguard duty. To stand up with other minority people to claim their places at the academic table. Seats on the best school buses. The freedom buses. She thinks schools like this, with all of their intellectual, historical, cultural, financial resources, must be brought—by hook or by crook—to acknowledge, respect and embrace diversity in all its forms. Not just by admitting token students of color or creating a titled position for a minority faculty member.

T-C and all schools like it have to become truly safe and nurturing for girls like Liberty Baker … Or they must be exposed for criminal neglect! Or worse.

"I said we're finished here, Dr. Patterson. Now if you'll excuse me …"

A knife scrapes the insides of her eyelids. "No … No, Dr. Sufridge! I will not excuse you. I know there's blood on your hands, and my lawyer will—"

"Out! Get out! I'll show you blood. You impudent, little …"

Strumpet, slut, squaw, nigger whore. She knows he wants to call her these names. Just barely catches himself. His face flushes in odd, rosy blotches. He grits his teeth. The jowls beneath the corners of his mouth shudder, as he lurches around the desk, stalking her.

She's reaching for a weapon to defend herself, the geode on Bumbledork's coffee table, when Denise Pasteur suddenly comes alive.

Steps between the headmaster and the ex-director of minority affairs, takes her by the arm.

"You can't fight this here, Awasha. Please ... come with me. Let me help you find your balance. Maybe this is for the best. You can get another job in the blink of an eye, and he's offering you a pretty sweet deal if you ... Please ... ? For me? Let's go."

She knows what Danny's trying to tell her. A year's salary and a first-rate recommendation is quite an inducement to just fucking walk on this whole dirty charade. And she knows that Danny is trying to apologize, wants her back.

But all she can think about is how warm it felt when Michael held her. And how cold it must be for Liberty, dead in the dark earth.

"Denise!" Bumbledork's voice cracks. "Must I call security? Or can you handle—"

"Come on, honey!" Danny takes her left hand between long, dry fingers.

She closes her eyes, lies, "OK."

* * *

3:47 a.m. The wee hours of April tenth. The night before T-C reopens for spring term classes. A night so still and prematurely warm that Gracie has left her window open.

She half wakes in her new dorm, a single room at the end of a first floor hall, when she hears a soft chatter as the window sash rises. Smells something like jasmine. Or maybe a more manly spice.

Her eyes are not yet open, the comforter pulled solidly over her whole body and head, when the first blow strikes her with a thud. Across her chest, her ribs. The second grazes her head. Someone's taking a bat to her. Blood seeps from her hairline, heading across her cheek to the corner of her mouth. Her tongue tastes the salt, the stickiness. She flails her arms, tries to throw off the covers as she leaps from her bed. And screams.

But almost no noise comes out. A strong hand is cramming a sock in her mouth, wrapping her lips, her eyes, in duct tape.

"This is just a warning, you little bitch." A voice—distant, garbled, hoarse. "Go home! Or you die."

By the time she tears the tape off her eyes, the room is empty. The only noise, the soft hum and chirp of her cell phone lying on her desk, signaling a missed call.

She presses a pillow to the side of her head, trying to stop the bleeding. Expecting that any second the pain will drive a spike through her brain and set her howling.

But the spike never comes, just a numbness, an odd vacancy of thought, that leaves her staring at the blinking light on her phone for who knows how long. When she finally gets off her bed, walks to the desk, flips open her phone, she sees that the missed call is from Doc P.

She turns on her phone, accesses the message.

Gracie—get out of that place. Now!!!!!!!!! Call Michael. We need help. He'll know what to do. Hurry ...

She hears a little pop. Message ended.

47

HE doesn't remember even a minute of his drive north from Nu Bej. Doesn't recall the jeep coming out of a sharp turn in a four-wheel drift, skidding, just missing two pedestrians, hitting a curb in front of the Braintree T-station. He only remembers the words of Gracie's call echoing in his head during it all.

Michael. Doc P's gone again. They fired her ... and someone just beat the living shit out of me!

Now here she is in her Red Army coat and Doc Martens, throwing her backpack and two huge suitcases in the rear of the jeep even before he can get out of the driver's seat. Then she is hugging him, pressing him against the fender. Her face fracturing into sobs. She flinches when he forgets about her head wound and strokes her hair. Dyed back to its natural black. Caked with blood.

Someone honks a horn, tells him enough with blocking traffic. Get a move on it, lover boy.

She releases him. "Fuck off!" Shoots the bird with both hands at the honker, her forearms low as if ready to neuter somebody. Ninja Girl.

"Let's get out of here." He's glad to be free of her arms. This is not like hugging Awasha. Gracie is dangerous. A wild child with the body of a woman. Taller, even more curves, than her mentor.

She jumps in through his door, scrambles over the shifter. "I'm running away, Michael." Her voice suddenly determined, giddy.

"You want to tell me where we're going?"

"We've got to find Doc P. I think she could be in trouble!"

"You're hurt," he says. "First, we have to get you to a doctor. We need to contact your parents before the school does ... so your folks don't have a melt-down."

"Not now. Listen. I heard this pop and then her phone just went dead."

"She got fired?"

The news was all over school last night. Kevin said Bumbledork busted her for having an inappropriate relationship with a student.

"Her? Who?"

"Me."

"What?"

"Exactly. Like Bumbledork is trying to make something out of our being stuck in that sauna together. Fuck, Michael. Nothing happened, you know?"

"None of my business."

"Yeah it is. I know you guys hooked up. You want to hear about the sauna? It was kind of weird. But we never—"

"*Cristo*, Gracie."

"I mean she's quite fit and all. Like everybody thinks she's a hottie. But you're a hottie too. And with her and me it's all about the—"

He slams on the brakes, pulls over to the side of the highway.

"Jesus, listen to me, will you? I'm not your therapist or your big brother. We're not going down this road. I really don't want to hear about that stuff."

"I make you nervous? Come on, Michael, you must think about sex. I mean—"

"Really! Have you no filter on what you say?"

She throws her head back, closes her eyes, squeezes her hands between her thighs. "I'm sorry ... Sorry, OK? We just have to find her. She could be hurt. And she could be almost anywhere."

"I don't think so."

"What do you mean?"

"She's scared. Threatened. And something happened to her cell phone ... or she's afraid to talk on it. Maybe she thinks someone is listening."

"She said you would know what to do."

"Maybe. But I think we should take you to a doctor first."

"You want me to tell you about the sauna?"

"No."

"Then let's go find Doc P before someone beats on her too."

"It's a bit of a hike."

"Where are we going?"

"You'll see."

"Huh?"

"We have to take a boat."

"No shit?"

"Call your parents. Tell them why you left school. Tell them you're safe. Tell them you are coming home."

She coughs. "You mean you don't want to know about the laundry tag I found?"

48

SHE thinks she hears voices. The treading of feet on broken shells. Knows someone has come looking for her. Probably followed her here. And, shit, it is at least a half day sooner than she could ever hope to see Michael. Even if he has talked to Gracie. Even if he figures out I'm hiding here.

When she looks out through the salt-stained windows of the bait shack, everything looks calm. Bird calls seem blue notes from distant woodwinds. The salt pond and upland meadows of Aquinnah glowing silver in the moonlight.

A herd of deer is scattering. The animals loping away from the pond, heading up toward the ridge and the lighthouse. Something has interrupted their grazing. Maybe coyotes, but she can't be sure.

She blows out the oil lamp on the table, then slowly, softly feels for the deadbolt on the door. Finds it frozen open with rust. So she slips out of her shoes and tiptoes to the closet, gropes in the dark for her father's old duck killer and the box of 12-gauge shells. It's an ancient Browning pump gun. There are only three cartridges, and she can't remember how to load them.

She thinks back to the days when she, Ronnie, and her father would sit in the pond blind, watch the decoys and wait. Their shotguns in hand, the chocolate lab Tibby resting at her feet. Loading up for the moment when her father called in a flight of blackbacks. Finally her hands remember the drill. The shells slide into the ammo tube. When she pulls the pump, the first cartridge clicks up into the firing chamber.

The moonlight slants through the windowpanes, makes a trail across the quilt where she drowned him a week past. In her hair, her hips. The cobwebs, tiny weirs, spread through the night. The air smells cool, suddenly very fishy, as she keeps to the shadows, slides along the walls, hides in the corner next to the hinges of the door. And waits. Her right index finger ready to pull the trigger if some girl-killer from Red Tooth or the Club Tropical dares to cross her threshold.

Still, what if it is someone else? Maybe Ronnie. He used to love this place, too. *But what would he be doing on the island?*

Probably she's just imagining things. Just scared since Bumbledork's unbelievable bullying, his veiled threats yesterday. Since Danny's slip later at their favorite lesbian bistro in the South End: *I wish you hadn't goaded him, Awasha, with that crack about blood on his hands. You want to end up like that girl in the attic?*

What girl in the attic? she had almost said. *I only told you about bones in boys clothes. Never told you about Roxy.* Shit. And double shit.

She had excused herself to go to the bathroom, and beat it out the back door. Got in her Saab and split for the Vineyard. Leaving her ex-girlfriend, a nearly full bottle of pinot grigio, a plate of scampi for the dogs.

Now she hears the burbling of voices again. Birds go silent. The crunch of feet on shells is clearer and coming along the trail circling the pond. She wishes she could just flat fucking break her self-imposed phone silence and call Michael. But that's probably just what her stalkers want. They want to hear her terror, feel her desperation as they pen her in for slaughter. Shit again!

But maybe the voices, the shadows out there, are just teenagers coming down to the pond to smoke some weed and swill some alcohol stolen from one of the summer places.

There's a female's voice, still muffled, but carping about the cold night, the blackberry briars. A deeper voice grunting. Possibly a third. Footsteps coming right up to the bait shack now.

She takes a deep breath, holds it as she does when she makes the cobra pose in her yoga class. Closes her eyes to gather energy. Feels the hair on her wrists rising as her hands tighten around the shotgun.

Then there are steps on the little wharf, right outside the door. Her eyes bolt open. She inhales. Steps back from the door and centers the barrel of the 12-gauge on it. Shouts at the darkness, her words ragged and shrill.

"Who's there?"

"Hey!"

"Michael?"

"And Gracie, Doc P. We came over on a big-ass ferry. Are you OK?"

"I almost shot you ..."

* * *

The three of them sit on the floor huddling close together around the open door of a small propane oven hissing in the corner. The old comforter pulled across their shoulders. Michael in the middle, females to either side. They pass a steaming mug of chamomile tea back and forth in the glow of the blue flames.

"First Liberty. Next we find the bones. Then someone runs the jeep off the road. Ronnie gets busted. An intruder clubs the hell out of Gracie. Bumbledork flat out threatens me. And Danny talks about a girl she's not supposed to know about in the attic."

"Danny?" He sounds confused. "Danny, your old boyfriend Danny?"

Shit! Thank god he can't see the hives rising on her chest, feel her ears burning. "I mean Denise."

"We can't just walk away from this now, can we? They know we know they killed Liberty … and Roxy. They are fucking after us." Gracie's voice has lost its usual fuck-all edge.

She can feel him take a deep breath, his flanks shiver.

"The problem is who are THEY? Kevin Singleton? His brother? His father? Your dear old headmaster? Other members of Red Tooth? Or those four guys who started the Club Tropical? And … and where does the good dean Denise Pasteur fit in?"

She gulps the tea. Her cheeks are boiling now, palms on fire. She knows he feels her sweat as he takes her hand, tries to deflect the attention. "We need a plan."

"You guys ever heard of dogfish?"

"What?"

They're little sharks, he says. Like two-feet long. Bottom feeders. Scavengers. Not much in the way of teeth. But when you get them in a net there's hell to pay. They can get in there by the hundreds in just a minute or two. And when you haul back, they will be stuck in every bit of mesh.

"I don't see what you're getting at."

"You can't get them out sometimes. You're better off just cutting loose the net. Kissing thousands of dollars away. Starting fresh. Like take your boat and go somewhere else to look for cod fish. Where the dogfish can't find you."

"You want to do that?"

"Haven't we already started?"

"Yeah but now what? We can't really stay here forever."

He sighs. "Can you guys just sit tight here for a day or so?"

"What? Why?"

"Maybe it's time to go on the offense. But first, I think I need to talk to Lou."

"Who?" Gracie asks.

"His cop friend ..." She feels the heat rising in her skin again, a stinging in her brain stem. Pulls her hand away. "But what do we do while you're off playing Batman and Robin? Bake cookies?"

He tosses off the comforter, stands up. "I don't know, Awasha. I really don't. But it was your idea to hide here. Isn't this some kind of holy place? Maybe you could come up with something spiritual and Indian to do. Or maybe you guys could start by trying to reach Gracie's parents. Trying to get her on a plane back to Hong Kong ... and away from this mess, you know?!"

Suddenly she's remembering why she thought women might be a better match for her.

"Hey," Gracie says. "Stop it you two! Like united we stand, divided we fall right? I'm in this to the end. The fucking dogfish killed my friend."

*   *   *

"It's really cold, Doc!"

"I'm sorry. But this is the only blanket."

They are lying on the floor of the bait shack, middle of the night, pressed as close to the sputtering oven as they dare. The moldy comforter folding them together into what she thinks of as a sort of a human taco. Gracie closest to the fire. Awasha lying a bit farther off.

"Maybe if you put your arms around me."

"I don't think that's a good idea." She imagines Danny's breath on her chest, her stomach, tries to push the urge for tenderness out of her veins. The need to melt away the fear. The quivering.

"I wouldn't mind."

"Just try to sleep."

49

"YOU look like shit." Lou Votolatto pours a cascade of sugar into his coffee cup. The last of the breakfast crowd at the Fishmonger's Café in Woods Hole is queuing up at the register to pay their checks. Now it's just the cop, eyeing the bum dropping down next to him at the counter. His jeans, flannel shirt, blue fleece vest are rumpled, speckled with lint and car crumbs. Cheeks dark with two-day growth, hair spiking in six directions.

"I slept in my car last night."

"The old Portagee hotel, huh? She throw you out?"

"Knock it off, OK? I'm worried."

The cop leans back on his stool. "Finally."

"What's that supposed to mean?"

"The shit's really starting to hit the fan, isn't it?"

"What kind of a person takes a club to a girl when she's sleeping?"

"The same kind that drugs a kid before he slits her wrists ... or disguises a chick as a boy before he stashes her body in an attic. Kind of the same M.O."

"Who are we looking for, Lou?"

"A coward. A planner. A cold-blooded killer."

"What about the guy who ran me off the road?"

"I don't know. Doesn't fit the profile. You're probably dealing with more than one vampire here, don't you think?"

"You sure are a comfort."

"Just telling it like it is, Rambo. You see your squaw last night, or is that someone else's lipstick on your neck?"

"It's not what you think. She's hiding on the Vineyard. Gracie's with her."

"You have to get them out of there."

"Why?"

"You remember what happened to her brother?"

"You're saying there's a connection?"

"You didn't hear that from me."

"Who have you been talking to?"

"Pocahontas' twin, your client, who else? One of her other boy toys?"

Suddenly he remembers her odd remark. *She said Danny when she meant Denise.* A slip of the tongue. As if they were one and same. As if Denise Pasteur had been her …

"Why am I always the last person to find shit out? Jesus Christ!"

"I don't know, kid. But maybe you better have a chat with Brother Ronnie, Nippe Maske, Water Bear. Or whatever he calls himself. Sooner rather than later. Know what I mean?"

*   *   *

The big man in the green chamois shirt and stained khakis smells of bourbon. He holds open the screen door to the tiny cottage on the cranberry bog in Yarmouth, welcomes Michael in with the sweep of his arm. Past the muddy deep-waders lying on their sides, the stretched-out moccasins, a paper bag full of Cheetos, Gatorade, cigarettes, and packaged lunchmeats that have not yet made it to the kitchen. The 30.30 rifle leaning against the door jamb.

"Imagine this. Johnny Cochran paying me a house call."

The sky outside has turned gray, drizzly. Inside, the weather seems the same, except for the violet light of a TV. Oprah doing her thing.

"We need to talk, Ronnie."

"Now what is the white man trying to blame me for?" His broad, tan cheeks are flushed. Eyes dewy. Black hair, having been cut short for his court appearance, is unwashed, speckled with dandruff. Clothes giving off the scent of sweat and ass. Hard to believe he's Awasha's twin. Or Indian. He looks like a brother.

"I don't think this is about what you did. Maybe not even about you. It's about your sister. You know she got fired?"

"Those bastards." He eases himself down into the only armchair in the living room. Motions for Michael to take the couch.

"Yeah."

"I heard about that girl who died. Liberty. Somebody killed her, huh?"

"Looks that way."

"And my sister won't let it go."

He nods.

"That's the thing about us."

"What?"

"We never know to quit when we're ahead." The Indian scoops his Winstons off the floor, shakes out a butt, lights it with a Bic. "We always have to go the distance."

"That can be a good thing."

"Not when you don't really know the rules."

He straightens up on the edge of the couch. "I don't understand."

"You want a drink?" Ronnie shifts his weight, seems ready to get up out of his chair. "I got some Jack and Coke in the—"

"Come on. Talk to me, Ronnie. What rules?"

"You know. The fucking Ten Commandments of Whitey's World."

"And what would those be?"

"That's what I'm saying. You got to ask Whitey. And he ain't saying. Just slaps us dark folk down when we cross the line. You're Portagee, you know what I mean."

"Like Thou shalt not look in the white man's closets."

Water Bear jumps to his feet. "I need a little Jack in my glass … if we're going down this road."

* * *

Midmorning, a Monday, late Spring. He brings her flowers. His second attempt, hiding them in his rucksack so that he looks just like every other G.I. out on patrol. The air buzzing with the sound of children playing street soccer. The scent of figs, dates, oranges. The blood of freshly butchered lambs from the cart vendors mixing with the fumes of Humvees growling along Haifa St.

"I came back," he says in a shaky voice when she opens the door.

"And you are most welcome." Her cheeks flush as she takes the roses from him. "Come in, Nippe Maske. Have some coffee and tell me about the life of my savior. Praise, Allah, my mourning period is finished."

He feels his breath stop. The light in her big eyes, the fine curve of her nose, the full bow of her lips may be the most beautiful things he has ever seen. Aaserah, in her black abaya. The curves of her hips showing as she cradles the flowers to her breasts. The pale blue hijab framing her face. He still remembers her long, braided, brown hair, almost as dark as his sister's. Saw it when he burst in on her so many months ago. Pictures that hair now trailing down her back.

And maybe she is picturing him beneath the battle gear, because she sets the flowers on a chair, and reaches for his face.

"Let me see you." Her fingers trace the chin strap under his jaw. Soft as the wings of a tiny bird, they brush his lips. Snap the strap free with a loud pop.

"Hey!"

"Take this off. Please."

* * *

"You fell for her, this Aaserah?"

Ronnie rises from his armchair and again heads for the kitchen table, the bottle of bourbon. Pours himself three more fingers of Jack. "I told Awasha never to ... Why the hell am I talking about Baghdad? I must be fucking wasted."

"Maybe, like you said before, you have to go the distance. Relive the pain to let it go. I don't know. Maybe that's your way. Maybe mine, too. Like in our genes or something."

"You're a philosopher now?"

He says he's sorry. Really sorry. Ronnie doesn't have to talk about Iraq. He just came here looking for answers that might put an end to all this hell. Might find some justice for Liberty Baker. Might help him work through some of his own shit. He thought maybe Ronnie could tell him something about his bust that ...

"Like what?"

"You were set up. Somebody planted that cocaine on your boat ... then called the DEA."

"Hey man, we already know this. I told you and that dick Voto-whoever about twenty times. Dog, is this not our defense?"

"Yeah, but maybe you left something out when you told me. Lou said—"

"You've been talking to the cops?"

He feels his back teeth grinding. *Shit.* "He just told me maybe I should go over the circumstances of the bust again with you. He said I might find something I missed before."

"Awh, Jesus."

"You ever think you could be taking the hit for your sister?"

"Like somebody dropped a dime on me to mess with Awasha?"

"Something like that."

"Why? Somebody wants to fuck with her, put her off all this Liberty Baker stuff at that boarding school, why not just get on with it? Cap her."

He winces at the image: Awasha's face a wreckage of blood, flesh, hair. "Maybe that's not Whitey's style."

"Fuck Whitey."

"Maybe Whitey knows your sister. Knows it's your pain that pushes her over the edge ... not her own."

Ronnie stares across the room, seems to fixate on the grocery sack, the bag of Cheetos, the carton of Winstons poking out of the top.

"Man ... that would be Awasha. You know what I used to call her when we were kids?"

"What?"

"Mother Teresa."

"Talk to me."

50

"WHAT the hell did you tell him, Ronnie?" She feels her hand tightening around the pay phone receiver.

Sweat oozes from her palms as she looks around to see if someone is following her. Or listening. Like Gracie who is heading out the door, up the street for her morning coffee and sugar fix.

The lobby of the ferry terminal in Vineyard Haven is almost empty. Just the folks behind the ticket windows. A mother and two young kids playing with stuffed bunnies. A young vagrant sleeping off a rough night, face under an open copy of a Vineyard newspaper.

"Nothing." His voice sounds small, childish.

"Bullshit. He's acting like ... I don't know. Some kind of spaz, some kind of Man In Jumping Hurry. He says he has to go to Beacon Hill. Like today. Beacon Hill. Does he want to see the governor?"

"I told him about Aaserah."

"Everything?"

"He doesn't know about what happened later after ..."

"God, Ronnie. Why?!"

"Are you going to lecture me? He's my lawyer. He's trying to help you. Maybe save your life, you know?"

"I can take care of myself."

"Yeah, sure, that's why you just lost your job, why you've been hiding in a bait shack in Aquinnah for days."

"I can't believe this. Are you trying to start a—"

"I don't know … I'm just worried about you."

"Wow … There's a new twist."

"Hey, Sis. Come on. Stop! Look around. Can't you see the fins closing in on you? Everyone around you has been taking hits since you started on this mission to find that Liberty girl's killer."

She pulls the receiver away from her ear, almost hangs it up.

"The sharks are circling."

"Damn it, Ronnie. Don't give me that Jimmy Buffett crap."

"I'm serious. Right before I got busted by the cops, I saw something."

"What?"

"Like for two or three days leading up to when the cops took me down, there was this car. Kind of parked off the landing."

"What do you mean *kind of?*"

"Pulled over on the side of the road. But not really in one of the spaces in the lot."

"I don't see what—"

"It was a silver Murano."

"A what?"

"A Murano. One of those fancy sort of SUV/station wagon crossovers."

"You lost me." Her free hand starts to claw the hair on the side of her head. Jesus, she needs a shampoo, a bath.

"What the hell was this yuppie car doing at the landing, you know? Two or three fucking days. Parked there with all the fishermen's pick-ups."

"You're so paranoid you notice that kind of thing?"

"Not paranoid, Awasha, Indian ... and ADD, you know? My mind is a sponge for details. Relevant and irrelevant."

She's watching the door, the sidewalk beyond. *Where the hell is Gracie? She should be back with my coffee by now ...* "So what makes you think this one is relevant?"

"Michael Decastro."

"He's wigging out."

"He says the car that ran him off the road could have been a silver SUV. Maybe a Murano."

"He also said it might have been a white truck. I've heard both versions."

"He says he knows some sketchy kid who drives a silver Murano."

Something is tearing, the sound of ripping Spandex or nylon deep in her head. "There was a teenage boy in the car? Tall? Messy, curly brown hair? Blue eyes, very anglo? Very preppie?"

"I saw someone. I don't remember the look."

"Jesus, Ronnie. Don't wimp out on me now."

"That's pretty much what Michael said."

"Well. Shit!"

"Who is this kid?"

"Liberty Baker's boyfriend."

"The girl who died?"

"One of them."

"Huh?"

"Never mind … Yeah, the girl who died."

"You think he killed her?"

Searching the sidewalk for Gracie, sucking on the inside of her cheeks, releasing. "I don't know."

"Michael doesn't like this kid."

"He was selling drugs to my girls."

"Like cocaine?"

She's silent for a long time.

"I don't see what any of this has to do with Beacon Hill."

He clears his throat. "I don't know, Sis. All that cola they found in my boat had to come from somewhere. Maybe this kid has a Beacon Hill connection."

Her gaze wanders around the terminal. Gracie's still not back. *Damn that girl.* The young vagrant's red eyes lock on hers. Blank, solar. "I wish you hadn't told him about Aaserah. He doesn't need to know everything about us. About her."

"I get lonely."

* * *

"Take these off." She's talking about his boots now, his pants, not his helmet. It's lying next to the green sofa out in the living room, next to his M-16, his ammo belt, his Kevlar vest, his shirt, the roses he brought. Her sandals. And her black abaya. The pale blue hijab drapes from the arm of the couch, a silk cascade.

He's lying back-down on her bed, the satin sheets growing damp beneath his bare back. She's beside him, kissing his neck, his chest. Her tongue hot, sticky. The fingers of one hand tracing his cheekbone, jawline. The other hand easing down his fly, pushing the pants below his hips.

His own hands massaging her shoulders. Those amber thighs. The delta of fine hair. Swamp Iris skin.

Suddenly she bolts upright. Stares into his eyes. Her brows rising with a thousand questions. Dark locks covering her breasts.

"Aaserah?"

"*Have you ever been so lonely you want to die?*"

"*For about twenty years.*"

"*After this we can never go back … Our bodies seal our fate.*"

"*You want me to leave?*"

"*I want you to cross the Tigris, Water Bear … I want you to love me. Like there is no sunrise. No East, no West.*"

Her hand feels for him, feels for what he calls his totem pole. Expert fingers. This widow of a warrior, this doctor's daughter. This Baghdad student of the law. Fellow traveler through the carnage. Woman with a thousand and one tales of the Arabian nights. Who most surely cannot be his enemy. Word.

51

"JESUS. Somebody does fucking brain surgery in one of these old Beacon Hill houses?!" Gracie's head is swiveling left, right, staring up at the cornices of the colonial and federal brick townhouses on Pinkney St. at Louisburg Square.

"We're looking for a doctor's office. Not a hospital. And, hey, if you can't stop dropping the F-bomb, we can put you on this afternoon's flight to Hong Kong ... As we promised your parents."

His voice cracks, warbles. The lack of sleep really getting to him. The nights curled in the front seat of the jeep, the tramping through the Vineyard moors at all hours. Those shots of Jack Daniels with Ronnie Patterson. *Cristo!* And now his sinuses clogging, a cold coming on.

"Fuck off, Michael. You need me."

Awasha nudges him with her elbow. "Stick to the script, OK?"

The three of them huddle together, the popped collars of their best spring topcoats shrouding their faces, backs to the east wind wafting down Beacon Hill. The daffodils in the little private park on the square dipping, juking, in the breeze.

"That's the place!" He points to a brass plaque next to a doorway on Pinkney.

Awasha takes his hand, Gracie's too. Says something softly in another language—Wampanoag maybe.

Nooshun kesukqut

Wuneetupantamunak kooswesuonk

Peyaumooutch kooswesuonk...

It sounds like the start of the Lord's Prayer.

"What's that, Doc?"

"War paint on, warriors!"

*   *   *

"You're here about Becca?" Dr. Marcus Snyder, celebrated neurosurgeon, T-C class of '75, ushers the trio into his examination room, cheeks flushing. He's in a white lab coat. "Is she alright?"

"We're not sure, Doctor." Awasha's voice flat, guarded.

Gracie pops up onto the examination table, adjusts her red suede skirt and black pantyhose with outstretched fingers.

Michael stuffs his hands in his pockets, speaks. "Gracie, here, has some concerns."

"I don't understand. I just talked to Becca two days ago, and everything seemed to be going fine. I mean—"

"Sometimes kids at boarding school don't tell their parents everything."

"What's going on?"

"We thought that maybe if we came here, talked, we could keep things off the record. You know, stay clear of the discipline system and the campus rumor mill?" Awasha takes off her camel hair coat, folds it over her arms in front of her, settles into a chair.

"Tell me who you are again?"

She pushes her shoulders back, the blood of warriors swelling in her chest, the invisible paint on her cheeks. And now she starts to lay her trap, starts to lie.

"I'm director of minority affairs. Gracie was on the swim team with Becca. She came to me worried about your daughter."

The doctor—lanky, longish charcoal hair, a fuzzy beard—closes the door behind him, falls back against it. His eyes searching the ceiling.

"What worries?"

Gracie's fingers straighten invisible kinks in her skirt. "Maybe you heard about the girl who died in February."

The doctor's face suddenly waxy-looking.

"Her name was Liberty Baker." The sound of his own voice surprises Michael. He told himself he would say nothing, try to act like Lou. Just watch the drama unfold, look for *tells* from Snyder as the females tighten the screws. But, *shit*, now he's in it. Man In Jumping Hurry. Both Awasha and Gracie are looking at him like *what up, dude?*

And he's in the doctor's sights. "You work at Tolchie, too?"

Now what? Another lie? Or the Truth? Quick! "I'm a detective."

A jolt passes over Snyder's face. He fishes in his pants pocket for his phone. "I think I want my lawyer here."

Cristo! This is all going south.

Awasha stands up, starts to put on her coat, turns to Gracie, Michael. "OK, let's go." *Plan B.* "Thank you for your time, Dr. Snyder. I'm sorry this isn't going to work out. You might want to warn Becca to watch her back ... at least until we can finish this conversation."

Snyder's eyes squint, trying to read between the lines. "What? I don't see how what happened to that Baker girl has anything to do with my daughter or—"

Gracie drops to her feet from the examination table. "Liberty was murdered. There's a killer loose at T-C."

"You think Becca's in danger?"

"We hoped you could tell us that."

"Me? How can I—"

"You want to talk to us about the Club Tropical?"

*   *   *

The three of them are stopped in the middle of the miniature suspension bridge. It spans the lagoon in the Boston Public Garden. They are taking stock in the aftermath of their close encounter with the good doctor. Wondering how long it will be before he tells his old club buddies that he ratted them out. At least, about the little pharmaceutical import business he and Jason Su set up at Club Tropical back in the Seventies.

One of the antique swan boats, the driver peddling it from his perch at the rear, glides beneath the bridge with twenty tourists aboard. All bundled up against the brisk, blue air of late April. But smiling. Inhaling the scents of forsythia blooming ashore.

On the tiny island in the lagoon a pair of swans trumpet at each other. Beat their wings. A domestic quarrel maybe, or a mating dance, sending a flurry of white down into the air, riding the breeze. Speckling Michael's coat. Catching in Gracie's and Awasha's hair.

"I'm sorry, gang. I almost blew that. Jumping in."

"Forget about it, Michael."

"I think we were a pretty good team." There's a lilt in Gracie's voice.

Awasha rolls her eyes. "Don't say it, OK, girl?"

"What?"

"What you're thinking."

"What's that, Doc P?"

"The Three Musketeers."

"How'd you know?"

She smiles. Taps the side of her head. "Indian Princess see everything."

"Please don't send me back to China."

"Why not?"

"Now you really need me."

"How's that?"

"Somebody has to talk to Jason Su."

"Yeah."

"Well … he's my second cousin."

"When were you going to tell us that?"

"Is the Ninja Girl still on the team?" She bats her eyes at Michael. Then at Doc P.

52

HIS back molds into the cotton mattress. He feels her draw off his boots, his pants. The rest.

Feels her warm breasts as she slithers from his toes up over his knees, his thighs. She lingers. Her hard tongue on his belly. Her lips soft little fish.

Until he is more than ready.

She glides, skin skating up his sweating chest until her breasts press his own. Her mouth opens into his. Tongues melt together. His hair buzzing wire.

The air pulses from her lungs as she lowers herself on him.

And now the rush and blare of traffic, the chants of street vendors soften. Weave a harmony to the music of powwows, fancy dancers, the drums in his head. Her pet Persian coiling and uncoiling in a discarded blanket heaped on the floor. Its purring rises, falls. Percussive. Ceaseless.

When she bends to nibble his throat, his ears, her breath is rich with scents. Stewing eggplant and bell peppers. Figs. Pomegranates. An undercurrent of coriander and something like fresh mint.

He wraps her in his arms, feels for the sinew of an athlete in the web
of muscles across her back, her shoulders. A toughness, the springs of flesh
he has touched in the shoulders of a doe.

"Allah akbar." She crushes his lips.

He breathes through hers.

Nooshun kesukqut. Our Father who art ...

The tribal drums, the flutes. Dulcimers pounding.

"Nippe Maske." Her voice more heat than sound in his ear.

"Nippe Maske?!"

Only the bear in his chest answering. Calling back to her questions,
singing. Singing her name. Aaserah. Aaserah full of grace. Aaserah of the
mighty Tigris. Aaserah of the Arabian nights. Allah akbar. Nooshun kesukqut, wuneetupantamunak kooswesuonk peyaumooutch ...

The drums. Dulcimers.

Suddenly she draws him to her chest, rolls him over her.

Now they fall. Surging, crashing right through the damp sheets, the
bed. Belly to belly.

Shattering the slate floor, piercing the apartment beneath. Pulling
down the concrete, the rebar, the plaster. Along with the sun, the stars,
the moon.

And half of Baghdad.

When the drums stop pounding in his ear, the flutes silent, the cat
run off to another room, he hears her whisper, "Heaven is waiting for us,
yaloog."

"What's that mean?"

"Wild donkey."

53

"YOU know how things are at that school, *byao-go*. When it comes to respect, these *lao wai* don't understand anything," she says.

Almost adds, *Like fuck them, huh, cuz?* But then she remembers where she is. On her knees. In bare feet. Eating moon cakes and drinking *oolong* at a miniature table in a nearly authentic Mandarin teahouse, hidden in the woods of Chappaquiddick Island, the Vineyard's high-rent zone.

This man is family. Old-school Chinese, what's more. Looking over her shoulder at something outside with the dull, steady eyes of a tiger.

She tries to get his attention. Flips her hair off her right ear in a suggestive way. Crosses, uncrosses her legs beneath her. Flutters her eye lashes. "All they ever think about is power and money, right?"

Her flirting has no effect.

He continues staring past her, out the window, grunts something in Cantonese. Then in English. "I hated that school!"

"I know what you mean. I just dropped out, Su Shen-San. Goodbye Tolchester-Coates. And … please forgive my intrusion. But mother always tells me that if I have trouble in America, call Cousin Jason. She says you will understand."

He nods, slowly, closing his eyes as he does. She thinks he looks much older than her father and mother, even though they are about the same age. Maybe it is the gray hair, the sunken cheeks, bare feet. Or maybe it is just that he wears a silk *chi pao* robe like her grandfather in Shanghai. Fills this teahouse retreat with expensive artifacts of the empire, decorative orange trees, and music CDs of the *guqin*, the ancient zither of the Imperial Court.

The man has become a phantom. Made his bundle in venture capital. Cashed out. Created his own private fucking version of the Forbidden City here in the forest. Ming vases and all. She would bet her sweet ass the dude smokes opium. Wonders what it would be like to take the lavender dragon into her lungs. Got to be better than the hash and weed she was getting from Kevin.

"You need money, a place to stay?" He pauses. "I am a bachelor, solitary. Trying to find, to follow, the way of the Buddha. You understand? This may not be the best place for a teenage girl, but I can make arrangements for you in Boston or New York until you and your parents—"

"I have friends. I'm staying with friends." *I think.* "But I need your help … Someone killed my best friend. Tried, is trying, to kill me … There is a killer loose at Tolchie."

She watches as his head snaps out of the dream he's having, watching a mother duck and ducklings paddling in his pond. When she feels his eyes beginning to tug on her, she says, "He's killing girls … You know what I mean? Like AGAIN."

Later she will tell Michael and Doc P, *his lungs just flat fucking stopped. Freaking froze, folks!* The blood so absent from his skin, she thinks she can see right into his soul. See the skinny adolescent boy hiding in there, the one his schoolmates called *Chop* or *Chop Suey*. See the boy copping an attitude, bragging about his contraband connections. Just to get a little credence from the fucking Spartans at Tolchie.

As a rebel of sorts. As a player with the new gang on the hill. Like fuck the Red Tooth types. The white ballcap boys.

"I'm a good student, *byao-go*. I do my research. I know about the Club Tropical. And you. The drugs you were bringing in to sell. The war with Red Tooth."

He puts down his little blue teacup on the low table in front of him and settles into the lotus pose. "I live in shame."

"The ancient ones say it is never too late for the horse to come to water. Help me. Please. My friend Liberty Baker is dead. Murdered."

"I always knew these things would come out."

"You know about the girl that died in 1975, don't you? You know what happened to Roxana Calderón."

"It's too late."

"I don't think so. My friends and I found her body hidden in the attic of Hibernia House. Where you had your club room. Where you ran the poker games."

He squirms, begins to rock back and forth. "It was not MY club room. I did not run the poker."

"You just supplied the drugs, *byao-go?*"

"You are too young, too free to understand. That school thirty years ago was a viper's nest. No one was safe. Alone. Ever. You had to have your clique, what you call your *posse*. Or the older boys, the richer boys, the *lao wai* would eat you for lunch."

He wants to tell me something. He wants to clear his conscience.

He rocks slowly, an emaciated monk, eyes closed now.

"You're right. I cannot understand what it was like for you. But you have to know, it is not over. They killed Liberty in February. She was black. Someone nearly clubbed me to death in my sleep. Like kill the nigger, slap down the chink, you know? Want to see my bruised ribs?"

"Fascists!"

"Who, Su Shen-San? The Red Tooth boys?"

He nods.

"Red Tooth killed Roxy Calderón?"

"It's not that simple …"

"What do you mean?"

"I don't really know how that girl died."

"Club Tropical guys killed her? Is that what you mean?"

There are tears in his eyes. "Such terrible shame. I should never have …"

"What?"

"We were just boys. Stupid boys. Playing gangsters. All for fun. All for a sense of defiance and protection." A memory wrinkles his face. She cannot tell whether he wants to laugh or cry.

"*Byao-go?*"

"Please, I must be alone now." He stands up.

She stands too. The custom for a good Chinese girl, an act of respect for her elder.

"Give me something to go on. *Byao-go.* Something to stop this killing. To save myself. Please! I'm scared." Her eyes plead. Teeth bite her lower lip as she fumbles with the black slicker that she borrowed from Michael.

"May the Buddha be with you, cousin." He's actually backing her toward the door, pressing his palms together in prayer. Bowing. Repeatedly.

Fuck, I'm losing him.

She remembers the list of the Club Tropical members. *The judge, what was his name?* Maybe if she can just throw it out there, the way desperate detectives do in cop shows, she'll get this ghost to toss her something back. Maybe not a confession or a map. But possibly some bread crumbs to follow.

"Maybe Thomas Merriweather can help me, then."

He squeezes his eyes shut for a second.

"*Byao-go?*"

"Make him tell you about the pink pantyhose ... and Puerto Rico."

Bingo! Ninja Girl scores.

She smiles. "Just grant me a favor or two, OK Su Shen-San?"

"Please, just go."

"First, if my parents call, tell them I will be staying with you for a couple of weeks until I can get everything arranged for a transfer in good standing from Tolchie."

"Pleaaaaaaaaase!"

"Second, can I use your bathroom?"

54

THE ex-lawyer/ex-fisherman stands on the work deck of the *Rosa Lee*. He's waiting for an acknowledgement from his father ... who is trying to splice a new eye in the winch cable.

"Want to give me a hand here, Mo, or what?"

He shrugs. "I'm not exactly dressed ..."

Caesar looks at his son. A stiff in a blue suit, white topcoat. "What the hell ... ?"

"Don't ask, OK?"

"You going to let me in on the secret? Or just stand there like one of those *palhaços* on *Law & Order*?"

"What can you tell me about the *crioulos*, about the Africans in our family? About Vóvó Chocolate?"

"You think she has something to do with these dead girls? Or ..." Caesar Decastro drops the steel marling spike in his hand. It hits the deck with a clang. He stares at Michael with slits for eyes, tries to read him. "Or is this about another attack of *saudade*. About that girl in the Bahamas?"

"She was my first time."

*   *   *

The beach. Her arms tightening around his back. Holding him against her. The African body. Slippery. Tasting of salt, gin. A basket of limes. Her breath on his neck.

Her pelvis pressing against his hips. They kiss. Long, slow. Her hand between his legs. His fingers under the hem of her bikini, gliding along the curve of her thigh.

He doesn't know how they get nude. Only that this is his first time, mamãe de dios, and her long legs are struggling to clutch his hips to hers. As he sucks on her neck. Here where waves break and river away into the dark. Stars on her face. Chocolate cheeks tilting toward the moon. Her body a mermaid's. Jesus. Surf thundering offshore on a reef.

She frees her hair, lets down the thick ponytail so he can bury his face in the black curls, the hot jungle of the Bahamas.

Cristo. The first time. Kissing. Deep. Deeper. Harder. Legs cradling him, wrapping him in abraços. *Loins churning together.*

The blood of cheetahs and gazelles scorching his veins. And hers. Silky, oiling skin. Taught muscles binding them, their souls.

"Don't go. Don't ever go, sweet Callaloo! Sweet baby."

*   *   *

"I don't want to hear the details, buddy boy. Really." His father snaps his Zippo out, ignites a Merit. Leans back against the deckhouse in the shade of the bridge deck, takes a deep drag.

"Sorry ... But you asked, you know?" He drops back, rests, his butt on the steel bulwarks of the boat. Stares at his feet in the cordovan Bass tassel loafers. Thinks he must look as foolish as he feels. A fisherman in lawyer's gear ... faking he's a cop. *Um palhaço.* A clown.

"What do you want me to say?"

"I don't know."

"Yeah you do. You came down here asking me about the *crioulos*, and your Vóvó Chocolate. I don't know how we got off on this Bahamas thing. Really, man, I ..."

Her eyes black, wet. Begging a question he can't hear. Can't imagine.

"I feel like this stuff is all connected for me. I just don't see the pattern."

"Pattern? *Cristo*, you think you can read life's patterns. Are you talking about fate, Buddy Boy?"

He hears disbelief in his father's voice. "No. Yeah."

"Jesus. You used to be such a happy, simple kid before you started in with studying the law. We used to talk about the Sox and the Bruins. Fish, beer, and coffee. Now it's like you want a road map to happiness, the rules of the universe."

"I just have questions."

"Yeah, like what?"

"Like how come nobody ever talks about Vóvó Chocolate in our family?"

"She was your mother's *mamãe*. I don't know, kid. We sort of lost touch with that side of the family."

"Are you ashamed because Vóvó was black?"

"Cape Verdean. Like you said."

"She's African."

"You think that ever bothered me? Look at me and your mother."

"Yeah, but how come nobody ever talks about it?"

"What's to talk about? Your mother and me, we grew up in New Bej. Portagee capital of the world. White, black, Indian. Who ain't a mix? And who gives a squid's shit?"

"But ..."

His father says the races have been mingling in New Bej since the whaling days. Probably back to the Indians and Pilgrims. The Decastros even have the blood of South Seas Islanders, like that harpooner in *Moby Dick*. Queequeg. Michael's great grandfather came from some island in …

"The central Pacific. How can I forget? You must have told me about a thousand times."

"Well, there you go."

"Not really."

"What?"

"We never talk about the Africans. We must have family there. But … but it's like Vóvó dropped into New Bej from another planet."

"Actually, she came on a packet from São Vicente … A mail-order bride."

"Really?"

"Your grandfather paid fifty dollars for her in 1936."

"He bought her? She was a slave?"

His father exhales a huge smoke ring. "That's how it was done back then."

"Weren't there plenty of available women in New Bej?"

Caesar shrugs. "Beats the shit out of me. Maybe he had a thing for brown sugar."

"Maybe I do too."

"You think that's something to be ashamed of?"

"I get the feeling some people think it's the kiss of death."

"You don't really believe that?"

"How did Vóvó die? Or my grandfather?"

"Maybe you ought to get out of that suit and find a real job, forget about the dead and gone. You think they care about you?"

"I've got to see someone in Provincetown."

* * *

When he wakes, water's rising around him—cool, black. What's left of the beach is little more than a slurry of wet sand beneath his back. The stars are gone. The moon. So is she. A sultry wind blows off the island. Dried sweat crusting in his eyes. Lips, chest, tops of his legs covered with fine white sand. Fumes of gin, lime, something rank etching the insides of his mouth, his nose, vocal cords. Waves piling up seaweed in his crotch, armpits. The roar of the surf. How long has he been here? Hours maybe. Alone. Fucked. Left for dead. Refugee of his first time. Survivor of Africa. Of the Bahamas. The tides of blood.

No Cassie. No Island girl. No kissing cousin. No mermaid.

Cristo! *He must have passed out.*

From the bar he hears Marley singing "One Drop." Then another song, "Africa Unite." A wave runs up the beach, licks his neck, ears. He never imagined it could feel this lonely to be the one left behind. The Callaloo Baby.

55

IT'S only sixty degrees at noon, and windy, in Provincetown. But she feels the sweat rising on her scalp and at the back of her neck. The knot in her stomach that always came just before she lay down with Danny.

The first thing she thinks as she sees the studio is *this guy must be rich*. Not that she really knows what a sculptor's studio is supposed to look like, but it doesn't take a real estate broker to tell her that anybody who owns his own wharf in P-town is worth way more than seven digits.

This is not one of the massive commercial wharves in the center of town. The Rausche Studio is a warren of gray-shingled fishermen's cottages and sheds mitered together, a miniature village atop huge timber pilings. It looms high above the tides of Cape Cod Bay at the West End of Commercial St. Exterior walks cluttered with a funky collection of nautical castoffs. Anchors, mooring bits, a steel wheelhouse, life rings, air scoops, dories, docking lines, a dozen rusting navigational buoys of different sizes and shapes. Not the stuff tourists think is quaint. More like salvage from ship breakers.

One of the largest sheds halfway out the wharf has its barn doors propped open to the sea breeze. A man inside is cutting up something that looks like a small rocket ship or a bomb. The acetylene torch shoots sparks out the door.

"That's our boy," says Michael. He stares into the studio, nearly hypnotized by the blue flame, orange sparks.

"I'm not getting good vibes." She feels the urge coming on to pray again in the language of her ancestors. "Maybe we should be talking to Judge Merriweather first."

Michael's voice is barely audible over the crackle and hiss of the cutting torch. "We've got nothing yet beside the club list, Snyder's stories about drugs and poker, and Su's obscure remark about red panty hose and Puerto Rico. We go to the judge with that kind of stuff, he's going to laugh in our faces."

She frowns, feels the heat rising in her cheeks … while Gracie seems lost in the image of the welder himself.

He is tall, slender. Wears white denim overalls, a flannel shirt. Bright pink. A lime green bandana over his hair. A large diamond stud in his right ear. Fashion Minnie Mouse goggles.

"I told you he was gay."

She feels her cheeks tighten. "Can you just leave it be, Gracie? Not everything's about sex."

"Maybe it's important, Doc." The girl pops a coy smile.

Michael shrugs. "Really. She has a point. I had this murder case in P-town, you remember the one with the drag queen from Bangkok? In the end, everything came down to—"

"Great Spirit, not you, too?"

"Well, it did. It all came down to sex. Or love."

She shakes her head, rubs her eyes. *Maushop, what have I gotten into?* Now she really wishes she had never agreed to bring these two to P-town today. Or shared that motel room in Welfleet with them last night. Yeah, she and Gracie had their own beds, and Michael slept wrapped up in a comforter on the floor. But it just wasn't right. She barely slept. She could feel their bodies, maybe even her own, sending off silent blues riffs. *Why?*

"Come on, Doc. Lighten up. How come all of a sudden you've gotten so uptight? Since when have you—"

She stomps her foot. "Just drop it! OK, Gracie?!"

The stomp shakes the wharf.

The welder feels it. Looks up from his work, lifts the Minnie Mouse goggles onto his forehead, eyes the trio looking at him from ten yards away.

"Can I help you?"

She shoots Michael and Gracie a fried look. "All right! I'm going to talk to this guy. I'll do it, OK? But give me some space."

"Come on, Michael take me to lunch." Gracie's voice is suddenly indifferent. "Call us when you're in a better mood, Doc."

She waves her hand in the air. "Whatever!"

"Excuse me?" The welder looks confused.

She goes with the curious fact Ninja Girl dug up online last night. "Isn't Denise Pasteur your half sister?"

He shuts off his torch, sets it on the ground. Surveys her. Deep blue eyes moving slowly over her. The long brown hair, the copper/cinnamon skin, the perfect breasts beneath her red cardigan, the small muscular body in the tight black jeans.

"So you're the Indian she's been fucking, love?"

She feels her lower back lock. Tells herself this is going to suck, but she'll do anything at this point to find and stop Liberty's killer.

* * *

RANDALL PEFFER

"I can see why Denise has a thing for you. You've got all the goods, honey."

She cringes, circles the rocket/bomb thing he has been welding. *You call this art?* Keeps it between her and the sculptor. "I really didn't come here to discuss my personal life."

He presses his hands together. "How cute, you're blushing! Let me guess, you used to think you were straight. But now darling Danny has got you turned all inside out. Dangling from a string."

"This isn't about Danny."

"Yeah right? She show you her collection of rubber *schlongs*, yet?"

"Maybe you could stop deflecting."

"Oh, sweetie, nice word. Does she love it when you talk all therapy to her?" He does a soft *salsa* beat with the palms of his hands on the rocket/bomb. It sounds like a timpani.

Maybe I have to lie, she thinks. "You know that guy who was with me? He's a cop."

He licks his lips, winks. "Cute. Kind of rough around the edges, though. Right? Dark, Latin cowboy. But maybe that's how you like your boys. Rough. Maybe …"

She glares at him. "I'm sure you know why I'm here. I'm sure one of your old pals from the Club Tropical has told you what's going on."

He puts his hands on his waist, bats his eyelashes. His Little Miss Muffet impersonation.

"Cut the shit, Jean-Claude." She has her cell phone open in her hand. "Or I'm going to get the cop back here. You can explain to him about where you were the night Roxy Calderón turned up dead at the Club Tropical."

"Ouch! Danny know you bite, sweetie?"

"That girl with the cop—she found a tag from Tolchester Laundry-Clean in a garment bag that held Roxy's body. The tag had your name on it." She watches his face for some flash of recognition. Or guilt. Or fear.

But nothing. He just beams a Bette Davis half smile. Tight lipped. Eyes amused. Possibly considering options. "So ... those bastards at Red Tooth are at it again? I heard about that black girl."

"She was one in a million."

He shrugs.

"I need to know about Roxy. And Club Tropical. I need to know how she ended up wearing boys clothes in your Brooks Brothers garment bag."

"Red Tooth plays for keeps."

"What's that supposed to mean?"

"Why don't you ask the Singletons or Malcolm Sufridge? You really think he fired you because you were playing find-the-fairy-cave with that little Chinese hottie in the sauna?"

For the second time since she's gotten here, she feels her cheeks scorching. Doesn't know what to do, maybe call for reinforcements? *How does he know I've been fired?*

She pulls out her phone. "I think you better tell your story to the police."

He shakes his head, lets a laugh out as he reaches down to the floor, picks up his torch in one hand, fishes a lighter out of a chest pocket in his overalls. "I'm not talking to anybody, sweetie. I've already had my ass-whipping from the Red Tooth boys."

"Are you talking about Roxy Calderón?"

"She was an insecure little tramp. And she got caught in the crossfire."

"In the war you were having with Red Tooth."

"You have no clue." He turns on the acetylene. Snaps the lighter. The torch pops to life. A long blue flame.

She has to say something, get some credence from this jerk. "I know about the pink pantyhose ... and Puerto Rico."

He gives her the Bette Davis smile again. "And I know your brother Ronnie would never survive prison again ... that your dark, Latin cowboy is no cop."

56

JUDGE'S chambers. Edward J. Sullivan Courthouse, Middlesex Superior Court, Thorndike St., Cambridge, MA.

The Honorable Thomas Merriweather leans back in his chair, hands folded under his chin. Looking like a smaller, delicate clone of Supreme Court Justice Clarence Thomas in his robe. Except that Merriweather's skin is as light as *mochaccino*.

"You think I don't know why you're here, Counselor? You think I won't have you booked for criminal harassment if you even think of coming on to me the way you came on to Mark Snyder?"

"Criminal Harassment? I—"

"That would be Chapter 265, Section 43A of the Massachusetts Criminal Code, Mr. Decastro. In case you missed that in law school. 'Whoever willfully and maliciously ...'"

"Your Honor, with all due respect, I know the statute. I've only requested this meeting in hopes of protecting the safety and well-being of my clients—Mr. Patterson, Ms. Patterson, and Ms. Liu—and sparing you and your high school friends, at the least, extreme embarrassment if what I know gets out."

The judge exhales slowly, his belly sagging beneath his robe. "I have court in ten minutes."

"You know about the girl who died at Tolchester-Coates in February?"

"What of it?"

"Her name was Liberty Baker. She was black. She grew up just blocks from your old neighborhood in Roxbury."

"I don't see where this is going."

"You went to that school. You know what she must have gone through, being poor and black amid all that wealth and privilege and whiteness."

"I'm not somebody who dwells on the negative."

"The school and the local police dismissed her death as suicide. They said that she buckled under the pressure. Under the culture shock."

A marble stare is creeping into the judge's eyes. "What does this have to do with me?"

"You were there. You lived through four years at Tolchester. You didn't buckle under the pressure. Why?"

"I wasn't going to give the bastards the satisfaction of thinking that I didn't belong, that I couldn't make it in their school."

"So why would it be any different for a girl like Liberty who, by all accounts, was excelling in every arena of the academy? She was a tough kid."

"People are different, Counselor. Hearts different. Souls. Maybe she didn't have allies. I had allies."

"The Club Tropical. Its poker table, the drugs—"

"Are you threatening me?"

"All I'm saying is that Liberty Baker was like you, Judge. Smart. Talented. Resilient. Ambitious. A survivor ... And two other things."

"What?"

"One, she was emotionally incapable of slitting her own wrists because she was terrified of blades. Two, there is strong evidence that someone slipped her a date-rape drug to knock her out before they killed her."

"Why aren't the police looking into this?"

"Maybe it has something to do with the fact that Tolchester-Coates pays no property tax on its two hundred acres of prime real estate because as a non-profit the school is exempt from the tax rolls. Instead the school makes a donation of $1 million annually to the town's budget as a gesture of good will. A donation that the school can modify or withdraw at anytime."

Merriweather flexes his jaw muscles, knots rising under the dark skin at the base of his ears. "What do you want from me?"

Whoa. Have I finally got his attention? Is he finally feeling the blood of Africa, the blood of warriors surging in his veins? Feeling me? Maybe he—

"Hey, Counselor. Snap out of it!"

He shakes his head, refocuses. "My clients think the same person or people who killed Liberty Baker are the ones who have been threatening and harassing them. Maybe the same person or people who made your life so miserable back in the Seventies. Maybe we're dealing with the killer or killers of Roxana Calderón."

The judge rises up from the chair. "We're done here, Mr. Decastro."

"The Calderón disappearance was a Federal case, Judge. I found Roxy's remains hidden in the Club Tropical. You want me to go to the U.S. attorney with what I know? Or do you want to tell me about the war with Red Tooth? The pink pantyhose and Puerto Rico?"

"Sometimes I take a martini after court at the Green St. Grille. About five-thirty."

*   *   *

A wave runs up the beach, nips his neck. The beach a slurry of wet sand beneath his back. No Cassie. No Island girl. No Africa.

Dried sweat crusts in his eyes. Jesus, for a cup of water. Just plain water. Fresh water. And, meu spirito santo, the black girl.

The barman's eyes look at him like the ghost of midnight past when he reaches the beach pub, asks for a glass of water. "You look like you need a whole ocean, mon."

He tries a swim off the beach. The salt stinging him. Ten thousand needles. And the surf rolling him, wrapping him in a net of white bubbles. Until he is clean laundry.

When he emerges the barman has two white pills and three tumblers of water lined up for him. "I seen bitch-bit a thousand times. But you something special, mon. That girl she got you bad. I can see the teeth marks on your neck."

57

"I never liked that girl." The judge's eyes stare at the richly finished wood of the bar. An ambulance bleats its way along Green St. outside. Another early May evening. Cambridge, Central Square.

"She was Puerto Rican."

"We only found that out in the end. She told everybody she was from Argentina."

"Really? Why?"

"Argentina sounds more exotic to a teenager than Puerto Rico. Don't you think?"

"You mean like Eva Perón."

"Something like that. She acted like she was hot stuff."

He takes a long swallow from his glass of ice water. "What do you mean?"

"She dressed like some kind of *Playboy* bunny. Big hair, lots of make-up, skirts as short as the house mothers at Coates would let her get away with, fashion boots."

"A looker."

"She used to hang out down at Factor's."

"Factor's?"

"The frappe shop in town back then. Juke box. Pinball machines. Sold cigarettes under the counter to a lot of boys from Tolchie. The girls from Coates would cruise in to size up the horseflesh. Single-sex schools … They tried to keep us apart, the boys and the girls."

"But you found a way."

"Not me. I was way too shy. Too scared."

"Did Roxy ever come on to you?"

He looks away down the bar. "She specialized in rich, white boys."

"Like the Red Tooth crowd?"

"Among others."

"Let me guess. Jean-Claude Rausche."

"He was straight back then."

"And he got it on with Roxy?"

"I have no evidence."

"You don't have to protect him."

"I said I have no evidence."

Time for a little lie. "You know, he's the one who told me about the pink pantyhose and Puerto Rico."

"I sort of doubt it, Counselor."

"You want to tell me what you remember?"

Merriweather swallows off the last of his martini, takes a toothpick, toys with the olive in the glass. "I don't remember much."

"Was she into Jean-Claude for drugs? Was he supplying?"

"I wouldn't know."

"What was in it for him? Couldn't have been the sex, right?"

"He always bragged about how much he was getting laid."

"You believed him?"

"He was a stud. Tall, blond, blue-eyed. The girls went for him like steel to a magnet."

"But he was faking it? Like Roxy and the Argentina thing. Posing."

"That's pretty much the conclusion I came to later."

"When he came out."

Merriweather's face is suddenly a waxy shade of oatmeal. A shadow fallen over it. "No ... After we found her."

"What do you mean?"

"It was spring exam week. Right before commencement. We went up into the clubhouse for one last buzz before everybody headed off to college. And to celebrate. Jean-Claude said we should celebrate. The four of us. Mark, Jason, J-C, me."

"Celebrate graduation?"

Merriweather signals the barman for another martini. It was more than that, he says. The boys had all made a lot of money. They thought they were rich. Each of them was going to walk away from Tolchie with something like twenty-three thousand dollars and change.

"From the poker and the drugs."

"It was a good business."

"I thought you guys had gotten your butts kicked in a territorial battle with the Red Tooth boys. I thought they were running the drugs and games."

The judge smiles, slips back into his old ghetto voice. "Naw, man. That's how come we had all that money. We whooped their asses. I mean whooped them bad. Put them out of business ... for a while."

"What happened?"

He says that right after spring break a bunch of those Red Tooth boys got their balls trimmed in a hotel room downtown while they

were doing a deal. Some folks held them up for a big bag of money.
They owed everybody. Never recovered. So the Club Tropical had a
corner on the market for the last two months of school. You can sell a
lot of drugs at a school when the weather turns warm.

"You guys, Club Tropical, took the money?"

"Naw, J-C just put the word out on the street about this deal going
down. He had inside information, you know? Someone had told him
the exact time and place. The street took care of the rest."

"*Cristo.*"

"I gotta tell you, it felt good. Those bastards had been fucking
with us for more than two years."

"So score one for the little guys."

"Yeah, that's what I was thinking when I went up into the clubhouse the last time ... Until I saw the body."

"Roxy."

"Lying there in the middle of the room like a big old dead bitch
dog. A little blood coming out of the corner of her mouth. All dolled
up like a cross between Farah Fawcett and Diana Ross. Dressed for a
plane ride home ... And graffiti written across the club banner over
the mantle. I remember part of it said something like RED TOOTH
ROCKS!"

"Rules."

"What?"

"It says Red Tooth Rules. They killed her, put her there, right?"

"The final fuckover. They got us good ... The banner is still there
in that attic?"

"Who would move it?"

"Just like the body?"

"Bones."

*   *   *

He eyes the barman, takes the pills. Chugs the first glass of water, feels his throat for the bites. The raw tender spot below his Adam's apple.

The barman laughs, "What you gone tell you mama now? The old rose tattoo. She marked you for life?"

Maybe so.

Now this new girl. The Indian princess in the seal skin. The scent of scallop shells, cobwebs, the light filtering through salt-soaked windows of the bait shack, the oboe calls of seabirds.

Her raw nakedness calling to him. From deep in the currents of a thermal vent. Drawing him to the planet's molten core. Volcanic annihilation. Where his *vóvó* and his mother hold him to their breasts and sing the lullabys of Cape Verde. Africa.

* * *

The judge on his third martini, the lawyer his fourth water. Dinner crowd starting to fill the tables, seats at the long bar.

"It was Jean-Claude's idea to dress her like a boy, put her in the garment bag and hide her under the eaves?"

Jean-Claude had this gray, stony face, says the judge. Like he was trying to freeze out all emotion. The whole time he undressed her. Changed her clothes. Each of the boys contributed some old Tolchie gear so that no one of them could be implicated if anyone ever found her. She had this mane of bleached blond hair. J-C cut it off with the scissors on his Swiss army knife. "It took forever … She looked like a little kid when we zipped her in there."

"You want to talk about the pink pantyhose?"

"They were on the poker table, we had piled all of her stuff there. We were going to bag it, get rid of it and the hair. That's when we found out about Puerto Rico."

"I don't understand."

"Mark was going through her handbag, and he found the ticket to San Juan. Then J-C gave me this funny look. Kind of smiled."

"Why?"

Jean-Claude had an idea. A way to shunt Roxana's death away from Boston and the school.

"'Try on her clothes, Squeaky,' he said. They used to call me Squeaky because I was so small and I had this voice like …"

Something clicks in his head. The pink pantyhose, Puerto Rico. He sees where this is heading. Roxy's last scene. "So you dressed up like Roxana, pantyhose and all. Got on the plane to San Juan."

That very afternoon. After J-C got him a blond wig from the costume closet in the Drama Tank. He was scared as shit. He still had her hair in his carry-on. Had some rum and cokes on the plane just to stop shaking. Back then any good-looking chick could get served on a plane. Jesus, he was a wreck.

"But you pulled it off."

"I changed out of her clothes in the lavatory just before we landed. Caught a flight back to New York that night. Dumped her stuff in a trash can in Penn Station before I caught the train back to Boston."

"So much for the case of the magic airplane."

"The worst day of my life."

"It wasn't so great for Roxy Calderón either."

58

SHE said she would wait for him to finish up with the judge. They would have a date. Sort of. Before they made the drive with Gracie back down to the Cape to crash with Ronnie.

So here she sits. But now it's sunset, and a chill is starting to settle over her shoulders. She's holding down a table at a Mongolian *smorgasbord* called Fire & Ice just off the Harvard campus in Cambridge. A glass of sauvignon blanc not enough to take the chill off her here on the outdoor patio. Christ, when she looks up, she can see the first of the evening stars. Or maybe it's a planet. Venus or Mars.

The phone beeps in her purse. When she fishes it out and scrolls to her missed calls, she sees five in the last four hours from Danny. And one from Ronnie. She's wondering if she should be returning those calls, finding out what Danny wants, checking in with Ronnie. Wondering if she did the right thing by sending Gracie off by herself to see a fest of classic Fellini flicks at the Brattle. Wondering whether this son of a fisherman is going to show any time soon. Whether she even wants to see him now. Whether she was thoroughly out of her mind when she thought maybe she'd get him a little tipsy over stir-fry.

Maybe drag his tight little Portagee ass into the women's room, lock the door. Give him the loving of his life.

Or does she really miss a woman's touch?

And just this instant, she's wondering what the connection is between pangs of mortal fear and the craving in her loins ... when she sees him talking to the hostess, scanning the room for her. And the blood starts buzzing in her thighs. *Oh sweet Jesus. Nooshun kesukqut ... Wuneetupantamunak kooswesuonk ...*

* * *

He looks soooo good! Smells so good in the starched white shirt and tie, the navy blazer. She's lingering in his hug, there above their table, inhaling the scent of Canoe on his neck. Shifting her shoulders just enough to remind him of her breasts, her perked nipples ... when two men the size of gorillas push through the crowded room. And grab him. Each one seizing an arm. Each stinking of stale coffee and cigarettes as they pry him free from her embrace.

He flails. Breaks loose. Fists pulled tight to his chest, elbows jutting out. Head tucked. Like one of those ball carriers for the Pats who Ronnie admires. Shaking his tacklers.

One of them dives, gets an arm around his left leg.

The other tries to throw a headlock on him, but he elbows the guy in the eye, knocks him back.

Chairs tipping over. Diners clearing off the patio. The hostess—a pale-faced blondie, eyes big as clams—is backing away toward the bar, shouting into her cell phone, probably at the 911 operator.

She doesn't know these monkeys, doesn't know if Michael knows them. But it's clear he wants to get away. His eyes fierce as he tries to beat off the guy clinging to his leg.

But now the other ape, still holding his injured eye, is reaching into his jacket and pulling out a pistol. Pointing it at Michael.

"Stop! Put your hands over your head or I'll shoot!"

The second Michael looks to the gunman, stops wailing with his fists, the guy on his leg throws an upper cut smack into his balls.

And Michael hits the floor. Flat, bang, down. Eyes rolled back in his head.

The gorilla with the gun now waving his open wallet, a badge inside, at the crowd. He's shouting, "Police! Nobody move!"

She starts to run to Michael, but the leg grabber/ball slugger, still on his knees, throws an arm around her, drags her to the ground. Twists her right arm behind her back.

"Don't move a muscle, don't say a word! Or I'll break your fucking arm, honey."

* * *

It's after ten when Lou Votolatto meets her and Gracie at the McDonalds at the traffic rotary next to the Cape Cod Canal.

"The bastards cuffed him while he was still out cold. Then picked him up and dragged him out the door. His blazer sleeve ripped off. Blood all over his shirt. And me just standing there. Like I can do nothing but see him open his eyes a little and mouth the words *Get Lou*."

The detective stares into his coffee, then looks up across the table at her and Gracie. "Didn't I warn that dumb bunny the shit would hit the fan if he keeps on letting people think he's some kind of cop?"

"That's what this is about?" She rubs her eyes with her fingers.

"What do you think?"

"I think it's about revenge. I think this is about us getting too close to the killers. I think Liberty Baker and Roxana Calderón are shrieking in their graves."

He takes a long sip of coffee, looks over her shoulder, out the window at the headlights of cars as they appear, disappear in the dark. "I made some calls."

"OK."

"Our boy just got collared by two of Cambridge's finest. Seems like some doc in Boston filed a complaint. Impersonating an officer, harassment. That kind of thing. Suffolk D.A. issued a warrant. Cambridge P.D. got a tip Rambo was going to shake down a superior court judge. So they staked out the judge and waited. Michael walked into their trap. They grabbed him on the rebound with you at the restaurant. Like no sense bringing the media down on the good judge's head."

"Now what, Detective?"

"He's in the Middlesex County lock-up. You got to get him out … Shit happens in a place like that."

Gracie reaches out, grabs Awasha's hand. "You mean someone kills him."

"The three of you have stirred up a hornet's nest."

"How much is this going to cost?" Gracie asks.

"Probably a lot more than you have, young lady."

"Is seventy-eight thousand dollars enough?"

59

SHE hears Gracie gasp. Then feels the girl's hand grab her right arm, squeeze so tight, she almost loses control of the Saab. "Look at all those fire trucks!"

The lane leading to Ronnie's cottage on the cranberry bog in Yarmouth is a maze of emergency vehicles, pumpers, ladder trucks, hoses, firefighters in slickers and helmets. Cops. The foggy night lit with flashing red and white and blue lights. Small plumes of smoke rising from the charred walls, merging with the fog. Roof, windows, front door gone.

"Something terrible's happening." Her foot presses hard on the brake pedal. One hand instinctively grabs for Gracie's, feels the deepening hollow in her guts and the girl's.

"Don't let go." The voice wavers, fades. She's not sure whether it's Gracie's or her own.

Then she sees Ronnie up ahead, wandering among the police and firefighters, the shadows, the strobing lights. Black T-shirt and boxer shorts. Swigging on a bottle of Wild Turkey.

* * *

She doesn't remember letting go of Gracie or leaving her behind in the Saab. All she knows is that she has him in her arms, wraps him in a hug. Right here in the middle of the lane, the scent of burnt pine, melted roofing tar clotting in her nostrils.

"My god, are you alright?"

He's crying. No, sobbing. His huge head pressed against her tiny shoulder. The tears hot, soaking her blouse.

"What happened?"

"I'm fucked. Totally fucked."

"You had an accident?"

He tries to speak … but his body convulses. Shakes his head no. "I was asleep on the couch."

"I don't understand."

He suddenly pushes himself free of her, takes a step back, glares at the wreckage of his cottage, takes a sip of bourbon. "When I woke up. I thought I was back in Baghdad for a minute. And all hell had broken loose again."

"Your house burned down."

"Somebody torched it!"

Gracie is out of the car, homing in on them. "They tried to kill you?"

"I don't know … Maybe they weren't after just me."

"What are you saying?"

He looks at his twin sister with cold eyes. "You and your pals been staying here off and on for a week. And you've made some serious enemies."

"Jesus." She reaches out for his bottle.

He pulls it away, afraid she's going to take it from him.

"Ronnie! Nippe Maske!"

"What?"

"Give me a drink, goddamn it!"

*   *   *

The fire trucks are gone. The remains of the cottage, the bog lost behind a curtain of fog. The dark so complete here in the Yarmouth heath, the inside of the Saab feels like a tomb. Except for Ronnie snoring in the back seat.

"This is a nightmare. Michael in jail … Ronnie's place a pile of ashes. And us sleeping in a freaking car," she says. "Can anything else go wrong?"

Gracie takes a pull from a bottle of Evian. "I think I lost Michael's bail money."

"You what?"

She feels the girl fussing in the shotgun seat. Fishing in the pockets of her army fatigues, huffing, pulling something out. Handing over a wad. Bills. "Nope. Found it!"

"Can I ask you where you got all that cash?"

Gracie takes another sip of water. "Let's just say my cousin Jason might be missing a little golden statue of Yamantaka."

"What?"

"A little household god. From the second Tibetan Dynasty, the broker said."

"You stole it?"

"From his bathroom."

"And sold it?"

"While you thought I was at the movies."

"Unbelievable."

Gracie leans back, snuggles against Awasha's shoulder. "I really miss Liberty."

She smells the oil in the girl's hair. "Me too."

*   *   *

The tribal drums. Flutes. Dulcimers.

And now Aaserah's whispering. "I feel so lonely ..."

He's lying on her bed, the sheets still damp beneath his bare back. She's beside him, kissing his neck, his chest. Her tongue slick. Soft. Tasting every inch of him. Fingers tracing his cheekbone, jawline. He knows she's trying to commit him to memory.

"You cannot come back here again, Nippe Maske. The isabaat mus-allah, the militia, has been here. They suspect us. They have their spies, and we are being watched. I am afraid of what they might do."

"We could run away. I heard that in Dubai we ..."

She puts her fingers to his lips, kisses him on the mouth. Slides her body on top of his, helps him enter her.

But he's unable. The bitterness, the fear numbing him. As if she is already gone. Already smoke ...

Later when they are dressed, pressing together one last time behind the closed door of her apartment, she hands him her cell phone. "Wait for me. It may take some time. But I'll call you, my love. When I find a way out of Baghdad."

60

THE secretary picks up the phone, glaring at him, Awasha, Gracie. As the ancient redhead whispers into the receiver, he can hear Lou's voice rumbling through his head.

"Count your lucky stars, Rambo, that little Chinese cutie made your bail. Or you would be pulling a train a mile long by tonight. Middlesex County jail's newest bitch on the block. Now stop dicking around, and go public with those fucking bones in the attic before you or one of your *posse* gets whacked!"

So ... why is he here, ignoring the man?

Why has he let Awasha and Gracie talk him into coming back to Tolchester, diving into the volcano? Going face-to-face, head-to-head with one of the Grand Dragons of Red Tooth himself, Malcolm Sufridge? The man Red Tooth's old boys on Tolchie's board of trustees no doubt imported from among the English brethren to steer their ship for them.

Because it's worth the risk. Because Roxy's bones and her story are our only leverage against Liberty's killers and her own.

The secretary glares at him, Awasha, Gracie again. "Dr. Sufridge says he will see you now." The huge oak door springs open, but no one is visible in the doorway. Or beyond.

*   *   *

The butternut-paneled office seems particularly Gothic with the harsh light of a May morning cutting the room into cubes of gold and dark recesses. Shelves of leather-bound books tower to the ceiling.

Bumbledork sits in a shadow behind his immense desk in his black academic robe. The Windsor knot of a red necktie just visible above the robe's collar.

"You have a lot of nerve, Dr. Patterson, coming back here like this. I should call security and have you—"

"Is that a Red Tooth club tie you're wearing, Dr. Sufridge?" Gracie lands her first strike below the belt.

The old don blanches, seems to choke.

"It's quite simple, Doctor." Awasha takes the lead. "We know about Red Tooth, the drug dealing, and the death of Roxana Calderón."

"Roxana who?"

"Come on, Doc. The girl who died in Hibernia House in 1975." Michael's voice echoes with his impatience.

"Who the hell are you?"

Your worst nightmare, he thinks. But what he says is, "Legal counsel."

"Am I supposed to feel intimidated?" The posh Midlands accent is regaining some of its timber.

"That depends on whether you care that we let the media and the Middlesex County D.A. know that you're a Red Tooth boy, that your cozy brotherhood still exists at this school and that it has been covering up a murder for almost thirty-five years."

"Don't be absurd."

"I'll bet you one thousand dollars you're missing a twelve-year molar ... and the police can find it on your key chain." Gracie strikes again.

"You're talking nonsense. I don't know anything about ..."

Michael shakes his head. "You really think anybody will believe that, Doctor Sufridge, when I can summon multiple witnesses to expose all the horrendous things your band of brothers has been up to?"

"Balderdash."

Awasha says she can provide incontestable evidence that points to Red Tooth boys killing Roxana Calderón. And the trail of evidence will show Red Tooth's hand in Liberty's death too. Then there is this mess of recent dirty tricks. Including the burning of her brother's house and now Bumbledork's firing her.

"You're speculating, Dr. Patterson."

"I don't think so," says Gracie. "Not as far as Roxy Calderón is concerned."

"Bunk."

"Then how do you explain this?" Michael opens his brief case, unrolls a green nylon banner. The words on the banner in large orange script: CLUB TROPICAL. Beneath the words, scrawled in pink paint, SUCKS SHIT. And in fuzzy red lettering, RED TOOTH RULES!

"That doesn't prove anything."

Time to drop the A-bomb. "Tell that to the crime lab that has matched the pink letters in the graffiti to the nail polish found on Roxana Calderón's finger."

*   *   *

Sufridge inhales deeply, leans back in his office chair, puts his hands together as if to pray. Beams a thin smile at the three people across the desk from him.

"Here's the truth. Trust me. Red Tooth has had nothing to do with any of these events. The brothers are extremely upset that someone has been implicating Red Tooth in Liberty's death and all these dirty tricks you refer to, Dr. Patterson."

"Yeah right!" Gracie's cheeks are coloring.

"Not so fast, young lady."

He says they've just had a slight misunderstanding. The membership has authorized him to say that as an act of good faith all of Ronnie Patterson's problems will soon disappear. Awasha's old job is hers if she wants it … or he knows of a position at a school in Seattle, with many Native American students, that could be hers for the asking.

Awasha's jaw drops.

"And you, my spirited young Gracie. Your dorm room still awaits you."

Her teachers will not expect her to be making up any work missed in the last two weeks. Her name is already being engraved on a Tolchester-Coates diploma. She can graduate in June. A year early. Won't that save her parents a bundle of money and make them happy?

"What about justice for Liberty Baker?" Michael feels indignant, fears Awasha and Gracie may start to waffle in the face of these bribes.

"Show me where the bones are, where you got this banner, and I will make sure that the police are notified. That they will find the person or people who killed these girls."

"Yeah, right. The police you've been paying off to the tune of more than a million dollars a year?"

Bumbledork stiffens. Shoots him a look to crush an elephant. "Does this mean there's something else you want the brotherhood to—"

Gracie surges toward the headmaster's desk. "Fuck you, old man. Just fuck you! My friend is dead!" The spit from her words catches on the breeze blowing through the window, showers them all.

Michael winces. *Code red!*

61

THE afternoon sun is scorching when he heads down the wharf at Sesuit Harbor, East Dennis, in search of Lou Votolatto.

A classic Lyman runabout is tied to the town float. The detective's in the boat, bent over the Chrysler Crown Special engine. Votolatto sips from a can of Bud, stands up, shoots a sideways glance at Michael. Grimaces. Burps into his fist.

"Don't even start, Rambo. It's my goddamn day off. The blues are running. I should be out there right now, two lines in the water ... But my engine's fucked. You want to tell me what you know about fixing bum carburetors, start talking. Otherwise, please just leave me in goddamn misery."

"I think we got the killers on the run. It's just that Gracie kind of went off on—"

"Ah, Jesus H. Christ! What did I do to deserve you?"

He pictures jets, needle valves, floats, choke plates, idle screws. The outboard engines he's rebuilt. The Chevy 357 he had in high school. Yeah, he can do carburetors. It's just all this murder stuff, and romance, that short-circuits him. Maybe he needs to take a deep breath. Right here, right now. Change the polarity.

"This could be your lucky day."

"Sure thing. The patron saint of cluster fucks is paying me yet another surprise visit … and I'm supposed to be overjoyed."

Michael rolls up the sleeves of his white dress shirt and steps into the Lyman. "Want to crank the engine?"

"Don't fuck with me today. I'm not in a happy place. You know what I mean?"

"Please. Crank the engine."

The detective hits the ignition, the engine spins. Doesn't even cough. Michael puts his ear next to the carb air intake, listens for the wet hiss of gas and air. Doesn't hear it, smell it. No fuel. Smiles.

"Yeah?"

"How bad you want to go fishing?"

"I'm not in the mood for games."

"I can get you on the water in ten minutes. Guaranteed."

"But—"

"Just talk to me a minute or two about this other stuff."

The cop rolls his eyes, settles back with his butt braced against a seatback. "You better not be fucking with me, Rambo."

"The headmaster's dirty as hell. He tried to bribe Awasha, Gracie, and me this morning. Wanted us to just walk away from the Roxy Calderón mess. But here's the weird thing. He didn't seem to know where we found her bones."

"So he's stonewalling. Fronting for someone … probably a bunch of people in that club of his."

"He said if we told him where the bones are, he would bring in the local police."

"The ones who rubber stamped the Baker girl's death a suicide."

"Yeah."

"And you think that kind of mischief is going to happen again."

"Or someone's going to drop a mountain on me and my friends."

"I'd say the avalanche has already started. Have you forgotten the night you spent in jail, the fire at Ronnie Patterson's place ... or that you, Ronnie, Pocahontas, and the Ninja chick are now sleeping in a fucking tent in Nickerson State Park?"

Something is burning behind his eyes. "I feel like I'm so close to these killers, I can smell them."

"Yeah and they are going to eat you alive. Listen, kid, why don't you let me have a little talk with the U.S. attorney. She'd love to be the one to crack the Magic Airplane Case. How many times do I have to tell you to stop dicking around? Go public with those bones before you or one of your sweeties gets whacked. It's way past time, you know?"

"That's not going to help Liberty Baker."

"Whatever. We still get the bad guys off the street, right? The headmaster and his Red Tooth bunch."

"Things still don't add up for me."

"Jesus Christ. This isn't math class. You got to let this go. For everyone's sake."

"If someone was stonewalling, how would you get around him?"

The detective finishes his beer, tosses the can in a rubber trash can in the back of the boat. "Find the weakest rock in his wall."

"That's what I thought. Thanks, Lou."

"Hey, hero! What about my engine?"

"Someone's got to talk to Kevin Singleton."

The detective pulls a .38 special out of the pocket of his fishing jacket. "How about I take you to the U.S. attorney right now, bub?"

"Maybe you want to change the fuel filter first."

"What?"

"I thought you'd rather be fishing."

62

KEVIN Singleton, baggy jeans/Jimmy Hendrix T-shirt, slouches in his metal chair in the courtyard at Au Bon Pan in Harvard Square. Looks up with blue, hungry eyes as Gracie drops her backpack to the ground and settles into the chair across the table from him. It's after seven o'clock in the evening, the shadows are long, but the air is still unusually warm for May.

"You're late."

She can feel his gaze on her. Phantom hands feeling the weight of her breasts through the tight, rayon turtle neck, the thighs flexing in the green tights. Her denim mini riding up so high as she sits down. Ninja Girl better cross her legs immediately ... or his eyes, those phantom hands, will be going right up her legs. *Even scared, he can't stop thinking about booty.*

"Where have you been?"

"Chill, Kev. I'm here, OK?"

"Yeah. Like whatever. This is your gig."

She thinks, *He's touchy. Try another tack, girl.* "Come on, cutie, don't be like that."

He raises his brows, purses his lips, James Deans her. "You're not really my favorite person right now."

"Give me a chance. I just got here."

"That's my point. You up and vanish from T-C one day. No goodbye, no nothing. No calls. No email. Now all of a sudden, weeks later, I'm your favorite person. Like hey, Kev, meet me for coffee in the Square. Tonight, dude! Like this is 'life or death.'"

"I didn't say life or death. All I said is that we need to talk. That you need to watch your back."

"What the hell's that suppose to mean?"

She pops the top off her latte, stirs it. "Look. As far as Red Tooth is concerned you're low man on the totem pole."

"Did you tell that cop that was hanging around with Doc P that I sold you stuff?"

"He figured it out on his own."

"Thanks a lot, Gracie!"

"So now this cop's coming for me or what?"

"He knows that Red Tooth is your pharmaceutical connection. And he thinks somebody in Red Tooth killed Lib."

"What?"

"You know how she really died, Kev? Someone put a shit-load of GHB in her Red Bull. Knocked her out. Then dropped her in the tub, turned on the water, and slit her wrists."

"No."

"Yes! Good old Fantasy, Liquid E, Cherry Meth. Same stuff we were mixing with our drinks that night with Tory and your bro in SoCal."

"Are you trying to freak me the fuck out?"

She takes a long sip of her latte. "Hey, I'm here because you're my friend. I don't want to see you take the fall for something you didn't do. Know what I mean? Like I know you really cared about Lib."

"Aw Jesus."

"I know you guys were having some off moments. But she loved you, Kevin."

Tears are welling in the corners of his eyes. "Shit. Fuck. I don't know."

"Listen, OK? This morning Michael and Doc P had a heart-to-heart with Bumbledork. He's ready to give you up for the murder. It seems your alumni brothers want to feed you to the sharks. They got lots of stuff to hide, and they don't like feeling the heat."

"I'm dead. I'm just fucking dead. Those dick weeds. I don't even like their stupid-ass society. It's a lot of old-school horseshit. You know that?"

"Don't let them fuck you."

"Why … ? How … ?"

"Michael doesn't think you killed Liberty. But he thinks maybe you have an idea who did."

He puts his face in his hands. "I don't know shit."

She can't help herself. She reaches across the table, strokes his wild brown curls, his neck. Hears Michael's voice in her head. *Maybe this poor slob doesn't even know what he knows. You're going to have to dig, Gracie.*

Yeah, dig, Ninja Girl! She draws her hand back from his hair.

"Who beat on me the night before I left school?"

"What?"

"Why did you run Michael's jeep off the road back in February?"

"Huh? I never. —"

"The car that hit him from behind was a silver Murano. Just like yours. Fact."

He rubs his eyes. "That's my father's car."

"So your father ran Michael into the woods?"

"No!" A sudden flash in his eye. "I remember something. We didn't even have that car then."

"Yeah, you did."

"No. That was like the last week of winter term. I wanted to use the car one day. My dad said no dice. He lent it out. Somebody was having car trouble."

"Who?"

He looks away. His eyes following a bus up Mass. Ave. "I don't know."

"Come on, Kevin. You want to go down for murder? Jesus Hell. Don't hold out on me. These people aren't going to protect you!"

His eyes still on the bus. His teeth suddenly gnawing on the knuckle of his thumb. "Can I ask you something personal, Gracie?"

She looks at him, wonders where this is going, what secret she's going to give up for the killer's name. "Like truth or dare?"

"Yeah."

"You know who borrowed the car?"

"Maybe."

"One question."

"Did you and Liberty ever …" He puts the fingers of both hands together, squeezes them in and out, like an accordion. "You know?"

"Get it on?"

"Yeah."

"Fuck you, Kevin."

"Hey, be nice."

"What? Why would you ask that? It get you off?"

He shakes his head no. "I don't know. I got the feeling Lib was see-ing someone else. You know, besides me? Those last couple of weeks. She seemed distracted."

"You know smoking too much weed can make you paranoid. The girl was mad deep into our history paper. That's all."

"I really loved her."

"Then tell me who borrowed the car."

He stares at his feet. A pair of red Chucks. Size twelve. "The dean."

"Denise Pasteur?"

63

"I didn't think I would ever see you again." Danny's voice breaks as the words burst from her mouth. Wet ghosts of memories, desire.

She thinks the dean's face has been transformed. The confident butch gone. Danny now a gawky adolescent girl again. Jeans and a violet fleece. Eyes darty, lips thin and pale, trembling like the fingers she takes in her hand.

"I'm here ... I had to come."

"But why here? Of all places. We never ..." She leans forward, bends down so she can press her forehead to the small woman's. Strokes Awasha's long black hair with her free hand.

"Why not? A fantasy. Maybe if we had come here sooner ..." There's no way she can finish this sentence. She hates regrets, and now she's caught up in the scene around her.

Mid-afternoon. A hot Saturday in late May, and Provincetown is already in summer carnival mode. The weekend crowd of lesbian couples, gay dudes, straight day trippers clot Commercial St. The drag queens are out in the street in front of the Crown & Anchor touting their shows.

A bass beat pounds from a boutique, blends with *bossa nova* filtering out the front door of an erotica shop. The scent of Portuguese pastries, fried clams, perfume, rising tide, mammals in heat swirls among the crowd. The horse-drawn carriages, the women jugglers tossing their pins in front of the town hall.

And Awasha's here in the middle of it all. On the steps of Vixen, a girl's club. Light blue peasant blouse. White clam diggers that grab her hips just right. Ruby lips rising to kiss away Danny's fears. Eyes just catching a glimpse of Michael and Gracie watching from a table in a bistro across the street ... And her mind wondering if she's playing her part right. Her heart trying not to feel her confusion about where this all is heading. Trying not to seize with the cold blood of dead girls tightening in her veins.

She steps back from the embrace, still holding Danny's right hand. "Walk with me. Let me see P-town through a girlfriend's eyes."

So they walk. Arm in arm. West. Past the fudge shops. Past the army surplus place. Past the boy bars. Past the skateboarders hanging in front of Spiritus Pizza.

Until they hit the Pied Piper.

"Let me buy you a drink," says Danny. The old tennis-pro handsomeness starting to stiffen and color her cheeks, chin.

They get *mojitos* and take a table where they can look out at the harbor. Sip. Hold hands.

"I'm not a fool. I know you want something from me."

She's not ready for this. Not yet. Danny's tough shell growing back so quickly. The imperious, take-charge, nō-bullshit Amazon just minutes away from total regenesis.

Great Spirit, what a little hand-holding can let loose. Michael ... I think I need you!

And now, she's without the right words, feeling off balance. But Wonderwoman is on the move. Leaning across the table. Putting a strong hand behind her neck. Drawing her face close. Kissing.

Mashing her. Crushing her lips. Sliding a hot tongue between her teeth. And, *fuck*, her own tongue's rising to tango. The old larceny of stolen moments.

Her thighs are starting to sweat, when she suddenly hears Gracie howling in her head.

Did you see the blood? A barrel of wine poured out of Liberty. Poured over Liberty ... Her head, her black hair, her long braids ... She was sticky with it. Her nose and mouth buried in it ...

Aaserah whispering. You cannot come back here again, Nippe Maske. The isabaat musallah *has been here...*

And Michael. Sweet Michael touches her. It is the first time all over again. She pulls him tight against her hips, slides her hands over the lobes of his buns. Knows the ecstasy of seals.

She breaks the kiss. Searches Danny's eyes. Just inches away from those gray-diamond teasers. Clears her throat with a little gasp.

"I need you to be honest with me. I need you to tell me what you know about Roxana Calderón. Or ... Or Michael's going to tell the police that he has proof you were driving the Singleton's car the day it ran him off the road."

A fire flares, fades in Danny's eyes. "You met my half brother, didn't you? You get a sense what a bastard he is, baby?"

* * *

"Jean-Claude used Roxy to get at those assholes in Red Tooth."

"How?"

They are sitting on the Long Point dike now. Talking, watching the sunset, the last of the flood tide rushing through a culvert beneath the massive granite blocks into the salt pond.

"She was a Latin bombshell and a flirt. Loved attention ... And they were a bunch of privileged, arrogant, horny boys who thought the world was their oyster, that pussy was their prerogative."

"Jean-Claude used her as a spy?"

"A prep school slut. She would fuck anything that moved ... for a price."

"A price?"

"Information she could use in trade with Jean-Claude."

"Trade for what?"

"Roxy liked her drugs."

"So I've heard. But couldn't she get it from her lover boys in Red Tooth?"

"Jean-Claude had some kind of nearly magical control over her."

"He was blackmailing her maybe."

Danny shrugs. "I don't think so. It was a chemistry thing. She craved him, for some sick reason. What a total fucking waste of her time!"

She feels the heat in these last words. Actually leans away. "What?"

"The little bitch loved playing his secret agent games. Sucking his cock. Taking it up the ass for him."

"But he's gay."

"He kept that in the closet, honey ... 'til later."

"Because he wanted that power over her. This was all about controlling the gambling and drug profits at the school? About Club Tropical trouncing the Red Tooth boys?"

"That was part of it, for sure. And controlling Roxy. Feeling superior over females. He likes that. They made her an HONORARY member of their stupid-ass little club in the attic of Hibernia House. The only girl they ever let in."

"Their pet?"

Danny gives another shrug, stares at the green and red afterglow of the sunset lacing the clouds on the horizon. "Roxy was handling this dweeb from Red Tooth, the winter before she died. Went to the Tolchie Snowball with him, spent an illegal night in a Boston hotel with him. Just to get information about a drug deal Red Tooth was working."

"The one that went sour. The one where Red Tooth got jacked by some guys from the street."

"You know about that?"

"Jean-Claude set up the hijack, right?"

"After Roxy came through with the details. Where. When. Who."

"It was quite a victory for Club Tropical."

"Those assholes were elated. Jean-Claude thought he was king of the world."

"How about Roxy?"

"She was impossible to be around."

She hears something in Danny's voice. Not bitterness. Something else. Something raw. "You two were friends?"

"She lived right next door to me for two years at Coates."

"You introduced her to your brother?"

"How stupid was I, huh?"

"Did you have a crush on her?"

"Please."

"How did she die?"

Danny looks at her with vacant eyes. The gray diamonds now flat, shadowy pools. "You think those are Roxy's bones you found in Hibernia House?"

"Don't you?"

"Those stupid little shits! When we came back for our senior year at Coates, the school told us that she had disappeared. On her flight home."

"You never thought Red Tooth or the Club Tropical had anything to do with it?"

She has tears in her eyes. Stands up. Turns to walk back across the dike toward town. There's a deep purple cast to the air now. And a chill. "My heart hurts. It just fucking aches!"

She watches Danny start to weave her way over the collage of the dike's granite boulders toward the lights of town. "Hey!"

"Yeah?"

"I have to know. Why did you borrow the Singleton's car and run Michael off the road?"

Danny turns, faces her. Bites her lip. Doesn't answer.

What seems like minutes pass.

"I was jealous, OK?"

64

WHEN he and Gracie finally find Awasha, she is wandering along the edge of MacMillan Wharf, staring vacantly down at the fish boats rafted alongside.

"Are you OK?" He sees waves of emotion surging over her face. Feels her trembling as she pulls him into a hug.

"Do you guys need to be alone?" asks Gracie.

He nods.

"Give us a couple of minutes." Her voice is wet, broken.

* * *

So they are alone. As alone as any couple can ever be in P-town. Locked in an embrace on the end of the wharf. Fog drifting in off the bay. The boats, the piles of nets, just shadows. Red light flashing from the end of the breakwater. A warning horn groans at long intervals from the lighthouse at Long Point. Or maybe Wood End. He can't tell.

He wants to ask her what happened, wants to know whether that witch hurt her. Or whether she's suddenly missing the love of women. Whether their night in the bait shack, the hours of love the next day, were just some kind of rebound. Whether those hours rocked her heart the way they rocked his. Or is she going to leave him when this quest for the killer is over? Leave him like Cassie left him. Like Filipa left him. *Cristo,* even Tuki, the drag queen client from hell, left him.

Where do we stand? His heart wheedles for an answer. His tongue aches to pose the question. But his soul tells him to just hold her until she stops shivering. His dead mother's voice counseling as always. *You have a good hug. Don't be cheap with it, Mo.*

Cristo, I'm trying. But is it enough to quiet the dead?

Her lips press against the tender spot below his Adam's apple. The rose tattoo.

I seen bitch-bit a thousand times. But you something special, mon.

He's not sure when he first feels her tongue on his throat, his chest. Or when she spreads her legs and pulls him down with her onto a mound of old fishing nets.

"Don't say anything," she says. "Just kiss me."

And he does.

A long, desperate kiss. The air heavy with the musty scent of scallops, fish. The thick night. The oboe calls of seabirds. Almost as before in the shack.

When they went down like seals.

She unbuttons his shirt, tastes his breasts. His neck again.

His arms cradling her as she slips out of her thong. Releases the belt on his jeans. The fly. Kisses him until he sees lightning behind his eyelids.

And then she raises her dress and guides him to the place where they meet, join.

"Let me feel you. Good god, let me feel you."

Her legs, short as they are, stretch, wrap around his waist.
Rock him.

He hears himself moan.

All his blood burning out through his pores.

And her lips, teeth, feast on his neck.

Like before ...

Their torsos surging, plunging.
Spiraling creatures,
diving through schools of silver
fish. Racing the currents into
the planet's molten core. A place
of bones and no bones. Back
to his *vóvó's* breast, his mother's,
the driving rhythms of Africa. Until
they break the surface. Whole
once more. Together.

"Could you ever love me?" Her voice a breathless whisper.

"Could I ever not?" he says.

Then he opens his eyes. Sees Gracie standing on the other side of
the wharf, just now turning her back to them.

What you gone tell you mama now?

65

NINJA Girl has a theory. She thinks Denise Pasteur is covering for her half brother. Thinks that Red Tooth is not the only villain in this mess. That they haven't found Liberty's killer yet. She says, like here we are in P-town, somebody ought to talk to that welder again.

Not me, says Awasha. She's way past burned out. And you can't send a high school kid in there, not to that cruel and arrogant man. "He's a world-class bastard."

So ... at ten o'clock at night ... it falls to Michael to put Gracie's theory to the test. Alone, a refugee of love. Solo. While Awasha and Gracie vanish into the mardi gras of the weekend crowd on Commercial St.

The blue flame, the sizzling torch, draws him into the studio. He thinks about those dead girls. Thinks, *maybe if I just flat-out shock this dude, he'll crack.*

So he goes in firing. Not so much as a howdy-do.

"You want to tell me why you murdered Roxana Calderón?"

"I beg your pardon."

"Your half sister says the Red Tooth boys didn't kill Roxy Calderón. You did. May 31, 1975."

The welder shoots him a cock-eyed look. "I don't have to talk to you. You're not a cop. You're not even a real lawyer anymore. I know all about you. You're a fisherman, Jazzbo. And you can tell Danny she can go piss up a rope for all I care."

"She's ready to go to the U.S. attorney with a story about how you used Roxy to spy on Red Tooth and knock them out of the drug trade at good old Tolchie."

"Like hell she is!"

"She's not the only one who has fingered you. I know all about how you cut off Roxy's hair, dressed her …"

The welder turns his torch on Michael. "Get the fuck out of here. I already told your switch-hitting girlfriend Red Tooth plays for keeps. Go knock on their doors."

"What's that supposed to mean?"

"It means they got Roxy. It was revenge for her helping me, the club. OK, got it? Now they're at it again. That black girl who died. She probably found out something she shouldn't have. Something they couldn't let her live with." There's a big grin on Jean-Claude's face.

"Bullshit." He lets fly with more of Gracie's hunch. "You really enjoy pinning it on the Red Tooth boys, don't you? It's such an easy way to slither out of this mess … I just don't see where killing Liberty Baker fits into this all. But I'm …"

The welding torch pointing again. "Out! Go back to your twisted little harem, Romeo."

"You and Snyder and Su and Merriweather. You had a plan. The ultimate turning of the tables on your arch enemies. You faked that Red Tooth graffiti in your club room in case anybody ever found Roxy. You really hated those bastards."

"You're out of your mind!"

"After all these years, you're still at war with Red Tooth, aren't you?

"You haven't a fucking clue."

"I think Roxy realized that you were using her, maybe that you prefer boys. She finally had enough. I think she was going to tell Red Tooth how you set them up to get hijacked. And I think you killed her to keep her quiet."

"In your dreams!"

"And maybe Liberty Baker figured it out. After all these years. So you had to eliminate her too. Red Tooth is the fall guy here. Not you."

The welder turns off his torch. Pulls the goggles off his forehead, sits down on his rocket/bomb sculpture. Suddenly it looks like a giant dick to Michael.

Jean-Claude throws back his head and laughs. "Fuck. You're cute … but you're dumber than a post!"

He feels a well opening inside his heart. The blood just rushing out into his chest. His vision going blurry.

"Think about this, hot stuff. Just for starters. How could I have killed Roxy Calderón when I was off campus for more than a day while someone was killing her? I just got back to school a half hour before we found her in the club."

"You expect me to believe that?" He can't hide the strain in his voice.

"Ask Marcus or Tom. I know you've been hounding them. Or ask Jason. Yeah, send your little China girl in to talk to Cousin Jason again. Let Chop open her innocent little eyes. He was with me."

"What? Where?"

"We took the bus and the ferry to the Vineyard. Chappaquiddick Island, actually. There's a place Jason liked to camp. We were probably fucking each other on South Beach when Roxy died … She was one stiff little piece of fluff when we found her."

So much for Gracie's theory.

J-C is beaming that arrogant grin of his again. *But why is his hand shaking as he lights a cigarette?*

"THERE'S something he's not telling us," Awasha says when she hears what just went down with Jean-Claude. Michael has her on the cell phone as soon as he's ten steps out the studio door. "Don't leave there, Michael. Watch that bastard!"

"Watch?"

"I got a really bad feeling about this guy. I think you spooked him, and he's going to bolt. Gracie and I will get my car and meet you!"

Suddenly flames are surging through her fingers, toes.

Nooshun kesukqut. Our Father. *Wuneetupantamunak kooswesuonk.* Who art in Heaven…

*   *   *

The Saab's rolling slowly toward the Rausche Studio, its head-lights off, when she spots Michael. He's hiding in a shadowy garden outside an Italian restaurant across the street from Jean-Claude's.

When she pulls to the curb, cuts the engine, he slips into the back seat. Gracie has shotgun.

"What's happened?" Her voice a husky whisper.

"He just turned out the lights."

"Hey, is that him?" Gracie asks.

A shadowy figure emerges from the gate in front of the wharf/studio. Tall, slender. Jeans and a white T-shirt. Carrying something bundled in his right arm. Maybe a jacket or a hoodie. He crosses the street, unlocks the door on an Eighties, black Porsche 911. Gets in. Starts the engine.

"That's our boy."

She's pumped. Images of street racers from *The Fast and the Furious*, screaming through dark city streets, flick through her head. The flames from her fingers, toes, now rising behind her eyes as she slips the Saab into first gear.

But even before J-C has the Porsche out of P-town, she sees that there will be no Hollywood chase scene. This is worse. Despite the hot Porsche, Jean-Claude is a slow, steady driver. He drives less than the posted speed limit as he heads west down Route 6. His taillights are so easy to follow, she wonders whether he knows she's back here. Whether he's making it easy for her to tail him. Leading them all somewhere.

The Saab's low beams barely cut the darkness as Gracie quizzes Michael about what happened in the welder's studio.

But she can't listen. Doesn't notice the car behind her. Something else, other sounds, are filling every corner of her head. And she can't tune them out. An approaching army.

*   *   *

Tribal drums. Then Flutes. Dulcimers … Beating. Again.

And Aaserah's voice, after three weeks of no contact, pleading from the cell phone she gave Ronnie. "Do you still love me?"

He tells her yes, beyond all reason.

"Would you leave everything you know and love to be with me?"

In a heartbeat!

For a long time she says nothing, as if she is trying to feel his love rising from her phone.

Finally, she speaks. "Then, Allah akbar! I have found a way, Nippe Maske. When all is ready for us, I will come to you. Wait for the call. It will be soon."

He pictures the internet images he has seen of Dubai, its high-rises, streets of gold, discos, banks. With his skills he can get a job in security. Or, maybe there is lobster fishing in the Persian Gulf. He wonders how much a boat would cost. Wonders if he is fortune's fool.

67

IT'S not until she has followed the Porsche down a winding road near Wichmere Harbor in Harwichport, sees it stop in front of a shingled summer mansion, that she realizes she's in a driveway. There's a car rolling up behind her, its quartz headlights glaring. She can't turn around, or back up. Like Ronnie that day in Baghdad. *Shit!*

* * *

He's in the make-shift gym spotting for a buddy doing bench presses— when the phone buzzes in his shorts' pocket. He takes the call in the men's room where no one will see, hear.

"I'm in my blue hijab," she says. "Outside the gate to your camp, I think. I can see the concrete barricades across the road. And the guards."

"Stop," he says. "Don't come any closer."

The sentries are nervous. The last two weeks two other FBOs have been attacked. One when someone drove a van full of explosives right into a convoy of Hummers leaving the base. Another when a teenage flower girl, a bomb hidden beneath her abaya, approached a checkpoint at the Green Zone and blew herself up, taking three marines with her.

"Tell me you love me!" Her voice sounds strange, desperate.

"I'll be out with the next patrol."

* * *

The headlights sear them from behind.

"Jesus!"

Suddenly she thinks she sees what is happening here. What has been happening ever since Christopher Columbus used the Caribs to supply his men with Arawak concubines. Since the Pilgrims enlisted the friendship and good will of her ancestor Massasoit, sachem of the Wamponaogs, her namesake Awashonks, squaw sachem of the Sakonnets… Only to hoist the head of Massasoit's son Metacomet on a pike to rot for years as a warning to bad Indians. Only to drive Awashonk's people from their homelands.

"Goddamn it!"

"What?"

"If you know your friend Lou's number, now would be the time to call him."

"Why?"

"You ever heard of Wounded Knee?"

* * *

By the time he's gotten his weapon and dressed in his cammies, vest, helmet—his civies hidden beneath, twenty-six hundred dollars in his pocket—his skin is oozing sweat. He's burning to go. But he can't just walk out the gate. No one gets off base without a pass. He's got to wait, fall in with a patrol that's heading out. Just as he always did when he was going to see her. Blending with the crowd, traveling under the radar. Old-time survival skills for an Indian.

It's more than a half hour before he sees a group of boys from Bravo company assembling for a foot patrol, two platoons massing at the gates. He joins them.

"Hotter than hell," *someone says as a sentry waves them out onto the sun-bleached street.*

"Global fucking warming."

"Fry City, man," *says a black G.I.*

"Word, dude!"

Suddenly he sees her. She gets out of a shit-brown Nissan parked up the block, starts walking toward the clutch of three dozen Americans. Her black abaya *blowing in the blistering wind.*

"Hey, heads up," *calls a sergeant.* "Check that bitch!"

"Lock and load," *says someone.*

"Here we go again."

One of the grunts makes a sound like a police siren.

What the hell is she doing?

He wants to pull out the cell phone, tell her to get out of the street. These guys aren't taking any chances, several of them already have their weapons pointed at her as she walks toward them. A hundred yards away. Right in the middle of the street.

"What's she doing?"

"Crazy fucking gash."

"Stop. Hey, lady, stop right there!"

Then in Arabic, "Qiff. Qiff! Stop goddamn it!"

But she keeps coming. Her hands seem to be cradling something that is beneath her abaya.

"Nippe Maske?"

"We got a situation here, Lieutenant!"

Is she nuts? Right here? Middle of fucking Baghdad? How in all hell does she ...

"Hey, hey lady. Stop. Stop! Qiff!!! You understand? Down on the ground!" *A sergeant is screaming, pointing at the street with both his M-4 and his free arm.* "Down!"

"Jesus Christ," *someone says.* "She's crying."

She's only about thirty yards away. He can see her cheeks glistening with tears. Her eyes searching the soldiers.

"Nippe Maske?"

"Fuck. She's got something under that robe!" *A G.I.'s voice screams,* "She's packing!"

He shouts her name.

She hears him. Her eyes widen as they find him. Her lips moving in prayer, maybe love.

"Bomber!!! Take her out!"

"NO! DON'T SHOOT!!!"

He's running toward her when someone fires.

Then a hail of bullets hit her. She staggers, eyes sewn on her Indian brave ... as she topples. Something, her guts maybe, squirming, bloody, spilling from under her abaya *as she goes down.*

* * *

"This is a trap, Doc P?"

"I'm soooooooo sorry."

"Aw fuck!"

* * *

She's dead. Along with the Persian cat she had hidden under her abaya.

And him with a broken nose, concussion, five broken ribs. After the squad turned on their brother-in-arms. Fucking madman Indian traitor.

When the MPs come to him in the hospital he says, "Yeah, OK, I knew her. She was a widow and a law student from the neighborhood. A kind person. All she wanted was a life. A little kindness and understanding."

"You got her killed, asshole. How's that make you feel?"

*   *   *

Recognizing the car jamming up against her rear bumper, she finally—fully—hears the truth in her brother's secret, Aaserah's death. In the blood of warriors beating through her heart. She gets it. At last. The old tribal lesson. About friendship and love, jealousy and revenge. About sleeping with the enemy.

She knows the killer who has come for them all.

68

HE hears the crack of the gun, smells the smoke, sees the tears freeze on Gracie's cheeks as the muzzle blast parts the hair above her right ear. The round just missing her scalp before it hits the ceiling with a thud, a puff of plaster.

Now the hot barrel of the Beretta is burning a red crescent on her temple. A long forearm chokes her neck.

He knows at this rate they'll all be dead before Lou and his crew get here.

"That was just a warning. The next bullet goes through her head! Everybody sit on the rug, hands behind your necks!"

Awasha is the first to drop to the floor of the nearly dark living room. Just a table lamp with a stained-glass Tiffany shade lit in a corner. He settles beside her on the worn red and blue oriental, their backs almost brushing a coffee table.

"I said sit, Jean-Claude, make yourself at home. Just your bad luck, mother's not here when you come running home with another pack of your problems … But she would want you to be comfortable in her house. Didn't she tell you she was going to be in New York this week?"

"Piss off, Danny. If mother were here, she would disown you once and for all. You think she still doesn't know you're queer."

"You should talk!"

"Hey, I'm out. Mother may not approve of me. But she admires my courage."

"She calls you a fiddlestick!"

"You know, she always suspected you had something to do with Roxy."

"Shut up and sit down or this girl dies right now."

He ignores her, swaggers over to the grand piano, looks at the sheet music propped above the keyboard. Debussy.

"Fucking shoot her, love. You think I care about these people? It's because you can't keep your dildo in your pants they're here. Because of you the spotlight's back on your lovergirl after all these years."

"Sit! I swear to god I'm going to blow the top of her head off!"

"Doc P, help me!"

"Don't do it, Danny. Don't make things worse than they already are."

"Shut up, Awasha."

"It was you. You killed Liberty didn't you? She found out about your secret life. So you—"

"Just shut the hell up. I trusted you. I loved you. And you threw all that back in my face. For what? A third-rate Lancelot? A fisherman?"

Jean-Claude sits down on the piano bench, kicks his legs out in front of him. "Oh, sweethearts, this is getting good. Don't you think, hotstuff? An honest-to-goodness cat fight. Right here in Mother's living room. Gun and all."

His half sister pinches the girl's neck harder in the vice of her forearm. Gracie's eyes start to glass over as Danny points the gun at Jean-Claude. "Get on the floor. Now, J-C!"

He makes a show of sliding off the chair, a man of rubber. "Have it your way, bitch."

"Michael?" Gracie's voice is little more than a gasp. A faint plea from a distant beach.

Her eyes black, wet. Begging a question he can't hear.

But he can imagine it.

After all these years of wondering. Of putting Cassie's face on it. Of asking his father tiresome questions about his mother, about Vóvó Chocolate. His African blood. He sees. It's not a black question, a white question, an Indian question, an Arab question, an Asian question. It's just a human question. About compassion. The one we ask when we find our fate bound dangerously with others. A call to take a stand.

Like now.

He looks around for a weapon, a distraction, sees nothing. But knows he has to do something. Knows as surely as he knows his mother's been dead, gone, for more than a year. Everyone in this room except the shooter is going to die if he doesn't act now.

He puts a hand on Awasha's shoulder, rubs it gently. Gets to his feet.

Danny points her gun back at Gracie's head. But something about her has changed. Her skin's paler, her chest heaving a little faster beneath her violet fleece. Eyes jittering around the dark room.

"Oh god, please ..." Gracie says. A faint prayer.

Awasha puts her hand on his. The blood is burning out through her pores. His pores. As before ... when they were diving through silver fish together. Racing into the planet's hot soul.

But now a child is calling. Children pleading. Some from their graves, secret attics. From Over-the-Hill. The heart's molten core.

Tribal drums. Flutes. Dulcimers. Pounding. Surf thundering off-shore on a reef. Marley singing from the bar. About Zimbabwe. About Revolution. The blood of cheetahs, wild seals scorching every vein. And Aaserah's shouting to Nippe Maske and her god.

He's lowering his head, shoulders. To make a smaller target. To charge. To kill ...

When she leaps. Awasha. Springs toward Danny. A blaze of torment, anger, rising from under his left hand. Howling. Black hair flying out from her scalp.

Her arms, hands, stretching. To tackle, choke. Tear.

The first shot breaks the air.

Then a second. A third. A fourth.

69

WHEN Lou Votolatto finally pulls him off the witch, pries his hands from her throat, someone has turned on a lot of lights in the room. And Danny looks dead. Her tongue choked out, sagging from the bloody corner of her mouth.

Awasha lies on the floor in a pool of blood. Three EMTs pressing enormous gauze pads to her right cheek, chest.

Gracie sits hunched over on the couch. "Oh, no. Oh, no ..."

There's a burst of bloody tissue on the far wall where Danny's last bullet scattered pieces of her half brother. His left kidney, to be exact.

"I tried to stop her, hotstuff," he says as two cops lift him onto a stretcher and start out the door toward an ambulance. "But you were the one nailed her."

Something ruptures in his chest. His throat gags. He heaves in his hands. Blood the color of wine. Liberty's last bath.

* * *

Dead. That's how he feels.

He's standing on the sidewalk at the top of the arch of the Paradise Island Bridge connecting the resorts on the island to downtown Nassau. Cassie's world. The rose tattoo throbbing now on his neck. The sailing yachts sliding beneath the bridge. Bum boats grinding up and down the harbor servicing the cruise ships at Prince George Wharf. And the water below clear, pale blue. He thinks he can see the fish schooling even from up here. Wonders what it would be like to jump. Die among their silver sides, fins flailing him. Their hard little lips nibbling at the rose on his neck.

*　*　*

"The bullet went through the top of your right lung. Came out just beneath your shoulder blade." It's not a doctor telling him this. It is Lou Votolatto. His dad is there, too, beside him in the surgical recovery room.

"I dreamed I was being eaten by a million little fish. I dreamed of the Bahamas."

"You're going to be just fine, Mo." His father squeezes his hand, turns his face away as it folds up in tears.

"You're a lucky son of a bitch, Rambo." Lou is trying to distract him from his father's melt-down.

He closes his eyes. Tries to remember. Feels Awasha rise again from under his left hand. Sees her spring.

Howling. Black hair flaming from her scalp. Her arms, hands, stretching. The first shot breaking the air. A pool of blood. EMTs pressing gauze to her cheek, chest.

"Where's Awasha?"

"You've been through a tough surgery, kid."

"Dad? Lou?"

"Everything's going to be OK. They're going to give you a sedative to help you rest."

A nurse is fiddling with his IV drip.

"Is she alright?" His voice only an echo ... slipping away.

* * *

He's in a hospital room when he wakes. Got to be Cape Cod Hospital in Hyannis. He can see the gulls wheeling on the wind outside the window. And his dad is there. Not crying now. A frozen look on his face. The look he gets when the *Rosa Lee* is just about on the fishing grounds, when he's staring at his fish finder, deciding exactly where he wants to set out for the first haul. It's the Caesar Decastro that always reminds him of a picture he once saw of the bullfighter Manolete. Stoic. Resolved.

"Is she dead, Dad?"

"The one you choked? No. In jail."

"I meant Awasha."

His father's eyelids flutter. Twice. The only show of emotion. "Hell of a woman. She probably saved your life ... Her brother took her to the Vineyard."

"Dad?!"

"She never regained consciousness ... I'm sorry, son."

He remembers something she told him about the Vineyard, scattering her mother's ashes on Squibnocket Beach. Alice's beach. Black Squirrel's beach. He sees it.

The wind is up, churning the waves. Coating her cheeks with brine. Lifting strands of black hair off her back. Her cheekbones high, prominent. Nose fine and proud. Eyes set on the horizon. She stands in the bright sun balancing on jagged granite ... in her yellow fleece pullover and jeans. Petite, almost anorexic except for full breasts. In the land of Maushop. Aquinnah ...

And now Ronnie. With the hatbox containing the ashes, clutched to his chest. Plaid work shirt, khaki pants. Moccasins. The wind is driving tears over his face.

Gulls swoop. Dive on the bait fish. Screeching.

The air almost too hot to breathe. Scorching his lungs. Air from a desert. And Africa.

A convulsion starts to rise in her brother's chest, in his own. Black rattling.

Ronnie's hand lifts the cover, opens the box as he swings to face downwind. The breeze starts to swirl the ashes out of the box, scatter them. Until they are nothing but a small cloud drifting away over the rocky beach, the breaking waves. Vanishing. With no word, no sign of hope or pardon.

"I wish Mom were here," he says.

His father stares out the window. "She would know what to say."

70

HE'S asleep when he feels a heavy hand shake his shoulder.

"Hey, kid, I brought some people to see you."

He pulls the pillow off his face, blinks his eyes open.

Lou Votolatto is standing over him. Two females next to him:Gracie and a black woman he should know, but does not recognize.

He catches her eye, tries to read her face. If her skin were lighter—and she weren't wearing go-go boots, a faux leopard coat—she could almost be his mother.

"Tedeeka? Teddie?"

"Hey, cha cha cha, baby." She brushes past Lou, bends down and gives him a kiss on the lips. "You the man!"

Gracie, huge smile on her face, drops onto the other side of his bed, hugs him. Nearly pulls the IV out.

"Careful, ladies ..." Lou sounds a little short of control. "The boy's just four days out of surgery."

"We can't hurt him, He's our knight in shining armor."

More kisses. A nose-full of trashy perfumes. For the first
time since his interlude on the fishnets with Awasha, he has the
urge to bark.

*   *   *

By the time his guests leave, he has the picture. Well, part of it.
Actually has a transcription of taped testimony he can read over. And
over. As if anything it contains will ever make any sense. Ever compen-
sate for what he's lost.

He can see it all: Jean-Claude, his mother at his bedside in the
hospital, ratting out his half sister. Big time. Bette Davis smile on his
face. While Lou Votolatto's tape recorder rolls.

JEAN-CLAUDE RAUSCHE

The little bitch broke her word, Mother. She said she would
never tell anyone about Roxy and me and the club ... if I never
told anyone about her own sick obsession with that Puerto
Rican *puta*.

I know how Roxy died. Danny told me one night in the
Harwichport house. Summer of '75. She told in return for my prom-
ising to never go public about her thing with that little tart ... Roxy
died by accident.

Sort of. She pulled a train for the Red Tooth guys. Just for the
hell of it, I guess. Because Roxy was Roxy. Or maybe she was pissed
because I had stopped paying attention to her.

Anyway, Danny heard about it. She couldn't stand it because she hated those arrogant bastards ... and she was sick
in love with Roxy. Pissed. Jealous that Roxy had given away to
Red Tooth what she would never give up to her. They got in a
shouting match the day Roxy was supposed to leave school for
the summer.

The fight ended with Danny heading over to my room in Hibernia House, over to the Club Tropical. She was going to tell me what Roxy had done, how Roxy had betrayed the club. Roxy chased her. Screaming, begging.

They had another fight at the top of the steps in Hibernia House. Danny pushed Roxy. She fell down the stairs. Broke her neck. Then Danny dragged the body up into the club room. Left Roxy for us (like "fuck you pricks") to deal with. Just lovely.

LT. LOUIS VOTOLATTO

Where does Liberty Baker's death fit in?

JEAN-CLAUDE RAUSCHE

Danny called me in early April and asked me if I had heard about the black girl who died at Tolchie. She said her girlfriend Awasha was on a mission to prove it was murder ... and it had something to do with secret societies at the school. She said the Red Tooth gang was already starting to freak out. I might want to tell the Club Tropical guys to watch their backs.

LT. LOUIS VOTOLATTO

How does this implicate your half sister in a murder?

JEAN-CLAUDE RAUSCHE

Because I asked her why she was being so generous to give me this heads-up. It's not like we've been close since boarding school, since Roxy died.

She said the stuff about Roxy and the drug dealing might come out. She didn't think Red Tooth could go for that. They might try some dirty tricks or sick the police on my boys. Or her. They aren't like the Club Tropical. They're still alive and well. Flourishing, if you believe Danny.

LT. LOUIS VOTOLATTO

Come on Jean-Claude. Get to the point. Your half sister and the death of Liberty Baker?

JEAN-CLAUDE RAUSCHE

Danny said that if the heat came down on either one of us that we had to cover for each other. That we had made a promise that summer after Roxy died. She said we had to stand by our word. She said we both had a lot to lose. She sounded nervous.

LT. LOUIS VOTOLATTO

So?

JEAN-CLAUDE RAUSCHE

So I asked her if she had something to do with this black girl's death. She said she was trying to protect her girlfriend. The Indian sweetie.

LT. LOUIS VOTOLATTO

Did you believe her?

JEAN-CLAUDE RAUSCHE

No. Didn't make sense. First she says the Indian chick is out to prove there's a murder. Then she all of a sudden says she's trying to protect her girlfriend. Like now her flavor-of-the-month is a player in this death. See?

LT. LOUIS VOTOLATTO
Was your half sister involved with Liberty Baker in some way?

JEAN-CLAUDE RAUSCHE
You think this is about jealousy again?

71

"MY parents are taking me back home to Hong Kong tomorrow." Gracie reaches across the table for his hand as he sets down his glass of *vinho tinto*. "I don't think I'll ever be coming back. My dad's pretty pissed at America."

They are in the *churrascaria*, called Vinho Negro, near Inman Square where he took her so many months ago when Liberty's death was so fresh it was all either of them could think about. The pain.

"Maybe it is the best thing. Get away from all of this. I wish I could go to the other side of the planet right now."

"You have your fishing with your dad. It's kind of the same thing."

He nods, thinks that within a week he will be offshore in the *Rosa Lee* at the canyons with Caesar and Tio Tommy. Sun hot. The birds circling in the air, watching for a free meal. Radio broadcasting the Sox game. The blue sharks will be out there too. Basking. Probably humpback whales. Maybe right whales. And the schools of silver cod. Smelling like a certain kind of heaven. He wonders why he would ever want to be any place else ... But there won't be any seals. Not out there.

"You know, I've really had a massive crush on you, Michael." She squeezes his hand.

He's going to pretend she didn't say this. "I heard Sufridge— Bumbledork—is getting fired. Lou says the U.S. Attorney's Office is looking into Red Tooth."

"Sometimes I was so envious and angry about what Doc P had with you. Sometimes I wished one of you was dead. Like that night I saw you two on the fishnets in Provincetown. And now …"

He feels her eyes on his, looks away. "You hardly touched your *moqueca*."

"Hey! Earth to Michael. Did you hear what I said? I just wanted you to know before I go, OK? I had thoughts about your body. And hers. Together. And sometimes I hated it. OK? Hated being the one left out. The kid. I wanted to be Ninja Girl, you know? I wanted you to see me as someone special. The way you saw her. And now, I don't know. I feel dirty. I feel like shit."

He withdraws his hand, lifts his wine glass. Stares at the purple fluid back-lit by the candle burning on the table. Sets it back down.

"I don't know what to say, Gracie. None of this was your fault. You've been a superstar. There could have been no justice without you."

"Jesus. Jesus Hell! You're avoiding, Michael! I offer my heart, my soul. My deepest secrets! And you give me back what? Some fucking detached compliments?"

"What do you want me to say? You want me to tell you that if I were eighteen, I could fall hard for you? It's true. But … but, Gracie, I'm not even a little like eighteen any more … And I seem to have lost my heart to …" He shakes his head. Can't say Awasha's name.

She pulls her napkin off her lap, throws it on the table. "Shit! Shit! Shit! How do we get them out of our minds? Everywhere I turn, every time I close my eyes. I hear their voices, see them. All the dead. Especially Lib. Sometimes I even smell them. It's just fucking hard."

"I don't know … I guess I should say that they have gone to a better place. They are not suffering. We have to let them go." *Like Vóvó. Like my mother, Maria. Alice. Awasha. And the living who will never come back. Cassie. Filipa. Tuki.* "We have to believe they are at peace."

"While that bitch is still alive?"

He feels the bullet go through his lung again. "Remember what Teddie Baker said to us in the hospital? 'Justice will be served now. She just takes her own sweet time.' I want to believe Teddie's right."

"You mean like what goes around, comes around? Doc P probably would have some trippy Indian way of explaining that. Circles of life or something."

He stares into his wine glass again. Sees nothing.

"Come on Michael. I need some closure here. Help me."

He lets out a long, slow breath. "I saw Lou Votolatto this afternoon." As soon as the words are out of his mouth he knows they were a mistake. He shouldn't be getting into this with Gracie. Not with her so touchy, so raw.

"So?"

"Yesterday Denise Pasteur confessed."

"To killing Liberty?"

"Manslaughter in the death of Roxana Calderón."

"What about Liberty? Liberty's why we went through this hell."

"It doesn't matter anymore."

"I can't stand this! There's something you're not telling me. Fuck, Michael!"

"The cops found out stuff we didn't know about. Denise Pasteur wanted to be the next head of Tolchester-Coates. She had been promoting herself behind the scenes for years. Back in January the trustees of the school made her an offer in private. They were going to force Sufridge to retire, and crown her."

"What's that have to do with Liberty?"

"The D.A. thinks that history paper you two were doing on the secret societies opened up Pandora's box. On multiple fronts. Danny Pasteur was advisor to the school newspaper. She must have heard about your and Liberty's investigation into the clubs from the student editors or writers. Maybe she even saw that video Liberty had on MySpace, the Old School Bones one."

"You mean it could be the school paper was planning to tap into what Liberty and I found and do their own exposé?"

"She had to have felt threatened, feared you guys would find out about Club Tropical, Roxy … and her. Wreck everything she had been working for. Totally tarnish her in the eyes of the trustees, especially the Red Tooth types."

"Or maybe some of the editors are Red Tooth and they were sworn to protect club secrets. They have a good thing going supplying drugs, right? No Club Tropical to challenge them now. And Red Tooth could be in hundreds of these kinds of schools. Like the goddamn mafia."

"The police are looking into it."

"So Red Tooth killed Liberty after all?"

"The D.A. thinks not. He thinks Red Tooth set up Ronnie Patterson for the drug bust and burned his house. Maybe even beat you in bed that night. And got Awasha fired. All to stop our investigation, shut us down. They thought we were the threat. They didn't know about Denise Pasteur."

"Who felt threatened by us too."

"She saw the big picture. Saw that our investigation was as big a pain to Red Tooth as to her."

"You think Denise Pasteur could have put that awful message in Liberty's physics book and the boast about Red Tooth in the headlines herself … to make Red Tooth look bad? Take the spotlight off her?"

He shrugs. "If she could weasel a car from the Singletons and use it to nearly kill me, I guess she could write a racist threat and doctor some headlines to hide her tracks."

"And kill Liberty."

"We're speculating."

She stares at the plate of *moqueca* in front of her. "That bitch tried to fucking kill us all. I was there!"

For a second he tries to reflect on Denise Pasteur's ambition, decades of anger at an aristocratic male hierarchy, her tortured love life, an abiding jealousy of the boys, a desperate need for credence.

But his head fills with the crack of gun shots again. First one. A second. A third. Fourth.

"She murdered Liberty." Gracie is suddenly sobbing.

"We'll never know for sure," he says. The words just fly out.

"Why? Just tell me why, Michael! Why won't we know?"

"Denise Pasteur hung herself with her sports bra in her cell this afternoon."

"Fuck all!"

Exactly.

EPILOGUE

"SHE really loved it here on Lighthouse Beach," says Ronnie. "I'm glad you could come. I wanted to thank you for everything you did for me and my sister."

"I just tried to help." What else can I say? I'm goddamn dying inside?

"Aquinnah was ground zero for her. But this beach, Chatham, she never got enough of them when we were living out here as school kids. She adored the seals in the winter and spring."

He nods, tries to keep pace with the big Indian striding south at water's edge. Thinks about when he lived over Alice Patterson's liquor store on Main Street, used to walk this beach. "Me too."

He feels the hot sun, southerly breeze on his cheeks, thinks about when he was last here to clear his head. Back in March. The pair of gray seals basking together on a pillow of sand, nuzzling. Nipping. How he felt the urge to bark at them. Feels it again now. Even though the seals are long gone. Following the herring north to colder waters ... It's late June, after all. The solstice. Summer people—couples, families, teenage au pairs with toddlers—replacing the play of seals here on the beach.

"What are you going to do now that the feds dropped your case, Ronnie?"

The Indian shrugs. "I've hauled my pots. Since I got no house anymore, I figure I'll go fishing for a while. I got a site on a sword boat out of Hyannis. We leave Wednesday afternoon with the tide."

He pictures the *Andrea Gail*, her crew. Lost at sea. *The Perfect Storm*. Not George Clooney, not actors in a movie. The guys. Real fishermen. Pros. His father and Tio Tommy met them once at the Crow's Nest in Gloucester when the *Rosa Lee* had come in from fishing Jeffries to repair the ice machine.

"Tough guy, huh, longlining?"

"Oh yeah. Maybe it will keep me out of trouble … They're starting up a twelve-step thing for Iraq War vets in Hyannis. I'm going to try it out when I get back ashore."

"I hear it can help."

The Indian shrugs. "You fishing again?"

"We just got back. Sold off the catch at Friday's auction. I'm rich for a week. Then we go back out. Summertime. Fish when you can."

"Going to stick with it? Take over your old man's boat?"

"He'll never give it up. And my Tio Tommy's mate-in-perpetuity. So … I don't know. I got to find something. You and I got this cop friend says I ought to stay away from the law, claims it'll kill me sooner or later."

"What do you think?"

"I got a pretty toxic score card the last couple of years."

"She wouldn't have cared."

"What?"

"Awasha. She would have stuck by you. Lawyering, fishing, whatever. You were the one she had always been looking for. I could tell!"

He's stuck for words again. Can't say the crazy shit running through his head. *If only I had brought the cops in sooner as Lou had suggested. Maybe the lab would have found Danny Pasteur's prints on the can of Red Bull earlier ...*

Maybe the cops would have searched her apartment at Beedle Cottage and found the vial of GHB she hid under the bathroom sink ...

Maybe before anybody else got hurt, some real detective would have found a way to prove Denise lured Liberty into Awasha's apartment with an offer of Red Bull and sympathy. Then killed her to keep her quiet.

Maybe I wouldn't have to live with this riptide in my chest. This sau-dade. This compulsion to bark until my voice is gone ...

"You believe in ghosts, Michael? What the old Wampanoags call *tcipai?*"

Suddenly she's there. He sees her.

Almost close enough for shouting. Down the beach fifty yards, where the tide pools are filling with the silver sea. Her cheeks sparkling with brine. The wind lifting strands of black hair off her back. She stands in the bright sun balancing between land and sea ... in her yellow fleece pullover. Jeans. One hand on her waist, her eyes fixed on a collage of black shapes slewing, tumbling in the waves in Pleasant Bay. Seals. A congregation of seals ...

"Michael, ghosts?"

"I carry my share."

"You think they're ever any good? You know, any use to us?"

He can hear the shudders of pain in Ronnie's voice. But his eyes are still on the seals, on her.

"Yeah ... I have to. Have to believe ghosts are not just here to torment us. Why? Why do you want to know if I believe in ghosts?"

Ronnie stops. Shuffles his feet in the sand. Looks out. Maybe sees the seals. Smiles. "There was a girl once ..."

"Tell me about it."

DEADLY RIDE

Sam stopped walking halfway down the aisle between the cars.

"Sam?" she called.

Nerves pressed her heart up against her rib cage when he let out a sharp gasp.

She was moving toward him when his hand came out, signaling her to stop. She didn't.

Molly's stomach cramped. It wasn't until she got closer that she saw, in the deep shadows of the barn, that there was someone sitting in one of the cars.

"Jet?" Sam called out. He was still a good four feet from the car, and Molly was behind him, frozen on the cement-covered spot.

"Is he all right?"

When they reached the side of the car, they both stopped, hand in hand by the open door. He looked so normal and peaceful, his head tilted to one side like he'd fallen asleep. But now that they were closer, it was easier to make out the dark stain and swelling on his temple. If it wasn't for the deep gash and the utter, immobile silence, Molly wouldn't have realized he was dead...

Books by Jody Holford

DEADLY NEWS

DEADLY VOWS

DEADLY RIDE

Published by Kensington Publishing Corporation

DEADLY RIDE

A Britton Bay Mystery

Jody Holford

LYRICAL UNDERGROUND
Kensington Publishing Corp.
www.kensingtonbooks.com

LYRICAL UNDERGROUND BOOKS are published by

Kensington Publishing Corp.
119 West 40th Street
New York, NY 10018

All Kensington titles, imprints, and distributed lines are available at special quantity discounts for bulk purchases for sales promotion, premiums, fund-raising, educational, or institutional use.

Special book excerpts or customized printings can also be created to fit specific needs. For details, write or phone the office of the Kensington Sales Manager: Kensington Publishing Corp., 119 West 40th Street, New York, NY 10018. Attn. Sales Department. Phone: 1-800-221-2647.

Lyrical Underground and Lyrical Underground logo Reg. US Pat. & TM Off.

First Electronic Edition: October 2019
ISBN-13: 978-1-5161-0868-8 (ebook)
ISBN-10: 1-5161-0868-X (ebook)

First Print Edition: October 2019
ISBN-13: 978-1-5161-0871-8
ISBN-10: 1-5161-0871-X

Printed in the United States of America

To my editor, John, and my agent, Fran, for believing in this series.
Thank you.

"I choose you over everyone."
—Rainbow Rowell

Chapter One

Molly Owens had a pretty strong grasp on vocabulary, but clearly she misunderstood the word *chilly*. When the locals, including her boyfriend, told her that the seaside town she'd taken up residence in would start getting chilly at the beginning of October, she wasn't concerned. As a former army brat, she'd lived all over and had known cold. She'd seen snow. Maybe she didn't remember it all that well, but she had survived low temperatures. Her brain must have blocked it out like a traumatic memory, though.

When she stepped outside the little cottage she rented behind a bed-and-breakfast, a gust of wind kicked up its heels and danced over every inch of her body. Her dog, a sweet, little, black-and-white fur ball, tugged on his leash, undaunted by the frigid air. He was ready for his morning walk by the beach whether she was or not.

"Oh. My. Goodness." She barely stopped her teeth from chattering. *Chilly* was "Grab a sweater for later when the sun goes down." This was "Where did I put my parka and earmuffs?" weather. Britton Bay, Oregon, was not simply *chilly*.

"It's freezing," she said to Tigger, who continued to tug. Wishing she had gloves, but really wanting to get the walk in, she tugged the sleeves of her jacket down, trying to warm her hands.

Tigger plodded forward, knowing the route from their cottage to the ocean.

She laughed through the shivers. "Okay, okay. Calm down. How are you not cold?"

Giving a bark of enthusiasm, Tigger led the way with his nose, sniffing at every inch of the path they took daily. Molly looked over to a two-story Victorian home. Its gorgeous, soft-blue coloring made it blend with the sky on a perfect day. No one was on the back porch today. *Too cold out.* Anyone smart would have stayed tucked under the covers.

Molly smiled when she thought of the man tucked under her covers. The one who sleepily asked if she'd wanted company for the walk, falling back asleep before she could reply. For someone who ran his own business, one that often saw early customers, Sam did not enjoy early mornings.

Before coming to Britton Bay, Molly hadn't cared one way or the other. She got up for work each day when she'd lived in L.A. Routine and repetition ground out having a preference. Since coming to this little dot of a town on the Oregon coast, though, seeing the sun rise over the water had become addictive.

She and Tigger crossed the quiet road and headed into the thicket of trees that parted only enough to create a walkable path. She'd found the shortcut to the beach her first week here, which was just over five months ago now. *Almost half a year. Where did the time go?* Tigger stopped to investigate what he must have felt was a particularly aromatic patch of flowers. The colorful petals were tipped with ice. The wind was getting stronger now that they were closer to the beach.

"Come on, you." She tugged him toward the rough pine steps that led down to the water. She could hear the waves through the trees. Increasing her pace, she all but jogged down the steps. It was only *just* October now, and they'd had a run of warm, sunny days to close out September. Hopefully, they'd get a few more before winter actually hit.

At the end of the steps, Molly's feet sank into the sand. She pulled in as much fresh air as she could, and despite the *chill*, her smile widened. The sky was a blurry wash of shades—red, orange, and yellow merging and overlapping. The water, deceptively still, shone with the reflection of cloud puffs and color.

Tigger sat on her feet, his favorite spot, and whined, looking up at her. She crouched down and rubbed his side, laughing when he nudged her with his nose.

"Worth the chill and the early hour, huh, boy?"

He yipped at her, then lowered the front of his body, wagging his tail with endless enthusiasm. As they walked the beach—she reveled in the quiet and he reveled in the scents—she thought being here, in Britton Bay, was worth a lot of things.

It was worth the long, roundabout way she'd gotten here. It was strange to think, but sometimes she felt like this little pocket of the earth had been waiting for her to show up and start her life. From the moment she'd arrived, she'd breathed better, her pulse had slowed, and she'd found something she hadn't in all of the other places she'd tried to settle: contentment.

As they scooted up the curve of the beach, taking the walking path up to the pier, Molly saw Bella, who owned Morning Muffins, working on her sidewalk chalkboard sign. Molly watched as Bella, using a bright yellow piece of chalk, made the shape of an L and grinned.

"Please say that's the start of you telling the world your lemon loaf is the special today." Molly pulled Tigger back when he started to prance forward on his back paws in his eagerness to see the baker.

Bella's musical laughter filled the air, and she looked up at Molly. "It's like you're a mind reader. Or sign reader, I guess. Hello, Tigger. Are you ever not happy, bud?" Setting the chalk down, she petted him and laughed again when he went belly-up.

Molly couldn't help but laugh at her pup's shameless bid for as much attention as possible.

"You guys are out earlier than usual," Bella said, returning to her lettering.

Molly crouched and got Tigger to sit with a little more dignity at her side. "I like to be at the paper early on Thursdays but didn't want to miss out on the walk. I don't think I'll ever get tired of the view."

"It's something," Bella agreed. She made a loop for the second L, then glanced over at Molly. "Sam excited about the car show?"

"He is. Stressed, I think, though he wears it well. But it's the first time I've seen him make an actual to-do list." Sam's auto shop was hosting and sponsoring the event, and her even-keeled boyfriend revealed nerves only in the subtlest of ways.

Standing and shaking the cramp out of her legs, she checked her phone and wondered if he was out of bed yet. They both needed to get to their respective jobs.

"It's so nice that we have one more event to look forward to before the town really shuts down for the winter," Bella said.

"It is. The official start is tomorrow, but the event organizers are arriving today. Jill is heading over to Come 'n Get It this evening to interview them."

Bella smiled as she stood up and wiped her hands on her apron. A few years younger than Molly, the baker never wore makeup and always had her hair tucked up in one of those buns that looked prettily messed. Today was no exception.

"I love that Jill is back in town. It's almost like she never left," Bella said. Jill was Sam's cousin and a good friend of everyone's favorite baker.

In typical small-town fashion, the connections among the residents were endless, and Molly realized she didn't feel like an outsider anymore.

"I heard you're offering a decorating class during the show." It was one of the many family-friendly activities being offered during the almost three-day event.

"I am. For kids. I thought it would be a unique way to showcase my food, but also that it would give the kids something to do. My dad used to drag me to car shows when I was a kid, and all I can ever remember thinking was how boring they were." Bella picked up her chalk and tucked it back in the box.

"I've never been to one," Molly admitted. She'd never had a reason before meeting Sam.

Bella glanced at the time through her shop window. "You want some lemon loaf? I need to open up."

"I absolutely do," Molly said. Tigger wagged his tail at the pitch of her voice.

Bella laughed and bent to pet him again. "I think I might have a dog bone for you, mister. Be right back."

* * * *

Lemon loaf in hand, pup leading the way, Molly was wide awake by the time she got back to her cottage. She loved it here, really and truly loved it. Her little house was tucked between evergreens, looking like it had sprouted naturally at the back of the property. It was a one bedroom with its own miniature front garden and a big enough fenced back area for Tigger to run around in.

Thinking she'd need to wake Sam up and resist the temptation of crawling back into bed with him, she was surprised to hear him moving around in the kitchen. She took the leash off Tigger and hung it, removing her shoes while the dog made a mad dash. She walked into the kitchen to the sound of Sam's laughter, and her heart flip-flopped along with her stomach. How could just his laugh brighten her day?

She inhaled sharply, seeing that he was still wearing just checkered flannel pajama bottoms. The smooth skin of his back and biceps, the disheveled state of his hair, and the way he grinned down at her dog was enough to make her mouth water. Yeah, she was definitely in the right place. As someone who was used to moving on, it was interesting to feel such a strong pull to stay.

The tattoo on his shoulder drew her attention, and even as he turned, those gorgeous green eyes zeroed in on her.

"Good morning," he said, his voice a little rough.

A shiver raced over her skin, and it had nothing to do with the weather. She walked to him, set the baked goods on the counter in front of him, and wrapped her arms around his waist. His came around her as though they belonged there, and she held on, breathing in his clean, crisp scent, which was more intoxicating than the ocean's.

"Morning. I wasn't sure you'd be up." She leaned back, accepted the sweet, gentle kiss he gave her.

Her hand moved up his arm, and she traced her fingers over the ink that he'd recently explained the meaning of. She'd wondered about the date, written in roman numerals inside a vintage Route 66 sign.

"Your dad would have loved knowing you brought the Classic Car Crawl here to Britton Bay," she said. Sam had started his auto repair shop using money from his father's life insurance after his passing. Sam spoke of his dad with so much love and respect, Molly was sorry she never got the chance to meet him.

"He would have. He took me to my first one in Las Vegas when I was nine. My mom was mad. Didn't think he should be taking me anywhere near the Strip. But once we got there, all we did was look at cars, and I couldn't get enough." His hands sifted through her hair.

"Jethro and Brian will be getting into town later today," she said, referring to the Classic Car Crawl founders. "Do you know if they're staying at the hotel?" Sam's mom, Katherine, ran the local bed-and-breakfast and hadn't mentioned it.

"Nah. They're staying at the RV park."

Molly scrunched her nose up. "I don't think I'd like knowing that much was behind me when I drove."

Sam grinned. "They've been doing this for over twenty years, driving state to state. They're used to it. And when I say RV, I mean miniature luxury home."

"I think I'm happier with just my Jeep. Unless you want to go camping sometime; then I think I could handle hauling a tent. Though I'd rather stay at a bed-and-breakfast than in either of those."

When he picked up a strand of her hair and played with it between his fingertips, she was momentarily distracted. He was always touching her, like he was part of her, and she was starting to get used to the feeling.

"I have to go. I was thinking I could bring you over some lunch later. You'll be busy. I don't want you to forget to eat."

Sam tugged her closer. "You taking care of me?"

The idea sent a warm feeling through her body, starting at her chest and moving all the way down to her toes. "That okay?"

Pressing his forehead to hers, he closed his eyes, then opened them and pressed a kiss to the top of her head.

Tigger flopped between them, on both of their feet.

Sam looked down. "Hey, buddy. Am I hogging all of the attention?"

Molly laughed and hugged him tight. "He got plenty of attention. From me and from Bella. By the way, your description of October weather was drastically understated."

He let her go and picked up the brown bag on the counter, opening it. "Cold out there? I don't doubt it. Even when the sun is shining, it's like a switch is flipped, bringing out the frost."

Pulling out a piece of lemon loaf, he took a bite. "Mmm. I could start every morning like this."

Molly grabbed a plate from the cupboard for her own piece. "With Bella's baked goods?"

He poked her side with his index finger, then snaked his hand around her waist and pulled her to his side, kissing her temple. "I meant waking up to have you *bringing* me lemon loaf."

Her heart trembled. She'd lived with a man before, and it had ended badly. Though she'd been careful to guard her heart with Sam, he'd easily snuck through all the barriers, and if she wasn't cautious, she'd ignore all of her previously learned lessons and forget about taking it slow. The truth was, she'd love to wake up next to him every day. But the truth was also that they'd only been together less than six months.

Taking the second piece of lemon loaf out of the bag, she grinned at him. "Maybe we can buy it in bulk and freeze it," she suggested.

"Right," he said around another bite. "Except that you're equally addicted to Bella's scones and muffins, so we'd also have to keep those on hand."

He wasn't wrong, and the immediate lurch of her heart settled, her pulse returning to normal. There was nothing wrong with enjoying the little things with Sam—like bringing him lemon loaf after a freezing morning walk. She could think about her future and know he wanted to be in it without second-guessing the thought. She'd never known anyone as loyal and innately kind as Sam. Other than his mother, Katherine, who ran the bed-and-breakfast and had happily welcomed her not only into the cottage, but into her family.

"You look too serious for not even seven a.m. You okay?"

Taking a small bite of the delicious lemon cake, she nodded. "I am. More than okay."

He reached out and stroked a hand down her hair. "Agreed. I need to shower and get to work. We on for later tonight?"

"Yup. Unless you get busy with stuff. But I can help if you need anything." She liked planning their day together.

Sam's smile chased away any residual chill from the morning. He stepped into her and kissed her again, before pulling her tight and burying his nose in her neck. When he pulled back, he kissed the tip of her nose.

"You should probably be careful, Molly Owens," he said with mock seriousness.

"Why's that?" She had to crane her neck to look up at him.

"Breakfast, lunch, and dinner with you? A guy could get pretty addicted to that."

Her heart nearly danced right out of her chest. *See? You're not alone in how you feel.* And since he was so free with his affection and feelings, she could be as well.

Going up on tiptoe, she kissed him, just a gentle brush of her lips across his. "I think I'm okay with that."

When he grinned, gave Tigger an extra rub, and then went to shower, Molly finished her lemon loaf with a grin on her face.

So much to look forward to. After a shaky end to the summer, Britton Bay was settling down again, and Molly was settling right along with it. The car show would be driving into town tomorrow, and she was excited to share in the town's enthusiasm—and, mostly, in Sam's. This was a big event for him. A big deal for his business. Molly couldn't wait to stand by his side as he pulled off one of his dreams.

Chapter Two

When Molly pulled her Jeep into her parking space behind the squat brick building that housed the *Britton Bay Bulletin*, the weather hadn't warmed any. She grabbed her purse and laptop and got out of her vehicle just as Clay East whipped his car into his spot.

She returned the wave he gave through the windshield and headed for the door. Clay wasn't her favorite person. *He's not anyone's favorite person.* Technically, he was their social media director and part-time photographer, but actually, he spent most of his time slacking off and making people uncomfortable. The small staff at the *Bulletin*—including her boss, Alan Benedict—put up with it because they all still felt bad for the loss of his father in June. Vernon East had been the lead reporter at the *Bulletin* for longer than his son, Clay, had been alive.

"Hey, Molly," Clay said, catching up to her. The heavy scent of his cologne didn't mix well with the ocean air. She unlocked the door but wasn't surprised when he scooted in ahead of her instead of offering to hold it open.

"Hi. How are you?" Molly was the one to find Vernon's body, and some nights the memory of that kept her awake, though not as much since Sam had been sleeping beside her. But between the memory of that event and the guilt of mistakenly suspecting Clay as the killer, Molly tried hard to keep the irritation out of her voice.

"Pretty good, according to the woman whose bed I just left," he said with a laugh.

And he made it so difficult. Letting the door close behind them, she didn't hide her eye roll.

"Charming."

"Aw, come on. I was just teasing."

Molly nodded, hoping he'd head straight to his desk and she could avoid him for the rest of the day. She took her time hanging up her jacket and was pleased that Clay was no longer in the small back room. Making her way to the kitchen that sat between the back room and the front office area, she was surprised to see coffee percolating. Elizabeth, their senior reporter, usually kept them all caffeinated, but she was in Vancouver, Canada, visiting relatives for another week.

Grateful she didn't have to make it, Molly grabbed a cup just as Alan came into the kitchen.

"Morning, Molly," he said.

She turned with a hello and a smile. His kind, tired eyes smiled back. With dark hair, peppered by gray at the edges, and his clean-cut suit, he was a handsome man, who was probably about her father's age. He loved his wife, his family, and this newspaper above all other things. Alan Benedict was an easy man to respect.

"Paper looks good. I checked the online edition. The sponsorship page Jill designed looks fantastic in print," Molly said. She turned back to the carafe and poured a mug of coffee, then moved so Alan could top his up.

"She did a great job—with that and all of the other stories she's covered. Unfortunately, I think doing her own stories and covering Elizabeth's right now has worn her out. She called in sick this morning." He filled his cup and then turned and leaned against the counter.

Molly's mind immediately started flipping through the list of things she'd need to switch around and organize to make up for Jill's absence. "That's lousy. I didn't know, but I haven't checked my phone. She probably texted me. I need to call her and ask her about the interviews with the Classic Car guys tonight."

"Do you want me to take the interview?" Alan oversaw everything, but mostly he dealt with the books and corporate sponsorships. He could and would step in for whatever they needed, but as editor in chief, Molly felt it was up to her to fill Jill's shoes.

"I can do it. I just have to juggle a few things," Molly said. She dug in her purse for her phone.

"What are we juggling?" Clay waltzed into the kitchen, heading for the fridge. He poked his head in and stared.

Molly noticed the way Alan's features tightened. He stiffened and pushed off the counter. She found her phone at the bottom of her bag, and sure enough, Jill had sent her three texts.

"We're trying to make sure Jill and Elizabeth's stories are covered. It would be nice if you could keep up on the social media this weekend with the car show. If you can't, I'll hand it over to Hannah," Alan said, referring to his niece.

Clay pulled a day-old box of Bella's treats out of the fridge and nudged the door closed with his hip.

"If Hannah wants it, she can have it. I hate that stuff."

Molly stared, her mouth dropping open. "It's what you're paid to do." Closing her mouth, she wondered if she'd overstepped.

Alan looked at her and gave a slight nod. Looking back at Clay, he shook his head and took his coffee back to his office—a clear signal that Molly was free to deal with their subpar worker as she saw fit.

Clay all but tossed the box on the counter, pulled out a muffin, and bit into it like a petulant child.

Molly set her phone and her coffee down. "Clay, we're all trying to give you the time you need. We know your father's death was hard on you."

His eyes darkened. "Nothing to do with me."

She knew his angry shell was a cover, but, God, he made it difficult to offer sympathy or feel empathy. "Regardless, grieving takes time. However, you opted to come back to work. You're letting a lot of your duties slip, and it's no longer acceptable. I'll have Hannah cover this week's social media because I'd like you to be out taking photographs of the event. But I think you should consider whether or not you want to stay at the *Bulletin*. Whether it makes you happy."

He crumpled the muffin wrapper and shot it across the small space into the garbage can. "You firing me?"

I wish. They were short-staffed as it was. Her preference would be for him to just improve his attitude. "No. Not yet. But there are expectations that come with your position. If you can't fulfill them, we'll have to discuss the outcome. For now, take photos for each of the days, and do what I said. Think about whether this is the place you want to be."

She'd had to consider that very question and was grateful that the answer was a resounding yes. This was her home.

Clay didn't look as certain. "Whatever. Guess I'm working the whole weekend." He popped the rest of his muffin into his mouth and left the kitchen.

Molly sighed. She hadn't even made it to her desk yet. Picking up her phone, she dialed Jill's number. If she was doing the interview, Jill's preliminary research would be helpful. Grabbing her mug and heading for her office, she hoped her coffee wouldn't be cold by the time she got to drink it.

* * * *

The Come 'n Get It Eatery was the reason most of Britton Bay liked to eat out at least once a week. Between the retro-chic atmosphere, the adorable couple that ran it, and the delicious food, it was a popular hangout for residents and visitors of all ages.

Molly waved to the few people she knew and smiled when she saw Calliope James, owner and waitress. With two plates of food in each hand—a feat Molly could not fathom pulling off—the vibrant redhead beamed in her direction.

"Hey, sugar! It's been too long. Grab a seat, and I'll bring you a soda," Calli called, heading toward the window, where bar-style seating allowed customers to gaze out through the front wall of windows.

Molly unzipped her jacket and hung it on the peg beside the booth before she slipped onto one of the padded, blue vinyl seats. Unsure if the two men she'd be interviewing would want dinner, she wondered if she should wait to order or grab something quick before they arrived. Sam would be joining her shortly, so she'd ask what he wanted to do.

Through a storm of coughing and sneezing, Jill had explained that she planned to interview the two men at the diner and invite Sam as well since he'd pulled everything together. It was busier than usual for a Thursday night, and Molly wondered how hard it would be to conduct an interview here.

Calli was at her table a quick minute later and slid into the booth; she sat across the table from Molly, making her laugh.

"My feet are cursing me out," she said, wiping the back of her hand across her forehead.

Molly glanced around. "You guys are jumping. I see you hired a new waitress."

The woman in question was laughing at something a man said to her as she took his order. As a new country song geared up, Calli sighed.

"It's a blessing and a curse. Thought we were done with the tourists, but this Car Crawl has a new bunch of them coming in. Where's your man?"

Molly's cheeks warmed. She and Sam were definitely exclusive, and anyone who knew them knew they were. But it still felt odd, how everyone just sort of knew her business.

"Look at you, blushing like a schoolgirl," Calli teased. "Mind you, I'd blush too if I was getting to kiss Sam good night."

Before Molly could say anything, or turn any redder, Sam appeared beside the booth.

"You'd blush, and I'd have a fist in my face. Pretty sure Dean doesn't want to share you, Calli. And no offense, but I'm a one-woman man."

Great. Molly was going to be the color of ketchup if the two of them didn't stop. The butterflies that her stomach set aside strictly for Sam danced at his arrival.

"Calli, get your cute self back on the floor. We've got orders up, and Molly didn't come to gossip with you," Dean, her husband, called from where he was cooking behind the pass.

The bubbly redhead slid out of the booth and patted Sam's arm as she walked past him. It took effort on Molly's part not to lay her head down on the table and hide from Sam's gaze.

Discarding his own jacket, he slid into the booth across from her and reached out to take both of her hands. "Aw, look at that. You're blushing."

"You guys are horrible. A whole conversation like I'm not even sitting here," she said. She wasn't mad. She wasn't really even that embarrassed. She just didn't know how to get used to everyone chiming in on her relationship. It was probably something she needed to do.

Sam's thumb swept back and forth over her hand and distracted her from her concerns.

"Calli's just teasing you. She wouldn't do it if she thought it bugged you." Sam's eyes softened, and her pulse settled.

"It doesn't. It's just weird, that's all. Having everyone…"

"All up in our business?" Sam gave her a goofy grin that made her giggle. Her embarrassment vanished, and she wished they were home, snuggled on her couch. Instead, he was meeting up with her before Jethro and Brian showed for their interview.

"I don't think you suit that phrase," Molly said, still laughing.

"As long as I suit you, I'm okay with that." He let go of her hand when Calli came back, two sodas on a tray.

"Sorry if I embarrassed you, doll. Can't help it. You two are almost as perfect for each other as myself and Dean."

Molly and Sam laughed, accepting their drinks. "No worries, Calli." He glanced at Molly. "We probably need a minute?"

Molly nodded, and they waited for Calli to head to another table. Sam pulled his hand back and grabbed his soda.

"Hope you're okay with a slight change in plans," he said, bringing the straw to his lips.

She picked up her own, arching her eyebrows in question as she sipped.

"Jethro and Brian just got into the RV park and wondered if we could come to them. Guess they had some trouble on the highway, and they want to settle in for the evening. Once we get started tomorrow, it'll be nonstop, so I said that was fine. I hope it's okay, but I mentioned we were together—that you were doing the interview—and I'd let you know about the switch."

Small-town grapevines were more efficient than any text or tweet. When she didn't answer, Sam frowned and set his drink down.

"Did I overstep?"

"No. Of course not. I'm fine with that plan. I just think it's funny that I didn't even have to speak to them to rearrange things. Small-town communication is something I both fear and admire."

Sam's laugh warmed her insides. He had a great laugh. A great smile. *Focus on your job.* "Do you want to grab a quick bite and then we can head out?"

His grin widened, and he picked up a menu, still looking at her. "Sounds perfect. Thanks for letting me tag along. I've never been behind the scenes on an interview."

Molly pulled her notebook out of her purse and grabbed her favorite black pen. Sam's eyebrow arched.

"Did I say something noteworthy?"

God. His grin was going to forever be a distraction for her...*forever?* Molly smiled.

"You've brought Jethro and Brian to Britton Bay. Jill wanted to interview you as well. Since she's sick, that falls to me."

Calliope came back to their table, her own notepad flipped open, pen at the ready. "What are we having, cuties?"

Molly didn't need the menu to order her favorites—double-dipped, sea-salted fries and a basket of popcorn shrimp. Sam hummed and hawed for another minute, like he didn't know the menu inside out. When he settled on a club sandwich, Calli promised it wouldn't be long.

Sam folded his arms on the table and stared at her expectantly. "No conflict of interest or anything?"

She laughed. "No. I'm just going to ask you about the car show and your involvement. You ready?"

"Shoot."

"From what I read, the Classic Car Crawl has been touring states for over twenty years, but there are other shows, other festivals. Why did you want this show to tour through Britton Bay?"

His smile hinted at a touching memory, but she warned herself not to read into his gestures or expressions based on her status as his girlfriend.

"My dad got me into cars. He loved everything about them, though mostly getting in one and driving. So part of it is nostalgic. My first show was a Classic Car Crawl. Now that I'm in a more stable place with my business, it seemed like a good time to bring the show here, to the place I love."

As she jotted down his words in shorthand, a smile touched both her lips and somewhere deep inside of her at the way he spoke.

The music swelled louder, as did the laughter, and a couple more people—teens—came through the door of the restaurant. Molly focused on the man in front of her, certainly not a difficult task.

"When I looked it up, I saw that the organizers tend to choose small-town venues. How does having an event like this benefit the community?"

He sat back, crossed his arms over his chest, making her eyes wander. When they made it back up to his, he smirked and winked at her. "No conflict of interest, huh?"

Laughing, she shook her head. "Answer the question."

His chuckle made her stomach dance, but he leaned forward again and got serious. "Doesn't seem to matter what hits this town, we stick together. The people of Britton Bay knew my father. They adore my mother, and a few of them are even partial to me."

Molly snorted, then bit her lip.

"They know this means something to me, so they're stepping up. They'll all put their best foot forward to make it a success. I think that Jet and Stoley—those are their nicknames—see the value and the heart in small towns and feed off of it. There's something about that extended family feel that makes something more meaningful. Britton Bay has a lot of that."

When Calli showed up with their plates, setting them down and chatting about the new hire, Molly's mind mulled over what Sam had said. The last few months had been a roller coaster for this small-town family. She had witnessed, firsthand, exactly what Sam mentioned. Good or bad, the folks of Britton Bay had each other's backs.

"Enjoy. You need anything else?" Calli looked at Molly, pulling her away from her thoughts.

"We're all good. Thank you. Oh, actually, are you busy Tuesday?"

"With the new hire, my nights are going to free up after this festival. Why?"

Sam was already digging into his fries. He slid the ketchup over to Molly. "Sarah Elwin? Chris's girlfriend?"

Calli nodded. "The artist, right? I haven't seen her in here yet, but trust me, I've heard about her. Supposedly cute as a button and just as sweet."

Sam shook his head around a mouthful of his sandwich.

"You're not wrong. She's lovely. She wants to try out a paint night with a small group, see what we think and get some feedback. You want to join?"

"Absolutely," Calli said. The bell from the overpass rang, signaling that another order was ready. "Text me and remind me, though."

When she left, Molly picked up a fry and grinned at Sam. "What are you laughing at?"

"Calli cracks me up. She knows everyone and everything." He took a sip of his soda. "It's nice that you're supporting Sarah. I think Chris is pretty gone over her."

They'd hung out as couples a few times, and Molly loved the way Sarah, who was quiet and sweet, pulled out the softer side of Sam's friend, Chris. As a cop, he was naturally suspicious and often overly cautious. He and Molly had butted heads more than once—unintentionally on her part. But she really liked him and was happy he'd found someone he obviously cared about.

"Do you two talk about how crazy you are about your girlfriends when you play poker or go for beers or whatever you two do on guys' night?" Molly popped a delicious, crispy fry in her mouth.

"Sorry. That's top secret. Can't have you disclosing the mystery behind guys' night to your readers."

Laughing, she picked up the ketchup bottle and shook it. "I'm not sure they want to know."

"We'd better eat up and head out to the RV park," he said, looking at his watch.

"The RV park. Another mystery. I haven't been there yet."

"Jet and Stoley have done web posts on their rides. They're decked out. You're going to love it."

She felt his excitement, and it fueled her own. She couldn't wait to meet the two men who'd created something that mattered so much to the man who was quickly claiming ownership of her heart.

Chapter Three

If Britton Bay had four corners, Molly had been to only three of them. She didn't realize, until Sam passed Main Street and the pier, that she'd never explored the entire eastern part of the town.

"I haven't gone past the pier. That's so weird. I felt like I was learning every little nook and cranny of this place, and I'm only now realizing I've left out a whole part of it."

Sam reached for her hand across the console that separated them in his truck.

"You haven't done any camping since you got here. You don't have an RV or a dirt bike, so it's not all that surprising. There are a few trailer and RV parks, and a skate park that used to keep the deputies busy and still occasionally does. Other than that, there isn't much to it."

She watched the ocean whip by out her window and thought about how hot the summer had been—hot enough to make the water a welcome reprieve. *Bet it's icy right now.* Though the weather was somewhat warmer than it had been earlier in the day.

Sam slowed to a stop at a sign that actually read "TOP." The "S" had been worn away, and Molly tilted her head, wondering how such a thing had happened. Weathering? Vandalism? It was interesting nonetheless. Sam took a right, but not before she saw one of the trailer parks he'd mentioned. Along the stretch of road they traveled, there were a few more trailer parks and some scattered, dilapidated houses.

Sam turned left onto a gravel road, and Molly smiled when she saw the bright, happy sign reading BRITTON BAY RV PARK: YOUR HOME AWAY FROM HOME. Excitement swirled in her stomach. Maybe it was an extension of the energy she could feel vibrating off Sam.

"You want me to let you be a fanboy before I get into the questions?" His laughter filled the cab. "Funny girl."

With another quick squeeze, he let go of her hand and stopped at the gate. A teen wearing a Portland Trail Blazers cap looked up lazily from his phone. He took his time standing and opening the window.

"Visiting?" he drawled.

"Lot thirty-eight," Sam answered, lifting up to pull his wallet from his back pocket.

"Ten bucks."

Sam handed the money over, and the teen sat back down, closing the slider window.

Molly laughed when they drove through. "He has about as much enthusiasm for his job as Clay does for his."

Sam glanced her way for a quick second. "Did I hear right? He started using his dad's last name?"

"He did. Seems weird since he still swears his father meant nothing to him." When Molly had started at the *Bulletin*, she hadn't known Vernon and Clay were even related.

The sun was setting in a darkening sky as they drove to the end of the gravel road they'd started on. In the corner, overlooking the water, were two RVs that were so big, other RVs could fit inside of them. Or nearly. One was significantly larger, but both were impressive.

"Wow," she whispered.

"I know. I was reading their blog, and those are both new. They house their cars in the back of their RVs."

"Seriously?" Her mouth was hanging open.

"Yup. Bet you'd camp in one of those," he teased, cutting the engine.

"I think I'd consider living in one of those."

They got out of the truck and met at the front. Sam took her hand, and though she didn't think it presented the most professional picture, she liked the feel of it too much—and how naturally it came to him—to pull away.

Wondering which of the RVs they'd knock on first, Molly was brought up short by the sight of a man reclining in a lawn chair, eyes closed, the brim of his ball cap pulled low, sunglasses shading his face. His feet rested on the metal firepit, which was full of debris and wood pieces. It took her a second for her to realize he must be sleeping because he didn't react to their arrival.

Before they could announce their presence, the door of the RV to their right swung open so hard it bounced off the side. A tall, angry-looking man filled the doorway. His full head of gray hair and thick gray beard hinted at his age, but it was more the road map of lines marring his face that made him seem older. That and the hard set of his jaw. As his eyes swung their way, his face transformed from tough-looking to gentle in a split second.

"Well, hello there. You must be Molly and Sam. Wake up, Stoley. Sorry folks. He naps more than he did when we were younger."

It didn't take much thought to realize that the man coming down the three metal steps, hand stretched out for them to shake, was none other than Jethro Harkaw.

"Jet Harkaw. You're the reporter lady? Would of dressed up had I known you were such a looker."

Behind him, Stoley—or Brian Stoleman—pushed off the lawn chair and gave a low grunt.

"Give her five seconds to get used to you before you hit on her, Jet."

Molly turned her attention back to the man still holding her hand.

"Molly Owens. Nice to meet you."

Jethro was smiling at her in a way that was far too familiar for someone she'd just met. A shiver traveled through her body, but she fought not to react. Now that he was closer and not shaded by the doorway of his RV, she saw the hint of bruising around his right eye. It could be a trick of the light, or lack of it, but the purplish tinge suggested otherwise.

Sam offered his hand, and Molly wondered if it was because he was eager to meet the man or he sensed her discomfort.

"Sam Alderich. Nice to meet you, sir."

Molly was happy when Brian shook her hand in a far more professional way. He and Sam exchanged hellos before Jet clapped Sam on the shoulder.

"Don't call us sir. Makes us feel old. You'll understand one day." His eyes wandered over Molly as he spoke to Sam.

Brian seemed all too aware of the inappropriate way his partner was greeting the woman who planned on writing about them in the local paper, and he stepped between Jethro and Molly.

"Thanks for coming out to us. Been on the road most of the day, and as much as we love cars, I didn't really want to take Mabel out before I need to."

Molly smiled as she and Sam followed Brian to what she assumed was Jethro's RV. Brian gestured for her to go up the stairs, but she stopped beside him. "Mabel?"

He grinned. While he wore his age in the lines on his face as well, they were much gentler and kinder. Less...lecherous. "My car. Your boyfriend didn't tell you all men name their cars?"

Sam laughed behind her and touched his hand to the small of her back. Warmth replaced the chill she'd felt.

"Only when they drive something worth naming," Sam said.

She moved far enough into the RV that the others could follow and close the door behind them. She couldn't stop her mouth from dropping open as she looked around. *This* was the kind of luxury travel she'd only ever read about. While she had no desire to commune with nature or sleep outside, she could definitely see the appeal of touring around in this mini-mansion.

They'd stepped into the living area, which was a combination of a sitting area and kitchen. Plush white couches lined a wall under covered windows. The dark-paneled flooring made the white furniture seem even more grand. A stainless-steel fridge, stove, and dishwasher worked to make an L shape that defined the kitchen area, and there was a small bar-style countertop, complete with black leather swivel stools underneath.

"This is just breathtaking," Molly said.

"I've been inside a few, but none like this," Sam added. He stuck close to her back while Brian took a seat and Jet went to the fridge.

"It's something, all right. After you travel in one of these, you never want to go back," Jet said. He pulled a couple of bottles of beer from the fridge and held them up to Sam and Molly.

Molly shook her head. "I'm fine, thanks."

"I'm good, too." Sam's fingers brushed hers.

Jet shrugged and handed one to Brian, who accepted. "Bought this baby from the place where Dolly Parton bought hers. They cut me quite the deal when I said I'd be advertising them across the country."

Molly looked at Brian, who'd crossed one leg over his knee and leaned back, clearly less focused on the need to impress. "Yours must be just as beautiful."

He nodded and hooked a thumb toward Jet. "It is. Paid less than this guy, too, because I don't need bragging rights."

Jet's loud laughter filled the space. "Come sit down, darlin'. You're going to ask us a bunch of questions, you need to be cozy."

He sat, leaving room between him and his partner, then actually patted the seat beside him. Molly moved toward the kitchen countertop, and Sam followed.

"If you don't mind, I'll sit here. The hard surface makes it easier to work," Molly said.

Sam leaned against the counter beside her, and she leaned in to speak quietly. "Do you want to sit here?"

"I'm good. You do your thing." His jaw was tight, and his expressive eyes were dark, not the usual expression for him.

Molly pulled her notepad and phone from her bag and swiveled the chair so she was looking at the two men, who physically were similar but gave off very different vibes. Both had gray hair, but Brian's was cropped close, which suited the hint of stubble on his wide jaw. Jethro's hair was wilder and complmented the thick beard he sported. From a glance, they could be mistaken for brothers.

"Let's start with you telling me a bit about yourselves and your love for cars," Molly said. She didn't think she'd record most of the conversation, but she kept her phone out in case she changed her mind.

Brian sat forward, took a long swallow of his beer, then rested his forearms on his jean-clad knees. "Hard to talk about one without mentioning the other. My daddy sat me down at my first engine when I was three years old. Loved everything about cars ever since."

Jet also took a long drink of his beer but didn't look reflective or sentimental when he spoke. "Couple of things make a woman turn her head. Cars, motorcycles, and money. I've got all three." He grinned like he'd just told her he'd won a Pulitzer.

Pulling in what she hoped was a subtle breath, Molly did her best to respond as an unflappable reporter. "It's not uncommon for teenage boys to try to impress women. Would you say, since your fascination with vehicles started so long ago, that this would have been one of the reasons behind your interest?"

Jethro chuckled and extended his arm along the back of the couch cushions. "Absolutely. Didn't hurt that I was good with my hands. Never cared much for school and knew early that I wouldn't be going to college. Working with cars brought in decent money. Working with old cars—classics—brought money and satisfaction."

Jotting down notes, very aware of the tension evident in Sam's body beside her, she smiled up at Brian. "Even with all of the new fancy gadgets and sleek styles, classics are still your preference as well?"

Brian's smile was nothing short of grandfatherly. "Absolutely. I'll take a classic over new any day of the week. When I love something, it's forever. Won't see me changing my mind. I'm a Chevy man, and I like speed and convenience, but I'll take a classic Mustang over a new one every time."

Sam murmured an agreement. "Can't make them like they used to."

"You got it, son," Brian said.

They chatted a bit longer about cars, favorites, their blog, and the show before Molly slipped into more personal questions. Human nature would have readers wanting to know who the men behind the cars were.

"Being on the road so often must make having a family life tricky. How do you navigate that?"

Jet finished his beer and got up for another. "Never let your women run into each other. That's the trickiest part," he said. He laughed loudly as he opened the fridge and pulled out a second bottle.

Brian groaned. "You better finish up your interview, dear. He's this obnoxious after one; you don't want to see him after a few."

His smile was tight, but he spoke without rancor toward his partner.

Molly tried to smile, but she wasn't sure Jet was joking, and she had more questions. "Are either of you married?"

"I'm on my second," Jet replied, taking his seat. "Likely my last. Was married close to thirty years to my first wife. And while I like the classics, let me just say, that works better with cars than with women."

Though Molly was able to bite her tongue, Sam's growl of irritation did not go unnoticed. Jet laughed and leaned back again. Brian shifted in his seat but kept his eyes down, focused on peeling the label off his bottle.

"Don't get all upset, son. I'm just joking with your girl. I love my wife. First one, well, I loved her, too. Just not enough to stay married to her."

"I've never married. Didn't seem fair since, as you said, we spend so much time traveling. And as you can tell, having this one here as a partner, it's like having a full-grown toddler around to watch over. No time for the commitment marriage takes."

Molly smiled at the attempt to lighten the mood, but she was finished. Oddly enough, as much as she hadn't enjoyed the interview, she was glad Jill had been too sick to do it. If she hadn't been, Sam's cousin would have ventured out here alone tonight, and though she had no doubt Brian was a good man, she couldn't say the same for Jet.

Molly closed her notebook and tucked it into her bag, along with her phone and pen. When she stood, Sam's hand went immediately to the small of her back again, like that's where it belonged.

"Thank you for your time, gentlemen. We should let you rest up for tomorrow. Should be a fun weekend."

She wasn't entirely sure she believed her own words. They left the RV, and as Jet and Brian walked them to Sam's truck, she stopped and turned, then looked at Jet.

"One more question. How'd you get that black eye?"

Brian's eyes widened marginally. Sam, who was opening the passenger door for Molly, stopped as well. In the overhead lighting of the RV park, she saw Jet's quick glance at Brian before he met her gaze.

"I'm old and clumsy. What can I say? Walked right into my closet door. Those RVs are roomy, but they aren't a house, you know?"

Molly nodded like she believed him. Back in the truck, on their way into town, Sam pulled over on a quiet stretch of the road.

"You okay?" She turned in her seat to see him.

He put the truck in park and undid his seat belt. Taking her hand, he kissed her palm, sending shivers up her arm and chasing away the last vestiges of an unpleasant experience.

"I need you to know that for all of the years I spent admiring those two, all of the time I've wanted to bring this show to Britton Bay, I had no idea that Jethro Harkaw was such a chauvinistic pig."

Molly smiled her first real smile in over an hour. She undid her seat belt as well and leaned across the console, putting her free hand to his slightly scratchy jaw.

"That is not something you needed to say for me to know it. The kind of man you are shines through every single day, Sam. I'm sorry that one of the two men you looked up to seems unworthy of your admiration."

He pressed his cheek into her palm, closed his eyes, and inhaled like she did sometimes. Like he was trying to breathe her in.

When he opened his eyes, he stared at her with the kind of intensity that made her stomach twist up in knots at the thought of not being with him. He'd really done a number on her resolve to stay single and unattached. And he was completely worth it.

"I would never knowingly admire a man who talks that way about women, and to be honest, I'm a little appalled that I have to spend a good portion of the weekend in his presence."

"Brian didn't seem so bad."

His smile was only a smidge of its usual brightness. "Silver lining."

He leaned forward and kissed her long enough to make her forget what they were talking about. When he pulled back and rested his forehead against hers, he asked, "Your place or mine?"

She sighed. "Doesn't matter. As long as we're together."

He gave her another quick kiss. "My thoughts exactly."

Chapter Four

A year earlier, Molly had spent a long afternoon trailing her now ex-boyfriend around the Lancaster Auto Mall. It was a mind-numbing activity—one she knew the outcome of before they spent hours checking out the interiors and exteriors of overpriced vehicles she'd never buy. That memory, along with purchasing a couple of gently used cars before splurging on her Jeep, was the extent of Molly's experience with cars.

So, as she stood outside the large, barnlike building that was to be the Classic Car Crawl display room on Friday evening, she was completely blown away. Standing along the sidelines with what felt like half of Britton Bay, she watched car after car, types she'd never seen, roll into the structure.

There were two outbuildings on the multiacre fairgrounds. This one, the older of the two, had double doors on either end, opened to allow the exhaust from the vehicles to escape. The drivers were to drive through the doorway and park in an assigned spot. Sam had reached out to the high school, who'd recommended kids for volunteers. Each car owner had at least one student who would basically be their host for the weekend in Britton Bay. This included knowing their assigned spots, helping to keep the owner on the schedule Sam had created, and giving them a thank-you card and small gift at the closing ceremonies on Sunday. Like the cars, this event was a fine-tuned machine.

Sam had a microphone and was chatting about the car in front of them, a 1952, baby-blue Chevrolet Bel Air. Molly started to list the awards each vehicle had won, but decided that not only were such accounts too tedious, they weren't what would really capture the *Bulletin* readers' attention. Using one of the two newspaper cameras, she took a photo, as she'd done with the twelve cars preceding this one.

Molly was enjoying listening to Sam's voice tell the audience about the vehicle and the owner. He had a strong, quiet cadence that was made for storytelling. It wasn't until the next car, however, the one idling as it waited to pull forward, that she'd realized he had a preference.

When the next in line pulled forward—a shiny, navy-blue one with a thick, white pinstripe down the hood—she heard the change in his tone.

"And this, ladies and gentlemen," Sam said, a smile tilting the corners of his lips, "this here is a 1965 Shelby Cobra. The sleek lines and curves, along with the 306-horsepower engine, were made for speed. Our driver, there, Brad Templeton, has tested the theory and is the first-place winner of several classic car races across the states. This one is a thing of beauty."

Molly grinned in Sam's direction. He caught her eye, and the look of pure joy on his face sent butterflies somersaulting around in her chest. He was adorable. She'd definitely be teasing him later about whether or not he'd drooled on the microphone as he introduced this one. The driver, Brad, waved to the lines of people on both sides as he revved the engine.

After watching a few more cars load in, Molly decided to chat with some of the drivers who'd parked in the building and were milling about their vehicles as the rest loaded. People walked past in either direction, moving in pairs and small groups as they laughed and talked. Molly didn't spot anyone else with a press badge, but that didn't mean they wouldn't show. For now, she had the advance scoop. By tomorrow, a few of the outside media sources would swoop in and get their sound bites.

Heading along one side of the long barn, Molly smiled and waved to a few people she recognized. It still surprised her how many of the townspeople she didn't know. Britton Bay seemed so small—especially when everyone knew everyone's business, including hers and Sam's—but really, there were over five thousand people in this area, and she couldn't know them all.

As she neared the back of the barn, Brad, the driver of the Cobra—what a weird name for a car, she thought—was leaning against one of the open doors. He was chatting with another man who Molly was pretty sure drove one of the first convertibles that had parked. The pale purple one. The inside of the barn was a rainbow of vehicles.

She approached the two men. Brad, who looked to be younger than a lot of the other guys, smiled at her, and his eyes wandered to her press lanyard.

"Hi, there," he said. He smoothed a hand over his dark beard. Little wisps of gray poked through, just like at his temples.

"Hi," Molly said. Before she could introduce herself, the other man, who was the kind of bald that made a person wonder why they didn't just shave off the last few tufts, stuck his hand out.

"Hi, there. Wondered if there was any press in this tiny place. I'm Herman Besbrewer. 1963 Ford Galaxie."

Brad stuck out his hand. "Brad Templeton. 1965 Shelby Cobra."

Molly bit the inside of her cheek, shook both hands, and then said, "Molly Owens. 2005 Jeep TJ. Also, editor for the *Britton Bay Bulletin*."

Both men laughed, so Molly felt comfortable with the joke she'd made. Her Jeep might not be a classic, but she loved it, though perhaps not as much as these men loved their cars. She wasn't planning to name it or anything.

"Do you two mind if I ask you a few questions for our local newspaper?"

Herman nodded his head as Brad pulled out a vape stick. Molly worked not to scrunch up her nose at the sight. It always surprised her how an action, a harsh word, or a particular habit could change the level of someone's attractiveness. While a moment ago she'd thought him handsome in a cowboy sort of way, now she planned to make her questions quick. She jotted down both of their names and vehicles, double-checking the spelling.

"Have either of you ever been to a Classic Car Crawl event before?"

"This is my fifteenth one," Herman said. He gazed over to his vehicle and smiled. "You build an extended family at these events. When too much time goes by in between, it feels like you're at a reunion." She could feel the family and friend vibe. These people, men and women alike, were in their element, and they were ready for a good time.

A small smirk played behind Brad's beard. "I haven't been around that long. I inherited the Cobra from my dad after he passed away two years ago. But I've attended several events. This is the second time I've been to one of these. This'll be the year I take best newcomer, though. Unless someone has already greased Jet's palm." He inhaled deeply on his metal stick and blew out the vapor.

"You just don't let things go, do you?" Herman said, laughter in his tone.

"Not when I'm getting ripped of titles," Brad said. There wasn't any laughter in his words.

He didn't appear angry, but he wasn't joking. Molly tilted her head, gave him a minute to gather his feelings, then asked, "Are the awards and trophies a big part of this for you guys?"

She'd need to make a note of the cars that were recognized. Sam would have a list.

Herman shoved his hands in his pockets, stepping out of the way of Brad's puff of vapor. "For me, like I said, it's the family and friend aspect.

I like getting out here and meeting up with people who understand how much I love my car. Some of my best memories are from the times I've spent in Harriet."

Molly grinned, remembering what Brian had said about naming his car. "That's your car?"

Herman nodded, smiling unabashedly. Molly turned to Brad. "Yours have a name?"

He nodded, his eyes scanning the crowd milling around the cars. "Of course. Winnie. Short for Winner."

One-track mind, she thought.

"Does it affect your desire to come back and participate in the show when you don't get the accolades you feel you deserve?"

His eyes lasered in on hers, startling Molly with their intensity. "I'm here because my car deserves to be shown. To be shared. You don't keep that kind of beauty to yourself. My daddy did that, and it was a waste. But a lot of these things, they're popularity contests more than accurate judgments of how fine a machine is."

Herman clapped Brad on the back. "Boy, you've been to two of these. I was attending these events while you were still in diapers. Knock the chip off your shoulder, and enjoy it for what it is." Herman waved a hand around them. "Look at these beauties. I've known Jet and Stoley a long time now. You might not like 'em too well, but they're good guys, and they know their cars."

Brad rolled his shoulders and tucked his vape stick back in his pocket. "You're right. I'm just tense from the long drive, I guess." He flashed Molly a genuine smile, making her realize the others had been forced. "Driving usually relaxes me, but I got lost on the way. They don't exactly have Bluetooth and GPS in these babies. To answer your question, the trophies don't matter much, but the recognition? Yeah, it's important. As much as these people are like family, I don't really wanna be the middle child who always gets looked over."

Molly didn't know what to say to that. It was such a strange way to look at an event she'd thought was just for fun. Clearly, it mattered on a whole other level to some of the players.

Several more people began to mill about, and when Molly peeked into the barn, she saw they'd finished loading it.

"They really are beautiful," Molly said. Both Brad and Herman turned their bodies to look.

Herman nodded, crossing his arms over his chest. A satisfied smile spread over his face. "Damn right they are."

There were twenty-four classic vehicles, all different colors or shades. Some convertibles, some hardtops. All shiny and gleaming from front to back. Sam was winding his way up the middle, and she figured she should interview a few of the other drivers.

"Thank you for your time, gentlemen," she said.

"Anytime," Herman said. He smiled and walked toward Jethro, who Molly saw was standing by one of the convertibles, laughing with another man.

Brad shoved his hands in his pockets, and Sam neared. "They'll all tell you the accolades don't matter, but everyone wants their fifteen minutes, you know?"

She turned her head, looked at Brad. "What's your end goal? Where do you see yourself and your vehicle landing?"

He smiled, like he admired her ability to read into him. "I want my own show on television. One of those reality deals. Taking classics apart and putting 'em back together. Maybe even a traveling one where I find hidden gems that have been hiding away in some backwoods county. I've talked to Jet about it. He said I'm young yet, but I'm approaching forty. Once you get to be their age, everything seems young."

He smiled when he said it, but he sobered immediately. "The more awards I win, the better it looks on my CV. This is one of the bigger, more elite events. But it's not enough just to be part of it. You need to stand out. Jet and Stoley have become complacent. It's more of a good ol' boys club than a proper festival. Jet never does what he says he will. Told me he'd give me his seal of approval if I got myself a meeting with some television execs."

Interest piqued, she glanced over and saw that Sam was shaking hands with someone. Turning back to Brad, she didn't waste time and asked, "Did you get a meeting?"

Brad inhaled from his vape stick, and Molly schooled her features so she didn't appear impatient.

"I did. Jet's idea of helping me out was telling them I was a newbie but had potential."

Which likely killed his deal if the bitter tone told a story. She didn't get to ask a follow-up question, but it wasn't the story she wanted to tell anyway.

Sam approached, his smile shining like a beam of sunlight. "Hey," he said. He didn't lean down to kiss her because she had her press badge on, but he stood close to her side.

"Hi. You look like you might burst with excitement," she said.

Sam grinned at her, then turned to Brad. "Sam Alderich. I own Sam's Service Station and organized the event. I'm really glad you're part of it. Love your car, man."

Brad preened at the praise. Molly nearly laughed. Her man—as Calli would say—was adorable. And clearly in his element.

"You want to take her for a spin? We'll be doing some driving later, right?" Brad asked, returning Sam's shake.

Molly watched Sam's jaw drop. It took him a minute to find his words. "I...that...I really want to."

Brad clapped him on the shoulder and laughed. He pulled the vape pen out of his pocket again. "I'll find you a bit later. Nice to meet you, man. Molly, a pleasure."

When he turned, Sam stepped closer, glanced down at her lanyard, and hesitated. She ignored his concern and stepped into him, wrapping her arms around his neck. His hands came to her hips, and he leaned down to accept the kiss she offered. When she pulled back, they were still nose to nose.

"You look like a kid who woke up in Santa's workshop."

Even his laugh was tinged with excitement. "That's how I feel. It's going great. I was worried last night," he admitted.

"I know. You tossed and turned for most of it."

His forehead touched hers. "Sorry."

Tightening her arms around him, she pressed closer. "Please don't be. I'm so glad today is going well. I should interview some of the others."

He nodded, but neither of them dropped their arms. Sam lowered his head and gave her a sweet kiss that intensified the already blooming happiness inside her chest. When he pulled back, she blinked several times. He had a way of making her forget where she was.

"I'm glad you're here," he said, one hand rubbing up her back and sifting into her hair.

"Me too. But we'd both better get back to work," she said. Molly was all too aware of Sam's ability to draw her focus. He did so without even trying.

"Meet up with you later?" Stepping back, he ran a hand down her arm, taking her fingers in his and pressing a kiss to her palm.

"You got it. I'll either be interviewing drivers or seeing how many of Bella's mini donuts I can eat without making myself sick."

His laughter floated behind him even when he'd wandered back into the fray of drivers and observers. Molly smiled and decided donuts first, interviews second. As she drifted through the crowd, she wondered if tomorrow would be busier. Sam had put a lot of hard work into this weekend, and from what she'd seen so far, it was likely to go off without a hitch.

Chapter Five

Molly had been to several Britton Bay celebrations—there'd been a wedding a couple of months ago, the end-of-summer festival, and a number of outdoor markets and activities since she'd arrived. She'd never seen a crowd like the one dancing inside the heritage-style barn on the fairground property. She'd thought the night before couldn't be beat.

The drivers had done some showing off with their vehicles, inside and out. To Molly, it was a bit too much of the same, but she enjoyed watching Sam drive Brad's car. It was a highlight for her, and she planned on framing the picture she'd taken of him behind the wheel.

The day had been successful as well. While Molly had wondered if it would be all about the cars, it was more of an all-ages event. Families showed up from other counties, people toured the car barn, drivers talked about their cars, chatted about the businesses many of them owned. It was a cross between the biggest social event she'd seen here and a cross-county networking session.

A platform stage against the far wall had been set up for a four-man band. The lead singer was blasting out an Old Dominion song like his voice was made for the lyrics. Molly sang along, leaning against the wall, taking it all in, and then realized, when the chorus hit, that in less than six months, Britton Bay had turned her country.

Fortunately, years of her dad's rock playlists blaring through the car speakers as they traveled from one place to the next ensured she'd never be a full convert.

Sarah, who was newer in town than Molly, joined her at the back of the room. "I can't believe how busy it is," she hollered over the music.

Molly nodded in agreement, leaning in. "I think the entire town is here, in addition to folks from a few other counties."

The ones who weren't dancing to the music were outside selling or sharing their products or enjoying the action. There were four bouncy houses for kids, face painting, games, a small midway, and an assortment of food options, including Bella's and Calli's. Things were wrapping up shortly, but people were still having a great time.

Sam had been running himself ragged for a full two days. The evening before had been all about the cars, and today was all about the socializing. Since Jill was still sick and Elizabeth was away, Molly took notes for stories and snapped photos. She was pleasantly surprised Friday evening and earlier today to see Clay walking around taking pictures.

"Sam and Chris were grabbing a bite to eat when I closed up my table. Sam was doing rounds with all the vendors, checking in," Sarah said.

Of course he was. He was going to crash tomorrow evening. Sarah pushed a hand through her light brown, pixie-cut hair. Once upon a time, Molly had thought of cutting her dark auburn tresses short, but she didn't have the bonus features Sarah did that helped her pull it off—angular cheekbones, dark lashes, and bright green, happy eyes.

"I figured Chris would be working the crowd," Molly said. The music stopped, and the crowed clapped and cheered. A security firm was working the event, but to her knowledge, Chris was never truly off duty.

Molly's ears were ringing. "Why don't we go outside?"

They walked side by side, through the crowd, waving and saying hello to people.

"You know everyone. I've been here almost three months, and I know you, Chris, and Sam." Sarah laughed.

Molly smiled. "You know more than that. And you'll get to know people better on Tuesday. I've invited a bunch of the women I know. Katherine— that's Sam's mom, Calli from the diner, Bella, who you know, Sam's cousin Jill, and one of my co-workers, Hannah. She's seventeen and is going to try and get her mom to come. It'll be a full house."

Sarah's smile was nearly as bright as the stadium lights shining over the fairgrounds. She started to respond but was bumped, hard, from the side. Tripping, she knocked into Molly, who was barely able to steady herself before banging into someone else.

"I am so sorry, darlin'," a thick voice drawled. The sound alone made Molly's skin quiver unpleasantly.

Turning her head after apologizing to the woman she'd almost crashed into, she saw Jethro looming over Sarah, his giant hands gripping her shoulders.

"You okay, beautiful girl?" He lowered his face, bent his knees, and Molly frowned. Saying sorry was one thing, but he was practically holding her up against him, and that was not.

"I think she's okay, Jethro," she intervened.

Sarah nodded, her mouth in a tight, grim line. "I'm fine."

Jethro loosened his hold, but only to move his hands up and down Sarah's arms. His eyes wandered. "You are definitely fine."

Molly's jaw dropped open, and her stomach sank. Before she could say anything, she felt and sensed Sam at her back.

"Everything okay here?" He moved to her side, his fingers touching hers. He held two cans of soda in his other hand. The hard expression on his face, the tight set of his jaw, surprised Molly. It wasn't typical for him to show anger, but he was clearly beyond irritated.

Chris, one of Britton Bay's deputies and Sam's good friend, quickly and confidently extricated his girlfriend from Jethro's hold.

"You okay?" His eyes were on Jet, and they weren't friendly. Molly knew that Chris, like Sam, was even-tempered and friendly. But his badge made him wary of people in a way she and Sam weren't. He did *not* like Jethro's hands on his girlfriend.

"I bumped into this gorgeous woman, and I was just making sure she was okay. I'm Jethro Harkaw." He put out a meaty hand, and Chris shook it, his expression not softening.

Jet put his hands in his pockets and turned to Sam. "Quite the turnout."

Sam placed his hand on the small of Molly's back, and she leaned into him. "I'm pleased with it. There are lots of out-of-towners. We hit the right crowd with our advertising. Brian was chatting with one of my mechanics and said this was one of the best and liveliest events he's seen."

Jethro looked around. "Yup. I'd have to agree. Definitely going to have to come back here some other time." His eyes roamed over Molly and then Sarah before he spoke again. "Excellent view no matter where you look."

Chris stepped forward, his eyes dark and his stance rigid. A woman Molly didn't know—one she'd have remembered if she'd met—sidled up to Jethro. In her low-cut, pale-pink tank top, she was underdressed for the breeze in the air. Thick, teased, and curly brown hair fell over her shoulders when she leaned into the tall man, pressing her front to his side. Jethro's eyes lit up when he looked down, his arm snaking around her shoulders immediately.

"Well, hi there, darlin'. I thought I'd lost you to the band. I know how you like to dance," Jet said, a warm affection in his tone. He looked at the four of them, staring at him, and gestured to the woman. "This is my wife, Amber."

Molly nearly choked. Amber looked more like she could be Jethro's daughter.

Her cherry-red lips tipped up in a smile. "He gets a kick out of saying that, but I know better than to leave him too long. He's a horrible flirt."

No one said anything. Amber turned to Jethro, her hand on his chest, and batted thickly coated eyelashes at him. "Come dance with me. The night is almost over, and you've been too busy."

With a grin that made Molly's stomach clench uncomfortably, Jethro waved a hand.

"Happy wife, happy life. Am I right?"

Neither Chris nor Sam said anything in response, but Molly caught the look they exchanged.

"I think I need a shower," Sarah said. The sound of the band starting up again drifted around them, but at least they could hear each other speak without shouting.

"Sorry about that," Sam said.

Molly looked at him and reached for his hand. "Why on earth would you apologize?"

"Yeah, man, that guy's creepiness isn't on you," Chris said, his arm sliding around Sarah's shoulder to pull her close.

Sam frowned, his brows furrowing together in a way that made Molly want to hug him and smooth out his concerns. "I guess I'm just disappointed to find out what he's really like. Every time I've interacted with him since Thursday, it's been a disappointment."

"That's not your fault, Sam," Sarah said.

He smiled, but it wasn't his usual. "This is the band's last set. Most of the vendors have shut down, but I'm going to do one more walk around, make sure. I need to chat with security, too, make sure they're ready to do a final walk-through."

"I'll help. I can chat with security if you want," Chris offered.

Sam looked at Molly, his head dipping to touch her lips. "I'll see you a bit later?"

"Of course. Anything I can do?" She wanted to put a real smile on his face but worried that wouldn't happen until this weekend was over.

"You want to check in with the band? I already paid them, but just make sure they don't need anything before they go?"

"No problem." When he pulled back, she went up on her tiptoes and kissed him again.

He took a minute to wrap his arms around her and give her the hug she'd wanted to give him.

"Sometime tonight, man. You're not the only one who wants to take their girl home," Chris said, shoving Sam's shoulder when Molly released him.

Sam laughed, as did Molly and Sarah.

"Meet you at the front of the barn when we're done," Chris said, pressing a kiss to Sarah's forehead.

When the guys walked away, Sarah and Molly wove their way back the way they'd come, following the steady thump of the drums.

"I don't think I'm supposed to fall so fast," Sarah murmured.

Molly turned her head, looking at her smitten new friend, and realized they had more in common than she thought. "I hear you. Trust me."

As they made their way back into the crowded barn, the music drowned out any further conversation. The music slowed, and Molly noted that several couples had taken the dance floor, including Calliope and Dean. They must have closed down their booth already. She couldn't help smiling at the way they stared into each other's eyes as they swayed back and forth. Not too far from them were Katherine and the town sheriff. Though Sam was coming to terms with his mother dating, Molly was glad he'd missed this view—the two of them impossibly close, smiling at each other under a thousand twinkling lights as the lead singer sang about falling in love.

Molly and Sarah split up. Several couples were heading out the door, their happy energy pulsing in the vibrant room. It had been a long night, but other than the unfortunate run-in with Jet, a very pleasant one. Molly was looking forward to crawling into bed and curling up with Sam and Tigger, who liked to lie right between them.

Moving behind the enormous speakers, hoping to catch the lead singer as soon the song was over, Molly stopped short. She recognized the back of Jethro, but she was pretty sure the woman he was pressed up against was *not* the wife she'd met ten minutes ago.

This woman, who Molly could barely see thanks to Jethro's wide back and shoulders, was wearing a long-sleeved floral-print shirt, and an almost white blond braid was in Jethro's fist. If the way her hands clutched the back of his shirt was any indication, this woman did not mind. Backing away slowly, hand covering her mouth, as if she might make a sound they could hear over the thump of the music, Molly made her way back to the sidelines of the makeshift dance floor.

Looking through the crowd, she couldn't spot Sarah. Molly figured she'd meet up with her friend the next day if she didn't run into her again tonight. The room was emptier than it had been only a little while earlier, so it was easier to see. Maybe she'd gone outside. Molly decided the band would contact Sam if they needed anything else. Unsure if it was the combination of perfumes and colognes mingling with sweat or what she'd just seen, Molly was desperate for some fresh air.

Outside the barn doors, she inhaled deeply. Jethro Harkaw was a one-man soap opera. Molly was glad he and his partner were only staying for the weekend. Leaning against the side of the red barn, she stared up at the sky. The stars danced like they could hear the music, and her stomach began to settle.

"I never take the time to stop and look at the stars. Wish I'd learned to hit pause at your age," Brian Stoleman said, walking toward her.

Aiming for a smile, she was pretty sure what she gave was more of a grimace. "They're beautiful. Hard to miss." Though she'd missed them plenty when she'd lived in a bigger city. Now, she couldn't imagine looking up and not seeing them.

"You're not wrong. Quite an evening. It's a nice town you've got here," Brian said.

Molly bit down on the urge to thank him for the compliment. "I love it here. You ever get tired of traveling?"

Kicking the toe of his boot into the gravel, he shoved his hands into the pocket of his leather bomber jacket and looked at the ground. "Off the record?"

As though a match was held to a flame, her interest sparked. "Sure."

He looked up, his eyes meeting hers. "This'll be my last ride. I'm tired of touring around. I'm getting too old for this…"

Molly wasn't sure how he planned to finish that sentence, but she had several ideas on what it was he was tired of. "What will you do next?"

People started coming out of the barn in pairs and groups. The music had stopped, but voices filled the air. Brian stared up at the stars she'd been studying.

"I've got a sister in Nashville. A couple of nieces and nephews. Might head there."

He sounded so…lonely that Molly's heart ached. How did two men who were so incredibly different form a bond that spanned decades?

"I think you're never too old to figure out what you want," Molly said softly.

Brian smiled at her. "Oh, I've known for years what I want. What you learn, when you get to be my age, is you don't always get what you want. So you make do with what you have. Fortunately for me, I don't need much more than Mabel and the open road."

They settled into a reasonably comfortable silence, looking up at the stars. She glanced his way when he pulled on light-gray, wool gloves. He gave her a sheepish expression. "It's cold here. Old man like me, lousy circulation, my fingers turn into ice."

She laughed. "I didn't expect it to be this cold here either. I used to live in California. I don't even own gloves."

He smiled, and they went back to star gazing. Molly was thinking she should give her parents a call—it had been too long—when loud laughter barked out from behind her.

"There you are. Wondered where you'd slunk off to," Jethro said, breaking away from the throng of people he'd exited the barn with.

"I was just saying good night to my girl," Brian said, smiling at Jet.

Jet looked at Molly. "That's what we call our cars. Our girls. Mind you, they're having a big old sleepover tonight, aren't they? You have a favorite, Molly?"

Every time one of the cars had passed during the parade the evening before, she'd thought, *that's the prettiest one*. Then the next one would roll into the space, and she'd change her mind. All of the cars were nothing short of beautiful, and that was the opinion of someone who knew nothing more than color preference when it came to vehicles.

"I tried to choose one yesterday but just couldn't. The only conclusion I came to was that if I were to pick, it'd have to be a convertible." Feeling like she should slip back into work mode, she asked, "Tomorrow is prizes and closing ceremonies?"

"You got it," Jethro said, glancing around over Molly's head. It was hard not to wonder who he was looking for in the crowd. His wife or his mystery kisser. His gaze came back to her face. "Last run of the year. We tuck 'em up tight for the winter after this. Makes me restless just thinking about it."

Brian clapped him on the shoulder. "Breathing makes you restless."

Both men shared a hearty laugh while Molly stifled a yawn. Time to call it a night.

She stared to say just that when Jet's eyes widened, and he looked at Brian. "Uh, do me a favor? Candice is here. Best if she and Amber don't connect."

The happy fatigue she'd noted on Brian's face disappeared. "Candy's here? Since when?"

Jet spoke through gritted teeth. "Since she showed up. Don't need to be getting into it with her. She's still in the barn over there. Here comes Amber. I'll get her back to the RV." Jet had pointed to someone in the barn but opened his hand as if he'd been reaching out for his wife, who took it and joined him by his side.

"I'm tired, baby," she said in a whiny tone. Phone in her hand, she looked down at the screen and started typing before she'd finished talking.

Jethro kept glancing back and forth between the barn and Brian. "Then let's get you home. See you all tomorrow." He guided Amber away from the barn and moved toward the exit with several others. Most of the drivers hitched rides with each other in additional vehicles that had been rented for the event. It seemed strange to Molly that they didn't drive their cars back and forth but was told the less they travel for no reason, the better.

"Who is Candice?" Molly asked Brian, who was staring over her head. Jaw clenched, hands on his hips, he didn't meet her gaze when she spoke.

But as she followed his line of sight, he said quietly, "Jet's ex-wife. I gotta go. See you tomorrow, dear."

Molly watched as he moved around the few stragglers and headed in the direction Jethro had pointed. When Brian stopped in front of someone, Molly's breath caught. The woman smiled up at him, throwing her arms around his neck. The sleeves of her floral shirt were every bit as familiar as the long, white-blond braid that swung as Brian twirled her in a hug. Why would Jet make out with his ex-wife? Or anyone who wasn't his wife?

Shaking her head, she turned, right into Sam's space. He smiled down at her, grabbed her arms to steady her from her surprise.

"Hey." She beamed up at him. He was a great guy, plain and simple, but what she'd witnessed this evening gave her a new appreciation of what made a good man. And having one in her life.

"Security will do the final sweep after we're all gone, but I want to shut down the gallery. I told them I'd make sure it was locked up."

"The gallery?"

His arms slipped around her, and he pulled her close. They were off to the side of the doors, a semi-secluded spot that allowed him to bury his face in her neck, pressing his mouth to the soft skin there. He pulled back just enough to talk into her ear, his breath tickling her and making her sigh at the same time.

"That's what we're calling the car barn. All the vendors are shut down, and we closed up the doors there a half hour ago, but I just want to make sure I have everything ready for tomorrow."

"And say good night to the pretties?"

He laughed. "Yeah."

She didn't know how to assimilate all of the thoughts she had on Jet or Brian or anything she'd seen. Part of her wanted to tell Sam about Jethro kissing someone else, but she didn't want to make Sam feel bad again by saying something negative about Jet.

"Want company?" She stepped out of his embrace, slipping her palm against his and tightening her fingers.

Even in the muted darkness, she saw the warmth in his eyes. "Yours? Always."

It took them a little while to wander through the dispersing crowd. A few people stopped Sam to chat about cars or the evening, or to congratulate him on a great job. The farther they walked on the fairgrounds, the more isolated their surroundings felt. With all of the vendors shut down, the lights had been cut. The lights from the dance barn still cast a glow, but it faded as they walked to the gallery. When they got closer, the lights from that barn lit the way. One of the doors was ajar, creating a path for them to follow.

"Sorry this is taking so long," Sam said, giving her hand a squeeze.

"No problem." She was tired but still excited from the evening, so she'd last until they made it home. Or at least to Sam's truck.

Sam pulled the door a little farther open so Molly could go through. There was only one overhead light on, and the back doors were completely open.

Sam frowned when he saw that. "Security could have at least shut that." There was an eerie quietness that made Molly's chest tighten. The cars sat, pristine, in their rows.

"I think I'll leave the one light on, because otherwise it'll be too dark to lock up. But let me grab the other doors."

Molly wrapped her arms around her stomach, unable to shake the unease creeping over her skin.

Sam stopped walking halfway down the aisle between the cars.

"Sam?"

Nerves pressed her heart up against her rib cage when he let out a sharp gasp.

She was moving toward him when his hand came out, signaling her to stop. She didn't.

"Jet? Jet?"

Molly's stomach cramped. It wasn't until she got closer that she saw, in the deep shadows of the barn, that there was someone sitting in one of the cars.

"Jet?" Sam called out. He was still a good four feet from the car, and Molly was behind him, frozen on the cement-covered spot.

"Is he all right?" She shuffled closer, barely moving her feet. Sam inched closer to the car.

She couldn't see any identifying features from where she stood. The cars closer to the back doors were all shrouded in darkness. But Sam could obviously identify the person.

"I don't know. Stay there," he said.

A swell of nerves crested in her stomach. "Sam. Something doesn't feel right."

She was beside him by the time he started walking closer to the vehicle. Their fingers locked around one another's.

"He's probably just sleeping after having too much to drink." Sam's tone made his thoughts on that clear. He stopped, looked down at Molly. "Why don't you stay here a minute?"

She arched a brow at him, and one side of his mouth quirked up. "Worth a shot," he said.

Together, they walked closer, neither of them rushing. "Jet? Jet. Party is over, guy." Sam's voice was loud enough that even someone deeply ensconced in a vivid dream would have heard. Or stirred.

But Jet didn't. When they reached the side of the car, they both stopped, hand in hand by the open door. He looked so normal and peaceful, his head tilted to one side like he'd fallen asleep. But now that they were closer, it was easier to make out the dark stain and swelling on his temple. If it wasn't for the deep gash and the utterly immobile silence, Molly wouldn't have realized he was dead.

Chapter Six

A chill that put the early-morning ocean air to shame invaded Molly's body. Her eyes went to Sam's, and he stepped forward, crowding in front of her, one arm turning her from the view. She glanced over her shoulder as he went to Jet, leaned in with one hand, and pressed two fingers to the man's throat. Sam came back to her, now crowding behind her, using his body as a shield.

"He's dead. Call 9-1-1. I'm going to call Chris. See how far away he is." Then, as though he realized the implications of what was happening, his head whipped from one side to the other, and Molly did the same.

"We're alone," she whispered.

Sam stroked a hand down her hair. "All the same, stay by the hood where I can see you. I'll call Chris."

She nodded, swallowing past the lump in her throat. Her fingers clutched at the strap of her purse, but she was frozen.

"Call 9-1-1, Molly."

Unzipping her purse, she fumbled through it a second before noticing that her hands were shaking. When she found the phone and her fingers clasped around it, a couple of pens and a pack of gum fell to the concrete floor.

Sam was talking to Chris behind her, and his steady voice reminded her that help would be there within minutes. She took a deep breath and bent to pick up her things. One of her pens had rolled just under the hood of the vehicle, but as she reached out to grab it, she saw a silver, cylindrical object. She squinted. She'd seen the object more than once in the hands of Brad Templeton. It was a vape stick.

"You okay?" Sam crouched down, picked up her pens and her gum, and put them in her purse. Taking her elbows, he stood. She needed to pull herself together. What was wrong with her? Unfortunately, she couldn't even say she'd never seen a dead body before. But the blood and the way it congealed against his skin and beard where it'd trailed down…how had he managed to look peaceful with that kind of injury?

"Molly?"

"I'm okay." Her brain was swirling at a quick tempo, one that matched the storm in her stomach, but she was okay.

Sam pulled her into a hug, and she pressed her face into his chest, focused on breathing in and out.

He spoke into her hair. "Chris has units on the way. He said not to touch anything and stay in a well-lit area. I'm not turning on more lights, though."

She wasn't sure if his train of thought was the same as hers, but less light was better if there was any possibility that the killer was still nearby. Fear wrapped tiny, cold fingers around her heart.

Leaning back, she looked up at Sam, kept her gaze focused on his. "There's a vape stick under the hood. Brad Templeton had a vape stick. From the way he spoke about Jethro, he also had a grudge against him."

Sam closed his eyes, pressed his forehead snuggly to Molly's like he could push better thoughts into her brain just from the contact. When he opened his eyes, his brows furrowed.

"Molly." Just the one word in a tone that said so much.

"We're the first people here, from the looks of it. We need to give Chris all of the details we can."

Sam's lips tightened. She knew he worried about her safety, and maybe she'd given him reason a couple of times.

"I'm pretty certain that part of police training includes sweeping a scene and looking for clues. So why don't we just move to the side and wait. Like we were told to do?"

She walked beside him, despite the fact that she wanted to scan the area around the car and see if there was anything else they hadn't noticed. Molly had no desire to look at Jethro's body again, but there might be something in the passenger seat or on the floor of the car that could give them information. It was too dark to look for a weapon. It had to have been something heavy. Hard. But without more light, she couldn't see anything anyway.

When they reached the wall, Molly leaned against it, very aware that Sam was still shielding her by standing in front of her. His wide shoulders blocked her view. Normally, she wouldn't mind because looking at Sam was fast becoming one of her favorite hobbies.

"I'm okay," she told him again. "Are you?"

Still watching her closely, he nodded. "Not how I thought the night would end."

Headlights shone into the barn a second before doors slammed. Chris led the way, but four uniformed officers followed directly on his heels.

"Ryan, gather up the rest of the security guards and sweep the grounds. Enroy and Patrick, secure the scene. Wills, get ahold of the Portland ME's office and get someone down here."

He strode their way, barking orders in a way that surprised Molly. Chris was good at his job, and she'd had the chance to see this several times. But he was usually more...reserved. Stopping in front of them, his eyes roamed over both her and Sam.

"You guys okay?" His eyes were on Molly.

"We're fine," Sam said.

Chris turned to look at him. "I'm taking the lead on this one. Saron is either grooming me for his retirement or he's getting lazy."

Molly and Sam both laughed, as they knew Chris intended. Sheriff Saron was anything but lazy, and Britton Bay was his home. If he was putting Chris in charge, he had the utmost confidence in him.

"Need I ask why, once again, you're where the dead bodies are, Molly?" He ran a hand through his dark hair.

Sam's arm immediately went around Molly's shoulder. "Don't be a jerk."

Chris's eyes widened, but he nodded and locked eyes with Molly. "Sorry."

She shook off the irritation and, knowing they only had a few minutes before Chris made them leave the scene, shared her thoughts. "Brad Templeton, one of the drivers, has...had an issue with Jethro. I interviewed him and another man yesterday. He vapes. A lot. Brad, not the other man." She was talking too fast and realized her adrenaline was still on high. "There's a vape stick under the hood of the car."

Chris closed his eyes very briefly, then looked at Sam. "Take her home. I'll send a deputy out to take both of your statements."

Molly bristled. Tired, irritated, wound up, and a little offended, she shook off Sam's arm. "Take me home? I'm fully capable of taking care of myself, thank you. And just because you have some sort of issue with me being here doesn't mean you shouldn't take me seriously."

"Molly, he's not blowing you off," Sam said. His tone was hard, his comment a suggestion to his friend that he hoped what he said was true.

Chris looked over his shoulder, and Molly saw that one of the deputies was crouched taking pictures under the hood of the vehicle.

Looking back at Molly, he hooked a thumb over his shoulder. "We're on it. I'm not blowing you off. At all. I just want you two away from the scene. Both of you. Seeing this kind of stuff is never easy, and I'd actually prefer that you let Wills take you *both* home, and he'll do your statement while he's there."

Lights flashed on, bright and startling. One of the deputies called out. "Think I found a weapon, boss."

All of them turned their heads in his direction but couldn't see what he was looking down at. One of the other deputies walked over, looked back at Chris.

"Crowbar. Out of place, but it's clean from the looks of it."

Chris swore, looking back at Molly and Sam. "I'll get Wills to take you home."

"I can drive, man." Sam took Molly's hand. She linked her fingers in his, grateful his were warm.

"Fine. I'll send him out as soon as he contacts the ME. I'll touch base with you when I can." Chris had gone into full-on cop mode. Officer Beatty. That was how Molly had been introduced to him the first time she'd found a body. She shivered, and Sam turned to her.

"Come on. Chris is right. Let's go home."

Molly couldn't help her tone when she said, "Thanks for coming so quickly, Officer Beatty. Let us know if there's anything else we can do."

He rolled his eyes, and the corners of his lips quirked. "Thank you, Ms. Owens."

Sam tugged on her hand, a touch of a smile on his lips. "He's going to lock you up for irritating an officer."

"That's not a thing," Molly said. Almost confidently.

"Chris, I hate to be insensitive about this, but what about tomorrow?" Sam asked, his eyes darting to where the police officers were cordoning off the area.

"Go home, let Wills take your statements, and I'll come by after I finish here. It might be a while, but I'll know more later."

Sam nodded, and he and Molly left through the far end of the barn, both of them not looking back toward Jethro's car. Molly didn't need to look at it to remember it with startling clarity. They wouldn't be sleeping tonight. Sadness washed over her as Sam held the passenger door of his truck open for her to climb in.

Jethro Harkaw was not a nice man. But he had a wife, friends, and even an ex-wife who would miss him. Fans and followers who still had reason to admire him would mourn his passing. And suddenly it didn't matter that he was a jerk or a chauvinist.

Sam climbed in, gripped the steering wheel. Looking over at him, Molly reached out and put a hand on his forearm, staring at his profile in the dark cab.

"I can't believe someone would do this," Sam said. "Who would do this? I didn't like the guy on a personal level, but why would someone do this here? In such a public way?"

"I don't know," she whispered.

While she'd unfortunately been up close and personal with not one, but two killers, she couldn't fathom hurting another person. After her arrival in Britton Bay, she'd been the one to find Vernon's body and also the one to uncover the secrets that had led to his death. It hadn't prepared her for finding the killer of a small-time celebrity chef a couple of months ago. The chef had been in town for a wedding that was supposed to be at the bed-and-breakfast.

Thinking about both of those events now, after seeing Jethro, she could understand Chris's frustration with, once again, finding her at the scene of a death. It wasn't like she *wanted* to be there. Molly definitely didn't want the nightmares that would ensue after she witnessed the worst of mankind.

"I'm so sorry you had to see that," Sam said. He still hadn't started the vehicle. Turning, he reached for her, putting a hand around her neck and pulling her close.

"It's definitely not your fault, and I feel just as horrible that you saw it. I don't think it's something either of us will forget anytime soon."

"Whoever did this was brave enough to do it while people were still wandering around." The truck's cab was dark, only bits of moonlight dancing in through the windows, but she could see him, the intensity of his gaze.

"Or desperate enough."

She put her hand to his jaw and felt it clench.

"Until Chris finds out who did this, I don't want you to go anywhere alone."

She smiled, despite the situation. While she appreciated his concern and loved that he wanted to protect her, it wasn't logical to think anyone would hurt her. She had nothing to do with the car world. Whoever killed Jet did. Which meant she was in less danger than, say, Sam. Telling him that, though, wouldn't penetrate while he was flipping "what ifs" over in his head.

It was easier to soothe him in the only way she knew how. Pressing a kiss to his cheek, breathing him in, and feeling incredibly grateful neither of them had wandered into the barn alone tonight, she whispered, "We'll just stay glued to each other's sides until we feel like it's safe."

And because she believed that whoever hurt Jethro was part of the car world, which put Sam at risk more than her, saying this, and having his agreement, soothed her as well.

Chapter Seven

Molly didn't warm up on the ride home or when Katherine let them into the bed-and-breakfast. With the busy chaos they'd expected for the weekend, they'd all come to the agreement that Tigger should stay up at the main house with Sam's mom. What that actually meant was that Molly insisted she couldn't take advantage and Katherine had insisted she'd have it no other way.

Tigger greeted her and Sam with his usual pouncing and a tornado tail wag. Molly crouched down in the spacious foyer of Katherine's home and accepted the love her pup gave so easily. She rubbed his ears, laughing when he tried to get into her lap. Sam lowered beside her and added his hands to the greeting. His eyes met hers as they said hello to her dog.

"You okay?" His voice was whispered.

She was. Or she would be. "I am. You?"

He nodded, but his gaze was shadowed with worry. They both stood, and Tigger flopped down across their feet.

Sam's laugh went a long way toward pushing back the chill she couldn't shake.

"How about you let us all the way in, buddy?" he said.

His mom went up on tiptoes and brushed his cheek with a quick kiss before folding Molly into a hug.

"What is happening to our small town?" Katherine asked, squeezing tight.

Molly pulled back, steadier now. "I'm not sure. I hope I didn't bring bad luck with me." It was partially a joke, but not entirely. Three murders in six months?

"Don't say that," Sam and his mother said in unison. They shared caring eyes, and all four were on her.

"I was teasing." But it wasn't the time or place, and she shouldn't have. They moved into the dining area. The house was decorated with a rustic, country vibe. Homey. Comfortable. Welcoming. Like Katherine herself. She'd set out cookies and tea on the ten-foot-long, wood-planked dining table. There was an electric fireplace on the faux-brick wall, along with handmade wooden signs that said things like HOME IS WHERE THE TEA IS and SIT * REST * READ * REPEAT.

"Is that one new?" Molly pointed to a narrow sign that held an arrow pointing to the kitchen. Underneath the arrow, it said, BLISS…THAT WAY.

Katherine poured them tea while Sam gave the dog a bit more attention.

"It is. Sarah made it for me. She said if the paint night goes well, she'll do a workshop on how to make your own wooden signs."

The conversation was normal, and normal was necessary. Molly needed the time to get her brain wrapped around everything that had happened. She and Alan had talked about establishing a stronger social media presence, but she couldn't very well post something about what they'd just witnessed. But she also couldn't shut her brain down.

"Come sit down and have some tea, Molly," Sam said softly. He took the cup from his mom and passed it to her.

She sat beside him on the long bench instead of on one of the six chairs available. Closer was better. The image of Jet flashed into her mind, and she shook it off. She couldn't think emotionally right now. They needed to give their statements, and she needed to catalog the facts for later. As if he sensed her thoughts, or just knew her well, Sam's arm came around her shoulder. She rested her head in the crook of his arm for a moment while he filled Katherine in on the barest of details.

"That's just horrible. I can't believe something like this has happened. Again."

The word hung in the air, and again Molly thought of how she'd lived twenty-eight years without seeing a dead body. Now, in six months, she'd seen twice as many as she'd ever wanted to. She should have felt scared. Instead, she was angry, furious that, once again, this sort of thing had touched the town she loved. The place she called home.

"I hope the police pick up Brad Templeton. But I know for certain that Jethro's ex-wife is in town as well. Do you think most people are staying at the hotel?"

There was one go-to hotel in Britton Bay. There was also a motel and several bed-and-breakfasts, along with camping and RV sites. Most visitors who didn't choose the personal type of lodging that Katherine offered went for the hotel.

Molly saw Sam and his mother exchange a glance. Avoiding the look both of them wanted to give her, she reached down and petted Tigger, who'd curled up in his favorite spot on her feet.

"I'm sure the police will do everything they need to. I hate saying this, I really do, but if I have to close down the show tomorrow, I need to get ahold of people."

Molly looked up again, and she knew Sam was thinking the same as she was when she said, "Brian," and he nodded, his lips tight.

Where had he been? *With Jethro's ex.* She'd watched Brian and Candy go one way, while Jet and Amber had gone another. Jet must have gone back to his car for some reason. Had Amber been with him? *The police will talk to her. They'll talk to everyone. This isn't your job.*

A knock at the front door sent Tigger into a frenzy of barking. That wasn't typical for him.

"He must sense your moods," Katherine said when Sam went to let the deputy in. "You two could stay here tonight. I have no guests, and the rooms are all made up."

Sam came back in with Deputy Wills—Molly didn't know his first name—and must have heard his mom.

"That's sweet, Mom, but I think we're okay. In fact, we should let you get to bed." He looked at Molly, his gaze softening. "You want to go down to your place?"

She nodded and stood up. Tigger leaned against her leg and seemed torn when Katherine walked them to the door. Molly wondered, belatedly, if Katherine had asked about them staying more for her own peace of mind.

At the door, Molly turned and gave Tigger a pet, then looked up at Sam's mom. "We're going to be busy with this. Could he stay again?"

Maybe it was her imagination, but she was fairly certain relief washed over Katherine's face. "Of course. No trouble. Let me know what's happening, okay?"

Sam promised, and so did Molly. When he leaned in to kiss her cheek, Molly heard Katherine's whispered "Be safe, sweetheart."

"Don't worry, Mom," he said.

Molly laughed at the look his mom gave him. Sort of an "as if" look.

Outside, on the covered porch, Deputy Wills stopped and turned to Molly. "We haven't met officially yet. I'm Deputy Trevor Wills."

Molly shook his hand. "Molly Owens. Are you new in town?"

"I am. This is actually my first week on the job here." They walked toward the cottage as he talked. "I was Boise PD for the last five years."

Molly unlocked the door to her cottage, thinking he didn't look old enough to have that much experience. Or maybe she was just exhausted and her judgment was faulty.

As they went into the kitchen, she offered the two men a drink. Both declined, and she suggested they sit in the living area. Sam stayed close to her side, and she liked the feel of his body next to hers, a quiet show of support, the two of them leaning on each other. Deputy Wills took the armchair and flipped open a notebook.

Molly had a flash of Chris doing the same thing not too long ago. When Vernon had died, he'd come to interview Molly, and like he did now, Sam had stuck to her side.

It felt like hours of questioning, recalling, and explaining details. In truth, it was a little over an hour. By the time they walked Deputy Wills to the door, Molly didn't have any words left in her, and Sam had withdrawn in a way she hadn't expected.

Knowing that rumor traveled faster than news, Molly had no doubt word of Jet's death was getting around. Despite the late hour, she texted Alan. He texted back almost immediately that he'd picked up some chatter on the fire station's radio. She heard the shower turn on and figured she had a couple of minutes at least. Dialing, she waited for Alan to answer.

"Hi," he greeted, his voice low.

"Hi. What a terrible end to the evening. I still can't believe it." She leaned against the counter, her body nearly as weary as her brain.

"I can't believe you were there."

She rolled her eyes. "I do seem to have a habit of wrong place, wrong time."

"Unfortunately, yes. How's Sam?"

Glancing toward her bedroom—he'd gone to the en suite bathroom to shower—she frowned. "He's worried about the implications. Sad that one of the men he grew up admiring is dead."

She didn't share what else had disappointed him about Jethro. She'd have to work to keep the reporting neutral as far as his personality went. Thinking about how he treated people, she wasn't surprised someone had issues with him. But who would want him dead?

Grabbing a pen and a piece of paper, she chatted with Alan about what they should share on social media and when. On the paper, she wrote: *Brad Templeton. Amber. Ex-wife.* Tapping the pen for a moment, she couldn't think of a reason off the top of her head, but wrote down *Brian* because he was close to the situation as well.

"Let's not do anything until we have an official statement from the police," Alan said.

"I'm so glad you said that. Sam isn't sure what's going to happen with the closing tomorrow or if Brian's even been notified. That's his partner."

"Okay. Touch base with me in the morning. Don't worry about coming in. We'll work on the layout using the stories we have so far and leave room for whatever we decide to share about the car show. For now, we'll use the photographs Clay took. He got some good ones of the cars on Friday."

Maybe talking to him had done the trick and reminded him that having a job actually required work.

They chatted another minute before hanging up. Molly was staring at the list of names, her pen tapping the paper, leaving little blue dots.

"What's that?" Sam spoke from the doorway of her bedroom. He wore a pair of lounge pants, his arms crossed over his chest. He'd towel-dried his hair, but it was still damp.

Molly crumpled the paper and tossed the pen down, walking toward him. He'd been a rock for her in the last several months. He'd made her laugh when she'd needed to, given her patience, kindness, and understanding. He'd single-handedly—well, he used both hands—rebuilt her confidence as a desirable woman. As a person. Sam made her feel stronger, more capable, and more sure of...everything. She wanted to do everything in her power to make sure she gave back what he'd so effortlessly given her time and again. Support. Whatever *he* needed.

Stopping in front of him, she watched her own hands as they trailed up and over his chest, along his wide shoulders, and around his neck. His hands went to her waist, one pulling her closer so their bodies fit together, like perfectly placed Tetris blocks.

"Nothing. It's nothing," she said. Because she knew he wouldn't like the fact that she was already building a suspect list in her head.

"You sure?" He whispered the words against her mouth.

Her arms tightened around him as he lifted her and turned, walking with her in his arms, her feet dangling, his biceps crushing her against him, and she nodded.

"I'm positive."

Chapter Eight

The scene was cleared in the early hours before dawn. Chris didn't drop by, but he texted Sam and said he'd meet him at the fairgrounds and update him. When they arrived, Brian was there as well. His eyes were red and puffy. Molly wondered if he'd slept at all. Had he spent the night at the station?

She couldn't help thinking of Candy and Amber as well. The three of them were the last people Molly had seen Jet with. *But the vape stick.* Either Brad had seen him again that evening, or maybe he'd dropped it earlier in the day. Her brain was too tired to be swirling so hard at this hour.

"Molly. Sam. Morning," Chris said.

They returned the greeting, and Molly went to Brian, giving him a hard hug. "I'm so sorry."

She felt his nod against her shoulder when he bent to hug her back. When she stepped away, Sam shook Brian's hand and offered his condolences. Chris ran a hand through his dark hair and breathed out a heavy sigh. She watched his eyes dart to Brian, unreadable, then he looked at her. Knowing it would get his back up didn't stop her from what she needed to do.

"Can I get a statement for the paper?" She pulled her notepad and pen out of her bag, trying not to stare at the spot where Jethro's car had been. Despite the fact that the barn still housed twenty-three bright, beautiful cars, the air was heavy with a hovering darkness. Where had they taken the car?

"Jethro Harkaw was found dead in his vehicle last night at approximately 11:43 p.m. At the moment, we're treating the death as suspicious and ask that any members of the public who saw anything that might be useful in solving this crime call our tip line."

He gave Molly the number, and she was pleased that he was reaching out to the community for help. The sooner the police figured out who killed him, the sooner their lives could get back to normal. Even now, as Molly spoke with Chris, she saw Sam pacing.

"Do you have any suspects?" Molly asked.

"We're collecting statements." Chris's tone was hard to read.

She arched her brows at him. "What about Brad Templeton?"

"Brad?" Brian stepped forward, into their space, but Molly didn't miss the way Chris narrowed his eyes at her. "Why would you suspect Brad?"

"I'm not at liberty to discuss details of the case, but I assure you *both* that I'll update you when I can."

"Brad ripped a strip off of Jethro before we got started yesterday," Brian said, more to Molly than Chris.

"Please don't write that," Chris sighed.

Sam joined them again. "Can we ask about Jethro's wife? I'd like to know how to proceed today with as much sensitivity as possible for his family. Brian, if you want to shut it down, I can make that happen."

"Amber is at the RV. She's got her sister coming in. She didn't love any of this stuff, so I wouldn't imagine she'll want to be part of it. Jethro would want us to close out the show properly. In the past, when we've lost someone connected to the Crawl, we've all honked our horns at the same time. We could do that for Jet today." The man's voice broke at the end. While Molly's heart pinched for him, she couldn't help but wonder if Amber had been questioned and released as well. *Let Chris do his job!*

Sam nodded enthusiastically. "Of course we can. We will. If that's okay, Chris?"

He gave a curt nod, checked his phone, and glanced up at them. "It's fine, but I have to get going. I'll be back later as I might need to follow up with some of the car owners. I'd appreciate it if none of them left. Deputies are touching base with each of them now so they know, but maybe give them a reminder. What time are you done?" He looked at Sam.

"Drivers should be here at nine. Fairground opens at ten, and there'll be festivities all day, but the award ceremony is at eleven. We'll close everything down so that drivers can get back on the road by noon."

Molly jotted down bits of everything. She could at least update social media. It was taking the town some time to get used to checking their website, Facebook page, and Twitter accounts.

She'd driven in with Sam but needed to go in to the *Bulletin*. When Chris turned to talk to Brian, she pulled him to the side.

"I'm going to go in to the paper for a bit. Will you be all right?"

Sam smiled at her and touched his hand to her jaw. "Yeah, babe. I'm okay. Stop worrying about me. Go to work, and I'll see you later today."

Stepping into him, she wrapped her arms around his waist and rested her head on his chest for a moment. It was the first time he'd used the endearment, and it felt so...intimate. Like they'd been together for longer than they had. Like they'd be together. For good. The thought didn't scare her the way it might have once.

"I'll be back later to do some more coverage of the events. I just need to upload some pictures and get something on social media."

His hands wrapped around her shoulders, and he rested his chin on her head for a moment.

"You want a ride, Molly?" Chris asked.

Pulling away from Sam, she turned. "Please."

"A question-free ride," Chris warned with an almost-teasing tone.

Molly stopped herself from sticking her tongue out at him. Because she was a professional and an adult. She didn't have siblings, but every now and again, she thought being around Chris was like having an annoying older brother.

"Brian, can we do anything?" Molly asked, giving him another hug.

"No, dear. I'm just going to help Sam close this down in a way that would make Jethro proud."

A lump rose in her throat. He clearly didn't approve of the way Jethro behaved, but he missed his friend. She felt guilty about putting him on her list last night, but until everyone close to Jethro had been ruled out, she knew everyone was a suspect. When Molly stepped back, Brian reached out to shake Chris's hand.

"Thank you for all your help. I want you to catch whoever did this."

He took in a shuddery breath, then seemed to steel his shoulders, giving Chris another serious look. "You'll update me?"

Chris didn't answer right away. When he did, his tone was flat. "When I have information that pertains to you, yes. For now, I need you to make sure you stick around as well."

Sam flinched at Chris's words, and Molly knew he was feeling bad for Brian. Between him and his partner, he was definitely the easier one to like. But she also understood Chris's point of view—being likable didn't make a person innocent.

* * * *

The drive from the fairgrounds to the *Bulletin* was under fifteen minutes. Molly lasted seven without breaking the silence.

"Jethro's ex-wife?"

Chris sent her a wary glance across the cab of his police cruiser. He said nothing.

"Candy. Or Candice. I saw her kissing Jethro last night. Behind the speakers."

"We met and questioned his wife, Amber Harkaw."

She turned in her seat. "I know. But Amber wasn't by his side while he was making out with Candy."

"Did you include this in your statement?" He gave her a more thorough glance when he stopped at a red light.

"No. I forgot about it. We talked about finding the body."

Pressing the gas when the light changed, he surprised her with his next question. "You doing okay with that? Seeing a body is hard. You've seen more than one. It wouldn't be a bad idea to talk to someone, Molly. And before you accuse me of thinking you're weak or anything else—because I do *not* think that—I'm going to suggest the same thing to Sam. It's not something that you forget quickly."

"I don't know how you do it," Molly admitted.

He pulled onto Main Street. "Honestly? It hasn't been something we've had to deal with much since I joined the force. It's definitely not my favorite part. Just let me know if you want a recommendation for someone to talk to, okay?"

He pulled up in front of the *Bulletin*. The wide front window was dark, making the white stenciled words BRITTON BAY BULLETIN seem brighter. Molly released her seat belt.

"Thanks for the offer. I'll let you know." She opened the door but turned back to him. "Don't get irritated, but if Amber, Jet's current wife, knew about Candy…"

"Molly." He sighed. "Go to work so I can."

She nodded. Right. They each had their own jobs. She waved as he drove away, knowing that part of her job was connecting dots, just like Chris's. To do that, she needed a time line. Letting herself into the *Bulletin*'s office through the front door, she locked it behind her and placed a call to a very sleepy Clay.

After insisting that, yes, she needed him to e-mail his photos *now*, she got to work on the official statement. When her e-mail pinged a short while later, she pulled up the photos Clay had taken, printing them along with her own.

Maybe there'd be something in the pictures that would give them more to go on. *More to give the police to go on, you mean.* Yup. Sure. That's what she meant.

Chapter Nine

BRITTON BAY BULLETIN @THEBULLETIN*48 MIN
CLASSIC CAR CRAWL FOUNDER JETHRO HARKAW HAS DIED.

Molly posted a picture of Jethro standing with Brian outside the fairgrounds. They each leaned on their respective cars, smiles on their aging faces. She attached the story she'd written, giving the barest details but asking the public for whatever help they could give. She also tweeted the number for calling in tips. She had no doubt that, whether the tips were valid or not, there would be plenty.

Alone in the office, she spread the photographs she'd printed out on the layout table. It was a large table, taller than usual, that let all of them gather around and share their ideas. Molly liked to put the dummy pages on the table so they could get a more accurate feel for what the paper would look like when it was printed.

Now, however, she used the photos to create a visual time line between her interview with Jethro and Brian on Thursday and the events of last night. Hearing the alarm beep, she wondered who was joining her and hoped it wasn't Clay.

"Molly?" Jill's voice called out, still a little scratchy.

"Up front," Molly answered. She glanced down at the photos. If it were someone else, she might shuffle them together and tell herself to stop looking for clues that weren't hers to find. But Jill would be every bit as curious as Molly.

"Hey," Jill said. She walked into the office area, which was separated by dark gray dividers. Wearing a pair of loose jogging pants and a hoodie, and with her blond hair in a ponytail, she looked like she'd just rolled out of bed.

"Should you be here? You feeling okay?" Molly came around the table. Jill dropped her bag on her desk.

"I'm feeling better. What the heck? Jethro Harkaw is dead?"

"Twitter?"

Jill nodded. "Yeah. I was going to text you and figured I'd just come in." She rounded the table, looked over the photographs, then sent Molly a look. "Tell me what you know."

Of everyone on the staff, Jill was the reporter. Being the editorial director suited Molly, but she loved discussing stories and ideas with her staff. She especially loved working out puzzles and sorting through her thoughts with someone whose mind worked in a similar way.

Molly sat on a stool and pointed to the first picture of Jethro. It was the one she'd used for his and Brian's interviews. Because the *Bulletin* came out only once a week, they often updated their stories online and then decided which key pieces of news to include in the print addition as follow-up. Next week, the interviews would be heavily overshadowed by Jethro's murder. A pang of sadness made her heart lurch.

"Okay. So, starting from Thursday, we figured out Jethro was pretty smarmy. I honestly thought Sam might walk out."

"He mentioned it after you texted me, that he was glad I hadn't gone alone," Jill said.

Jill had been away at school for the last few years, but Sam had recommended her to Molly as a feature reporter when she'd moved home. She was a perfect fit for where Molly was trying to take the aging newspaper.

"I was glad of the same thing. So, he's married to this woman, Amber Melner Harkaw. They've been married for eight months. She's twenty-four to his sixty-eight."

Jill raised her eyebrows and said nothing. Molly pointed to a picture of Candy that she'd found online. "This is Candice Harkaw. Still goes by that last name even though she and Jethro divorced fifteen months ago. They were married for over twenty-five years."

"What a slap in the face that'd be. Being married for longer than his next wife has been alive." Jill shook her head, then examined the photograph Molly had taken of Brad and Herman.

It took effort not to color her tone with her feelings, but she wanted Jill's objective opinion. "This is Brad Templeton. He and his friend, Herman, talked to me a bit about the show. When Herman walked away, Brad made some references that suggested he wasn't a fan of Jethro's. He vaped almost the whole time we spoke, and a vape stick was found under Jethro's car."

Jill sat on the stool beside her, moving a picture closer. She pulled another photograph close, putting them side by side. "Who's this?"

She pointed at both pictures, but it was the same person. "That's Brian."

Jill glanced at Molly, then pulled the picture of Brian down into line with the other three. "Why isn't he with these guys? The police already rule him out?"

"No. They haven't ruled anyone out yet. I'm pretty sure all three were questioned last night, though I'm not positive. But obviously there wasn't enough to hold any of them. Brian is close to Jet, but I just can't think of a reason, whereas these three," she said, pointing to Candy, Amber, and Brad, "seem obvious."

"But I guess," Molly said, aligning Brian's photo with the three she suspected, "wanting out might be a reason. He told me last night, off the record, that this was his last ride."

Jill frowned, her fingers resting on the photos. "That's a lot of players already. Officer Beatty give you anything?"

Shaking her head with a wry smile, she said, "No. But that doesn't mean you can't do your own digging."

Jill smiled, then covered her mouth and coughed. When she finished, she looked wiped. "I do like to dig."

"You don't have to today. You still don't sound great." She meant it, but her attention was drawn back to the photographs.

"What are you thinking?" Jill leaned closer and examined the pictures with Molly.

"When we were getting ready to go, I ran into Brian. We talked, then Jethro showed up saying he didn't want Candice and Amber to run into each other."

"Of course. Who wants that kind of awkwardness?" Jill's tone was dry, making Molly smile.

"So what happened between Candy and Brian leaving and Jet and Amber leaving? I saw Jet leave with his wife."

"He could have doubled back. Here's one of Jet dancing with Amber." Jill pushed the other photos back into the time line. "Why doesn't Clay time-stamp his pictures?"

"Why does Clay do or not do a lot of things?" Shaking off the negative thought, she glanced toward her office. "I didn't print all of the photos. I just selected some I thought might give us a visual."

"I'm not fit for the outside world yet. Why don't I go through the rest of them, see if anything looks out of place? I'll make notes of what I can look into, starting with Brad Templeton since your face scrunches all up when you say his name. You're heading back to the fairgrounds, right?"

Molly stood up, smiling at Jill's intuition, and gathered the photos into a pile. "I am. That's perfect. You sure you feel okay?"

"I'll be fine." Jill stood up and went to her own desk, unloading her laptop. "How's Sam? He must be sad. And probably a little worried?"

"He's both. He was already feeling guilty about Jethro. And now this. He doesn't want this to be how the event is remembered. He especially doesn't want the last Crawl and the death to be synonymous with Britton Bay."

"We can keep the media focus on facts rather than the setting. But I'm guessing we'll get some more outside reporters in today."

Molly frowned, remembering the last large-outlet reporter who had come through when the celebrity chef had been killed. He'd labeled the staff of the *Bulletin* small-town from the second he set foot in the door, and though he'd wanted information, he hadn't been keen on sharing.

This was definitely not what Sam needed. They could control their own reporting, but once it hit beyond Britton Bay, Molly worried that Sam's name would come up only in conjunction with the death—the absolute opposite of anything he could have wanted or imagined.

"I'm going to go. I'll be there covering the closing of the event, but if I can learn anything from people who were there, maybe I can pass it on to Chris and they can close this case more quickly."

Jill gave her a sympathetic look. "Try not to worry. Sam isn't going to lose customers because someone who has no connection to our town died."

She was right, but he wouldn't necessarily gain them either.

"I'll text you if I find anything new," Molly said.

"Same goes here." Jill pulled her chair in and leaned closer to her laptop, already scrolling through images that Molly and Clay had shared.

They weren't stepping on toes, Molly reminded herself as she bundled up for the walk home. It was early enough in the day that tourists weren't crowding the streets. If they were still enjoying summer, there'd be throngs of people picking their spots at the beach or out already touring the shops. The people who were in town for the car show were a different breed of tourist for this area. As she walked down Main Street, heading for the bed-and-breakfast, Molly thought about what Jill had said. *No connection to our town.* It definitely made sense that whoever killed Jet wasn't from Britton Bay. No one in town had reason to want him dead. No one even knew him.

The most common motives for murder are love, money, and revenge. "I have a suspect for each," Molly whispered to herself. The wind whipped her hair across her face as she neared the ocean.

If Candice still cared for Jet—and that kiss indicated she did, at least to some extent—she might have murdered for love. If Amber stood to gain what had to be a sizable inheritance from her husband's death, she had the money motive. Molly's thoughts wandered back to Brad Templeton. What if he'd somehow gotten hold of the winner's list? When was that decided? If he wasn't going to place in this year's Crawl, would he be angry enough to murder for revenge? *Don't rule out Brian.* She didn't mean to keep dismissing him, but she couldn't pin down a reason. *What if he and Jet argued over him wanting out of the show?* She thought of the black eye Jet had sported. Perhaps they'd argued before the show as well. The only thing that was vividly clear was that no one could be entirely dismissed. Which meant that she needed some more answers.

Molly turned down Wilmer Street, which would let her cut across to LaMonte. Gorgeous, thick trees lined both sides of the street. The cloud-filled, baby-blue sky filtered through little openings in the still-green leaves. It would be breathtaking to see the colors change to reds, oranges, and yellows. The weather in California was fairly consistent, but here, she'd get to witness and enjoy each of the seasons. She wanted that, more than she would have thought that she could.

Walking up to the bed-and-breakfast, she stopped short. First, because Tigger saw her and came barreling toward her, but also because Katherine was on the front lawn, helping a new arrival with luggage.

Molly crouched, ready to greet Tigger. She'd missed the little guy this weekend.

"Hey, buddy. How are you? Oh, I missed you, too," she said around a laugh.

Katherine gave a wave, but even from a distance, Molly saw the tightness of her smile. The woman whose large bag Katherine was holding turned. Molly's stomach cramped.

Apparently, Amber Melner Harkaw was checking into the bed-and-breakfast.

Chapter Ten

Calling Tigger, who easily fell in step beside her, Molly joined the two women.

"Hi, dear. How are you?" Katherine greeted her.

Molly gave her a brief hug, whispering that she was fine, before turning to Amber.

"I'm so sorry for your loss," she said. Those words changed absolutely nothing, but what could she say? There was nothing *to* say in moments like this.

Amber's eyes were red, and even with the layer of makeup she wore, her skin was blotchy, her nose pink.

"Thank you. I met you yesterday, right?" She looked down at Tigger, who sniffed her high-heeled shoe as she shook her leg to warn him off.

Molly leaned down to pet Tigger. He lay over her right foot. "Yes. Jethro introduced us. My boyfriend, Sam, organized the event. Everyone feels just horrible about what's happened. Are you…checking in?" Molly glanced at Katherine.

"I am. I can't stay in our RV. Not with him not there. And not with Brian letting that, that…*woman* stay in his RV, right next to me. My sister is flying out from Oklahoma today to be with me. The police won't say how long it'll be before they'll release Jet's body. I kept asking, and they just focused on where I was and what was I doing, like I'd hurt my own husband. Why would I hurt him? I loved him. Now, I just have to wait around for them to find some small shred of fake evidence to accuse me. So, I can't…I can't make any arrangements until—"

Her voice broke off on a hard sob, and Amber lowered her chin to her chest, her shoulders shaking. Katherine's eyes widened, and she put an arm around the young woman's shoulders.

"Let's get you in and settled. Molly, come in for some tea?"

Molly couldn't get an accurate read on Amber. The sobs wracking her body were real. But the little speech she'd just given felt rehearsed, defensive, as if she'd been insulted by her questioning by the police rather than realizing that they were obligated to question everyone.

Molly only shook her head but realized Katherine wasn't looking at her. "I can't. I just came for my Jeep. I need to get back to the fairgrounds."

Amber turned, dislodging Katherine's arm. "You're going back there?"

"Yes. I work for the *Britton Bay Bulletin*, the town's newspaper. I'm going to cover the closing ceremony. They plan on honoring Jet. Would you like to come with me?"

Amber shook her head, swiping at her tears. "No. I don't want to be there. I can't face it. I was at the police station until three in the morning. I need some sleep."

Molly took the woman's bag from her, gave Katherine a glance, and walked with them, hoping neither would mind. "I saw you just after the band finished. Jet, too. He mentioned getting back to the RV as quickly as possible."

This was the part that didn't make sense. If Jet and Amber were on their way out, how'd he end up back in the gallery?

Walking up the stairs, looking between Molly and Katherine like she was grateful someone wanted to hear her story, she nodded. "Yes. We were on our way, but then Herman Besbrewer texted Jet. Insisted he meet him before he left. Jet asked one of the other drivers to drop me off at the RV. I figured he'd get back not long after me, but instead it was the police who showed up." Amber's breath hitched.

Katherine opened the door to the bed-and-breakfast, and Tigger raced in ahead of them. Molly set Amber's bag down in the foyer.

"What did Herman want to meet him about?" At almost midnight.

Amber looked around, not focusing on any one thing as she answered. "Oh, he and Jet were always fighting. I'm not sure about what. I try to stay out of it, you know?"

Katherine put Amber's suitcase down and folded her arms across her chest. Molly knew if she looked at Sam's mom, she'd be on the receiving end of a very "mom" look. Katherine knew exactly what she was up to.

"You told the police about Herman?"

Amber stopped looking around and glared at Molly through red-rimmed eyes. "Of course. They said they'd speak with him, but they won't tell me anything. They're too busy asking me about my time when they should be finding my husband's killer."

"I'm really sorry, Amber." Makeup and tight clothes could distract from a lot of things, and Molly was embarrassed to admit to herself that she'd let those things overshadow something glaringly obvious right now— Amber loved Jet. Whatever had brought them together, however strange their pairing seemed, she was truly mourning her husband. There might be more to the story, but she cared that he was gone.

"Thank you. Sorry, what was your name again?"

"Molly. I'll check in with you later." Amber had already started looking around, her heels tapping against the floor. Tigger followed at a distance. *Smart dog.* Even if the widow's grief was real, her personality was definitely in flux.

* * * *

The fairgrounds were packed when Molly arrived just before ten o'clock. She parked a good distance away, grateful she'd taken the time to change into her sneakers. With her press badge visible over her jacket, she bypassed the crowd waiting to get in, keeping her head down. She wasn't in the mood for conversation at the moment. Too many thoughts were bouncing around in her head, and she wanted to see Sam, check on him and make sure he was holding up okay.

The vendors had already set up for the day. Bella was adjusting the setting on a portable heater when Molly approached.

"Hey," Molly said, her stomach growling just at the sight of Morning Muffins's display of goods.

Bella turned, her high ponytail whipping back. "Hey. How are you? How's Sam? I can't believe all of this. What happened? Do you have any idea who would do this?" She came around the table she'd set up, so they were standing in each other's space.

Her friendship with Bella had been a sort of mini roller coaster. When she'd first arrived in town and fallen head over tummy in love with Bella's baking, she'd befriended the woman. Then Molly had mistakenly accused the baker's ex-boyfriend of murdering Vernon. But when the celebrity chef had been killed a couple of months earlier and the police had suspected Bella for a half a second, she'd reached out to Molly. Since then, their friendship path had smoothed considerably. Since Bella and Jill were good friends, it made Molly happy to no longer have barriers in the way. For now, at least. She knew very well that her curious nature had a tendency to rub some people the wrong way.

"Have you seen Sam?" Molly asked, skipping over all of the other questions.

Bella looked around, waving at Mr. Elbury, who owned the pet store. "He gave us a brief overview of what happened when we got here. Said to expect the police coming around to interview some of us. Officer Beatty already interviewed me and most of the vendors in this row. You think Sheriff Saron is cutting back on cases because he's retiring or because he wants time with Sam's mom?"

Bella, who was typically sweet and kind, seemed like she was in overdrive this morning. As if she realized Molly's surprise at her rapid-fire questioning, she gave a lopsided grin. "I'm sorry. I didn't sleep well last night and made up for it with three espressos. Feel free to run away screaming."

Molly laughed and picked up her camera. "I'm harder to scare off than that. I have no idea what's happening with the sheriff, but I trust Chris. Do you mind if I get a picture of you and ask a couple of questions?"

"About the event?" Bella's brows raised. The baker knew, like many of the people Molly had connected with since arriving, that she had a tendency to dig into details even if her job was editing the stories others wrote.

"Sure. How is this event different than the others, such as the Summer Wrap Up, that happen in Britton Bay?"

Bella thought about the question a moment, and once she'd written her answer, Molly asked the same question of several of the other vendors. Each one asked her opinion about what had happened. It wasn't until she made it to the end of one row that she saw Sam. He was chatting with Chris, and though she figured if it was anything that shouldn't be overheard, they'd have moved somewhere more private, she still hesitated to join them.

Sam's eyes landed on hers, and a smile lit up his face. He held out a hand to her, and she walked forward.

"Hey," she said, coming to his side and wrapping her arm around his waist. She leaned into him, and he pressed a kiss to the top of her head.

"Hey, yourself." He sounded tired, and her heart twisted. Hopefully, Chris and his deputies were making headway.

"How's it going, Officer Beatty?"

Chris sighed, glanced around the fairgrounds. "Slow." His gaze returned to her, and he arched his brow as if waiting.

"Jethro's wife checked into the bed-and-breakfast," Molly said.

Sam leaned away and looked down at her, his eyes wide. "Seriously? Why would she do that?"

Molly looked at Chris, hoping that if she easily shared information, he might do the same.

"Said she couldn't bear to be in Jethro's RV, and I guess Brian has Jet's ex-wife staying in his RV, so she didn't want to be around her either."

"Candice Harkaw is here. Has been all morning," Sam said.

That seemed strange to Molly, but she directed her question to Chris. "Amber also said Herman Besbrewer was the reason Jethro sent her back to the RV with another driver. Apparently, he had something to talk about that couldn't wait?"

Chris's shoulders lifted and dropped in another deep sigh. "No comment."

Molly's brows scrunched. "You've spoken to Brad Templeton?" Sam's arm tightened around her shoulder.

"No comment," Chris said.

Molly looked up at Sam. "Are all of the drivers here today?"

He nodded, and she looked at Chris with a smile. "Guess I'd better do a few last-minute interviews."

Chris's lips tightened, and he seemed to be struggling with what to say. Finally, he bit out, "Let us do our jobs, Molly."

"Back at you, Officer Beatty."

Sam shook his head and dropped his hand. "Am I always going to be telling you two to knock it off?"

Both of them looked at Sam, and Molly felt a hard stab of guilt. "I'm just going to interview the drivers about the show. I won't print anything about the murder that I don't check with the department." She turned to look at Chris. She didn't mind going head to head with him. He pushed her, she pushed back. But she never wanted Sam to feel torn between them.

"I appreciate that. Stop by the station a little later, and I'll update you with a formal statement," he said.

Sam clapped Chris on the shoulder. "There. Was that so hard?"

The three of them laughed, but Sam sobered quickly. "I need to do the closing ceremony. Candice and Brian both want to speak."

"I'm not going to stick around," Chris said. "I need to run down some leads and touch base with my deputies. I'll see you guys later."

He wandered off, and Molly was about to do the same because she knew Sam had things to do. Things that had seemed so exciting only a few days earlier would now be tinged with a dark sadness no one could have predicted.

Sam turned Molly, pulling her up against him. There were people walking and chatting. They were nowhere near alone, but Molly felt like it was just the two of them in a private bubble.

Sam smoothed her hair back from her face with both hands and touched her lips with his in such a gentle kiss, her breath caught. When he pulled away, just enough to speak, she put her hands on his wrists and stared into his troubled eyes.

"We don't know who the murderer is, babe. I know you have a job to do. I get that. I also know you're…curious." He paused.

Her stomach and heart took a tumble, slamming into each other. Molly tried to make light of it with one of her favorite *Alice in Wonderland* quotes. "Curiouser and curiouser."

His smile was shadowed with concern. "I need you to be careful. More than your usual careful. I have things I have to do, and you're wandering around with a camera and questions, and everyone is here today, which means, in all likelihood, whoever killed Jet is here. It would make my day easier if I knew you'd keep yourself safe."

"I will," she said. He didn't need to be worried about her on top of everything else.

"I mean it, Molly. You…" He stopped, closed his eyes, and pressed his forehead to hers.

"I what?" She wasn't sure why she whispered.

Sam opened his eyes, looked into hers with such a concentrated focus, her heart beat more heavily. "You're everything to me. I need you to be safe. To watch your back when I'm not there to do it."

Her heart flatlined for a full two seconds, and then she sucked in a breath. "Back at you." Going up on tiptoes, she pressed her mouth to his, hard, hoping she could show what neither of them wanted to say at a crowded fairground.

He returned the kiss, his fingers sifting through her hair. When he pulled back, he pressed a kiss to her forehead and said he was going to double-check the microphones.

She said she'd see him shortly, but as she stood there, watching him weave his way through the crowd, she took a minute. Pressing a hand to her heart, she gave herself some time until it slowed its frenzied pace. Wants and needs tugged at her from all sides. She wanted to run to him, to stay by his side. She wanted them both to walk away from the fairgrounds and forget that, once again, someone had died in their town. She needed to do her job, and she needed to do it in a way that let her keep her promise to Sam.

Heading for the gallery, knowing many of the drivers would be chatting while they waited for the closing ceremony to begin, she wondered if she was, indeed, about to rub shoulders with Jet's murderer. Would not knowing who it was help her keep her vow to Sam? She sure as heck hoped so.

Chapter Eleven

The drivers seemed to have broken off into groups. There were several women present. Whether they were wives, groupies, or children, Molly wasn't sure. Sam had told her there were people who traveled from one event to another, even if they weren't showing a car. It was a lifestyle.

Sam, Candice, and Brian chatted beside the podium. Brian's eyes scanned the crowd, as though he also wondered who among them could be guilty. She took it all in—the crowd, the subtle pulse of grief, the barely there hum of excitement—because this was still an event they were happy to attend. Did Jet personally know every driver involved? Could some of them be unaffected by his death?

Over the last two days, Molly had said hello to each of the drivers and gotten their names and vehicles for the paper. She and Jill had chatted back and forth about putting a roster of sorts in the paper to share who was who with the town. At the moment, however, she felt like it was a suspects list.

A chill hovered over the somber tone in the outbuilding. Brad and Herman were talking, heads close, and neither of them looked particularly happy. Some of the drivers were staring down at their phones. Everyone's attention was on other things, and that gave Molly a chance to keep looking around. No one looked twitchy or worried. There was no one glancing over their shoulder or trying to escape.

What did you think? That the killer would wear a shirt saying, "It was me"? That was as likely as her figuring out who it was just from their behavior in this room. She sidled closer to Brad and Herman, the only two she'd chatted with about anything beyond basic questions. Intending to ask their opinions, Molly stopped when she heard bits of their argument.

"Don't lie to me. I saw that stupid stick you suck on. I accidentally kicked it under the car and knew you'd been there." Herman was using a harsh whisper.

Brad glared at him. "Well, guess what? That means you were there *after* me. I saw you fighting with him. Want to explain that? I already spoke to the police."

Molly inched closer. She immediately wondered if he meant physically fighting or just arguing.

"And they told *you* to stay in town," Herman said.

"I'm pretty sure they told all of the drivers that," Molly said. Both men turned and looked at her, their mouths closing as they visibly worked to rein in their tempers.

Neither of them looked willing to talk. Their anger—whether it was with each other, the situation, or something else—vibrated off of them.

"Both of you saw Jet before he died?" Molly glanced up at the stage, where Candy seemed to be comforting Brian. Sam looked down at his phone. She couldn't catch his eye, but she knew they'd be starting soon.

"We did. But I didn't kill him," Brad snarled.

Herman bristled. "I didn't kill him either, you sniveling—"

Molly held up a hand. "I didn't suggest you did. Did the police?"

Brad crossed his arms over his chest, almost defiantly. "They questioned me. But they hear what they want to hear."

"Did you argue?"

Brad's jaw tightened. He shoved his hands in his pockets, making Molly wonder why he was so restless if he was innocent. "No. God, you sound like them. He wasn't there to see me anyway." He sent Herman a pointed look.

Before Molly could follow up on that, Sam got the crowd's attention.

"Hi, everyone. Thanks for being here this morning. It's with deep regret and sadness that I tell those of you who might not know that Jethro Harkaw passed away last night." Sam paused, found Molly's gaze in the crowd. She tried to smile, but her throat went tight, making it difficult to swallow or offer reassurance.

With the murmur that moved through the crowd, Molly realized some people actually didn't know what had been going on. Even if they'd been questioned by the police, they might not have been given any particulars.

Brad and Herman stared straight ahead, and Molly followed their gaze as Sam thanked the drivers and talked about Jethro's impact on the car world.

Brian stood next to Candice, and she was whispering something in his ear. He was hunched over to accommodate her shorter frame. Even though she wore high heels, he had to come down a fair amount. His hand slipped around her waist, and she leaned into his side as Sam made the crowd laugh by sharing a Jethro story.

It said a lot about her boyfriend that he could remind the crowd about Jethro's good qualities while still struggling with learning about the other side of his one-time idol.

"Before we assign the awards and prizes, Candice Harkaw and Brian Stoleman would like to say a few words," Sam said.

Sam gestured to the two, who pulled apart. Candice walked up to the small podium and picked up the microphone.

"Hi, everyone. Thank you for being here. Jethro loved everything about cars. He loved being in them, driving them, taking them apart, and talking about them. His greatest source of pride was the Classic Car Crawl."

Candice spoke eloquently, not a waver or break in her words. Molly was impressed with the way she held herself together and couldn't help comparing Jethro's ex-wife to his widow.

They were opposite ends of a spectrum, as different, from the outside, at least, as two women could be. Candice wore her long blond hair in a low ponytail which highlighted the fact that she wasn't wearing makeup. She was natural. Soft. Classy. Molly knew from experience that those qualities didn't rule her out as a killer. But she'd been with Brian. And Amber had been with Jet. *Until he sent her home. Then it was Herman.* She stared at Herman as Candy spoke.

"I was by Jethro's side for most of this journey. Up until the last little bit, when he decided to trade me in for a newer model with a younger, trimmer package," she smiled when she said it, clearly trying to lighten the mood. "But we stayed friends and business partners. There won't be a day I don't miss him."

The crowd clapped. Looking around, Molly saw sadness on many faces. A couple of people still scrolled through their phones, seemingly bored. Brian stepped up to the podium.

Molly wrote down the words "business partner" on her notepad. Was Candice a big part of the event? Was that why she was here? *Friends.* They'd certainly seemed more than friendly last night. As Brian cleared his throat and stared out at everyone, Molly made a couple more notes. Herman said Brad had talked with Jet before him. That established a bit of a time line. Amber said Herman had texted him. The time line was tripping her up.

"There are no words to express the hollowness I feel knowing that I'll never share another Classic Car Crawl with Jet. He was my best friend, the brother I never had, and we promised each other we'd do this to our dying day. I guess he kept his word." Brian looked up, tilting his head back, and took a few breaths. When he spoke again, he didn't do it into the microphone. "I'll keep going, brother. You are gone, but you are not forgotten, and I'll make sure your name lives on."

Stepping back from the podium, he looked out at them, but Molly got the impression he wasn't *seeing* anyone. Grief had a way of blinding a person. Remembering what he'd said the night before about this being his last event, Molly wondered if Brian now felt obligated to have this not be the last show.

Sam shook Brian's hand when he went back to the podium and began sharing the various awards that would be handed out. Molly had what she needed for now, as far as the car show went. She had to get to the station and get another statement, though.

Herman caught her eye, and she moved closer to him. "Amber said you texted Jet last night," she said as Sam spoke to the crowd.

"I did. What's it to you?"

Molly flinched. He'd certainly lost the friendly persona he'd put on yesterday.

"I was just curious. I'm sure you want to find out who did this as much as everyone else. Did he say anything about meeting anyone else?"

Realizing that she wasn't pointing a finger at him, he relaxed. The crowd clapped as one of the trophies was claimed.

"No. But we weren't exactly having a friendly conversation." He ran a hand over the top of his almost hairless head. Molly frowned and stepped closer. He had bruising under his eye and what looked like a cut lip. She hadn't noticed before because his tea-colored skin hid it until she was really focused.

Molly stared at him, and he fidgeted, dropping his hand, which had three knuckles crusted with blood. "You fought physically?"

Herman's gaze went dark. "He punched me first. I've put up with enough from him. Guy went crazy when I told him I was done waiting for him to pay me back. I told him I was going to expose him for the fraud he was. He sucker-punched me, we fought, I left. *With him alive.* But he gets the last laugh as usual."

Herman clapped along with the crowd when the winner of the "Best Newcomer" trophy went to receive the award. It wasn't Brad. Had he known?

Molly couldn't figure out how Jethro had had the last laugh or how any of this could be seen as funny. Then the words settled in her brain. "Wait, he owed you money?"

Herman folded his arms across his chest. "Fifty thousand dollars. Don't think I'll be getting it back now."

Chapter Twelve

BRITTON BAY BULLETIN @THEBULLETIN*2 HOURS
AMBER HARKAW, CLASSIC CAR CRAWL FOUNDER'S WIDOW, OFFERS REWARD
FOR INFORMATION LEADING TO AN ARREST OF HER HUSBAND'S KILLER.

Other than Amber reaching out to PBN, the Portland Broadcasting Network, to announce that she'd offered a monetary reward for leads, Monday was relatively quiet in Britton Bay. Sam returned to work, and since he'd stayed at his own place Sunday evening, Molly missed him by mid-afternoon. When she stopped by Come 'n Get It to grab him some lunch, she realized she'd have a bit of a wait.

A good number of the people hanging around because they'd been instructed to by the Britton Bay Police Department were in the diner. Molly recognized several drivers and their partners. She still couldn't figure out the dynamics of who was who, but wedding rings made a few of the relationships clear. Then she thought about Candy, Amber, and Jet and realized the wedding rings didn't necessarily tell the whole story.

"Hey, Molly." Calli greeted her, both hands grappling with delicious-looking sandwiches and fries. "Find a seat, hon."

Two other waitresses worked the floor with Calliope, and there was a teen behind the counter who looked familiar but whom Molly couldn't place. He was laughing at something Dean said from the kitchen.

"I'm just placing a to-go order," she said to Calli, walking between the full tables and booths to get to the counter.

The counter guy turned when Molly approached. Hovering somewhere between boyhood and manhood, he had thick brown hair that fell across his forehead and a happy smile that brightened her otherwise dreary day.

"Hi. Welcome to Come 'n Get It. What can I get for you?" His grin made Molly smile.

"I'll take a clubhouse sandwich on brown with fries."

"You got it," he said, then stared at the computer for a moment, his index finger hovering over the screen as his eyes scanned.

"I'm Molly. I work at the *Britton Bay Bulletin*. You're new here?"

He looked up as he pressed in her order. Dean caught her eye from behind the silver pass and waved.

"Hey, Molly. This is my nephew, Greg." Dean said.

Greg smiled at her, then turned to his uncle. "Order up. Less talking, more working."

Dean laughed, and so did Molly. "Kid wants a car, so he begs for a job; now he thinks he owns the place."

Molly paid for her order and slipped onto one of the retro, vinyl-covered spinning stools. "You look familiar."

He smiled, glancing at her as he slipped the money into the register. "You're working the Car Crawl, right?"

She nodded.

"I volunteered there Saturday night. We have to have a certain amount of volunteer hours to graduate."

"Oh. That's a great idea, though. Volunteering, I mean. Gives you a look at different job choices."

He shrugged. "Those cars were sweet, but I don't really want to work with vehicles. Doesn't matter if the hours are in keeping with what you want to do with your life. Guess they realize maybe all of us don't have it figured out."

His laugh was sweet and happy. She certainly hadn't known what she wanted to do when she graduated.

Molly wondered if the police had questioned the teens who helped out. There'd been several. "Did you work with a specific driver?"

He shook his head, looking back at the kitchen, then turning to Molly again when he saw he wasn't needed. "Nah. Just floated around. Grabbed food and water for some of the drivers who were busy chatting with people. Walked a bunch of people to their pickup vehicles at the end."

She smiled. "Guess if you're not into cars, you didn't meet any idols, huh?" Had it been Sam walking people to cars or floating around at Greg's age, he'd have been in his element.

Greg's laugh was cut short when he had to ring up several takeout orders in a row. A couple people slipped onto stools along the counter, but a few just waited by the register. Greg came back to Molly when he finished.

"I didn't have any idols, but I got to meet one of the people who ran it. Not the guy who died. The other one. I walked his girlfriend or whatever to the car."

Molly's ears practically twitched at his words. "His girlfriend?"

Someone else approached the counter. "Uh, seemed like his girlfriend. Could have been his friend, I guess. I left her at the car and had to go walk a few others out to the lot. Sorry, I gotta help this person."

Molly let the conversation go verbally, but in her head, all she could think about was the fact that both Candice and Brian had been alone after saying good night. Which gave either of them opportunity.

Greg smiled at her when the customer left after paying, but she didn't probe anymore, and that seemed to relax him.

"Busy time to start a new job," Molly remarked.

Greg nodded just as Calli came behind the counter. "Wasn't supposed to be. These folks staying in town means there's no time to stop and chat, doll, but I'm looking forward to catching up tomorrow at Sarah's."

"Me, too," Molly said.

Calli showed Greg how to do something on the computer as the other waitresses came to pick up orders. Spinning on her stool slowly, Molly noticed that neither Brad or Herman were in the diner. She wondered how many of the drivers were staying at the RV park. Looking around, she saw that Brian and Candice weren't around either.

She wasn't looking when someone slid onto the stool next to her, but she turned back toward the counter, wondering why, with all the empty stools, the person would slip in right beside her so they were elbow to elbow.

"Molly Owens, right?"

Molly turned her head to look at the speaker, a man about her age. He looked familiar, but she couldn't place him.

"That's right. And you are?"

He offered his hand. "Ed McLaren. PBN News."

Molly shook his hand. "You here specifically because of Jethro's death or because of the car show?"

He smiled. "Direct. I like it. Planned on doing the car show, got caught up in other things. Showed up late Saturday."

She nodded. Greg came over to ask if they wanted anything to drink while they were sitting. They both said no, and Molly checked the time on her phone.

"You're sticking around?" she asked. "Waiting to see what comes of Amber Harkaw's reward announcement?"

She thought about the fact that Jet owed money. "Do you know if she has the funds to support the reward?"

He smiled, leaned his elbow on the counter. He was attractive in a polished sort of way. Slicked back, sandy-brown hair and a camera-ready smile. She didn't like the way he crowded her personal space with just a look.

"Her last husband left her a sizable inheritance."

Of all the things she thought he might be about to say, *that* wasn't one of them. Without meaning to, she leaned in. "Amber was married before? To someone who died? How do you know that?"

"We have resources. Amber's first husband died of a heart attack. The death was ruled natural. She was young when she married him. But yes, I'm positive she has the money."

Molly's lips pressed into a pout. Amber was young *now*. Before she could think about all of the implications, someone tapped her on the shoulder.

She looked up and saw Sam standing beside her, his brows scrunched, a not-so-happy look on his face. It was then she realized how close she and Ed were physically. The information he'd shared had done exactly what he'd hoped—drawn her completely in. But Ed, even with his slick looks and handy information, couldn't hold even the weakest of candles to Sam.

Slipping off her seat, she stepped into him and wrapped her arms around his waist. "Hi. This is a coincidence."

His arms wrapped around her, but when she looked up, she saw his gaze was on Ed. "Thought I'd grab some lunch."

Ed and Sam stared at each other. The air went thick, and despite the noise of patrons and clanging dishes, Molly felt like she'd been pulled into a vortex of strange silence.

"This is Ed McLaren. He's a reporter for the Portland Broadcasting Network. Ed, this is Sam Alderich, my boyfriend and owner of Sam's Service Station."

It took them a second longer of staring, but Sam released one of his arms to shake Ed's hand.

"Your shop sponsored the event?" Ed knew his stuff even if he'd arrived late.

"We did." The arm still around Molly tightened.

"Rough go. Sorry about Jethro. Did you know him outside of the Crawl?" Sam shook his head.

A bell rang behind them. "Order up. Hey, Sam." Dean waved.

Sam smiled, his body relaxing. "Hey, Dean. I was craving your fries."

"That's what they all say. Pretty sure this order is yours, so you're in luck."

Greg grabbed the bagged-up order and set it on the counter. "There you go, ma'am."

She smiled and grabbed the bag. "Molly."

His cheeks went pink. "Right. Molly. Hey, Mr. Alderich."

"Hey, Greg," Sam said.

Molly looked up at him and offered the takeout. "Great minds. I was just about to bring this to you."

Sam's gaze, his stance, and the set of his jaw all softened, and Molly's heart gave a hard tug.

Taking the bag with one hand, he hooked a hand around her neck and pulled her closer. "Share it with me?"

She nodded, her heart rate speeding up. She glanced at Ed, who was watching them. "Nice to meet you."

"You too, Molly. I'll see you soon, I'm sure."

Sam glared at him and didn't say goodbye as he took Molly's hand and led her out of the diner.

"Bye, love birds," Calli called as the door swung closed behind them. Molly bit her lip to keep from giggling.

Sam glanced down at her as they walked, hand in hand, toward his shop, which was only a few doors down from the diner.

"Are you trying not to laugh?" One side of his mouth quirked up.

"A little, yeah." She let the wide grin take over her face.

Sam stopped abruptly, and she turned so the front of their bodies were touching. The breeze from the ocean slid over and around them, but standing on the sidewalk, looking up at him, she didn't feel the chill.

"Sam."

He sighed. "Molly."

Putting her hands on his chest, she stared a moment longer. "Are you okay?"

Sam brought a hand up to her hair and smoothed his palm down the length of it. "I just feel out of sorts, I think. I wish Chris would update us. I've got a bunch of the drivers hanging out at the shop. It's cool, but it's like Jethro's death is hovering over every conversation."

"I'm sorry." What else could she say?

"It's not your fault. In any way. Let's do something tonight. Head out of town and see a movie or something. You've got the paint thing tomorrow night, right?"

"Yes. I'm sure it's still on. Tonight sounds good. I'd like that."

He pulled her into a hug, and she held on tight, wishing the last few days weren't weighing so heavy on him.

"You go have your lunch. I'm going to head back to work and get some stuff out of the way so we can forget about everything else tonight."

Sam leaned back. "Thought you were sharing my fries."

"Next time."

"Not tonight, though. Let's go somewhere that doesn't serve fries," he suggested.

"Oh. That sounds intriguing. I like it."

She kissed him goodbye, and her heart tumbled a little more when he watched her cross the street. She waved when he was outside of his shop and then headed back to the *Bulletin*.

Jill was at her desk. Elizabeth would be back from her vacation by the end of the week.

"Hey. Where are Alan and Clay?"

Jill looked up from her computer. "Alan is in his office chatting with ad people. Clay said he was going to take photos."

Molly stopped short of rolling her eyes. They might need to let him go after all. The paper came out on Thursday, which meant it was all hands on deck every Monday and Tuesday. They were already short several pair of hands.

Glancing at Alan's closed office door and knowing they'd be tied up for the rest of the afternoon getting the paper ready, she gestured to her own office with a tip of her head.

"Got a minute?"

Jill smiled. "Sure."

Without a word, they went to Molly's office and shut the door.

"What's up, Nancy Drew?" Jill sat down in the chair on the other side of Molly's desk. She ignored the teasing and grabbed a piece of paper and a pen, and sat in the chair beside her friend and colleague.

She wrote down Jethro's name in the center of the page. Jill leaned in as she drew lines to Candice, Amber, Brian, Brad, and Herman. She put down each of their connections to Jethro and then a possible motive for each.

Jill traced the line that led to Herman. "Wait, Jethro owed Herman money?"

Molly nodded. "A lot of money. And he admitted to being there after Brad was in the gallery on Saturday night. Amber said Herman texted Jet, and she caught a ride with another driver."

Staring at the paper, Jill tapped her finger on the desk. "Okay. So Herman may have murdered him because he owed him money. Doesn't really improve his chances of getting paid."

Molly tapped her fingers. "Jet and Herman got into a fistfight about the money. Tensions were obviously running high, but he said he walked away with Jethro standing."

"Well, he wouldn't say he killed him. But I thought you didn't think Brian was likely. And didn't you say he was with the ex?" Jill pointed to Candice's name.

Molly nodded. "But the kid I just talked to at the diner said he walked Candice to the pickup van, alone."

Jill rubbed her forehead. "Okay. So that keeps them both in it. And the fight with Herman explains what I found out from the ME. Jethro had severe bruising in the abdomen, likely from a fist, and several facial bruises. One was older than the rest. I don't know why, and neither did the ME."

Pushing back from her chair, Molly stood, wishing they were outside, walking on the beach, like maybe the fresh air could help filter her thoughts. "Jethro said he hit his face in the RV. He had a black eye on Thursday night."

Leaning back in her chair, Jill picked up the pen and twirled it between her fingers. "Okay. Herman could be lying. Maybe he took the fight to a new level, picked up the crowbar, smashed Jet with it, but didn't intend to kill him? Wiped it down and left."

It was definitely a possibility. As Jill said, Herman wouldn't be getting paid anytime soon, if at all. His best chance of getting paid was if Jethro was alive.

"What about the ex-wife? You said they were kissing. Maybe she went after Jet once the kid walked her to the car. He tells her to leave because, as he told Brian, he needed to get current wifey home. She gets mad. Swings the crowbar at his head when he tells her he can't choose between her and Hawaiian Barbie."

Walking back and forth in the small space was not productive, so Molly took her seat again. "Jet was a big man. It seems so difficult to imagine a woman having enough force behind a swing to kill him."

Jill waggled her eyebrows comically. "Sexist, but not if she distracted him."

Molly smiled. "True. Scorned lover?"

A knock came about two seconds before the knob turned, and Alan popped his head through. "Girls' club meeting?"

Molly and Jill laughed. "Not so much. Just talking about Jethro."

He came all the way into the room. "Of course. What other topic is there? You solve the murder yet?" He smiled at her affectionately.

"Of course not," she said, shooting Jill a look that she hoped said *shh*.

"We need to get going on the paper. We'll do the feature on Jethro that Jill wrote, but I'd still like to include some lighter pieces about the show. Your interview, Molly, and the list of drivers and vehicles. Maybe we do something fun like a game to match the car to the driver?"

Grinning, happy with the distraction, Molly stood up. "That's a great idea. Very fun."

"Perfect. I'll put a pot of coffee on. Won't be as good as Elizabeth's, but it'll get us through the next few hours."

Jill poked Molly in the shoulder as they went back into the main office space. "Put it out of your mind for a bit. Sometimes things fall together on their own. Plus, I bet those guys with badges are still poking around."

Molly's laugh cleared the last of the cobwebs from her brain. "I think your cold left you with a stronger sense of humor."

With a mischievous smile, Jill nodded. "I was always funny. You're just paying more attention now."

Molly was always paying attention, sometimes to too many things at once. She needed to learn how to compartmentalize better. Newspaper now. Sam later. And everything else could wait.

Chapter Thirteen

The space Sarah had rented for her shop was adorable. It hadn't been when she'd taken over the lease a few months earlier, but Molly, Sam, Chris, and several others had chipped in to make it cozy and bright.

In addition to offering lessons in a variety of mediums, Sarah did paint nights, sign painting, pottery, and jewelry workshops. Those could be private events or public ones. She had her first bridal party booking next week, which was the reason behind the Tuesday night gathering.

"Thanks for coming, everyone," Sarah said. There were four, large rectangular tables with stools around each. Sarah stood between the two tables at the front of the room. "I've put all of the paint supplies out. I just need to grab the canvases, and I'll show you the painting I've created. I'll walk you through each step, and it really doesn't matter if you've painted a hundred times or never. We'll work together, but each one will be unique."

"Mine will be uniquely garish," Priscilla joked. Pris worked the front desk at the police station. She was good friends with Bella.

Calli nudged Pris in the ribs. "You can paint right over it if it's too bad."

The others laughed, and Sarah smiled, waiting patiently. She'd swept her hair over to the side with a bobby pin and looked more like a student than an artist, business owner, and teacher. Molly scanned the room and was pleased to see everyone had shown up. Katherine was perched on one of the stools, Calli beside her, standing. Pris and Bella were leaned against one of the heavy tables. Even Alan's wife, Vicky, and their niece, Hannah, had come. Jill held up her wineglass and saluted Molly.

Sarah gestured to Jill. "Special thanks to Jill for supplying enough wine that no matter how anyone feels about their paintings, we might all think they're masterpieces."

When the laughter quieted, she also gestured to Bella. "And thank you, Bella, for bringing snacks. I haven't decided whether or not to offer a small appetizer menu, sort of like what Bella brought tonight. I might just allow parties who book events to bring their own snacks. Maybe that can be one of the things you offer an opinion on tonight."

"We could work something out so it's a choice for the booking party. I can create a small party package that you could offer on top of the paint nights," Bella said.

"I can't provide wine for all of the parties, though," Jill quipped.

They chatted for a few minutes while Sarah went into the adjoining room to grab the canvases. Jill poured wine for everyone, and they caught up on local gossip, which was a refreshing change from talking about Jethro's murder. Calliope updated them on what was happening at the diner, and Molly could not help but notice the way Hannah seemed to perk up at the mention of Greg. *Something there maybe?* Hannah was a sweet and smart kid. She'd be graduating in June, and Molly was certain she'd have a bright future. The subject got a bit heavier when Bella told them that Callan, her ex, was still pressuring her to get back together.

"You can file a restraining order if it gets too bad," Pris said.

She was the eyes, ears, and hands of the department. She worked the front desk, answering phones, logging complaints, fielding questions, checking evidence, and as Molly had found out not too long ago, pretty much anything they needed her to do.

"I don't want to go that route. We went to high school together. We've known each other forever. But he wasn't happy with me either, so I don't even know why he's pushing to get back together." Bella took a sip of her wine.

"That boy has always wanted what he couldn't have," Calli remarked. She wasn't wrong, but the way she spoke—as if she was so much older than the rest of them—amused Molly. Calli was a mother hen, and the people in this room, along with several other residents, were her little chicks.

Wondering if Sarah needed help grabbing the canvases for this many people, Molly broke away from the group and wandered to the back room. The space was open and airy, even with the windows closed, because of the time of year. The main room was a bright, cheery yellow, with a mural Sarah had created of the town on one entire wall. It was incredible, and Molly had enjoyed watching Sarah work on it. There was a small bathroom and a mudroom area that would be used for cleaning supplies. Beside that was a broom-closet-sized office, and right next to that was the storage and supply room.

When Molly stepped in, Sarah sniffled loudly and whirled her way, a tissue in her hand.

"Hey. You okay?" Molly stepped forward. This room was perfectly square and completely cramped. One side held shelves upon shelves of supplies, all ruthlessly organized. The other side held a bench-like shelf with projects that Sarah was working on. There was a door that led outside to the alley.

"Yeah. I'm fine. Sorry. I was just trying to make sure I have enough canvases." Sarah turned again and counted the stack of them she'd put on the bench.

Another glance at the supply shelves reminded Molly of the evenings they'd spent helping Sarah get her stock ready. *Ruthless* might have been too mild a term for Sarah's level of organization. There was no way she went into tonight without having everything she needed.

"Sarah?" Molly stepped closer.

"Hmm?" She didn't turn around.

Putting a hand on her arm and keeping her voice low, since her new friend clearly didn't want an audience, she peeked around her shoulder. "Talk to me. What's wrong?"

Sarah huffed out a deep, almost shuddery breath, but her voice was even when she spoke. Turning to face Molly, she gestured to the canvases on the floor by the shelves.

"I was positive I checked and double-checked my supplies for tonight. I think I'm…I don't know…sleep-painting or something." Her cheeks went a soft rosy pink, and she glanced down, staring at her hands. "I know that sounds ridiculous."

Molly went to the canvases she hadn't noticed and crouched in front of them. With one finger, she pulled each one forward to rest against her knee. Some had a few squiggles and splatters on the edges. A few had what Molly would say were abstract designs, and still others were painted solid colors in varying shades.

Looking up at Sarah, she asked, "Is this the first time your supplies seem to have been used when you don't remember using them?"

Her cheeks flushed a deeper shade of red, and Molly wondered why she'd be embarrassed. "No. But, honestly, it's not a big deal."

Molly stood up, shaking out her legs. How did people crouch for extended periods of time? Looking at the blank canvases Sarah had put aside, she did a quick count. Eight canvases. It was enough, but clearly she'd had more set aside.

"What else has been touched?" She held her friend's gaze, trying not to push, but not wanting her to feel like she had to hide anything.

Sarah sighed and tossed her Kleenex into the small wastebasket by the door. "A week ago, I came in and my brand-new Copic markers had been used. I get distracted sometimes. I'll get off the phone with my mom and then see I doodled all over the cover of a notebook. I often forget things because I'm thinking about art or designs."

She was blowing it off, but it was clearly bothering her. Molly arched a brow. "What else?"

Leaning against the bench, Sarah gestured to the shelves. "I'm pretty meticulous about how I keep them, and more than once I've come in and felt like things were…out of place. That sounds so dumb."

"No, it doesn't. Have you talked to Chris?"

Sarah's eyes widened, and she gave a dismissive laugh. "No. And I'm not going to. It's not a big deal, Molly. Honestly. I'm super distracted. We haven't been friends for that long, but you'll see. Give it a few months, and the first time I forget to show up for something we planned because I fell into a drawing or painting, you'll see."

Giving her a smile, Molly leaned on the bench beside her. "I get that. I do. The same thing happens to me when I'm reading or editing. Or writing. I think creative types tend to function, at least partially, in their own little universe. But that doesn't make what's happening less real, Sarah. And it's strange. Maybe it's not a big deal, but you have to admit it's strange."

Sarah ran her hand along the bench. "I can admit it's strange without involving Chris. He has a lot on his plate right now. Things far more serious than some missing paints and used markers."

Unsure what to say or how hard to push, Molly gave her arm a comforting squeeze. "He'd want to know. Even if it's just part of telling him about your day. I'm positive he'd want to know."

Sarah shrugged. "Maybe. We…we're just starting out. I don't want to throw this at him. I'm not trying to be stubborn or silly. I just think he has more important things to think about."

Molly understood her reasoning but still disagreed. Pushing off the bench, she walked to the door. It wasn't dead-bolted, and there was no lock on the knob.

"You use this door?"

Sarah picked up the canvases. "Only for taking out the trash. It's got a coded entry pad on the other side."

Molly thought about that, but since Sarah was already heading back to the art room, she could only follow. The women had spread out between the tables and were laughing loudly. Katherine was telling them about one of the bed-and-breakfast guests who sleepwalked.

"I'm just glad I hadn't gotten ready for bed yet," Katherine said.

The laughter quieted as Sarah showed the picture they were going to recreate. It was gorgeous. Sarah put it on the easel at the front of the room and pointed to it.

"I wanted to choose something universal, and I thought that, with winter coming, the ocean is going to be beautiful. I also thought most of us are probably pretty partial to the view."

They nodded in agreement, all of them a little stunned at the level of her talent. If any of them were sharing Molly's thoughts, they might also have been wondering how the heck they were going to paint anything that resembled what Sarah had created.

The background was a mix of grays, blacks, and blues. There was enough distinction for viewers to see they were looking at the ocean meeting the sky on a cold day. The pier in the painting looked like a carbon copy of the one down the street. The picture was so realistic—a little dark and a little haunting—that Molly shivered.

"That is just amazing, Sarah," Katherine said.

"I'm going to need a lot more wine when I'm looking at mine because it's the only way it'll look like that," Pris said, lifting her glass to her lips. She finished off the last swallow in her glass and poured herself some more.

They each got top-ups for their drinks. Molly chose soda, and Hannah smiled at her, holding up her own can. "No wine for me," she said quietly.

"At seventeen, I would think not. Though, just between you and me, wine is overrated." Molly nudged her with her shoulder, and Hannah laughed.

Sarah explained how they were going to work toward the finished result and went over the supplies and the different brushes, and they each found a space at a table. With their canvases, paint, water, and brushes, they started the step-by-step process of recreating the painting.

The noise level fluctuated between loud laughter, quiet conversation, and intense concentration. The more Pris drank, the more verbal she became, making the others laugh. Bella and she took turns swapping canvases, and when Sarah came by to check Molly's progress, she looked over at them.

"I guess you'll get some who are more interested in the socializing than the art," she said quietly, smiling despite the difficulty of the task. How Sarah made this look effortless was far beyond Molly's level of understanding.

Sarah grinned at Pris and Bella. "They're having a great time, and that's what this is all about. They won't come back because they love painting—though a few might—but because they had fun."

"Oops. Huh. Guess I'll have a tree in mine," Pris said, snorting through a giggle.

The others laughed, and Sarah went to take a closer look. "You can definitely make that a tree. Or a lamppost maybe?"

Pris set her brush down. "I want to work here. It's more fun." She was still smiling, so no one shifted their attention.

"You could come work at the diner," Calli offered.

"Nooo. No serving food to others. I think I'd munch on their fries as I delivered them," Pris admitted.

"She helped me out at the bakery one weekend and ate all of my profits," Bella said.

The laughter felt good. Molly had been reluctant to come tonight, not because she didn't want to but because there was still so much up in the air and because Sam seemed withdrawn, down. And she hated it. But he'd insisted he was hanging out with Chris anyway. If Chris could get away from work, they planned to shoot some pool and maybe watch sports highlights. It was good for them both to get out and put the stress of the weekend aside.

"How's that tip line working out?" Calli asked. She'd put her brush down and was browsing the cookies and pastries Bella had put on one of the tables.

Priscilla sighed dramatically and sank onto her stool. "It's the stupidest thing ever. Hey, everyone in Britton Bay, call our station and tell me what you think you might have seen. It's tripled my workload. The city might not have the budget for any more deputies, but they need to hire another person for the phones at least."

"Have you talked to the sheriff about it?" Katherine asked mildly.

Pris turned in her seat, realizing belatedly it wasn't a spinning stool and wobbled a little. Bella laughed.

"I'll bring it up when everyone can breathe. We have weekly station meetings, and everyone does a little bit of everything when we're in the office, so it's not like they don't know."

Then, with the candor alcohol imparts, she bounced her eyebrows up and down. "Speaking of the sheriff...you're never too old to dish."

Katherine laughed. "Dish?"

Bella nodded. "Sheriff Saron is good-looking for an older man."

Katherine held her brush still and stared at Bella until Bella realized what she'd said. When she did, one hand flew over her mouth.

Vicky laughed. "It's okay to recognize a handsome older man, dear. I have one of those myself, and any of the men you ladies are interested in are going to age eventually," she said.

Sam's mom nodded, and Molly smiled and turned back to her painting, happy to just listen in on the conversation. Her thoughts drifted to Sam getting older. He'd be no less handsome, just with more laugh lines and touches of gray at his temples. *Oh boy. Slow down, Molly.* She'd lived with a man before and never imagined who they'd be that far down the line. It took falling for Sam to realize that she'd only been one foot into her last relationship. It wasn't her fault that he cheated—he was still dead wrong there—but maybe, if she'd felt for him what she felt for Sam, they would have been better for each other. Or she'd have left the relationship with fewer scars at least. *But if not for him, you wouldn't have Sam.* It was one of those situations that seemed impossible, because finding out her ex was cheating had sucked hugely. But if Sam was the reward for going through that? *Yup. I'd do it again.* She was so sunk.

"The ex-wife gets everything," Pris said, pulling Molly's attention.

"Whose ex-wife?" Molly asked, her fingers tightening on the thin-tipped brush.

"That car guy's," Pris said, her head swinging in Molly's direction.

Jill laughed. "I call the current wife Hawaiian Barbie and the ex Malibu Barbie."

"Those both fit," Pris said. "I'd be choked if my husband stayed in business with his ex-wife."

Bella and Jill murmured agreement.

"But if they had the business arrangement before the marriage, his wife would have known, going in, that he still had ties to his former wife," Vicky said. Her brow was scrunched in concentration.

"How do you know Candice gets everything, Pris?" Molly set her brush down.

"It's in the paperwork. She's his bene…ben…I never realized how hard that word was," she said, trailing off.

Jill laughed. "Beneficiary?"

Pris pointed at her, eyes brightening up. "That! Yeah. She gets it all. Everything. Despite that, it's the other one offering a reward to find the killer. Too much drama for me. Maybe I really do need to think of alternate employment," Priscilla said. She stared at her half-finished painting.

Molly noted the melancholy in Priscilla's tone and frowned. Taking a moment to stretch, she looked across the table. "I'm going to get some fresh air. Want to come?"

Pris shrugged. "Sure."

Molly looked around. "Anyone else?"

"I'm not sure walking around in the dark is a great idea with what's going on," Katherine said.

They wouldn't venture far, but Katherine's concern was valid. Still, Molly wanted to get her friend some fresh air now before her thoughts became maudlin.

"We'll stick close. Promise." Molly nodded to Pris. "Just a few minutes of fresh air."

Katherine nodded in understanding. Bella slipped off her stool, eyed her own painting, which was quite similar to Sarah's. It didn't have the same sophisticated technique, but it was very pretty.

"I'll come, too. Too much wine makes my head spinny," Bella said.

Sarah unlocked the door for them, and they stepped out into the frigid night air. Unlike many of the other businesses in this area, the Art Shop had its own parking lot. It wasn't huge, but it would make hosting groups easier and less cumbersome for the surrounding owners.

"I like Sarah. She's good people," Priscilla said. Her words fumbled over each other, blending syllables.

"You okay, Pris?" Bella asked, staring up at the starry sky. Eyes closed, hands in the pockets of her long, winter coat, Bella just stood.

"Yeah. Better than Jethro." Her voice got quiet, and while Bella kept her face turned up, as if meditating on the sky, Molly stepped closer to Pris.

"Are you really okay?"

Priscilla was professional and confident. She handled a bull pen full of cops and the front desk with ease and a smile. But this case seemed to be unraveling her a bit, and that worried Molly.

Pris looked down at the pavement. "My dad was stabbed," she whispered. Molly's heart clenched, and she put her arm around Priscilla. "I found him. I was eleven. Most days...I'm fine. Really, I am. I don't dwell on it. I'm happy. I know he'd be happy I grew up and became who I am. But seeing the crime-scene photos...I don't know. Jethro wasn't stabbed, I get that, but he was killed and just left there. To die alone. It just triggered something, you know?"

Molly nodded, her eyes filling with tears. "I'm so sorry. That's terrible for anyone, but to see something like that so young." She had questions but wouldn't ask. She couldn't get them past the lump in her throat.

"His pawnshop got robbed. He let the guys have everything. They still stabbed him. When I found him, he looked like he was resting. Except for the knife." She shivered, and Molly put her other arm around her friend. Priscilla leaned into her but kept her arms at her side.

"You saw the photos of Jethro looking like he was sleeping?" Molly felt her nod.

"It was like looking into a memory, Molly. They never found the guy who stabbed my dad." She pulled in a breath and stepped back. Molly dropped her hands.

"Since there were no prints on the crowbar, they won't find this guy either. How can they? I wanted to work with the police—not be an officer, but be part of the team that made the world a safer place. But it just feels like life gets scarier. More dangerous."

Molly didn't know what to say to that. Her heart ached for Priscilla. In the back of her mind, she tucked away the information, but she knew she needed to get her friend home before she divulged any information that she'd regret the next day.

She was just about to tell her she'd take her home when Bella spoke.

"I'm going to be sick."

Molly sighed, grateful she hadn't had any wine. She'd be taking them both home and hoping her Jeep didn't need to be detailed afterward.

Chapter Fourteen

Molly spent most of Wednesday morning proofing news articles and features. By noon, she was ready for a break and wondering how Priscilla was feeling. Jill was out of the office. She'd received a lead on a puppy mill just outside of town and wanted to follow up.

Since Molly had arrived in Britton Bay, she'd been hearing about this elusive illegal activity. Whatever tip Jill was following today, she hoped it led to something that could close the place down. Thinking about Tigger's eagerness on their walk this morning reminded her that, once again, something good in her life came from something unpleasant.

When she'd discovered Tigger behind a dumpster at the *Bulletin*, she'd tried to find his owners, but none had surfaced. Several people had suggested that her furry pal was a puppy mill runaway.

Pushing away from her desk, she went to find Alan and saw he had company. Ed McLaren smiled at her from the chair in front of her boss's desk.

"Hello, Molly. I heard you've met Ed?" Alan gestured for her to come in.

There was a leather couch to the right of his desk, but Molly didn't sit there. Instead, she walked to the desk and remained standing.

"We met yesterday. I heard the police station is being inundated with tips thanks to your story on Amber's reward," Molly said.

Ed smiled like it was an actual compliment. He opened his arms, spread his palms up. "Whatever I can do to help."

Alan leaned back in his leather chair, steepling his fingers under his chin. "Ed says he has some news he'd be willing to share about Jethro's history. Seems he's been following him for a while."

Irritation prickled at the back of her neck. "Google does make life easier."

Alan smirked but quickly recovered. Ed held Molly's gaze, unbothered by her less than friendly welcome. If he was offering something, he wanted something. Not only did they not have anything to give, but she was wary of giving anything to a regional outlet that was less concerned about their little town than they were with making headlines. *But if he thinks there's a headline here, maybe he does know something.*

Before he could comment on her dig, she sat in the chair beside him. "I don't think we have much to trade. I'm also not sure why you're so interested in this story."

Honesty was easier for her than playing games. From the way he smiled, Ed appreciated the candor.

"I can't get the local police to talk at all. Not even a statement. You have any sway there?"

Molly grinned and thought of how many times Chris had rolled his eyes at her and the way Sheriff Saron warned her off of...almost everything.

"Absolutely," she replied.

"Perfect. Then you can work together," Alan said.

Molly stood. "We can exchange information, and then I'm heading to the station. If I get an update, I'll share it with you."

Ed stood, straightening his shoulders, as if she needed the reminder that she was shorter. Especially in her preferred Converse sneakers.

"Maybe I'll share mine after you talk the police," he said.

"Is what you have worth my waiting?"

She felt Alan's gaze following their verbal volley.

"Candice Harkaw stands to inherit all of Jethro's money. Jet never changed his will, and since Candy owns part of the business, everything professional and personal is hers. Including the house Amber lives in. The police are taking their time, trying to rule out drivers so they can let them leave, but Amber has a life she needs to get back to as well."

Molly didn't react, since she already knew this, but she also wondered what Ed's angle was here. She stared at him, trying to read his intentions.

Alan pushed away from his desk and came around to join them. "The police have questioned her?"

Molly nodded. "She and Amber were both questioned. I think everyone has been, preliminarily."

"And now that they're doing follow-up interviews, things are getting drawn out."

Molly frowned. "Murder tends to do that. Make things inconvenient for the people impacted by it."

Ed grinned. "That's the truth. But with your little one-horse town, the delay is much longer. Candice Harkaw is the most viable suspect, yet your guys are running around chasing innocent women like Amber."

It took effort to unclench her jaw. "Britton Bay has a half dozen well-trained, experienced deputies, in addition to four reserve officers in surrounding counties, and a sheriff with one of the best reputations on the West Coast."

"Doesn't change the numbers. Now, I shared mine. I left my number with Alan. Touch base with me when you've talked to the police."

He tipped an imaginary hat to her and Alan, and left, leaving Molly staring at his back. Her teeth were definitely clenched.

"Sometimes I forget that you came from a big city," Alan said, patting her arm.

She crossed her arms over her chest, then dropped them. She poked her head around his doorframe to make sure Ed had left.

"What do you mean?"

Alan laughed, and they went into the main area. "You're so mild and sweet, but when the big boys show up, they don't stand a chance."

She turned and looked at him. "Um, did you not see that? Because I'm pretty sure he just got the last word." She pointed toward the door.

Shaking his head, Alan pulled his phone from his pocket. "Conversation isn't over, Molly. I have no doubt the last word will be yours."

His confidence loosened the tension in her shoulders. "Let's hope you're right. I need to head to the police station."

"Now?"

She glanced at her office. "Actually, I think I need to consult Google first. Once I do, I'll see if I can get an updated statement from Officer Beatty."

Looking down at his phone, Alan murmured his agreement. "I'm going to meet Vicky for lunch. She had a great time last night. Thank you for including her."

Any thoughts of the murder or the irritating reporter fled. She smiled at her boss and stepped closer. "It was really fun. I'm glad she came. Hannah, too."

His smile was a touch dreamy, and she knew he was thinking of his wife. They'd been through a lot in the short time Molly had been in Britton Bay. Alan's smile was replaced by a grimace.

"Vicky tells me Hannah likes that Greg boy who started at the diner. He seems a bit...mature for her."

Molly bit her lip and stared at him. "He's the same age as Hannah. I'm pretty sure they go to school together."

"Yes, but he's saving for a car. You know where that will lead."

Molly laughed, loudly. Alan did not look impressed. "Hannah's a smart girl, Alan. With a very bright future ahead of her. And for what it's worth, Greg seems very nice. Plus, he's Calli and Dean's nephew. So that's comforting, right?"

Alan didn't look convinced. "You weren't here when Dean and his brother were younger. Those two weren't exactly little angels."

Patting his arm, she tried for an empathetic smile. "But now Dean's been married, happily, to Calli for years. Hannah's a smart girl, Alan. I don't think you need to worry about her."

It was his turn to grin. "Sometimes I can't help it. She's really blossomed over the last year. Come into her own. With Jill being here—remembering when she went off to college—it makes me a little sad that Hannah will likely do the same."

"Just remember, Jill came back."

He nodded, and with one more smile, she went to her office and did a little social media digging. Edward McLaren was more careful with his profiles than most. His Facebook, Instagram, and Twitter accounts were locked and revealed very little personal information. Fortunately for Molly, Amber was not nearly as cautious.

By the time she was on her way to the station, she'd learned that Amber and Ed had been junior high sweethearts. She'd posted several pictures of herself with "Eddie M" from "back in the day," as the folder was titled.

Ed's interest in this case wasn't professional. It was completely personal. And if he and Amber were still involved or had been at any time during her marriage, it changed things. He'd come to get answers, but instead, he'd left Molly with a very basic question: Did Ed still love Amber enough to kill for her?

Chapter Fifteen

The police station was busier than Molly expected. Even the parking lot was packed. She had to find a spot near the street. The wind had picked up over the last two days, and as she pulled the neck of her jacket tighter, she thought about asking Jill to do some shopping. She needed warmer winter gear, including some gloves and a good scarf.

As she climbed the steps to the station doors, she stepped to the side as a few people she vaguely recognized exited. She held the door, but they didn't acknowledge her because they were busy chatting.

"I thought there was a reward for giving information," one of the guys said.

"Me, too," the girl said, her tone sulky.

"I told you guys it was only if it led to anything. You think they're just going to hand out twenties at the front desk?" the second guy asked them, scoffing.

They were probably in their very early twenties, if that. Molly wondered if this was just a snapshot of what Priscilla was dealing with every day.

Her pale pink Converses were mostly silent on the linoleum floor. The wide lobby of the station was larger than the outside of the building suggested. Though they were understaffed and probably underfunded, the station had resources. There were holding cells downstairs and several interrogation rooms behind the counter, and as Molly knew from personal experience, there were interview, fingerprinting, and mugshot rooms down a hallway to the left.

An assortment of people sat on the benches that ran along the wall in the waiting area. There were more standing in line at the reception desk.

Molly couldn't believe how many residents had come to give information. How did the police decide what to take and what not to take?

She ducked around the line, waving to a couple of people she recognized. Officer Beatty and Priscilla were both behind the counter.

"I'm not sure how telling me your sister-in-law met Mr. Harkaw twenty years ago helps the investigation, Mrs. Shilling."

The older lady, whom Molly had seen around but never met, shook her finger at Chris. "She's a sneaky one. You know she tried to turn my Timmy against me when we were dating."

Molly rolled her lips inward, trying not to laugh. This woman probably hadn't dated in fifty years.

"That doesn't mean she hurt someone. But I'll look into it," he said.

She smiled at him. "You're a nice boy, Christopher."

Molly smiled, and he caught it, sending her a glare that said he was finding it difficult to be a nice anything right now.

She walked away, but before the next person approached him, he looked at Priscilla. "I have to chat with Molly. You okay here?"

Priscilla gave Molly a weary smile. "They'll just have to be patient. You can do that, right, guys?"

Several people murmured agreement. Some didn't reply. Molly looked at Pris and mouthed, "You okay?"

"I'm good. Thanks for last night." Priscilla held her gaze a moment longer than necessary, and Molly knew she was thanking her for more than the ride home.

"Anytime."

Chris let her through the locked gate, and she followed him across the empty bullpen.

"Wow. You must really hate working the front desk if you're using me as an escape," Molly said when they were in his small office.

He closed the door behind them and leaned against his desk. "You have no idea." He smiled when he said it.

"How are you doing?" He was a cop, someone she needed information from and needed to give information to, but he was also a friend. A very good friend of the man she was in l—*whoa. Sam's friend. He's Sam's good friend. Sam. Your boyfriend, whom you like very much.*

"I'm all right. Between us—and I mean it—Sheriff Saron is going to run for mayor in the next election. That happens, someone from the outside might replace him, but he's angling to slip me into that spot."

Molly leaned forward, pushing her purse, which hung across her shoulder, behind her. "That's huge. That's incredible."

He pointed at her. "That's off the record."

She frowned. "However little you think of journalists, I would never betray the confidence of a friend, Chris." Which had her wondering if what Sarah had shared the night before counted as a confidence.

"I know. Or I wouldn't have told you. But honestly, with that on my shoulders—this murder, and everything else that still happens and needs to be taken care of—I don't have time to be working the counter."

Leaning back, Molly thought out loud. "Hannah might be able to help you. I mean, you don't have to be in law enforcement to write down information, right?"

Chris rubbed a hand over his slightly shadowed jaw. His hair was a bit messy, like he'd run his hands through it a few times today. "She'd have to sign a nondisclosure agreement. That's not a bad idea, actually."

Grinning, she pulled out her phone. "I get them occasionally."

He rounded his desk and took a seat behind it. "Ask her to come see me. That might work. I didn't think of hiring someone just for that, but I could, and Hannah is trustworthy. And I wouldn't have to worry about interviewing people."

"Exactly." Molly sent her a text, knowing she'd reply when she was out of class.

"Thanks. But you're probably here to ask for an official statement, right?"

"I am. You're very insightful."

He gave her a wry look, folding his hands on his desk. "It happens occasionally."

He let her pull out her notebook and pen. She should just use her phone and update her practice, but she liked writing things down. It helped her think and process the information people were sharing.

"So?" she prompted.

He let out a sigh. "We appreciate the community cooperation and support as we continue investigating the death of Jethro Harkaw. At this time, we will only be asking for information that pertains to the hours of nine p.m. to one o'clock a.m. on the Saturday of the festival. While we have not yet pressed charges, we do have several leads, and nineteen of the twenty-two drivers have been cleared to leave town."

Molly wrote quickly. She'd created her own shorthand over the years. "The drivers who have been asked to stay—are they suspects?"

"The investigation is ongoing."

She wrote it down, bending her neck so he didn't see her roll her eyes. When she looked back up, he had on his game face. His "I'm in full-on-cop, you-can't-break-me mode."

"Are Herman Besbrewer and Brad Templeton among the drivers who are staying?"

Chris leaned back in his chair, crossed one foot over his knee. "Now come on, Molly. I can't do your work for you. That should be easy information to find out."

"Funny. Okay. How about Ed McLaren? Thoughts on him?"

His smile slipped, and he leaned forward again. "Who the hell is that?"

Molly laughed, and he pointed at her, his eyes narrowed. "Don't you dare throw my words back at me."

"Fine. But you deserve it. Ed McLaren is the reporter who covered Amber offering her reward."

"Oh. That guy." A frown pushed his expression from irritated to mad.

"Yeah. Interesting fact? He and Amber go way back. Like further than Sam Hunt's Cadillac seats."

Chris surprised her by laughing. His eyes crinkled at the corners, and he looked younger. Happier. The same age as Sam, he was good-looking, with brown hair and dark eyes. He was what she'd call rugged. She had no trouble imagining him camping without a million-dollar RV. She liked seeing him smile. He'd done so more since getting together with Sarah, and again, she wondered if he and Sarah had spoken. If she'd told him.

"We really are rubbing off on you, aren't we? Did you even know any country lyrics before you came into town?"

"A handful of them, but nothing like I do now."

His smile didn't fade, but he returned to the topic. "Okay. So they know each other."

She nodded. "I did some digging. They grew up together. I spoke to a couple of their mutual Facebook friends through messaging, and according to them, he never got over her. Loves her to this day. Which makes the fact that he showed up here less surprising."

"It's a big story. He's a reporter. Why was it surprising at all?"

"It's not a huge story in comparison to what he sees daily. We're hardly downtown Seattle when it comes to news. He's here for Amber."

"Is he staying at the bed-and-breakfast?"

"I'm not sure. But I'll know in a few hours when I go home."

He wrote down Ed's name. "I don't see motive. You like to play detective. You must have thought of that."

Argh. How can he be funny one minute and so annoying the next? "I don't like *playing* detective. I'm a reporter."

"Editor."

"You're annoying."

He stood. "You just insulted an officer of the law."

She rose from her chair, tucked her notepad away. "You've surely had worse."

When he opened his door, he put a hand on her shoulder. "Seriously, Molly. Keep your head up when you're asking questions. Whoever did this is still here. I can feel it."

She nodded. "The crowbar? There were no prints?"

Chris's lips tugged down. "How do you know that?"

Oh. Don't get Priscilla in trouble! "I just wondered. You confirmed it."

She should have stopped pressing her luck, but she couldn't help herself. "With Candice getting everything, she had as much motive as Amber, who gets nothing. Do you think one of them is more suspicious than the other?"

"Bye, Molly."

"Chris."

"If you don't stop bugging me, I'm going to make Sarah take back the present she insisted I buy you for your birthday."

That brought her up short. She turned so they were facing each other. "What? You bought me a present? Hey, how'd you know it was my birthday?"

He leaned in, crowding her space. "Maybe I should get a nameplate that says 'detective' so you'd remember. Also, I'm friends with your boyfriend. You're friends with my girlfriend. These things have a way of coming out. Thirty, huh? That's a big one." He was baiting her.

"Twenty-nine."

He crossed his arms over his chest. "Sure. Sure. Twenty-nine. For the next fifty years, I bet."

She walked away before she got in trouble for assaulting an officer. His laughter followed her. The crowd had cleared some by the time she reached the counter. Priscilla was talking with a uniformed Officer Wills.

"I just came from there. I had to drop something else off. I'm headed back now," he said. He saw Molly approach.

"Hi, Molly. How are you?" He closed the file in his hand.

"Good. You?"

He looked over her head and then back at her. "Can't complain. I need to talk to Detective Beatty."

When he walked away, the words sank in, and Molly turned to Pris. "Detective?"

She gave a weak smile. Molly saw the dark shadows under her eyes and was glad she'd steered clear of the wine. "Yeah. He's not making a big deal about it, but he passed his exam. Things are changing around here."

The wistful way she said it made Molly want to hug her friend. "You doing okay? I mean, other than how you feel physically?"

Priscilla laughed and turned, leaning against the counter like she wanted it to hold her up. She was dressed impeccably—a runway model come to life. Her inky black hair was pulled back from her face. The dark shadows made her seem a bit paler, but her skin was beautiful. Her makeup was always magazine-ready. Knowing one of Pris's secrets reminded Molly that regardless of what people saw on the outside, it was impossible to really know their story unless they let you in.

"I look that bad?" Priscilla laughed.

Molly's mouth opened. Closed. "No. Sorry. I didn't mean it like that."

Priscilla waved a hand at her. "I'm joking. I'm okay. Thanks for letting me unload on you last night. I didn't say too much, did I?

Not in Molly's opinion. "No. You didn't. Even inebriated, you're professional. But were you serious about finding a new job?"

She shrugged. "I don't know. Something to think about. But while there aren't a horde of people here, I need to catch up on stuff."

"Right. Um…Officer Wills? He said he had some information?"

Priscilla turned to her computer, but side-eyed Molly. "Don't."

Molly leaned in. "Come on. Please? Just give me one tiny tidbit of information. I won't print it or anything. Just point me in the right direction. Pretty please?"

Whether it was because she'd let Priscilla lean on her the night before or because she was dealing with a hangover, her friend surprised her by inclining toward Molly.

"They found DNA on Jethro. It was the ex-wife's."

"What? Like on his lips? Because they kissed behind the stage that night."

Priscilla glanced toward Chris's closed door, then down at Molly. "Hmm. That might account for the hair they found on his clothes. But if that was during the dance, it doesn't explain officers finding her clothes at the scene."

"Clothes?" Molly hadn't seen clothing, but she was too focused on the body. She hadn't seen the crowbar either.

"Her jacket."

Molly remembered seeing Candice, more than once. Her floral shirt had identified her, but she didn't remember a jacket. She'd been without an escort for an undetermined amount of time. Molly needed to figure out what happened between the time she said goodbye to Jet and Brian and the moment they found Jethro's body. More importantly, she needed to know why Brian and Candice had gone their separate ways, even momentarily.

Chapter Sixteen

As Molly drove home, thinking about the different people involved in Jethro's life, she listed the reasons that made Candice a viable, solid suspect—over and above Ed McLaren, whose only real motive was anger on behalf of his ex-girlfriend. Candice had to harbor her own heavy load of anger, knowing that Jet had ended a quarter-century marriage for a woman young enough to be his daughter.

"That's one." She stopped at the traffic light.

Candice stood to inherit everything.

"Definitely a reason," she muttered, pressing on the gas when the light changed.

It could have been a crime of passion. Anger over not being his wife? Over him choosing, as she'd joked, a younger model. If the kiss at the dance had been a one-off—if they hadn't hooked up in the time since their divorce—it may have misled Candice into thinking there was a chance for reconciliation. *She tells Brian she forgot something? Her jacket? Goes to talk to Jet, and he says the kiss meant nothing. She gets angry, spies the crowbar, and whacks him with it, maybe not intending to kill him, but she wasn't in charge of the outcome.*

Pulling into her driveway, she was pleasantly surprised to see Sam's truck parked in one of the spots his mom had paved for the bed-and-breakfast. The second car there, one she didn't recognize, reminded her that Ed might very well be staying at the house.

Grabbing her laptop case and her purse, she rounded the hood and took the small gravel path to her home. When she checked the door, it was unlocked, so she let herself in, her pulse doing its "I'm going to see

Sam" dance. Tigger found her first and came sliding across the vinyl-plank entryway.

She put her laptop and purse on the hook by the door and crouched down. "Hello! Oh, it's like we've been apart forever, isn't it? Yes. I missed you, too." She laughed when he tried to bury his face in her hair.

Sam leaned on the arched entryway wall that separated the small area from the kitchen and the rest of the place.

"I missed her, too, bud, but have some dignity," Sam said, laughing. At the sound of his voice, Tigger raced across floor to Sam's feet.

Molly rose, going to him. He uncrossed his arms and folded her into them with one fluid movement as his mouth came to hers. As if that's what he'd been waiting for all day. She fell into the kiss and into *him*. His hands roamed up her back, pressing her closer, and then they went to her hair, his fingers tunneling through the tresses as he changed the angle of the kiss, deepening it. Her hands grew restless, so she moved them up and around his neck. One of his hands cupped the back of her head, while the other stroked down her back. When he finally pulled back, his nose still touching hers, she sighed, her breath uneven.

"Wow." She didn't have a lot of words left rattling around in her brain. And there was a good chance he'd just kissed her spineless because if it weren't for his arms holding her up, she thought she might melt into the floor.

"I'll say." He buried his face in her neck, extending the moment, sweetening it, by staying like that for a few minutes.

There was nothing else. Just them. And her dog lying across their feet. "I'm glad you're here," she whispered. Inhaling deeply, she realized something smelled very good.

"Hmm. Are you cooking?"

He grinned down at her and took her hand. "Good news and bad news," he said, making her laugh. Their ideas on what constituted *actual* bad news frequently differed.

As he tugged her into the kitchen, she saw the freshly made dinner rolls cooling on her baking rack, the one her mother had given her last Christmas that she never used. She wasn't much of a baker. Or a cook. But she loved to eat.

"Mmm." She reached for one, but he tapped her hand.

"They're too hot."

She looked up at him with a mock glare. "Good news?"

"I baked for you."

She couldn't hide her smitten smile. "Yes, you did. Because you're the best boyfriend in the world."

Sam smoothed a hand down her hair. "Wow. Maybe I'll take your birthday present back if that's all it takes to make you happy."

That was the second time today someone had mentioned her birthday. "Have you and Chris been gossiping about my age?"

He laughed, grabbing a couple of bottles of water from the fridge. "Gossiping? No. Discussing? Like the manly men we are? Possibly."

She laughed and took the bottle from him, taking a welcome drink. "Of course. That's what I meant. But honestly, I forgot it was even coming. I don't need you to make a big deal of it."

He took a drink of his water, eyeing her over it. When he set it down, he stepped into her space, which she was happy to share with him, and took her hand.

"What if I want to make a big deal of it?" His thumb stroked over her palm. *Don't get distracted by the feel of his fingers.*

"You don't have to," she said again. Though it was sweet that he might want to.

"But if I don't, I'll lose my best boyfriend status," he said, tugging a strand of her hair playfully.

She put a hand on his chest and stepped into him, looking him in the eyes so he got that she was serious. "That couldn't happen. You could skip my birthday entirely, and it still wouldn't happen. You are, without a doubt, the best man I've ever met. And I—" *Why do you feel weepy? Stop it. Breathe.*

"And?" His voice went husky.

She breathed in through her nose and out again slowly. "And you make me happier than I've ever been. The kind of happy I'm scared to lose. The kind I could get used to." *For the rest of my life.*

Sam lowered his head, pressed a kiss to her cheek, then trailed his mouth along her jaw, tiny kisses making a path to her ear. "Do that. Get used to it."

Before he could kiss her again, she asked, "The bad news?"

His eyes darkened. "My mom is getting tired of her guest. She's a little high-maintenance. I told her we'd come up for dinner."

Molly grinned. "Not the worst news I've heard." Though at the moment, she was hungry for something other than his mother's cooking.

"I guess not. But there's a silver lining," he said, walking her backward toward her bedroom.

Molly grinned and fastened her arms around his neck. "Oh, yeah?"

His lips found her jaw again, then her neck. "Mmm-hmm. She isn't expecting us for an hour."

Molly laughed, tilting her head to make it easier for him to kiss her in the way that made her legs feel like Jell-O.

As he came down over her on her bed, she smiled up at him. "That is excellent news, indeed."

* * * *

They packed up the dinner rolls and Tigger and headed up to the main house. Instead of heading through the back door, they walked across the yard, going around to the front porch. It was such a pretty house. The woman inside made it the welcoming place it was known to be, but aesthetically, the two stories, wraparound porch, and wide windows made quite an impression.

Sam opened the door, and Molly went through. They'd put a leash on Tigger in case Katherine's guests had issues with animals. Molly had thought of suggesting they leave him in the cottage, but things were so busy lately. She hated the thought of him being alone again, even for a few hours.

Sam closed the door behind them, and Molly heard voices to the left of the foyer. There was a sitting room and a small television area there. In front of her, a gorgeous wood staircase led to the bedrooms. To the right was a small hallway that opened to a spacious dining room with bay windows. Beyond the kitchen, Katherine had her own little area—almost a suite like Molly's—but she used the bed-and-breakfast's kitchen.

"Oh, good. You're both here," Katherine said, coming down the hallway toward them. Tigger strained against his leash. "Why are you trapped, buddy?"

"Mom. He's fine. We thought it would be best until we made sure your guests are okay with him."

Katherine petted Tigger but came to Molly with her arms open. When she hugged her, she whispered in her ear, "Thanks for joining me. I just need a little regular conversation."

Molly hugged her back as Tigger worked his way around and between them, leash tangling. "No problem. Uh—I think we're caught."

Sam laughed and helped them untangle as Ed McLaren joined them in the foyer.

"Look at that. It's a party. Hello again, Molly. Sam."

The two men exchanged less than friendly glances. Molly was determined not to let Ed get under her skin. And since she was right, and he was staying here, she'd use the time to find out more. She'd left the police station feeling like Candice was suspect number one—as far as the evidence went, things didn't look good for Jet's ex—but something about Ed and Amber's relationship was nagging her subconscious. Was it really just one friend helping another?

"You know each other?" Katherine asked. She looked back and forth between them. Sam stepped closer, passing his mom the rolls and putting an arm around Molly's shoulder.

Amber came into the foyer, a wineglass in hand, wearing a very fancy dress—it was teal, low-cut, and, from the look of it, satin. Molly's eyes widened, but she worked to keep her voice normal.

"Hi, Amber," she said.

The woman scrunched her brows in confusion. A second woman joined her, and it was clear from her nose, the set of her jaw, and the matching eyes that this was Amber's sister.

"Who's this?" Amber's sister asked, her eyes zeroing in on Sam and taking a leisurely look up and down, then up again. She stepped around Amber. She wasn't dressed as fancy, but her top was cut so low it almost showed her navel. "I'm Alicia, Amber's sister."

Sam nodded, held out his hand. "Sam Alderich. This is my girlfriend, Molly."

Molly looked at him and smiled. Looking back at Amber, she reminded her of who they were. "We met you the other night. Then I met you the day you checked in. I work for the *Bulletin*. That's our local paper."

"This is silly, all of us standing in my entryway. Please, come sit down. Dinner is ready," Katherine said.

Letting all of the guests follow Katherine, Sam tugged Molly back gently when she fell in line. Leaning in and down, he whispered, "See? Bad news."

She laughed, patted his stomach, and leaned into his side. "Okay. I'll give you this one. It's probably not going to be the most fun we've ever had."

They joined the others, and Sam held her chair out for her, sitting down beside her. Alicia sat on the other side of him, Katherine at the head of the table, and Amber and Ed sat side by side. Tigger sat beside Molly's chair for a minute and then decided to wander off to the kitchen. Katherine kept a dog bed there for him.

"This looks great, Mom."

"Thanks, honey. It's nice that you and Molly could join us. Please, everyone, eat."

No one said much while they passed around roasted chicken, salad, roasted potatoes, and buns. Once plates were loaded and everyone started to dig in, Molly wondered how to phrase her questions.

"Do you know if the police have found my husband's killer yet?" Amber asked Molly, pushing her chicken around on her plate.

Molly almost choked at the woman's abrupt question. She took a sip of water. "I spoke to the detective in charge this afternoon. They're definitely narrowing the field."

Sam nudged her elbow with his own. "Detective?"

She gave him a small smile. "Didn't you cover that in your *discussion?*"

He laughed and scooped up a bite of chicken.

"I don't see why they're looking anywhere other than at Candice," Amber said.

"Oh, sweetie, don't get all upset again. It's terrible for your complexion," Alicia said.

Ed's hand covered one of Amber's. "It's just a matter of time."

Jumping on the opportunity, Molly hoped her smile made up for her own abrupt line of questioning. "So, you two have been friends for a long time. Since you were kids. That's really great that you've stayed friends so long. Most people lose touch, but Facebook does make it easier to reach out. You said you were heading up here to cover the car show but got delayed, Ed?"

He released Amber's hand. She didn't seem bothered by Molly's words, but Ed's jaw definitely tightened. He averted his gaze when he answered. "With Amber living in Arizona most of the time, I take advantage of times she's close by. So yes, I would have come up. I'm so glad I did." Looking at her, he smiled. Molly's gut clenched. He was in love with her.

"I'm so glad, too. What would I do without you?" Amber asked.

"You'll never have to find out."

Molly watched the exchange, feeling like they'd forgotten anyone else was in the room. Amber's tears and sorrow over Jet seemed genuine. As genuine as Ed's affection for the widow. Was it possible she'd loved both men? Perhaps Ed had murdered Jet to get the competition out of the way.

Katherine set her napkin down. "Forgot the salt. Be right back."

Molly rose before she could and smiled. She needed a minute to sort out her thoughts. "I'll grab it. Sit."

Walking down the hallway and into the kitchen, she made a list of things she could ask Chris to confirm. He probably hadn't even looked into Ed. Molly wasn't surprised when she entered the kitchen and found it'd already been mostly straightened up. Katherine took care of everything with ease, no matter how many guests she had. She walked to the stove, opened the cupboard to the right, and took out the salt. It was nearly empty, so she grabbed the box of it that was on the shelf right behind it.

She was just tipping the box when a sound startled her, and she spilled it on the counter.

"Shoot," she said, turning to look over her shoulder.

Ed was looking at her with a strange expression.

Unease fluttered in her chest. "Do you need something? Salt?" She gave a weak laugh.

"You said you'd give me details," he said, coming closer.

She picked up the box of salt again, surprised her hands weren't altogether steady. Something about this guy didn't sit well with any of her instincts.

"Actually, I said I'd let you know if I learned anything. I didn't."

"Not true, Molly." He walked close enough that he was in her personal space. Encroaching on it. She could smell his overly spicy cologne. It made her stomach turn. "They have to have something. They're stupid if they think they can pin this on Amber."

The salt was taking forever to fill up, but she was moving so slowly, it couldn't be helped. "I'm sure that they'd like to *pin it* on the murderer."

Ed leaned his face uncomfortably close. "Which isn't Amber. You have any sway with the department, you'd better make that clear."

She set the salt down, wanting to push him out of her breathing space. "Trust me, I don't have any sway. And if Amber and you are innocent, then you have nothing to worry about."

"Excuse me?" Rage contorted his face, making Molly step back. "Are you insinuating I had something to do with his death?"

Not while he was looking at her like that—at least not out loud. He emitted a strange, growl-like sound and lifted his hand.

"What the hell is going on?" Sam stepped around Ed and leaned into him.

Ed put his hands up, shuffled back. "Nothing. Just two reporters disagreeing on a story. No big deal."

Sam glanced at Molly, and she saw the way his jaw flexed. He silently assessed whether or not she was okay, then turned back to Ed. "I find out differently, you'll need to find a new place to stay."

Ed said nothing, but he got the hint because he turned and left. Sam picked up the salt, screwed the cap back on, set the box back in the cupboard, then swept the grains she'd spilled into his hand. He did all of this while saying nothing. When he'd walked to the sink and dumped the salt there, he came back to stand in front of Molly.

"You're not usually forgetful," he said. He didn't move to touch her.

"Pardon?"

"I asked you to keep yourself safe. That didn't look safe to me. I don't like that guy."

She pointed at the counter. "I came to get salt. Not exactly a dangerous activity."

He grabbed the salt and her hand, pulling her out of the kitchen. "Maybe I shouldn't let you out of my sight at all."

She laughed at his gruff tone, pushing down the swoony feeling his words inspired. "Maybe you shouldn't."

He spun, backing her up to the wall, pressing against her, one hand coming to her hip. He dipped his head, kissed her. Hard. She gripped his shirt, clenching her fingers in the fabric. When he pulled back, his gaze was dark.

"I wouldn't be okay if something happened to you."

Touching her hand to his jaw, she stared at him, waited for his heartbeat to settle under her other palm. "I'm okay. We need to get back."

When they rejoined the group, the conversation stalled momentarily, but Alicia was oblivious to any tension. She batted her false eyelashes at Sam, and Molly hated the jealousy that prickled her skin.

"Sam, what do you do?" Alicia asked.

"I own an auto shop." He gave Alicia a brief glance, then focused on his dinner.

Molly was still looking at Alicia, so she saw the way the woman's nose scrunched up.

"Oh. That's…um…that's hard work," she said.

Katherine smothered a laugh by picking up her water and taking a drink.

"Molly, you said you spoke to the police?" Ed asked, his tone sharp.

She stared at him, shocked he'd bring it up again. Sam glared at him, and she put a hand over his. "I did. I've got a formal statement I can share with you, but they don't have any solid leads yet."

Ed thumped his hand on the table, startling everyone.

Sam sat straighter and glared at him. "You're going to want to cool your temper. Or you'll have a serious problem. Thought I'd made that clear."

Ed glared at Sam, neither of them breaking eye contact, but after a few seconds the reporter's hand relaxed, and he offered a stiff smile. "Sorry. I just get so angry when these fantastic small-town police stations don't have the resources to solve crimes. It's a shame, really. Because I'm sure that top-notch police officers are just flocking to this little mecca of happiness. With all that brain power, you'd think they'd be able to find a killer prancing around right in front of them." He swung an arm out as he spoke, his volume raising.

Sam set his fork and knife down, pushed his plate forward, and folded his forearms on the table. "You either check your attitude now and assure me you can do so for the foreseeable future, or I'll introduce you to the Britton Bay Police Department personally. I'm more than happy to have Detective Beatty drop by and show you how smart he is. How capable he is of spotting a bad apple when he sees one."

Molly slipped a hand onto Sam's thigh under the table, giving him a reassuring squeeze. She didn't blame him for being upset or protective. Katherine was staying in the house alone with these people. For the first time, Molly wondered what kind of background checks she did on her guests.

"Eddie, calm down," Amber whispered.

"I wouldn't mind meeting a detective. That job sounds exciting," Alicia said. She tore a bun in two pieces and took a tiny bite.

Ed set both hands on the table. "I apologize." He looked at Katherine. "Amber has been my closest friend since we were children. I guess I'm not handling things as well as I should be. I'm worried about my friend. I just want her to have closure and be able to move on with her life."

Molly had a few guesses about how he hoped Amber did just that.

Katherine nodded. "While I can understand and appreciate how you feel, for your friend and about the situation, that'll be the last outburst you have in my home or I will personally escort you out of it."

A grin so wide it made Molly's cheeks ache bloomed. She loved Sam's mom. Sam smiled, pleased with his mom.

Ed pushed back from the table. "I assure you, there'll be nothing to worry about. I'm going to retire to my room. Molly. Sam. Thank you for dinner, Katherine," he said, even though he'd hardly eaten any.

He tossed his napkin on the table and walked out of the room. Amber stared after him. "He really loved Jet, too. They got along great. I didn't realize he was hurting so bad." She stood up, crumpling her napkin and tossing it on her plate. "Thanks for dinner. I'm just going to go check on him."

Alicia sighed and leaned back in her seat as Amber rushed off. "My sister is never boring. I'll give her that. So, Sam, do you have any single friends? From the sound of things, I'm going to be in town longer than I'd like."

The three of them stared at Alicia until she grinned sheepishly and excused herself from the table.

Sam rose, collected the plates, took them into the kitchen, and came back a minute later.

He leaned over the table, pressing his palms flat, looking at his mom. "I don't like you staying here with them."

Katherine smiled, patted her son's hand. "I'm a big girl, honey."

"That guy could be a killer. So could the widow. You don't know them. And I don't trust him." He rose up and pointed after him, his mouth angry. It was strange to see him like this when he was always so even-tempered.

Love, affection, and loyalty pushed people to behave in ways that weren't necessarily typical. Not everyone, but a lot of people would go to great lengths to do something in the name of love or protection.

"I promise, Sam. I'm fine."

"He might be right, Katherine. I really don't trust Ed."

Sam gave her a smile of appreciation. "See?"

Katherine rose from her chair and looked down at the table. Taking a deep breath, she looked at Sam. "You really don't need to worry. Turns out you and Brandon have something in common. Neither of you want me alone with unknown guests. He's been staying here, and he'll be back in about an hour to do so again tonight."

Molly pulled her lip between her teeth and watched Sam process that information.

He ran a hand through his hair and held the back of his neck. "I don't like that either."

Katherine grinned, but Molly managed to bite down on her laugh.

"As I said, honey, I'm a big girl. Come help me dish up dessert. We don't even have to share it now."

Sam shook his head, sent Molly a frustrated glance, and followed his mom. While they were in the kitchen, Molly pushed the other chairs in around the table, gathered up the water glasses, and was about to carry them into the other room when her phone rang in her purse.

Setting the glasses down, she pulled her phone from the pocket of her hoodie. It was a text from Sarah. Molly frowned when she saw what it said.

SARAH
PAINT SPILLED OVER ONE OF THE TABLES, RAGS USED AND IN WASH-UP SINK.

Molly tapped out a reply quickly.

MOLLY
DO YOU HAVE CAMERAS?

SARAH
NO. I'LL LOOK INTO IT. HONESTLY, I DIDN'T THINK I'D NEED THEM.

Molly understood that thinking, but considering they were knee-deep in another murder, maybe more businesses should consider installing security cameras.

MOLLY
DID YOU TALK TO CHRIS?

Sarah sent the little monkey emoji with his eyes closed. Sighing, her thumbs hovering over her screen, she thought about how to convince her friend to talk to her police officer boyfriend, who would be very able to help.

MOLLY
WHAT IF YOU HAD SOMETHING MORE CONCRETE?

SARAH
LIKE WHAT?

Sam and Katherine came back into the room. Molly glanced up and sent them a smile, but it must have fallen short because Sam asked if she was okay.

"Sorry. Just texting Sarah back."

"No worries, dear." Katherine set the dessert down in front of her, and Molly sat, finishing the text.

MOLLY
LIKE YOU SAW SOMEONE? COULD POINT THE FINGER SOMEWHERE RATHER THAN JUST THINKING THINGS WERE GETTING MOVED AROUND IN THE SHOP?

SARAH
…
I GUESS. YES. I WOULD.

MOLLY
OKAY. I'LL TEXT YOU LATER.

She set her phone down and smiled at Sam, who was watching her.

"Everything okay?"

She picked up her spoon and scooped up a bite of something delicious and full of chocolate.

"Oh, my. Put things like this in front of me, and I'm more than okay."

Sam and Katherine laughed. The telephone on the buffet beside the dining table rang.

Katherine rose to answer it, and Molly stared, then looked at Sam. "I did not even notice that phone before. I didn't think anyone still had house phones."

He scooped up a bite of dessert. "It's for the guests to contact her from their rooms."

"Of course. I'll bring that right up." Katherine hung up and turned back to the table.

"I need to make some tea. Would you like any?" Her face gave away nothing.

Sam glanced at Molly, and she shook her head. "We're good, Mom. We should probably get going after this anyway."

"Okay. Back in a minute."

"They're really pushing things, huh?"

Sam's eyes darkened as he stared down the hall where his mother had disappeared. "I still think this a lot for her. She's doing too much."

Slipping her hand over his, she waited until he looked into her eyes. "She probably thinks the same of you when you schedule too many brake jobs."

Sam turned his hand over, linking their fingers. "You know I do more than brake jobs, right?"

Molly laughed. "Of course. Just don't ask me to name anything."

When he held her gaze, she leaned in and said, "Remember our first sort of date?"

His head tipped to one side, and his gaze shifted from enamored to wary. Definitely wary. "Uh-huh. We broke into Vernon's car."

Feigning hurt, she pressed a hand to her chest. "And we went hiking."

He grinned. "Right. Forgot that part."

Molly hadn't been able to let go of the feeling that she was somehow responsible for Vernon's death and had enlisted Sam's help in finding clues surrounding his murder.

"What are you up to now?"

She couldn't even pretend insult. Cupping his jaw, feeling the gentle brush of stubble against the soft skin of her palm, she lowered her lashes and looked up at him through them.

"How would you feel about a stakeout?"

Chapter Seventeen

Warmth lingered from the heated seat of Sam's car's passenger side even after he'd cut the engine. They were parked across the street from the back of Sarah's shop.

Sam adjusted the driver's seat so he was lying back a bit. "Too bad I don't have a sunroof. We could look at the stars."

Turning her head, she smiled at him through the darkness. The moonlight gave them enough of a glow to see each other, but anyone looking at the lone truck sitting there likely wouldn't see them. Unless they were looking.

Molly reached across the console and took his hand. "You're a good sport."

He hadn't asked a dozen questions about the why or the who. When she'd explained about Sarah's supplies, he'd suggested telling Chris, but Molly shared Sarah's thoughts on that, and it had been enough for Sam to agree.

She went with her gut on a lot of things. She was wrong more often than she'd like. But Molly couldn't ignore the feeling that if someone was going into the shop, they were getting in through the back door.

"I like being with you. Whether we're watching a movie at your place or mine. Hiking. Breaking and entering. You have a way of making things fun."

She laughed, squeezed his fingers. He tugged his hand free and reached out to thread his fingers through the hair at the base of her neck.

"Though I can think of a way to make sitting in a parked, dark vehicle a lot more fun."

Unable to quell the flutter in her chest, she leaned into the kiss, her eyes drifting closed. In the silence of the cab, she could easily get lost in the scent of his cologne, the feel of his mouth on hers, and the pressure of his fingertips at the back of her head. The words she felt ran around inside her like toddlers on a sugar rush, but she held them back. *Stop being so scared.* Why was she so scared?

Sam's low growl against her skin when his lips wandered down her neck sent shivers everywhere. Everything about him made her want more. *And that's why you're scared.* He pulled back, stared into her eyes.

"You drive me a little nuts. I don't think I've made out in a car since I was seventeen."

Her breath caught, and her chest felt tight. "Technically, we're in a truck."

"See? I don't even know what vehicle I'm in."

Laughing, she was secretly glad she wasn't the only one feeling the crazy rush of falling. *Who are you kidding? You fell the first time he broke into a vehicle for you.*

"If it helps, you drive me crazy, too. This is the first time I can ever remember enjoying it so much."

"Enjoying what? The making out?"

She laughed again, and they pulled away from each other, leaning back in their seats, faces angled toward one another. "Definitely that. But I mean, the...you know...the falling."

Maybe it was a trick of the moonlight, but it seemed as if his eyes darkened. "Maybe that's because the other...falling you did was just to prepare you for us. For something more than falling."

Maybe. Her pulse picked up. She'd definitely never felt like this for any other man. There was no other man like Sam.

As if the air had been sucked out of the space between them, Molly's chest tightened more. Sam leaned closer again.

"I think maybe the falling is done," she whispered.

His smile did nothing to settle her pulse. "On my side, it's definitely past the falling stage. Long past."

Right. Who needs to breathe anyway? If he says it first, it's not so scary.

He inhaled sharply. Exhaled and reached for her, his hand curving around her cheek. She leaned into it.

"Molly. I...I...wait, I think someone is coming," he said, his gaze turning toward the windshield.

"I love you, too," she breathed out, her voice about one octave from shrill.

Sam's head whipped back in her direction. "What? Wait. You do?"

OhmyGodohmyGodohmyGodohmyGod. Please, earth, swallow me up whole and spit me out on the other side of the country. She pulled away, released her seat belt in such a rush she almost banged her head into his. What if that was not at all what he was trying to say? *Oh my God. What have you done?* Trying with everything in her to pretend she hadn't spoken aloud, to pretend he wasn't sitting right beside her, she reached down and grabbed the camera she'd brought.

"Molly," Sam whispered through the darkness that she wished was darker.

"Shh," she said, pulling the camera up and removing the lens. There was definitely someone moving toward the back of the shop.

"Molly," he said again.

She pointed, clicked. "I can't tell if it's a guy or a girl." She looked through the viewfinder and zoomed. The person was wearing a black wool hat, tugged down low on their forehead. They typed in the code Sarah had shared with them and Molly realized she was right—whoever was vandalizing the shop was getting in through the back. The person disappeared inside.

Molly opened the passenger side, still doing her best to convince herself the last five minutes had not happened. Sam was at her side instantly and wordlessly, and they walked across the quiet street and entered the back lot of the Art Shop. Other than some trees, a few shrubs, and a large dumpster, it was empty. There were some weathered pallets leaning against the dumpster. Molly stood beside them, which would give her a view of whoever came out. *Which they have to do eventually.*

Sam was beside her, his arm brushing hers. "We should call Chris." He pulled out his phone.

"But wait, we want to see who it is," Molly said, the camera hanging heavily around her neck. She couldn't look at him, and she had no idea why she was whispering.

"We want this why? It's not like we can make an arrest," Sam said. It was then she heard the hint of irritation in his voice.

It took courage to look at him, but she made herself do it. "They haven't done anything yet. So far, Sarah said the person is just using supplies."

Sam pointed at the door. "And breaking and entering. I agreed to come with you, Molly. I didn't agree to putting you in danger. I'm calling Chris."

Her heart squeezed painfully. "Are you mad?"

Should she apologize? Tell him she didn't mean it? *You do mean it.* Sure, she meant it, but it was too soon. She'd been so scared of being scared that she'd probably scared *him. Breathe.*

Sam ran a hand through his hair but avoided her gaze. "No. I'm not mad. Let's just…let's just get this done." He finished dialing, and before he spoke into the phone, he pointed at her. "Get ahold of Sarah."

She nodded, tears burning her eyes. *Please don't cry. Don't add that to your list of acts of idiocy tonight.* She texted Sarah and asked if she was with Chris. When her friend said no, she explained what they were doing and told her to get down to the shop.

The fifteen minutes it took for Sarah and Chris to arrive separately were the only awkward moments Molly had spent with Sam since the second she met him. The thought of having possibly wrecked things by pushing too hard and too fast stole her breath, made her ribs ache with pressure, like they were poking into her heart.

Chris pulled up in his police cruiser, and Sarah pulled up a moment later. They both parked where Sam had and walked across the street to join them.

"I don't get why you wouldn't tell me," Chris was saying as they approached.

"I didn't want to bother you with something if it was nothing. You have enough going on," Sarah said, her voice quiet.

Chris stopped her with a hand on her arm a moment before they reached Sam and Molly.

"It's not a bother. You need to know that. My work will always invade our lives a little more than it should, but you can't let that make you feel like you don't matter to me. Because you do. And this," he said, pointing past Molly and Sam, "this isn't nothing. Even if it was, you need to be able to talk to me. Would you want me to hide something from you?"

Sarah didn't reply, but Molly saw her shake her head back and forth. Chris hooked a hand behind her neck, sort of like Sam did to Molly sometimes, and stepped closer. Molly couldn't hear what he said to her because they'd lowered their faces to each other and the conversation went private. But she could feel the emotion pouring off of the two of them, and her heart tightened for an entirely different reason. She was glad Chris wasn't mad. *And hopefully Sarah won't be mad that you got involved.*

Glancing at Sam, where he stood, arms folded, leaning against the brick building, she thought it might be better to deal with Sarah than Sam. It would have been so easy to spiral into a series of "What if I wrecked things?" thoughts, but Chris, holding Sarah's hand, walked over to them.

"Hey. Thanks for calling me," he said to Sam.

"No problem."

If Chris thought it was strange that Sam was standing ten feet away from Molly, he didn't remark on it.

"Thanks for doing this, Molly, but you really didn't have to," Sarah said.

Chris gave her *that* look. "Yes, Molly. You *really* didn't have to."

She started to defend herself, but he held up a hand. "I appreciate you caring enough to do so. Next time, though, maybe find a way that doesn't involve you getting hurt."

"I'm not hurt," she said. *That might not be true later when Sam tells you he needs some space.*

"Thankfully. You guys stay here." Chris let go of Sarah's hand and drew his weapon.

"Wait, you're going in without...backup or whatever you call it?"

Chris sighed. "Yes, honey. Pretty sure I can handle one prowler who likes to paint. Do me a favor and stay out of the way with Sam and Molly, okay?"

Sarah nodded and came to stand by Molly. When Chris punched in the code for the door, they moved over to where Sam stood by the wall.

"Hi, Sam," Sarah whispered.

"Hi, Sarah," he whispered back.

Molly was relieved to see the smile he gave her. She'd hate it if he took out his...whatever he was feeling...on her friend. Molly put an arm around Sarah's shoulder.

"I'm sorry that there's actually someone who's been vandalizing your shop," she said.

Sarah turned her head and grinned. She'd swept a piece of her short hair to the side and pinned it with a cute clip. She wore pajama bottoms and a thick jacket. "I'm not."

"What?" Molly dropped her arm and rubbed her fingers together. The wind wasn't reaching them behind the building, but it was still cold.

"Well, the only other explanation is that I'm crazy. This is much better."

Molly laughed, and though she didn't turn her head at the sound, Sam did too.

A moment later, Chris came out of the building; the person they'd seen go in walked in front of him, hands behind their back.

He stopped, watched the door close behind him, then looked over at their huddle of three.

"Meet Naomi Walsh."

Naomi didn't look up. Her cap was gone, and long hair spilled down around her face.

Sarah stepped forward, bent her knees a bit, trying to see the girl's face. "Hi, Naomi. I'm Sarah."

The girl looked up, and Molly nearly gasped. She really was a *girl*. She couldn't be out of her teens yet. It was dark, but the scared look in her eyes, the torn clothing, and the hard set of her lips gave away her youth and, possibly, her situation. She couldn't be positive but instinct told her this girl lived on the streets. Molly hadn't thought much about the homeless population of Britton Bay. She knew they existed but hadn't noticed many people. Maybe she hadn't been paying close enough attention. *Too busy putting your feet in your mouth.*

"Are you an artist?" Sarah asked.

Chris straightened, stepped back a step, taking Naomi with him. "She's a criminal. You'll be able to press multiple charges. Breaking and entering, vandalism, theft."

Naomi's head shot up. "I didn't steal nothing."

"Whatever, kid. Taking something that isn't yours is called stealing."

"Huh. Guess I missed school the day they taught that," Naomi snapped.

Sam came to stand by Molly, and though she was grateful for his presence, she wasn't ready to look at him.

"I'm going to take her in. You'll have to give a statement, but you can do it in the morning. There'll be paperwork," Chris told Sarah.

"But what if…" Sarah said.

"What if what?" Chris's tone was all cop.

"What if I don't press charges?"

It was too dark to be sure, but Molly would have bet money Chris just rolled his eyes.

"And you wouldn't do that why?"

Naomi was staring at Sarah.

"You're right, Naomi. You didn't steal anything. But why were you breaking into my shop."

The girl shrugged.

Sarah sighed loudly. "Okay. Maybe you're right, Officer Beatty."

Molly hadn't heard her call him that yet, and it felt weird.

Chris started to walk, but Naomi tugged and turned her head toward Sarah.

"I am. I am an artist. I didn't mean to wreck nothin'. I just wanted to try stuff out."

Silence covered all of them as the moon rose higher in the sky. The wind seemed to have found a way around the building because Molly was freezing. Her heart cracked a little when she shivered. There was no way Sam didn't feel it. But he didn't wrap an arm around her like he normally would.

"You know what? I'm not tired. I think I'll come down to the station tonight, and we'll clear things up," Sarah said.

"Sarah," Chris warned.

"Is that all right with you, Officer Beatty? Is there a reason you'd like me to delay coming down to make my statement?"

He sighed. "No. I'll meet you there."

When he left, Sarah turned to Molly and Sam. "I think she's just a homeless teen. How am I supposed to press charges against a teen?"

"If she wasn't of age, Chris wouldn't have said it, so she's at least eighteen," Sam said.

"That's still a kid," Sarah answered.

"What are you thinking?" Molly asked.

Sarah shrugged. "I'm not sure. I just...I'll feel better after I go down to the station and actually talk to her."

"That's definitely not going to be Chris's first choice of response."

Sarah tilted her head and gave Sam a friendly smile. "Yes, well, I have a feeling I can make him see things my way."

Sam gave a half laugh. More of a resigned sigh. "I don't doubt it."

They said goodbye, and anxiety pulsed inside of Molly like a living thing. Sam held her door for her but didn't hold her hand on the drive back to her cottage. She expected him to tell her he was staying at his own place tonight. That he'd call her in a few days. She tried to brace herself for the words even as she unlocked her door and they greeted Tigger.

Right. He'd probably come in and do it properly. He was a good guy. He'd tell her they should take a step back, and she'd be cool. *You can totally be cool.* She let Tigger out into the yard and back in a few minutes later. The silence between them was clogging her throat.

When Tigger grabbed a chew toy and pounced up on the couch to lie down, Sam stepped in Molly's path to the kitchen.

"Molly," he said.

"Uh-huh?" She reached out, rubbed her fingers over his hoodie. She held her breath. Waiting. *Be cool. Just don't breathe until he leaves.*

"Can you look at me?"

"I'm good," she whispered.

"Please?"

Biting the inside of her cheek, she tilted her head back, stared into the eyes that had hooked her from the first glance. Eyes that had flipped her heart upside down and changed everything. She blinked rapidly, feeling all of the cool she wanted to possess fly away.

Sam put both hands on her jaw, cupping it with exquisite tenderness. She bit her lip. *Hurry up. Make it fast. Rip off the Band-Aid. Just say goodbye.*

"I've never told a woman I loved her."

Right. Because they weren't words to be thrown around in the cab of a truck after a quick make-out session.

"Look at me, Molly."

Bringing her gaze back to his, she nodded, still biting her lip. His thumb tugged it free. "I'm glad I waited. Because I've never felt this before, and now I know why. I've never been in love. Until now. Until you."

Molly's jaw dropped, and her heart exploded like someone poking a balloon with a pin. "What?" Her voice was a harsh whisper.

Sam pressed his forehead to hers for a moment, then leaned back, bending his knees so that the two of them were eye level with each other. "I love you. I think I have since the minute I saw you. It doesn't really matter when it happened, I guess. But I do. I love you."

Her hands gripped his wrists. "But you...you couldn't even look at me. You didn't even stand next to me." He loved her? *He loves me.*

He gave a rough laugh. "Uh, yeah. The woman I'm crazy in love with, the one who scares easily when it comes to matters of the heart and relationships, tells me, *first*, that she loves me, just when I'm about to tell her the same thing? Of course I didn't look at you or touch you. If I had, Chris would have wondered why I was pressing you up against the building kissing the life out of you. It might have been awkward."

Her heart fluttered—actually fluttered like it had hummingbird wings. "Oh. Yeah. It might have been."

He laughed, and the sound shook off the haze of shock and surprise and elation. She wound her arms around his neck, pressing herself against him, wondering if he could feel her heart trying to beat its way out of her chest.

"I figured it was safer to wait until we were back here."

"Smart. Definitely smart."

They stared at each other, their breathing and Tigger's chewing the only sounds.

Her fingers touched the back of his hair, and his tightened around her waist.

"You could do that now, you know," she whispered.

"What's that?"

"Kiss the life out of me."

A low growl sounded from the back of his throat. Without warning, he scooped her up against him. "Trust me. I plan to."

Chapter Eighteen

The next morning, as she made her way to work and stopped at Bella's for muffins, Molly felt like she was one of those cartoon characters floating along with heart bubbles trailing after them. Every time she thought of Sam's words, of the look in his eyes as he said them to her again last night, warmth rushed through her blood.

Determined to focus, she schooled her features and went into the *Bulletin* office through the back, as usual. Grabbing a cup of coffee, Molly pushed thoughts of Sam into a little pocket of her brain. *Time to work.* There were several things they needed to discuss.

Alan and Jill were already chatting at the layout table when she came in, bearing muffins.

Jill hopped off her stool. "Yummy. Gimme."

Molly laughed and handed over the box. Alan lifted his mug in greeting.

Setting her coffee down, Molly went straight to the whiteboard and grabbed a marker.

"We're not going to bother waiting for Clay, but we can come back to a discussion on him later," she said.

She waited while Jill and Alan chose a muffin, then got started. She wrote the questions driving her crazy on the board.

1. Police kept some drivers in town. Who & why?
2. Why did Herman Besbrewer lend Jet money?
3. Why was Candice's jacket in the gallery?
4. Where was Brian while he and Candy were apart?
5. Where was Ed McLaren at the time of Jet's death?
6. Where was Amber at the time of death? Who drove her

back to the RV?

7. Who is Naomi Walsh, and why did she break into the Art Shop?

Before Molly set the pen down, Jill was speaking around her muffin. "Someone broke into Sarah's shop?"

Molly nodded. "Yeah. She mentioned when we were there on Tuesday that strange things had been happening. Misplaced supplies, missing supplies. That sort of thing. So Sam and I watched the place last night, and sure enough, this Naomi girl knew the code and let herself in."

"Did she destroy anything?" Alan asked.

Shaking her head, Molly selected a muffin. "That's the thing. She was basically breaking in to do art. Told Sarah she was an artist. Chris came and arrested her, but when he asked Sarah if she wanted to press charges, she wasn't sure. I'll touch base with them later today and see what happened, but I'm thinking that the homeless population in Britton Bay is larger than I suspected. Or, sadly and regrettably on my part, even thought of."

Alan broke off a piece of blueberry muffin but held off putting it in his mouth. "It was bad years ago, but things have been fairly good since the shelter went in on the outskirts of town. Actually, I guess you'd call it the next county. Like other cities, our population has grown. That shelter is probably bursting at the seams."

"Definitely something to explore and take a look at," Jill said. She gestured to the whiteboard. "With everything else going on, though, I think we need to put that on the back burner. Catch me up on Ed McLaren."

Alan grinned at Molly. "He's a reporter from Portland. He's taken an interest in Jethro's story and in irritating Molly."

She laughed even though he was partially right. "I think his interest started before Jethro, actually. I learned firsthand last night that he has a temper and a fondness for Amber. They have a history and—I have a very strong suspicion—a present as well."

"You think she was cheating on Jet?" Jill took another bite of her muffin, already eyeing the box.

"I think it's a definite possibility. But I want to speak to someone who knows her better than I do."

"Who?" Alan asked.

"Brian Stoleman. He and Jethro were close, so it makes sense he'd know Amber fairly well. I want to check in with him anyway. The last time I saw him, he was still so distraught over Jethro. Plus, I've recently learned that he and Candy didn't go straight to the van after the show. They split up, at least for a bit. Last I heard, the police were looking hard at Candice."

"The police interviewed both of them?" Alan looked at Molly, but it was Jill who answered.

She scooted off the chair and went to her desk. "I did a follow-up with him by phone. I called Monday." She scrolled through her laptop, staring at the screen. "Yup. They took him in after the murder, along with everyone who was still at the scene. He was released after giving his statement. I remember thinking, when I spoke to him, that he sounded so sad. We're so focused on solving a puzzle, and this man has lost his best friend."

Guilt tugged at Molly's conscience, remembering the way his voice had broken when he'd spoken of Jet. She was too busy pointing fingers at everyone to offer good, old-fashioned empathy. Perhaps she should ask Sam if he wanted to drive out to the RV park with her. If her brain had the ability to swoon just from a thought, it would have when her "Sam" envelope firmly burst open and she thought of him again.

"I'll go out there, if you want, to follow up on Herman or the other drivers," Molly suggested.

"I can do both. I need to make up for lost time," Jill said with a smile.

"I'm going to sort through the list of stories we have and prioritize," Alan said.

With a plan in place for everyone, Molly texted Sam to see if he was available to come for a ride.

SAM
BRAKE JOB UNDERWAY. I SWEAR I DO OTHER THINGS.

Molly laughed and typed back.

MOLLY
I KNOW YOU DO. OKAY. I'M GOING TO HEAD OUT THERE. I'LL TEXT YOU WHEN I'M BACK.

SAM
PLEASE DO.

She stared at her screen, her pulse scrambling when the little dots hovered.

SAM
I LOVE YOU. HMM. I LIKE TEXTING IT. YOU TRY.

Even as she laughed again, her heart swam in a pool of happiness. She wanted to hang onto the feeling and the moment. But there was something to be said about moving forward. It had gotten her here.

MOLLY
I LOVE YOU. YOU'RE RIGHT. IT IS FUN TO TEXT. BUT NOTHING BEATS HEARING IT.

SAM
AGREED.

* * * *

The drive to the RV park was quiet. There was no traffic in the middle of the day, not that Britton Bay ever had much, but weekends did get busier. Molly hoped Jill was able to get answers today. She couldn't shake the feeling that Ed McLaren was not what he seemed. But she'd been wrong before. And she had a tendency to remind herself of that.

The same kid who'd manned the entry booth on Thursday night greeted her now, and she had her ten dollars ready. There were several trailers and RVs in the park, but most of them were shut down for the season. A few of the more hardcore outdoor enthusiasts would probably keep coming right up until the end of October when it shut down.

Molly parked her Jeep in front of Jethro's RV. Her stomach turned over, and she was grateful she hadn't eaten too much. He'd shown up in town a week ago, and now he was dead.

Brian came out of his unit, which was to the left. The two RVs were parked so that their doors faced each other. He was wearing a hat advertising Sam's Service Station, making Molly smile.

He waved as she turned off the vehicle and got out. In jeans and a thick sweater, he wandered over and gave her a hug. "How you doing?"

"I'm good," she replied, returning the hug. "How are you?"

He pulled back and stared at Jet's RV. "I'm doing as well as can be expected. Trying to stay positive. Candice is stayin' in Jet's RV, so it's been nice to have the company."

As if she'd heard her name, Candice opened the door and descended the few steps. She looked at Molly, her brows scrunched as she tried to place her.

Molly stepped forward, hand out, noticing the dark circles around Candy's eyes. "I'm Molly. I work for the *Britton Bay Bulletin*."

Candice snapped her hand back as if Molly's palm was full of spikes. "I'm not up for any more questions. Why won't you people leave me alone?"

Brian went to her side and put an arm around her shoulder. Looking down at her, he told her, "Molly is Sam Alderich's girlfriend. Just because she works for a newspaper doesn't mean she's a snake, like that other guy." Brian looked at Molly. "McLaren's been harassing her. Between him and the cops and Amber trying to get Candy tossed out of the RV, it's been a nightmare."

Molly thought she was up on all of the events, but clearly they'd been having their own little sideshow. She wondered what Ed had asked Candice. He seemed as ready as the police to pin the death on her. They hadn't yet, though, so something was holding them back.

"I didn't come to ask questions, really. Well, not about you," she said to Candice.

The woman looked down her nose at Molly and shrugged out of Brian's hold. Moving over to the firepit, which wasn't lit despite the chill, she took a seat on a luxurious folding chair. Molly had never seen such a fancy one. It was basically an outdoor La-Z-Boy.

"I'm tired of this town and the people. I want to go home. I don't even know why I came."

Brian sat in the lawn chair beside Candice and gestured for Molly to choose one of the few others. "They'll have answers soon enough. You're here because you're the brains behind the entire thing."

Molly sat, trying to be unobtrusive, but that struck her curiosity. "I didn't know that."

Candice leaned back, measuring Molly. She must have found her worthy, because she gave a nod. "Back when Jet and I were first married, his obsession with cars drove me nuts. Not because I can't handle a man having a hobby that takes him away from me, but I didn't intend to be a pauper just because he liked to tinker with toys. I told him if he wanted to spend his days around cars, he needed to make it financially feasible."

Smiling over at Brian, she reached for his hand. "This guy backed me a hundred percent, and the two of them developed the Classic Car Crawl."

To Molly, it didn't seem fair to call her the *brains*, but perhaps a catalyst. "How did Amber feel about the Crawl?"

Candy wrinkled her nose. Brian dropped her hand and folded his on his lap, but Molly couldn't help noticing how he continued to stare at her as she spoke. Like he couldn't *not* look at the woman.

"Amber doesn't like anything that isn't about her." Candice rolled her eyes. While this woman still didn't feel like a murderer to Molly, she could definitely imagine Candice holding a heavy grudge. It was easy to picture her exacting a slow, meaningful revenge. But not murder.

Brian was still looking at Candy when Molly asked, "What do you think, Brian?"

Candice leaned forward. "Is there information we don't know? Are they going to arrest her? She tried to assault me, you know."

"Now, Candy, the police dealt with that."

She scoffed and leaned back. "They gave her a slap on the wrist. Blamed it on her emotional state. She nearly clocked me with one of those stupid high heels."

Molly couldn't help but think that if Amber was silly enough to strike this woman, she'd get struck right back. Candice did not seem the type to sit idly by while anyone put their hands somewhere she didn't want them.

"Brian, are you aware that Ed and Amber had a relationship years ago?"

He looked at Molly, not answering at first, but holding her gaze. "What makes you think it was years ago?"

Tension wound in her belly. "You think it's more recent?"

He nodded, putting both hands on the armrests of his chair, gripping the edges. "I know it for a fact. She wasn't shy about letting Jet know he wasn't enough for her. Especially if he was on the road. We told the police this, but they didn't make an arrest. Said cheating isn't a motive."

"She had plenty of motive," Candice said.

So do you. Molly bit her tongue. Telling Jet's ex-wife she'd seen her with him probably wouldn't win her over. "Such as? My understanding is that all of Jet's estate goes to you. What possible motive could Amber have?"

Candy leaned forward again. "Jet told her he didn't love her, but he'd never let her go. He knew even when he married her that she wanted Ed. Physically, at least. But she wanted Jet's money. Wasn't enough that she's still living high off her last husband, but she wanted Jet's, too. But that meant staying married to him because she wouldn't see a penny otherwise."

Molly processed that. Would she kill Jet just to get out of the marriage? She could have moved out. Was Jet abusive? Had he threatened her about leaving? Molly remembered that this was a man who openly cheated, reneged on deals, and made people feel uncomfortable for sport.

"What do you two know about the fifty thousand dollars Jet borrowed from Herman Besbrewer?"

"Excuse me?" Candice sat forward, and Brian's eyes went impossibly wide. She turned to Brian, fury emanating from her eyes. "Did you know about this?"

Brian washed his hands over his face, then looked at Molly. He pointedly avoided looking at Candice. "Jethro liked to handle things his own way. My understanding is it was a handshake deal and had nothing to do with his estate or our business."

Molly stared at him, uncertain as to whether he was admitting he knew something. "So, you know what the money was for?"

The skies opened up at that moment, without a second of notice. Surprise had them all frozen for about three seconds, then Brian rushed them into his RV.

Candy whipped her hands around like she could dry off that way. "God. This place is miserable. Unpredictable. Just ridiculous. My heavens, Brian. How are you living in this place?"

It was a good question, Molly thought as she shivered. Rain pounded against the roof and on the glass. She looked around the unit. It was beautiful, but nowhere near as grand as Jethro's. Laundry was scattered everywhere, from the front seats to the kitchen benches. It was a wide-open setup, the hallway narrowing down to a bedroom. She could see the end of the bed from the entryway. If she had to guess, she'd say there were a bathroom and a closet behind the two doors in the hallway.

Brian hastily picked up some of the items littering the table area. Old chip bags, a half-eaten sandwich, several cans of beer. He tossed things onto the counter, which was piled high with food packages. The sink was full of dishes.

"Sorry. We've been hanging out in Jethro's RV," he said. Molly wasn't sure which of them he was speaking to, but his cheeks brightened when Candice sighed and sat down like something might jump out at her.

"It's understandable that cleaning hasn't been on your mind," Molly said. He looked so embarrassed, and she felt bad for him.

"Still. Sort of let things get out of control. Just...haven't had the energy or the frame of mind to clean up." He was talking to her, but looking at Candice.

The quick, hard rain softened, falling on the windshield in a smoother rhythm.

"Sit," Brian said to Molly.

She sat, her eyes still scanning the space. It was so different from Jethro's. He was so different from Jethro. Molly looked at Candice.

"How much longer do you think you'll be here?"

"Until the police let me go. They're forcing me to stay here. I've contacted my attorney, and he'll be out here Monday if they haven't released me."

Brian sat down beside Candy and put his hand over hers. Despite her exaggerated response to the mess, she leaned into him, against him. They'd clearly been friends a long time. When Brian said something quietly, for Candy's ears only, a lump lodged in Molly's throat.

She'd been around love. Witnessed it. Felt it. Given it. She was *in* love. So she recognized the signs. Brian was madly in love with Candice. And if the affection she returned so easily said anything, she felt something for him as well. Molly couldn't stop herself, and part of her really wanted to.

Sitting forward, feigning a casualness she didn't feel, she asked, "I wondered about something. It's a little awkward to ask, but I feel like the more details we can get to piece things together, the faster you'll both be out of here."

They turned their attention to Molly. Candice gestured for her to go ahead with a wave of her hand.

"You two left right after I saw you, right, Brian? Right after you told me who Candice was?"

He nodded, glanced at Candy. "Sure. We went to the passenger van taking a group of us back to the park here."

Candice affirmed this with a nod of her own. Molly's heart hammered. "But your coat was found in the gallery. The police must have questioned you about that."

She straightened her shoulders and gave Molly an icy stare. "They did. Hard to argue with an alibi. Brian and I were together the whole time. As I told them, I must have forgotten my jacket there earlier in the day."

Molly nodded, still trying to remain calm and casual. "So you and Brian were side by side the entire time. You didn't split up at all?"

"What are you getting at?" Candice put both of her hands on the table.

"You didn't answer the question," Molly said.

"You said you weren't going to ask questions, Molly," Brian said softly. It made her think of Sam, the way he quietly stuck up for her. What else would he do for her?

"I know. But I also know that one of the high school students walked you to the van, alone."

Candice looked at Brian, her eyes wide. Scared. Brian smiled at her—an intimate, warm, more-than-friends smile. When he looked back at Molly, he spoke firmly. Confidently. "Candy told me she forgot her jacket. I said I'd run back and get it. One of the students walked her there, but within a minute or two, I realized going back in against the flow of people leaving was impossible. I was back at her side just a couple minutes later. Without her jacket. So it's my fault it's there. I should have just gone and gotten it for her. Maybe then I would have been able to help Jet." He paused, inhaled deeply. "If you need me to tell the police that I stepped away from Candice for less than five minutes, I will, but I think even if they knew that, they wouldn't be able to charge her anyway. She didn't have the time to get back to the gallery, kill him, then come back with me."

Brian and Candice shared a glance that Molly couldn't interpret. He met Molly's gaze.

"As for me, I ran into a couple of security guards on my way back in, literally. Younger guys. Didn't catch their names, but I'm sure if you checked with them, they'd tell you that right after that, I decided the crowd wasn't worth a jacket we could grab the next day. So our time is accounted for, Molly."

Candice said nothing to confirm or deny, and Molly could guess why. Candy had been alone more than long enough. And Brian was providing her an alibi.

Molly stood abruptly. "I need to get going," she said.

"Oh." Brian looked up at her. "Okay. Do you want me to amend my statement to the police? They'll likely swing by. It seems to be part of their routine, dropping in to place more stress on Candice."

"Uh, no. Don't worry about it." Now she knew why the police hadn't brought Candy in and charged her formally. They couldn't with the time line and alibi she had established.

Candice didn't say anything when Brian walked her to the door. He hesitated before opening it.

"She's the best woman I know, Molly. A *good* woman. Deserves happiness."

All she could do was paste a phony smile on her face. She had no right to tell him that he might be looking at her through love-tainted glasses. But she'd tell Chris and hope it wouldn't break Brian if he learned the truth.

Molly wasn't sure what she was feeling when she got into her Jeep. She needed to go back to the office. She needed to sort through some of the random thoughts running through her head.

Turning back onto the road that would lead her to Main Street, she wondered if she should head to the police station. If she told Chris about what Greg had said, Brian would just cover for the time Candy was alone. She would chat with those security guards after asking Sam how to get in touch with them, but a sinking feeling in her stomach told her she'd learn Brian had chatted with them for longer than he'd let on. Was he covering for her because he knew she intended to kill Jet or because she'd confessed to him afterward?

The crowbar was a tool of opportunity, which suggested Candy hadn't planned the murder. They'd argued, she'd picked up the crowbar, hit him, maybe even used the jacket she'd forgotten there to wipe the prints off of it? There'd been no blood on it, at least not that Pris had mentioned. But what would she have wiped the tool off with?

Molly had seen Candice's temper, could imagine the resentment she felt toward Jethro. He'd probably cheated throughout their whole marriage. Maybe she'd even known and looked the other way. But then he'd divorced her.

For Amber. The two women had more than a mild distrust and dislike of each other. Molly wasn't sure if Amber would open up to her, but she wanted to know more about the assault Candice had mentioned. Since she seemed fine with lying, there was a very good chance she'd been the one to instigate the argument. If it turned out that Candice had threatened Amber verbally and almost physically, it would add weight to the theory. And the knowledge that Candice had had opportunity.

Deciding she couldn't wait for these details, she turned left on Main Street instead of right and headed for the bed-and-breakfast.

Calling Jill on the way, she left a message. Hopefully the fact that her machine had picked up meant she was getting answers. Molly wanted to have some when they met up again as well.

When she pulled up to the bed-and-breakfast, shock had her slamming on her brakes. Chris was there with another officer. They were leading Amber out of the house. Though she couldn't hear him, she could see Ed yelling and Chris gesturing with his hand for him to back off.

Katherine watched from the porch, and Amber's sister was crying, tears streaming down her face. Molly parked across the street instead of going around to the back, where she usually parked. Getting out of her Jeep, she ran over in time to hear Ed threaten Chris.

"When I'm finished with you, you won't be able to get a job as security guard at a donut shop. You're going to regret this."

"Sir, I'm going to ask you to calm down one last time, and then I'm going to slap cuffs on you as well," Chris said, his voice completely even as though it was a normal, everyday conversation.

"Amber, baby, don't worry. I'm going to fix this." He got in Chris's path again, and the detective handed a hysterical Amber over to his deputy. He turned to face Ed.

"You need to calm down."

Instead of doing as he was told, Ed did the exact opposite. He shoved Chris, swearing at him. Katherine rushed down the steps when Amber's sister jolted forward.

"No, dear. Don't get involved."

"That's it," Chris said, easily maneuvering Ed, twisting him and shoving him up against the same cop car that Amber had just been put inside of. "You're under arrest for assaulting an officer. You have the right to remain silent, and I really, truly hope you'll exercise that right starting now. But if you can't shut up and choose to waive that right…"

He continued the Miranda warning, and Molly covered her mouth in shock. Belatedly, she realized this was why she made a better editor than reporter. Chris put him in the back of the cruiser with Amber and stalked over to her.

She wanted to take a step back, but stood her ground. "What are you going to put online?"

She ignored the snarl. Her entire theory collapsed in her brain. Chris would *not* make an arrest without solid, irrefutable evidence. "What do you want me to put?"

"Nothing would be my preference."

She didn't smile, but tilted her head. "That's unlikely. Is Amber under arrest for Jethro's murder?"

"Yes. We have reason to believe she lied about her alibi." His jaw tightened. He didn't want to share any information with her.

"What reason?"

Chris huffed out a sigh. "She lied about her alibi. She didn't get a ride home. The driver who was supposed to take her said she blew him off and went back to the fairgrounds. I need to deal with this. I'll update you later if you promise not to speculate on social media."

"Deal."

She watched them drive off, then turned to Katherine, who was just staring back, mouth slightly open, holding a sobbing stranger in her arms.

Chapter Nineteen

Molly watched as Katherine tried to extricate herself from Alicia's grasp. The woman was hovering on the border of hysterical and theatrical. Eyes wide, Katherine stared at Molly.

"Um, Alicia?" Molly said, coming closer.

Alicia lifted her head and turned to Molly, allowing Sam's mom to take a step back. The distraught woman brought a hand to her mouth and wrapped her other arm around her waist, her loud sobs sounding like a large animal dying in exquisite pain.

"Wh-wh-what?"

"Would you like me to drive you to the police station?"

She wailed louder. "Why would I want to go there?"

Molly and Katherine exchanged a glance that shared their silent surprise.

"Your sister must have an attorney, Alicia. Come on, dear. She needs your help now. You need to be strong for her," Katherine said, her voice firm.

The next sob was more of a hiccup. She nodded. "Oh. Okay. Sure."

It was doubtful that this woman would be any help to her sister, but Molly would take her and see what information she could glean.

Leading her across the street, Molly wondered if she had Kleenex in her Jeep. Checking the back seat while Alicia crawled in the passenger side, she found a box under the seat and passed it forward.

Alicia mumbled a thank-you and seemed to get herself a little more under control.

Molly started the Jeep and pulled into the street, fingers tight around the steering wheel.

"The police said your sister's alibi fell through. Do you know anything about that?"

Though she kept her eyes on the road, she felt the woman's glare. "My sister didn't kill her stupid husband."

Molly pressed her lips together.

"She didn't. But what was she supposed to say? Oh, I was making out with my high school sweetheart? It's not like Jet even cared. God. That guy was all over anything with a pulse. He was a pig."

Giving her a quick glance when she pulled up to a stop sign, she said, "Your sister said she loves him. Are you suggesting she didn't? Because honestly, that's not going to help your sister's case."

Alicia wiped her nose and pulled out another tissue. "She doesn't need help. She didn't do anything. She's innocent."

Molly had thought the same thing until only moments ago. "Well, she's going to have to give up her affair if she hopes to get released."

"I'll talk to her, but she probably won't listen to me. I told her not to marry that old jerk. But she was so dazzled. He could be charming when he wanted to be, and Amber had money, but she goes through it faster than hair products. If you want the truth, the way we grew up, it's not a surprise she fell for someone old enough to be her father."

With one hand, Molly rubbed at her temple. Her head was beginning to pound. These people made reality television look rational.

"Does she have a lawyer?"

Alicia pulled her phone out of the pocket of her designer jeans. "Yeah. We have one. She just spoke to him yesterday to contest the will."

As she turned at the light, heading toward the police station, Molly frowned. "There's no way the will has been read yet."

Looking up from her phone, Alicia shot Molly a bleary, red-eyed glance. "Of course not. But that didn't stop Jet's wench of an ex-wife from rubbing it in her face."

That she could easily see. It might have been when their fight occurred. Trying to breathe through her nose, Molly wondered if taking Amber's sister to the station would serve any purpose. Alicia greeted someone on the phone as Molly parked the Jeep. She continued to explain the situation in a far calmer voice to the person on the other line.

It was hard to offer privacy when she didn't lower her voice in any way. Holding the door to the station open, she cringed when Alicia's voice rose several octaves.

"That's what we pay you for, so why don't you get your lazy butt down to this nowhere town and deal with it?"

She jabbed her thumb on the screen, ending the call. "Useless."

Approaching the counter, Molly gave a small wave to Priscilla and wished she could shoot her a warning. Alicia stomped her high-heeled feet to where Pris was typing and slammed her hands down on the counter.

"My sister is being illegally detained by your police officers. I demand to see the person in charge."

Molly stepped back a little. She saw Ed and Amber sitting in chairs beside one of the desks, both cuffed. Ed's eyes found Molly, and his gaze seemed to fill with anger. Chris was standing near them, but even with him facing away, Molly could read the frustration in his body language. He put both hands on his hips and dropped his head.

Sheriff Saron came out of his office and looked at Chris. "You want me to deal with this?"

Chris's head rose, and he shook his head. Turning, the only indication he gave that seeing Molly surprised him was the slight flare of his eyes and nostrils. He focused on Alicia. Coming to the counter, he leaned over it, folding his hands together as casually as if they were old friends.

"Let me give you some advice," he started. Alicia opened her mouth, and Chris raised a hand. "Nope. This is the part where you listen. Your sister?" He hooked a thumb over his shoulder. "I'm going to talk to her and her idiot friend. You have two choices. You can stay on this side of the counter, ready to support them when the decision as to whether or not they'll be staying in our fine facility comes down the pipe. Or you can say one word—swear to God, just *one*—and I'll invite you back here to join them. But see, if that happens, I'm going to lose my patience and need a bit of a break. Which means instead of taking care of this now and getting some answers, the three of you can cuddle up in a cell until my blood pressure lowers. Do you understand your choices—and nonverbal replies are strongly suggested."

Alicia nodded, her eyes comic-book wide. Chris had delivered the entire speech with such a quiet authority, Molly was sure no one who wasn't standing right beside him even heard it.

Her fingers itched to high-five him. He glanced at her, saw that Alicia was going to hold her tongue, and turned back to the room. Sheriff Saron's lips twitched, and he headed back into his office.

"Uh, I'll just leave you here to wait. Good luck," Molly said.

Priscilla pulled her bottom lip between her teeth, and when her gaze met Molly's, she could see she was trying hard not to laugh.

Hurrying out of the station, Molly got in her car and rested her head on the steering wheel. The day's events were dizzying. She texted Jill and asked for updates, and let her and Alan know she was checking in with Sarah before heading back to the office. She could use a break from the crazy.

The police station was only about fifteen minutes from Sarah's shop, which was just off Main Street. There were a few cars in the lot. She parked and went through the front door. A woman and a little girl were painting mugs at one of the tables, and two other older women were painting ceramic animals.

As the bell jingled over the door, Molly froze. From the cleanup room, a slight, dark-haired woman with a streak of cobalt blue down the center of her head emerged. Sarah came right after her, and Molly arched her brows when her friend saw her standing there.

"Hi, Molly. I didn't figure you for a day painter." Sarah came over to her while the other woman took a dish of water to the mother and daughter.

Sarah whispered, "That's Naomi."

Molly whispered back, "I put that together. What happened?"

Naomi said something to the little girl that made her laugh, and it was impossible to swallow down her shock. She hadn't expected Sarah to press charges. Not really. In fact, she expected there'd be a little friction between Chris and his girlfriend when she didn't. But she sure as heck couldn't have predicted finding Naomi helping customers in Sarah's shop.

Naomi walked to the older women and asked if they needed help. Molly and Sarah looked on.

"What's your name, dear?" one of the women asked. She was wearing a bright white sweater covered in cherries. Her gray hair was curly and long. She held the paintbrush as though it was delicate, and her glasses perched low on her nose.

"Naomi," the woman said quietly.

Woman? Girl? Molly couldn't wrap her head around it.

"Sarah, how old is she?" Molly kept her voice low.

"Just turned eighteen. She stays at the shelter about twenty minutes from here. She's working off the cost of the supplies she used."

Naomi grabbed more brushes for the women, glancing sideways frequently to where Molly and Sarah whispered.

"Is that safe?"

Sarah grinned. "You sound like Chris. Even when she broke in, she didn't hurt anything. She's coming in a couple of hours a day, and I told her that at the end of each shift, she can have an hour to use the supplies."

Molly turned and stared at her friend with awe. "That's...so kind."

Naomi wandered over, hesitantly, as though fearing one of them might yell at her. "Um, sorry to interrupt, but the little girl wants to paint something else. Can she just choose something?"

There was a selection of ceramics on a shelf along one of the walls. "Yes. She can. Naomi, this is Molly, my friend."

Naomi eyed her warily. "You were here last night? With the car guy?"

"Car guy?" Molly folded her hands over her chest to hide her surprise.

"Yeah. He owns the auto shop, right?"

"He does."

"He's cute."

Molly bit back her grin. "He is. Sarah says you stay in the shelter."

If she'd had hackles, they would have revealed themselves. "So?"

Molly softened her gaze. "So, how long have you been staying there?"

The teen shrugged.

"Do you go to school?"

Molly figured it was a defense mechanism when the teen stared back blandly and answered sarcastically. "No time. I'm really busy these days."

"Hmm. I can see that." Molly smiled. "It's nice to meet you, Naomi."

Another shrug, and she walked away to show the little girl the choices.

Molly turned back to Sarah. "You know nothing about her."

She nodded. "I know. But to be fair, I don't really know anyone in town that well. I've only connected with a few people, and that's because those people have been kind and welcoming. What if you and Sam and Chris hadn't pulled me into your circle? I'd probably be standing here alone. Everyone needs someone to take a chance on them. Besides that, Chris put the fear of...well, of *him*, into her so I think she'll toe the line. Either that or just disappear. But I get the sense she wants to be here. There's no reason she can't be, and I'd rather it was during the hours when I'm open."

Feeling a new appreciation for her friend, Molly gave her an impulsive, hard hug. "You would have found your people with or without us. But I'm glad we became friends."

Sarah laughed, patted Molly's arm. "Me, too. But I should get back to work. Everything okay?"

Not wanting to share official news by word of mouth—seeing as she was working hard to make the *Bulletin*, online and print, relevant and important to the town—she shook her head.

"But check the *Bulletin*'s website in about twenty minutes," she said with a smile.

She left and headed back to the office. Sometimes things that seemed bad at first had a way of turning into good things. Like when her tires had the air let out of them and she'd met Sam. Molly was glad that even if not everything was falling into place, some good had happened in Britton Bay this week.

She'd report it, for sure. But there was another headline that would capture the attention. *Time to get back to work and write it.*

Chapter Twenty

BRITTON BAY BULLETIN @THEBULLETIN*19 MINUTES
AMBER HARKAW ARRESTED FOR THE DEATH OF HER HUSBAND.

Jill took care of the article online, but Molly updated the Facebook page and Twitter. Jill had touched base with Priscilla and confirmed that Amber had lied about her alibi, but would only say she'd been waiting by one of the fences for Jet to return. When he didn't, she'd hitched a ride with another, unnamed driver. Molly couldn't fathom not telling the police about the affair. Maybe Ed would tell them since he seemed to want to protect Amber so much.

Unless...unless Amber really had done it and Ed didn't believe she was capable. She still couldn't believe the turn of events, and though she wanted to see things solved, something wasn't settling correctly in her mind. It was like laying a blanket over rocks–no way to smooth things out without removing what was underneath.

Jill came into her office, waving a piece of paper. "So, I have a friend who is pretty good with computers."

Molly glanced up from her computer screen. "Do they want a job?"

Jill laughed and took a seat. "I don't think Alan can afford him. Anyway, you know how they always say 'Follow the money'?"

Closing her laptop, a grin on her face, Molly leaned back in her chair. "Do they?"

Jill nodded. "You know they do. Every good cop show does, anyway. Well, I had my friend follow the money. And guess where that fifty thousand dollars went?"

Excitement danced over her skin. "Tell me."

Jill slid the paper across. It was screenshots of two different bank accounts. One showed a deposit and withdrawal of fifty grand. The second showed a deposit from the first account for the same amount a few minutes later. Molly squinted to see what she was looking at.

"I suspected it was a payoff he didn't want to make public. This is Jethro's account, I'm assuming?" She pointed at the one on the left.

"Yup," Jill said, leaning forward and putting her finger on the second image. "And this one here is Ed McLaren's account."

Her friend's smile widened, and she tapped the paper several times. "He paid off his wife's ex. For what? I think it was a get-out-of-her life payoff."

"Makes sense." Molly wondered if she could find a way to ask Ed some questions. "I'm not sure who that makes seem guiltier. Ed takes money and promises to stay away from Amber, but never plans to and kills him instead. Or Amber finds out her husband paid off her ex and kills him out of anger? To get him out of the way? Because she's aiming to be a serial husband killer but has only one death under her belt?" Nothing was seeming too ridiculous or far-fetched at the moment.

A heavy sigh left Jill's lips. "I don't know. I really don't. I'm not as good as you are with solving these types of puzzles. Do you think the police know about the payoff?"

"They'd have Jethro's financial records for sure. They knew who inherited his estate. I still think the murderer had to be a guy. Chris wouldn't comment on it, but think about how much force would have to go into a blow that caused death." Though rage was a powerful emotion and if Amber had enough of it, it was possible.

"She did lie about her alibi."

That troubled Molly. If Ed and Amber said they were together, they'd essentially cover for each other. *Like Brian and Candy?* Unless the exchange of money confirmed the two had a motive to do it together. "Was that because she or Ed was killing Jethro or because they were together right under his nose, and for whatever reason, they don't want that to get out?"

Jill stood up and grabbed her paper. "I'm going to leave those questions to you, but at least now we know where the money went. I loved what you told me about Sarah and the girl who broke in. I'd like to do a human-interest piece. I'm not sure how shy the kid is, though. You think she'd be open to an interview?"

Since she was more used to skulking around in the dark and definitely had an edge of suspicion toward others, Molly couldn't say. "Why don't you call Sarah and feel her out. Maybe after things settle? I'm not sure where she'll go from here."

Walking to the door, Jill stopped and turned back. "I think I might head out to the shelter. I feel like there's more we can do as a community, and it's time someone reached out to them."

Guilt tugged hard. This was what they were supposed to be doing—tracking down stories that impacted their residents and supporting those in need by bringing awareness to them. *We are.* But she was also consumed with figuring out why it didn't sit right that Amber was under arrest for murder.

"Do that. We could maybe do a series of articles in the coming weeks."

"Okay. See you later."

Molly drummed her fingers on her desk, not opening her laptop again just yet. She wondered how long it would be until Amber's lawyer showed up.

Unable to just sit there, even if she did have copy to edit, layouts to organize, and story ideas to develop, Molly grabbed her jacket and her bag. Packing up her laptop, she told Alan she was leaving and headed to her Jeep.

Using the process of elimination, she drove to the Sea Side Shangri-La, Britton Bay's only hotel. The town also had a motel and several bed-and-breakfasts. By next summer, there'd be a new hotel; a large developer had purchased a large lot at the far end of the beach, opposite where Molly lived. The city council had posted plans and updates on their website; it was something else the *Bulletin* should be more focused on.

When she'd moved to the seaside town, she couldn't have predicted that murders would pull their focus away from small-town, local news.

Pulling into the parking lot of the hotel reminded Molly of the last murder. A not-quite-celebrity chef had been killed in one of the rooms. It had been at the very end of the summer, and Molly couldn't help but wonder if it would impact reservations next year.

She got out of her Jeep and went into the hotel. She recognized Kip Martin, who held several positions including front desk and concierge. He waved when he saw her, giving her a wide, friendly smile. With smooth, ebony skin and perfectly coifed black hair, he looked more like a *GQ* model than a hotel manager.

"Hi, Molly. How are you?" He closed the magazine he was reading.

"I'm good. You?" The last time she'd seen him, he hadn't been anywhere near as relaxed as he appeared right now. *Knowing there was a dead body in one's hotel tends to create internal chaos that spills over.* She knew that type of situation too well.

"Things are good. Quieter now than they were a few days ago. We've got several empty rooms. Hibernation season," he joked.

Molly leaned her arms on the counter. "Speaking of rooms, would you be able to ring Brad Templeton and Herman Besbrewer's rooms? I'd like to speak to them if they're around."

Kip's fingers flew over the keyboard. "I can call up to Mr. Besbrewer's room, but Mr. Templeton checked out this morning."

Interesting. The police must have cleared him. He definitely wasn't the strongest suspect in her mind, but it still bothered her that he'd been there, probably confronting Jethro. And Herman had followed after him. There was more of a story there. *Looks like you aren't getting Brad's side of it, though.*

"Okay. Just Herman's then."

Kip called up to the room and told him who was there. "He says he'll be down in a minute."

To the right of the front desk was a seating area. Molly pointed to it. "I'll wait over there."

Kip nodded and flipped his magazine open again. Pulling out her phone while she waited, Molly texted Sam to see if he wanted to meet up later.

"Molly?" Herman bent at the waist to get himself in her line of sight, then sat across from her.

"Hi, Herman. Thanks for coming down."

He shrugged. Dressed in track pants and a baggy sweater, he looked like he'd just rolled out of bed. His hair was messy, and there were several days of growth on his face.

"Nothing else to do. God, I'll be happy when they let me go home. I'm losing money every day I'm here."

Trying to offer an empathetic smile, she tucked her phone away. "I'm sorry it's taking so long. Have you spoken to the police?"

He leaned back in the floral-patterned chair. "Repeatedly. They've combed through my finances, my personal life, my business. I don't get why it's so hard for them to understand that with Jet dead, I stand no chance of getting my money back."

"Would you mind if I asked a few questions about that money?"

Wariness clouded his features, but he gestured to go ahead.

"Do you know why Jethro wanted to borrow it?"

Shaking his head, he stared at a spot behind Molly, perhaps thinking about the exchange. "No. Said it was for something personal. He didn't want it tied up in his business. We'd been friends a long time. He's helped me more than once. Didn't think it'd be a big deal. I mean, the guy has... sorry, *had* more in liquid cash than I have in assets. Who could have foreseen this?"

"But you argued, right? Fought physically?"

A scowl replaced his wariness. "I've been over this with the police. We did. It happens. We were both angry, but I needed to get away from him. I didn't want to use my contingency plan, but I'm going to have to. Shame, though."

Molly sat forward. "What plan is that?"

Herman smiled. "I might not have the money Jethro did, but I have some, and I'm no idiot. Guess what he used as collateral for the loan?"

Thinking for a moment, she sorted through what Jet could exchange for not paying the loan. Something that wouldn't impact Candice or Brian, who clearly didn't support the side deal that he'd made.

Her jaw dropped. "His car?"

"Yup. And if the cops ever wrap this up, I'll be chatting with Brian and Candice about collecting what's owed to me."

Looking down at his shoes for a moment, he crossed his hands in front of him. "That's what got Jet so upset. I told him to get me my cash in the next week or I'd go to Brian and tell him about the deal. Brian would have made sure he didn't renege."

"You have no idea why he'd want the money?"

He leaned forward. "None. Does this have something to do with the arrest made today? I saw online they'd arrested Amber and that reporter guy. Were they in on it together?"

It wasn't a bad question. Were they? "I'm not sure. I don't have any further details beyond what we reported."

"Well, since they've got someone to point the finger at, they should let me go."

"I'm sure Detective Beatty will contact you as soon as he can."

Molly started to stand, but stopped herself. "How well do you know Candice Harkaw?"

"They were a package deal forever, her and Jet. She was on the road with him every time. Part of that was because she knew he was a cheater, but I think she really enjoyed it. As much or more than Jet did. She loves cars. Loves people."

"Did she love Jet?"

His smile was sad. "Funny how some guys spend their lives looking for love, wishing for it, willing to do anything for it. And guys like Jet? They take it for granted, and it seems the more they do, the more they're wanted. One of life's sad truths."

She hated the sadness in his voice. He stood and smiled down at her.

"Nothing to do with you, but I'm hoping this will be the last time I see you. I think I'll go pack my bags in hopes of being given the green light to get out of this place."

As he walked away, she called out. "Brad left already?"

Herman tucked his hands in his pockets. "He's a grumpy one, but he wouldn't hurt a fly. I'm glad they let him go."

He walked back to the elevator, and Molly waved goodbye to Kip. She knew no more than she had before. And it was driving her a little crazy. She wondered how wrong it would be to suggest a dinner with Chris and Sarah tonight, then felt bad for even thinking it. She wouldn't use their friendship to her advantage, and Chris was no more likely to open up while they were hanging out than he was at the station.

Climbing into her Jeep, she decided that was her next stop. The town of Britton Bay had the right to know if a killer had been caught. And if she'd posted bail.

Chapter Twenty-One

Two things happened the next day, and Molly didn't know which story to go after. Early the next morning, Detective Chris Beatty confirmed, through the *Britton Bay Bulletin*, that Amber Harkaw and Edward McLaren were released on conditional bail when her lawyer had arrived at the police station.

Shortly after she had posted the information on their website and social media channels, Brian phoned her cell.

"Hi. You okay?" she asked.

She assumed he was calling because Amber had been released and he wanted more information. Maybe something that he could share with Candice to make her feel better. Molly still wasn't convinced of Candice's innocence, so maybe she was panicking that Amber had been set free and Brian was trying to allay her worries.

"I'm not," Brian said. "I should phone the police. I know I should. But I love her, Molly. I know you know that."

Her eyes widened, and surprise stole her breath for a second before she flailed her hand around, grabbing Jill's attention. Jill hurried over to where she was sitting at the layout table and leaned in close.

"I do know you love her, Brian. I can see it. But covering for her isn't the answer. Especially if she's done something illegal." Her heart beat heavily.

"I know. But we were going to be together. How could I turn her in when it was finally our time? Now she's run off. She turned her back on me, so now I have no choice but to tell the truth. She did it, Molly. She killed Jet. She couldn't stand that he'd married Amber."

Jill gasped, but the sound was covered by Brian's sob. "I don't want to see her come to harm. I don't know what to do. She went on the run.

Wouldn't tell me where she was going..." he trailed off, and she could hear his muffled crying. Her heart ached.

"Brian, we need to call the police."

There was no response. Molly pictured him hunched over, crying. He'd lost his best friend and the woman he loved, after trying to cover for her. The line went dead.

"Oh my God," Jill said.

Alan came out of his office. "What's going on?"

They caught him up to speed as Molly shoved her phone in her back pocket and grabbed her purse, rooting around for her keys.

"Where are you going?" Alan asked.

"Call Chris and tell him what Brian said. I need to go see him. He's so fragile. I wouldn't put it past him to..." She didn't even want to finish the thought.

"Suicide?" Jill whispered.

"You heard the line go dead. He's alone in the world. More now than ever."

"You shouldn't be walking into that, Molly. I'll come with you," Jill said.

"I'll go with you," Alan said, his tone commanding.

"No. I have a rapport with him. Too many people might overwhelm him and push him toward the ledge rather than pull him back from it. I'll head there now. Jill, you get hold of Chris and keep things updated. If you can get a license number for whatever Candice is driving, flood social media with it. Alan, you go get Sam at work. Take him up to the RV park. Brian cares about him, so maybe he'll listen to Sam if me being there doesn't work. Or maybe he isn't trying to hurt himself, and having Sam there will just be a comfort. Either way, I need to go talk to him. See for myself that he's okay."

She didn't wait for a response. Taking off through the back door, she got in her Jeep and took the alley road down to the end, grateful she knew a shortcut to the RV park.

* * * *

Molly pulled up to the site and released a breath she didn't know she was holding. Brian was sitting at the firepit, elbows resting on his knees, head in his hands. He looked up when she turned off her Jeep and got out.

"I was so worried you were going to do something you couldn't take back," she said as she approached him.

He didn't get up, just let his head fall back into his hands. She took the seat beside him.

"I shouldn't have let her go, Molly."

Putting a hand on his arm, she squeezed. "Brian, you did what you had to. There was nothing else you could do."

Turning his head to the side, he stared at her through bloodshot eyes. "That's the truth. There was nothing else I could do." He took a shuddery breath, and she was about to tell him that the police had been called and he didn't need to bear that burden anymore. But he continued. "I've loved her since we were kids. She was my girlfriend for about a week when we were fifteen. Bet you didn't know that. Then she meets Jet, and it's all over. She fell for him even though he jerked her around for *years.* I'd have treated her right. He treated her like dirt on the bottom of his most-hated pair of shoes, and still she loved him."

He shook his head, stood up.

"Brian," Molly said.

As he turned to look at her, anger and sadness fought to dominate his expression. "She used to tell me about their problems. Unload all of his garbage on me. I'd tell her, leave him. Send him packing. But she couldn't. Wouldn't. So I did the only thing I could. Loved her anyway. I was there for her every chance I could be. I stopped trying to turn her against him. Because the truth was, I think if she had actually up and left him, she would have said goodbye to me as well."

Brian paced back and forth in front of Jethro's RV, and Molly tried to think of a way to reach him. To explain that loving someone didn't mean you got to control their decisions. He couldn't change Candice's decisions by loving her more.

"I couldn't stand it, Molly," Brian whispered, leaning against the side of the fancy RV.

"Loving someone who doesn't feel the same is never easy, Brian." She knew that. And now that she had Sam and knew the difference between mutual love and unrequited feelings, she could truly empathize with him.

She stood and went to him, standing in front of him. Maybe Sam would be better able to help him understand that he couldn't change Candice's path. Hopefully he'd get there soon.

He shook his head. "Even with him gone, she wouldn't choose me. Oh, she loved me, she said. But only as a friend." He waved a hand in disgust and pushed away from the RV. "I didn't need another goddamn friend, and I'd waited thirty years for that piece of trash to have his turn." He pointed viciously at his chest, stabbing it with his index finger. "It was my turn. *Our turn.* My turn to show her what her life could have been like. What it felt like to be truly loved. Now, both of us, we got nothing. Not each other, not Jet, nothing."

Tears welled in her eyes at the agony in his voice. She started to reach out to him, offer a hug, but he opened the door to the RV, held it for her.

"You're probably frozen. Listening to an old man lament his stupidity."

Molly walked to the steps, but paused and looked him in the eyes. "Believing in someone isn't stupid, Brian. Especially when it's someone you love."

He smiled at her with that same grandfatherly affection he had shown the first night. "I think you're right. Everyone needs someone to believe in them. But it's foolish, don't you think, to see only what you want to see?"

Stepping up into the RV, she started to tell him it was no more foolish than it was stupid, but she didn't. Even as her eyes fell on the pair of gloves sitting on the kitchen counter, right where she'd done the original interview, it didn't fully register that something was off.

Molly felt Brian behind her, heard the click of the RV's door. Her attention had been naturally drawn to the left because of the wide-open space. Plus, she recognized the gloves from the night of the dance. She'd watched him pull them on. She wasn't sure why them being there in Jet's RV seemed odd, but a noise to the right of her pulled her attention.

Almost as if she were in slow motion, she turned her head, ignoring the bubbling panic churning in her chest. Something was very off. The driver and passenger seat were blocked from view by a pair of long curtains. Another strange sound and a fluttering of the curtains made the nerves in her chest spread like a fire, consuming her. She kept turning, looked at Brian.

"I'm sorry, dear. I really, truly am."

Molly tried to push him, to reach the lock or the handle on the door. He grabbed her effortlessly, gripping her biceps as if they were nothing more than straws.

"Now don't do that. I don't want to hurt you. I didn't want to hurt anyone. Just stay calm, and everything will be okay."

She blinked rapidly, and her throat went dry. "Where's Candy?"

Another noise, this one garbled and stranger than the last. Brian held Molly with one hand wrapped around her arm, tight enough that it would leave a mark, and dragged her to the curtain, whipping one side open. There, in the passenger chair, sat Candy. She was bound and gagged, squirming to get the ropes on her hands undone. Her eyes went wide with panic, and Brian reached out, smoothed a hand over her forehead.

"Shh, darlin'. It's going to be okay," he crooned.

Arm throbbing, Molly took advantage of his distracted state and kicked out, knocking him right in the knee, hard. He swore, buckled, but didn't release his grasp one bit. When he steadied himself, he glared at her and slapped her across the face. Shock stung worse than the feel of his palm.

"I didn't want to do that. Both of you, spitfires." He said it as though he was mad but also partially impressed.

From the corner of her eye, Molly saw Candy try to plant her feet. They made eye contact, and Molly did her best to communicate that they could work together. Just as the other woman was about to stand, maybe even launch herself at Brian, he pulled a gun from behind him.

"Neither of you wants to go this way. So you're both going to get those stupid ideas out of your heads, and we're going to do this civilly."

Tears burned Molly's eyes, and a headache crept up her neck, landing at the base of her head. Candy moaned quietly.

"At least ungag her," Molly said.

Brian looked at her and shook his head. "She won't shut up if I do. Won't let me make her understand my side of it. Now, I'm going to take my hand off you, but you do anything, I'm going to shoot Candy, and it's going to be your fault. You're a nice girl, Molly. Sadly, you wouldn't be here, be this involved, if you weren't. So I know you don't want to be the reason Candy dies, do you?"

Molly shook her head. When he released her, she stood still. She could bide her time. He obviously had a plan. He reached down and grabbed Candy's arm, yanked her up.

"Now Candy here wouldn't care if I shot you. So I'm not going to threaten her with that. She's not as kindhearted as you, dear. But Candice knows I'll shoot her somewhere painful if she does anything she shouldn't. Don't you, darlin'?"

Candice shot him a razor-sharp glare, but nodded.

Brian smiled. "There we go. Look at us getting along. Let's go have a seat."

He gestured to the couches with a tip of the gun. Not sure what to do just yet, Molly walked to the spot where Jethro had sat the night of the interview. Glancing at the gloves, she saw the blood staining them. *Oh God.* When she turned to sit, she saw that the oven was open. And turned on. Heat emanated, filling that small area of the RV. *Oh God.*

"You cleaned your fingerprints with the gloves." She sat down, her stomach clenching.

Brian pushed Candice into the seat beside Molly. "I did. Would have thrown the gloves out, but I always found it hard to part with anything Candy gave me. I thought I could get the blood out."

He stared at them a moment, then shook his head, like he was clearing his thoughts. Before he sat, he pulled a ring of keys from his pocket and pressed a button. Though it was whisper quiet, Molly knew he'd started the RV. He smiled at her indulgently, almost proudly. He looked at the stove, then back at her.

"You are a clever girl. Candy isn't as smart. Oh, she's good with numbers, but putting the figurative two and two together was never easy for her. That's how Jet was able to cheat on her from day one."

Candy made a noise from behind the gag and held up her bound hands, holding up one finger in Brian's direction. He laughed. A deep belly laugh.

"I love your temper, darlin'. Love everything about you. Hate that this is how it ends. In case she doesn't get it, and to make sure I know you do, why don't you tell her what's going to happen here, Molly."

Molly turned to Candice, saw the fear in the woman's eyes, and wondered if she looked as scared. She definitely felt it.

"Come on, dear. Don't have much time. Everything I researched says it doesn't take long this way. Then this will all be over."

Candy's eyes widened, and Molly had to blink back tears. "He has the oven open and started the RV. I'm guessing, since he knows cars, he found a way to route the exhaust into the RV and seal up any escape. We're going to die of carbon monoxide poisoning."

Brian slapped his thigh, startling both women. "Damn, you are smart. I really wish you didn't have to be part of this."

Her head hurt, her stomach rolled, but she still felt like she was in control of her thoughts. "It doesn't have to be like this. You can tell the police it was an accident. You got in a fight. Candy and I will back whatever you say. Just let us go. Don't do this, Brian. This isn't who you are."

Candice nodded emphatically, murmuring behind the black cloth tied between her lips.

"You might keep your silence, Molly, but how do you think we got here? I tried to tell Candy I did it for her. I'd do anything for her. She just got mad. Blamed me for stealing the love of her life. Even after he divorced her, hurt her in every way a man can break a woman's heart, she still loved him."

Molly stared at him, trying to formulate a plan. She couldn't think of anything other than needing more time. "I'm sorry, Brian. You deserve more than that. So much more. Despite this…situation, you seem like such a kind man."

He nodded, a sad smile on his lips. "I am. Never wanted to hurt anyone. Hell, even killing us all, I'm willing to do it gently. I didn't intend to kill Jet, either. Though, I'll say on that, I'm not sorry I did."

Molly nodded, wiped her hand across her forehead, and smiled at him through her teary eyes. "I see that. I can't breathe, though. I'm overheating. You've got the exhaust coming in. You don't need the oven, too. Let me close it? Turn it off? It's too hot. Please, Brian."

He glanced at the oven, back at her. "Having it on will make it quicker."

She kept smiling. "Don't you want as much time with her, even if it's the end, as you can get?"

His gaze went to Candy and softened. Turning back to Molly, he said nothing.

"I want to hear the whole story. Please, Brian, give us all a little more time."

He nodded, pointed the gun at her. "Nothing silly."

She rose slowly and walked to the small stove. Eyes darting around, she looked for anything she could use as a weapon. Her hands shook as she turned the knob on the stove, then lifted the door closed. The small window over the small sink let in some light. She could see the firepit and chastised herself for coming inside without one hint of an argument. He was right. It was stupid that she'd believed him. There was nothing on the counter. Nothing she could throw at him or use to inflict injury.

"No use, dear. Have a seat and I'll tell you the story."

Defeated, she moved back to the seat. Sitting close enough to Candy that their thighs touched, she stared at Brian. *Think, Molly.*

Brian crossed an ankle over his knee, the gun resting against his jeans. "Like I said, I didn't mean to kill Jet." He stared at Candice while he spoke. "I went back to get your jacket and heard fighting. I picked up the crowbar as a weapon, but only because I didn't know what I was walking into. Saw Jet and Herman pounding on each other. I was going to intervene, but Herman got a final shot in and took off. Don't even know why I held onto the crowbar. Adrenaline maybe?"

Candice squirmed, pulling at the bindings on her wrists. Molly watched, then looked at Brian. "Let me untie her."

He laughed. "No, darlin'. She'll be all over me like a cat on a mouse. She hasn't got near the calm you have."

"Brian, we're going to die, right?"

She wondered how long they'd even last. It was a big RV, but if carbon monoxide poisoning didn't take long, she was surprised she wasn't feeling sicker. Or more light-headed.

"We are. Together."

She looked at Candy, eyes wide and fierce. *Please play along. Please understand I need you to play along.*

Looking at Brian, she lowered her lashes and used the tears clogging her throat to her advantage. "You win. You get the girl. Wouldn't you rather she was wrapped in your arms when the moment comes? Let me untie her. She won't do anything. She doesn't want it to be more painful either. And I think she gets it. This is the end. Right, Candy?"

Candy's eyes locked with hers and held. Then she nodded, slowly breaking eye contact and turning to Jet. She went down on her knees and shuffled over to him, lay her head on his lap. A guttural sound left his lips as he lifted the gun out of the way and stroked a hand over her hair.

"Aw, darlin', this is all I ever wanted. You and me."

Molly inched along the bench. "You have it, Brian. Untie her."

Taking a deep breath, she did a physical assessment. Headache was moderate. Her stomach was tense, but calmer than it had been. How long would they have before the symptoms hit? Before they passed out and succumbed to the fumes they couldn't even smell.

Brian was stroking Candice's hair. Molly would wait until he agreed to let her be untied, and then, somehow, the two of them would overpower him.

"Okay. Untie her so she can curl her arms around me," he said. Molly started to move when a strange sound came from the doorway about a second before the door simply fell away from the RV.

Fully vested and armed men burst into the room, Chris leading the way. Brian saw them and pointed the gun at his own head. Candice reared up, out of his lap, knocking his hand hard enough to dislodge the gun from his hand. In seconds, Chris had him on the floor, hands behind his back.

"Brian Stoleman, you are under arrest…"

Molly collapsed onto the seat, Chris's words a blur in her head, tears spilling from her cheeks. One of the cops helped Candice up. Chris was leading a sobbing Brian out the door when Officer Wills sat beside Molly.

"Come on, Ms. Owens. We need to get you checked out."

"I thought carbon monoxide was quick," she said through tears. Her throat hurt.

"We cut the pipe he had leading in here. There hasn't been any exhaust coming in for ten minutes."

Before she could respond, she heard thumping footsteps and her name being yelled. Sam appeared in the doorway, eyes wild when they landed on her. Officer Wills stood.

"Looks like he'll want to help you," he murmured in an amused tone. He stepped aside so Sam could get to her.

When he did, he fell to his knees and ran his hands over her face, her shoulders, her arms, hands, thighs.

"You're okay? You're okay? Tell me you're okay?" His eyes were scanning her, his hands moving frantically.

"I'm okay." She took her hands in his to stop them from moving, then launched herself at him. He fell back so he was sitting on the floor and she was in his lap, his arms wrapped around her like a vice.

"You scared the life out of me," he said.

"I'm sorry. I'm so sorry."

Sam rocked her back and forth, murmuring that she was okay. That everything would be okay.

"Uh, guys?" Chris called from the doorway.

They looked up. Chris clenched his jaw, one hand on his hip. He pointed at her with the other one. Then he shook his head and lowered his hand with a deep sigh.

"We cut the engine, but you still shouldn't stay in here. Molly needs to get checked out by a doctor, Sam."

"I'm okay," Molly said.

Sam cupped her face in his hands. "Your face is bruising, and someone tried to poison you. Could you pick your battles? Please?"

Laughter bubbled up around the tears. "Okay."

"Hurry up," Chris said, leaving.

Sam rose, taking Molly up with him as if she weighed no more than feathers. Adrenaline. It was still coursing through her, too.

"I can walk," she told him.

When he was sure she was steady on her feet, he pressed his forehead to hers with enough pressure that her brows rose. "You really don't understand what careful means."

She hated that she'd worried him. She hated it more that she didn't really have a plan for escaping. Would she and Candy have been able to overpower Brian? Would they have died? She thought of how she'd feel if the situation were reversed, and tears spilled over.

"I'm sorry. I'm so sorry. I thought he was going to hurt himself."

They made their way out of the RV, and even though she probably hadn't ingested that much carbon monoxide, she took a minute to take a few deep breaths. The RV's door had been detached using the hinges. How they'd done it silently was far beyond her current level of comprehension.

Brian was in the back of a cruiser that Deputy Patrick was getting into. Wills was standing by the ambulance, talking to Candice, who was being looked at by a medic.

The air, while cool, was refreshing and welcome. Molly took another deep breath. Sam's hand linked with hers as he watched her trying to gulp in the fresh oxygen. Chris joined them.

"I have to deal with paperwork. Take her to the hospital, then come by the station."

"Yes, sir," Sam said.

Chris stared at Molly. She wanted to lower her gaze. He'd told her, several times, to let him do his job. If she'd just had faith, trusted someone she *knew* she could count on rather than seeing something that wasn't there with Brian, he wouldn't be looking at her right now like he wanted to throw her in a cell, too.

She forced herself not to look away. Sam's hand tightened on hers.

"Sarah can give you the gift she made me pick out," he said, his voice harsh.

Molly stiffened. "What?"

"For your birthday. I'm getting you a dictionary," Chris said, still mad. He pointed at her, wagging his finger like he didn't know what to do with her.

"I...*what?*" Molly stared, confused.

"For someone who spends their life looking at words, you have very misguided understanding of several of them." He held up his index finger, pointing it skyward. "Police." He held up a second finger. "Detective." A third. "Reporter." A fourth. "Meddling." Five fingers splayed wide. "Civilian. You don't know the meaning of *any* of those."

Sam chuckled. Fresh tears filled Molly's eyes, and she launched herself at Chris, hugging him hard. His belt dug into her, and his vest made it hard to get close, but she did her best.

"I'm sorry. I'm sorry I scared you. That I didn't call you first."

He wrapped his arms around her, and he squeezed, then released her, setting her back with his hands on her shoulders. "Swear to God, Molly. Next investigation? I'm putting you on house arrest."

Sam slipped an arm around her shoulder and pulled her to his side. "I'll stand guard," he said.

She looked up at him, relief, love, and happiness mixing with the vestiges of sadness still simmering within her.

"You won't need to," she said.

Neither of them looked like they believed her.

Chapter Twenty-Two

Molly tried really hard not to show how frustrated she was with the hospital doctor's insistence that she stay "for observation." After waiting to get the results of the bloodwork he'd ordered, she'd been certain he'd discharge her.

"Stop pouting," Sam said, helping her into the hospital bed. She wore two of those ridiculous gowns, so she was covered. Katherine was bringing her clothes of her own, but they hadn't wanted Molly to stay in the clothes she'd worn in the RV.

"I'm not pouting," Molly said, leaning against the pillows. The bed was raised into a sitting position, and she scooted over so Sam could sit beside her.

He tapped her nose. "You're totally pouting."

Tears burned her eyes. She didn't know why she was so emotional, but she knew she'd feel better if she was allowed to go home. Though at least Sam was with her. She tried to focus on that. Reaching out, she took his hand, and he folded both of his around one of hers.

"Sorry," she whispered.

With one hand, he reached out and stroked a finger down her cheek, where she knew the bruising had gotten worse. It didn't throb as much now, but that was likely thanks to the pain meds the doctor had prescribed.

"You don't have to say sorry. I know you don't want to be here, but I feel better that you are. Even with only low exposure to the gas, you were struck in the head by a man twice your size, and locked in an RV to die." His voice hitched on the last word. He dropped his hand.

Molly's heart tightened like it was locked in a vise. "I do have to say sorry. If the situation were reversed and you were putting me through this much emotional stress, I don't know how I'd handle it. I promised you I'd be careful, and even though I truly meant to be, I was reckless. I should have waited for someone to come with me. I really am sorry."

Sam put his hands on the bed on either side of her hips and leaned in. "You have a tendency to be reckless, and if I'm being honest, it scares the hell out of me. Other than my parents, I've never had anyone in my life that I was terrified of losing."

The tears welled, and blinking them away only caused them to fall. Sam leaned in and kissed the paths her tears made. She wrapped her arms around his neck and pulled him close.

Against her ear, he whispered, "I get that you have to be you, and I'll never try to change you. I just need you to remember when you're making decisions that I *need* you, Molly. I love you."

She tightened her hold. "I love you. So much. And I promise to work on not acting without thinking things all the way through." Molly pulled back and kissed him. "I need you, too. It's a two-way street. You know that, right?"

Still close enough that their noses touched, he nodded. "I do."

The words sent a shiver of delight and promise through her. *One day.*

Three quick raps at the door got their attention. Chris walked into the room looking like she felt: exhausted.

"How's it going?" He looked back and forth between them.

Sam straightened and glanced at Molly. "She's okay, but staying the night for observation."

Chris crossed his arms over his chest. He was wearing a sweater and a pair of jeans, leading Molly to think he was either off work or just tired of his uniform for the day.

"I'll see if I can chat with the doctor about that," Chris said.

Molly grinned. "Really?" Maybe he wasn't upset with her after all. She'd certainly given both him and Sam reason to be irritated.

"For sure. I'll see if he can keep you here permanently. At least then I can keep tabs on you, and you can work from anywhere, right?"

Sam laughed, which brought out Chris's grin. Molly tried to fight it, but her smile broke free. "Very funny."

Chris checked his watch and approached the bed. "You want a formal statement now or off the record?"

"Maybe call Jill for the formal one, and just tell me and Sam what's happened?"

With a nod of approval, a slight smile ghosting his lips, he checked behind him.

"Brian said he started to tell you what happened. He thinks you got him talking because you were trying to delay the inevitable," Chris said.

"I knew you and Sam would come."

"Appreciate the faith, as I'm sure Sam does, but I also know we'd both be happy for you to wait on us, preferably me, in situations like this."

Molly lowered her gaze and sighed. "I know."

Sam held her hand while Chris continued.

"He went back to get Candice's jacket and saw Jet heading to the car barn, followed him. He heard the whole thing with Herman and Jet arguing. Waited until they'd each gotten some punches in. Herman left before seeing Brian. According to him—Brian—he went in to see if Jet was okay, still holding the crowbar. Jet made some inappropriate comment about being well enough that he could have had Candy before going home to have Amber."

Sam swore under his breath and squeezed Molly's hand.

Chris gave Sam's shoulder a nudge. "Not on you, man. Not even close."

"It's disgusting," Sam said.

"I don't disagree, but men like this? They have their own set of rules. Brian wasn't happy with the comment either. Claims things went hazy, and he just wanted to shut Jet up. He did. Permanently."

"You think he'll try to claim insanity or something?" Sam asked.

Chris shook his head. "No. Can't be sure, but he was pretty cognizant and knows what he did. There's also the premeditation of what happened with Candy and Molly."

Again, Sam's features tensed. Molly reached out and stroked his cheek, the slight rasp of his five-o'clock shadow tickling her fingers.

"How is Candy?" Molly dropped her hand.

"She's probably in for a night longer than you. She was in there longer with the oven open. Smart thinking, getting him to close it. That definitely bought us some time to get there and cut the hose going into the RV. She said he told her he'd done it for her. She freaked out, said she was going to the police or to that nosy reporter lady."

"So he brought the nosy reporter to Candice." Molly sighed.

"Yeah. Said you were too curious to let it go, and he wanted the last word. Which meant dying rather than anyone finding out the truth. Now he feels like Jet had the final jab."

"Thank God this is over. I might never attend a car show again," Sam said.

Molly straightened. "Don't say that. You can't let bad experiences keep you from something you love." She stared at him until his gaze softened, and he gave an almost imperceptible nod.

"I need to go. I'll call Jill with my statement. Stay in bed until they release you, and then stay out of trouble after," Chris said.

"You act like I want trouble to come my way," Molly said, her irritation prickling.

"You don't exactly turn away from it when it shows up," Chris said.

"I'm staying behind my desk from now on. Elizabeth will be back soon, and then she and Jill can cover the outside world. I'll just edit it."

Sam and Chris both stared at her and then laughed.

Lifting a hand to say goodbye, Chris chuckled. "I should have written that down and made you sign it."

When he left, Sam and Molly had about ten minutes of quiet cuddling time before groups of people began to show up.

Alan, Clay, Jill, and Hannah were the first to show up, flowers and chocolates in hand. They told her their versions of what they'd heard through the town grapevine. Molly could neither confirm or deny but told Jill to expect a call from Chris.

Katherine and the sheriff showed up for a short visit following her colleagues, and Molly was grateful to change into her own pajamas.

Sheriff Saron—she couldn't get used to calling him Brandon—had listened to her story quietly while shooting her looks that made her want to squirm. He was firmly in Chris's camp of thinking Molly should be under house arrest for any future investigations. Katherine was softer and sweeter, but pretty clear when she informed Molly that she expected her to "keep herself a lot safer than she'd done so far."

By the time her visitors left, she was having a hard time keeping her eyes open. Sam pulled up a plastic chair that reclined but looked incredibly uncomfortable. His mom had brought him a pair of track shorts, a T-shirt, and a sweater.

"I'm going to ask the nurse for an extra blanket. You want anything? Something to drink or eat?"

She shook her head. "I'm not cold."

His brows furrowed for a second. "Oh. No, it's for me. I'm not leaving you. I'll sleep in the chair."

Happiness pushed away some of the fatigue. "I'm glad to hear you aren't going anywhere. I'd be sad if you did. But there's enough room in here for both of us." She threw back the blanket and patted the mattress, which probably wasn't much more comfortable than the chair. But at least they'd be together.

"I don't know about that. It's probably against policy; plus, it doesn't look big enough."

Molly smiled, fluttered her lashes, making him laugh. "If you stay really close, we'll fit. And as to the policy? I don't see it posted anywhere."

Running a hand through his hair, he came to the side of the bed. Molly turned on her side, and he slipped in behind her, wrapping his arm around her tightly. She tugged the covers back over them and snuggled against him, feeling warm and content. And safe.

They lay there, wrapped in each other, listening to the various beeps and noises of the hospital.

"You asleep?" he whispered.

"No. I'm tired, but it feels like I could stay awake. That's weird, I know."

He nuzzled her neck. "Babe, that's like the least weird thing about you."

Molly gave a gravelly laugh and swatted his hand. He squeezed her gently, but tighter, then linked their fingers over her stomach.

"I really am sorry that I keep scaring you. It's never my intention. You must have been horrified when you showed up at the RV." A shiver wracked her body, and Sam scooted impossibly closer, like he could shield her from her own thoughts.

"I was. Everything about it felt wrong. And I couldn't understand why you'd think you could stop him from whatever he'd decided to do. I was mad at first, wondering why you'd do that, why you'd run off and throw yourself into an unpredictable situation."

She flinched, hating that she'd made him mad, but understanding.

"But then I realized, it's part of who you are. You're so willing to see to others, to put them first, and do right by them, that you forget about yourself. That terrifies me. But it's also part of what makes you so easy to love. Your capacity to care is humbling. I'd really like you to be more cautious, to remember that you have people who love you back as much as you love them. But I won't try to change what makes you you."

Several tears escaped the corners of her eyes and dripped onto her pillow. "I think I'm going to nominate you for most wonderful boyfriend in the world award. I don't know how I got so lucky, but I promise to be more careful and try to give you less reason to worry. And maybe, if you wanted, you could help me follow through with that by keeping closer tabs on me."

She smiled into the low light the hallway fixtures cast into the room.

"What do you mean?"

She shrugged, even though she knew what she meant. "Just, maybe if you were around more, it would remind me not to be so impulsive."

"Around more, like how much more?" He inhaled deeply.

Her heartbeat went wonky, alternating between stomping and fluttering. "Every night?"

His breath whooshed out.

"Every morning?" he asked.

"I'd understand if you don't want that kind of responsibility. I'm turning out to be kind of high-maintenance."

He chuckled, and his breath tickled her neck. "I think taking on more responsibility at this stage in my life is exactly what I need. And what you need."

It took some effort, but she turned so she faced him. She felt like a kid hiding in a fort with the blanket pulled up tight and barely able to see the other person in the semi-darkness.

"You are exactly what I need," she whispered.

"You really want me around that much?"

Always, her heart shouted. Molly nodded, but worried it was too soon. "If that's too much, you could start with maybe leaving more of your stuff at my place."

He kissed her forehead. "Don't chicken out now. You can't take it back. You just asked me to move in."

"For my own safety," she said with mock graveness.

Around a laugh, he added, "And my sanity."

She ran her hand up his chest and around his neck. "I can't promise living with me will provide sanity."

He pressed his mouth to hers, taking his time to kiss her with such gentle affection, it stole her breath. "I can trade sanity for happiness."

She smiled around her yawn and burrowed her face into his chest.

"Sleep, Molly," he said, kissing the top of her head and tucking her closer. "Okay."

Her eyes drifted closed, but she was still conscious enough to hear him whisper, "I'll be here when you wake up."

He meant it. She fell asleep, and even though the bed was uncomfortable and noise flitted in the background, there was nowhere else she wanted to be.

Epilogue

Two weeks later

Molly ripped the shiny pink wrapping off the present Chris handed her, knowing from the feel of it that he'd kept his word.

She held it up, unable to contain her laughter. "A dictionary," she said, showing it around the circle of her favorite people.

Sam, sitting beside her on his mom's dining bench, took it from her hand.

Chris lifted his soda in salute. "As promised."

Chuckling, Sam pointed to the page he'd turned to. "He actually highlighted words for you."

Molly shook her head, oddly touched by the quirky and somewhat satirical gift.

"Remember, that's just from him," Sarah said.

Chris stood behind her chair. Bella, Jill, Katherine, and the sheriff were all gathered around the big farm-style table. They'd had a delicious meal of burgers, hot dogs, and potato salad. Sam said he knew, the colder it got, the more she was missing summer, so he and his mom thought a BBQ was needed.

Bella had baked a gorgeous, two-tier cake in the shape of a typewriter. A tiny piece of her wallowed in the sadness of not having her parents at the table, but they'd be coming for Christmas. That had been one of her presents when they'd phoned earlier that day. The others were in the mail. She couldn't wait for them to meet the people who'd become her family. To meet Sam, who'd become her everything.

"I promise to keep it right on my desk," she told Chris.

"I don't care where you keep it, just use it," he said, making everyone laugh again.

"My turn," Sam said, passing her a rectangular box wrapped in pale blue paper with a bright purple ribbon on it.

It was sentimental and silly, but she took more care with the paper on his gift. When she got to the box, she smiled when she read the Converse logo.

"My favorite," she said, leaning over to kiss his cheek.

"I hope they will be."

Confused, she opened the box and gasped. Inside, nestled in pink tissue paper was the coolest pair of shoes she'd ever seen. They looked like they were covered in newsprint.

"I've never seen these," she said, her voice low.

"They're custom," he replied.

"You had sneakers custom made for me?"

He nodded. "You like them?"

She blinked away happy tears. "I love them. They're perfect."

He kissed her and smiled against her lips. "You're perfect," he whispered.

Leaning back, he gestured to the shoes. "Look inside."

When she did, she pulled out a tiny square black box. Opening it, she smiled when she saw the tiny black Converse shoe charm.

"It's adorable," she said, thinking she'd need to get a bracelet to go with it.

"Glad you think so. You can put it on here," he answered, opening his hand to reveal a gorgeous silver charm bracelet.

"It's beautiful," she said, her fingers running over links. There was a charm already on the bracelet, and when she turned it to see what it pictured, her heart puffed up like a balloon. It was a plain, silver circle with tiny letters that read M + s with a heart around them.

Throwing her arms around him, she squeezed tight, then pulled back so he could put it on her wrist.

"This is the best birthday ever," she said quietly.

The others may or may not have heard her, but Sam was listening. He clasped the bracelet around her wrist and hooked the Converse charm on as well.

Taking her hand, he stared down at the delicate gift, running his fingers over the links and her skin.

"Just you wait, Molly Owens," he teased. "This is just the beginning."

"Time for cake," Bella declared.

Molly stared at Sam, overwhelmed with happiness. He leaned in as Bella rose to go to the kitchen and whispered against her ear.

"Happy birthday, babe. I love you."

She turned, pressing her hand to his cheek. "I love you back. When we get *home*, I'll show you how much."

Sam chuckled, and they turned back to the conversation until Bella came from the kitchen carrying the lit birthday cake. As the people she loved sang to her, Molly thought about how lucky she was to have so much, to be surrounded by people who gave their love and friendship without reservation or condition. That, more than anything else, was the gift she planned to cherish most.

CPSIA information can be obtained
at www.ICGtesting.com
Printed in the USA
LVHW041024161019
634268LV00002B/364/P